Task MATHS 5

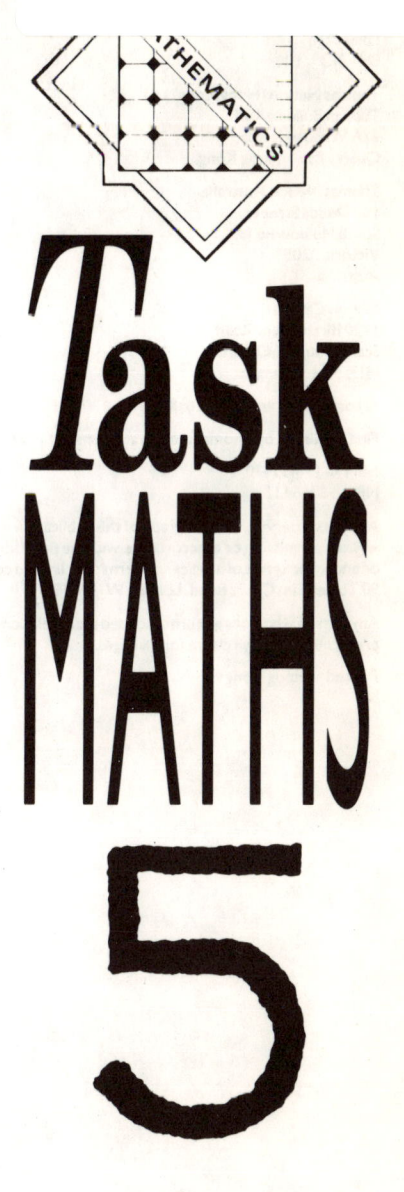

BARBARA BALL
& DEREK BALL

Teacher's RESOURCE BOOK

Thomas Nelson and Sons Ltd
Nelson House   Mayfield Road
Walton-on-Thames   Surrey
KT12 5PL   UK

51 York Place
Edinburgh
EH1 3JD   UK

Thomas Nelson (Hong Kong) Ltd
Toppan Building 10/F
22A Westlands Road
Quarry Bay   Hong Kong

Thomas Nelson Australia
102 Dodds Street
South Melbourne
Victoria 3205
Australia

Nelson Canada
1120 Birchmount Road
Scarborough   Ontario
M1K 5G4   Canada

© Barbara Ball and Derek Ball 1991

First published by Thomas Nelson and Sons Ltd 1991

ISBN 0-17-431430-2
NPN 98765432

All rights reserved. No paragraph of this publication may be reproduced, copied or transmitted save with written permission or in accordance with the provisions of the Copyright, Design and Patents Act 1988, or under the terms of any licence permitting limited copying issued by the Copyright Licensing Agency, 90 Tottenham Court Road, London W1P 9HE.

Any person who does any unauthorised act in relation to this publication may be liable to criminal prosecution and civil claims for damages.

Printed in Hong Kong

CONTENTS

INTRODUCTION 4

   1 How the course is organised
   2 The teacher's role
   3 How to use the introductory activities
   4 How to use the sections of questions
   5 How to use the Further Coursework Tasks
   6 How to use the Review Exercises
   7 Recording and assessment
   8 Matching this course to the National Curriculum
   9 Equipment and resources
  10 Computers and graphical calculators

Guide to chapter 14: **TABLE GAMES**	22
Guide to chapter 15: **COLOURINGS**	32
Guide to chapter 16: **EVERY PICTURE TELLS A STORY**	44
Guide to chapter 17: **MANAGING THE FUTURE**	54
Guide to chapter 18: **EQUABLE SHAPES**	64
Guide to chapter 19: **DISSECTING CUBES**	72
Answers to Review Exercises C	84
Guide to chapter 20: **REPEATING PATTERNS**	92
Guide to chapter 21: **HOW DO YOU DECIDE?**	102
Guide to chapter 22: **KNOWING WHERE YOU ARE**	108
Guide to chapter 23: **WHAT DO YOU BELIEVE?**	122
Guide to chapter 24: **TELLING THE COMPUTER WHAT TO DRAW**	130
Guide to chapter 25: **GETTING THE MOST OUT OF LIFE**	140
Answers to Review Exercises D	151
Running the computer programs	156
Task Maths Software for Key Stage 4	160

INTRODUCTION

1 HOW THE COURSE IS ORGANISED

> Using and applying mathematics, as represented in Attainment Target 1 and the associated elements of the programmes of study, should stretch across and permeate all other work in mathematics, providing both the means to, and the rationale for, the progressive development of knowledge, skills and understanding of mathematics.
>
> (National Mathematics Curriculum, *Non-Statutory Guidance*, D1.5)

The National Curriculum requires that mathematical knowledge, skills and understanding are learned in contexts in which they can be used. Attainment Target 1 is concerned with using and applying mathematics, and the other four attainment targets specify the knowledge, skills and understanding to be used and applied. One way of picturing the relationship between these is shown in the diagram.

Task Maths translates this ideal into practice, by providing 25 tasks within which students are able to use and apply all the mathematical knowledge, skills and understanding relevant to Key Stage 4 of the National Curriculum.

Task Maths provides one set of books which is suitable for *all* students. There are not different tracks for students judged to be at different levels of ability. This is closely in line with National Curriculum thinking and means that premature judgements about the final achievements of students do not need to be made. The student's books for this course are written so as to be manageable by students working at Level 4 and yet they make demands on students working at level 10. The way in which this happens is outlined in later sections of this introduction and explained clearly throughout this teacher's resource book.

The course consists of 25 chapters. Each chapter introduces a task by means of an introductory activity. There follow two or more sections, containing questions which develop the task, while at the same time they focus on specific mathematical content or skills. At the end of each chapter there are a number of Further Coursework Tasks (FCTs). By choosing to tackle one of these, a student will have the opportunity to explore further the task for the chapter (and to develop some coursework).

In addition to 25 chapters the course contains four sets of Review Exercises, organised by topic, to provide consolidation and practice. At the end of each book there is an information section.

The course assumes that calculators are constantly available to students, who can make use of them whenever they feel this is appropriate. The course also makes frequent references to the use of computers and graphical calculators, and students who are able to use computers and graphical calculators in the ways described will gain maximum benefit from the course. The computer symbol is used to indicate that a particular question or coursework task requires the use of a computer or graphical calculator.

2 THE TEACHER'S ROLE

Task Maths is not a 'teach-yourself' course. Although all the key skills and concepts are explained in the student's books, the teacher is still needed to support students' work and to give help in response to their individual needs. There might be occasions when you want to explain methods to the whole class, but most of the time you are likely to be responding to particular students' problems as they arise while working on the task.

The Non-Statutory Guidance for the National Mathematics Curriculum strongly advocates that students should be encouraged to develop their own methods for doing mathematics. For this reason *Task Maths* offers explanations of words and concepts, but not detailed explanations of methods. This leaves students free to develop their own methods and you free to explain the methods which students find easiest to use.

When students use *Task Maths* your role as the teacher is crucial. You know best what difficulties your students are experiencing, and can provide the appropriate detailed explanations which are required to fit in with the way a particular student is thinking.

The structure of *Task Maths* encourages students to make demands on themselves mathematically. You might want to see your role as supporting students to the extent that is necessary, whilst at the same time encouraging them to become as self-reliant as possible.

3 HOW TO USE THE INTRODUCTORY ACTIVITIES

Each chapter has an introductory activity. Its purpose is to introduce the task for the chapter. The introductory activity is suitable for students of all levels of ability. One way of starting most introductory activities is by means of a class discussion.

Introductory activities vary in length. You might only want to spend part of a lesson on some; others are more substantial, and you might find it appropriate on occasions to develop an introductory activity into an extended piece of work.

4 HOW TO USE THE SECTIONS OF QUESTIONS

Each chapter has several sections of questions, labelled A, B, C etc. These questions develop further the task which was begun through the introductory activity.

One function of the questions is to ensure that students cover a range of statements of attainment whilst working on the task for the chapter. But, although they ensure that the syllabus is covered, the questions are not dull and repetitive; instead they provide insights into the ways of developing work on the task. (Consolidation and practice, where required, are provided by the Review Exercises, as described in a subsequent section.)

The questions are of variable length. While one question might be straightforward and take little time to complete, the following question might involve a significant amount of exploration. Students should be made aware of this, so that they have appropriate expectations. Some of the more substantial questions, or groups of questions, can be used as starting points for extended pieces of work.

The questions are also of variable difficulty. Those which are unmarked can be managed by nearly all students working at Key Stage 4; those which are marked with a single bar are somewhat harder and should be appropriate for students working at about level 7 or higher; those which are marked with a double bar are more difficult still and some of them are very challenging indeed.

You might wish to decide which questions are tackled by each of your students. Alternatively, you might sometimes want students to determine the appropriate level of challenge for themselves. Some students might persist in tackling questions which are too hard. Some students, particularly if they are anxious about not over-reaching themselves, might need to be encouraged to omit easier questions and tackle harder ones. However, it needs to be made clear that the unmarked questions should not necessarily be omitted by more able students, because some of these questions stimulate interest by the ways in which they develop work on the task for the chapter.

Sometimes boxes appear within the sections of questions. Some of these are information boxes which help the student with a new word or concept, or explain a method or technique. Some boxes are advice boxes which suggest to the student how one, or more, questions might be tackled. Some boxes are

---

Levels of difficulty

Accessible to all students
(no bars)

Somewhat harder
(one bar) ▬

More difficult
(two bars) ▬▬

I Information boxes

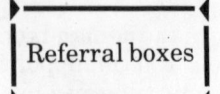

referral boxes, which direct the student to the information pages at the back of the book, or to a particular Review Exercise, in case further practice is required.

The computer symbol is used to indicate at a glance questions which require, or would be enhanced by, the use of a computer or graphical calculator. When students are invited to write a computer program to help answer a question, examples of suitable programs are provided within this teacher's resource book.

5 HOW TO USE THE FURTHER COURSEWORK TASKS

Each chapter concludes with several Further Coursework Tasks. These provide students with ideas for developing work already done on the task for the chapter, into an extended piece of work.

This teacher's resource book provides you with ideas about how each Further Coursework Task might be tackled. It is important that these ideas should be treated as illustrations only: the vast majority of Further Coursework Tasks can be responded to in a great variety of different ways and each student should be encouraged to be as imaginative as possible when deciding how to tackle the task presented.

The guides to the chapters provide you with advice concerning the levels of difficulties of the Further Coursework Tasks. Some tasks are described as neutral. These are suitable for students of all abilities, because the task is such that any student can produce work which indicates his or her level of achievement. Tasks which are not as suitable for students of all abilities are described either as 'easier' or as 'more difficult'. 'Easier' tasks are unlikely to provide the students working at the highest levels with sufficient opportunity to demonstrate their strengths. 'More difficult' tasks are likely to be inaccessible to some students. The computer symbol is used to indicate at a glance Further Coursework Tasks which require, or would be enhanced by, the use of a computer or graphical calculator. When students are invited to write a computer program to help with a Further Coursework Task, examples of suitable programs are provided within the teacher's resource book.

6 HOW TO USE THE REVIEW EXERCISES

Review Exercises are organised according to National Curriculum topics. Each exercise contains a set of questions, either taken from GCSE examination papers or of a similar type, which provide students with consolidation and practice. You might want to use questions from the Review Exercises when setting homework.

Sometimes information boxes appear within a Review Exercise. The purpose of these is the same as that of the information boxes appearing in the sections of questions.

Because chapters are *not* organised according to syllabus topics, several Review Exercises are usually linked to one chapter, and one Review Exercise is usually linked to several chapters. The links between chapters and Review Exercises are explained clearly in the guides to chapters in this teacher's resource book.

7 RECORDING AND ASSESSMENT

Recording and assessment are discussed here in general terms; more detailed advice is provided in the teacher's guide to each chapter.

The following section, which explains in detail the match between *Task Maths* and the National Curriculum will make it relatively easy for you to record your teacher assessment of each of your students.

It is difficult to provide this match in detail with respect to Target 1. Instead, illustrations of students' work are provided in the teacher's guide to each chapter. The students' work was produced in response to Further

Coursework Tasks, and demonstrates students' achievement of particular statements of attainment in target 1. The secret is to learn to use the statements in this target creatively. The examples of students' work have been chosen to show that the statements of attainment in this target can be interpreted in different ways to suit different contexts.

It is helpful, both to you and to your students, to make all your criteria for assessment, and particularly your criteria for assessing Target 1, explicit to your students. You might find it helpful to provide your students with simplified versions of the statements of attainment in target 1, and of any criteria produced by examination boards.

There is a cross-curricular aspect to the National Curriculum. Students might demonstrate some statements of attainment, particularly in Target 5, when working in other curricular areas. You might want to liaise with teachers of other subjects to avoid unnecessary duplication. It should be noted that some of the Further Coursework Tasks in *Task Maths* are essentially cross-curricular, and students tackling them might be able to satisfy attainment targets in science, history, geography or technology, for example, as well as in mathematics.

8 MATCHING THIS COURSE TO THE NATIONAL CURRICULUM

The Teacher's Resource Book uses the revised attainment targets published in May 1991. The charts in this section will be useful for Book 4 also.

As already stated, the chapters in *Task Maths* present tasks, and each chapter thus relates to several different National Curriculum attainment targets. Most statements of attainment appear in several different chapters. This type of approach is advocated by the *Non-Statutory Guidance*, which advises you not to work with students at one level at a time, or on only one attainment target at a time.

> Attainment Target 1 differs from the other targets not only in the matters which it covers, but in its relationship with other targets. As a consequence of the interaction between learning and using mathematics, work related to Attainment Target 1 cannot be tackled in isolation from the rest of the programmes of study. Similarly, work related to Attainment Targets 2–5 cannot be satisfactorily pursued independently from that related to Attainment Target 1.
>
> (*Non-Statutory Guidance* D1.5)

Consequently, all levels of Target 1 are integrated into every chapter of *Task Maths*.

The charts in this section show the correspondence between National Curriculum statements of attainment and chapters of this book. The example below explains how these charts are organised.

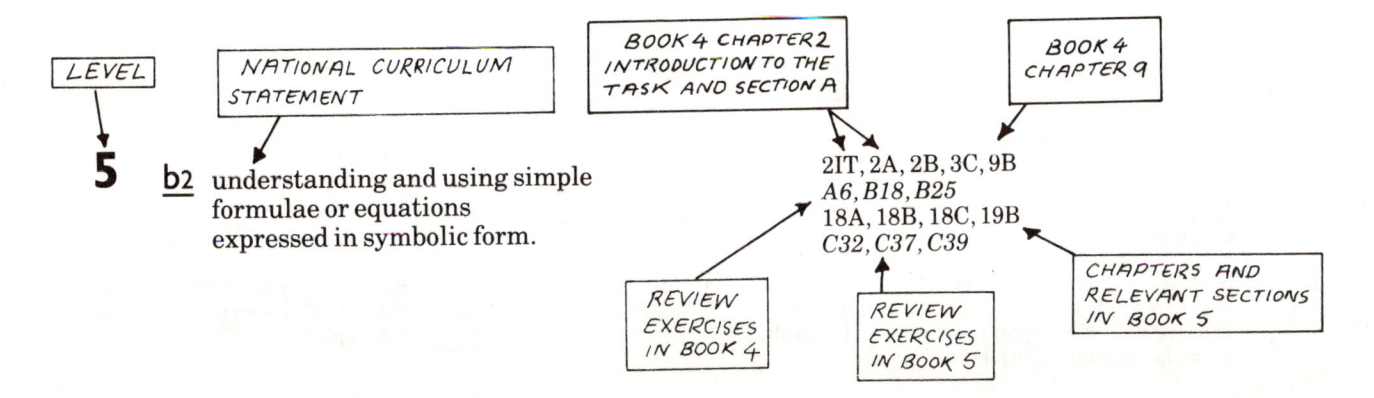

LEVEL — NATIONAL CURRICULUM STATEMENT — BOOK 4 CHAPTER 2 INTRODUCTION TO THE TASK AND SECTION A — BOOK 4 CHAPTER 9

5 **b2** understanding and using simple formulae or equations expressed in symbolic form.

2IT, 2A, 2B, 3C, 9B
A6, B18, B25
18A, 18B, 18C, 19B
C32, C37, C39

REVIEW EXERCISES IN BOOK 4 — REVIEW EXERCISES IN BOOK 5 — CHAPTERS AND RELEVANT SECTIONS IN BOOK 5

Attainment Target 2:
Number

Pupils should understand and use numbers, including estimation and approximation, interpreting results and checking for reasonableness.

Programme of Study	Task Maths	Statement of Attainment
Level 4		

	Pupils should engage in activities which involve:		**Pupils should be able to:**
a1	• reading, writing and ordering whole numbers.	3IT, 3A, 7IT, 7A A1, A4 21A, 25B	(a) Solve problems without the aid of a calculator, considering the reasonableness of the answer.
a2	• learning multiplication facts up to 10 × 10 and using them in multiplication and division problems.	1B, 2A, 3IT, 3A, 11A A9 18IT, 18A, 18C, 24B, 25B C33	
a3	• adding and subtracting mentally two two-digit numbers.	3A, 11A, 11D A1, A8	
a4	• adding mentally several single-digit numbers.	3A A1	
a5	• adding and subtracting two three-digit numbers, without a calculator.	11A, 11D A1, A8	
a6	• multiplying and dividing two-digit numbers by a single-digit number, without a calculator.	3A, 3B, 11A, 11D A1	
a7	• estimating and approximating to check the validity of addition and subtraction calculations.	3A, 5A, 11D	
a8	• solving addition and subtraction problems using numbers with no more than two decimal places, and multiplication and division problems starting with whole numbers.	3C A9 18IT, 18A, 18B, 18C, 25A, 25B C33	
b1	• understanding and using the effect of multiplying whole numbers by 10 or 100.	3C A4, A9, B16 C33	(b) Demonstrate an understanding of the relationship between place values in whole numbers.
b2	• understanding and using the relationship between place values in whole numbers.	3IT, 3A, 5A, 11A A1	
c1	• recognising and understanding simple fractions in everyday use.	5A, 13IT, 13A, 13D 14A, 14B, 16IT, 16A, 19A, 19B, 21A, 23B C27	(c) Use fractions, decimals or percentages as appropriate to describe situations.
c2	• using, with understanding, decimal notation to two decimal places in the context of measurement, appreciating the continuous nature of measurement.	5IT, 5A, 7A, 7B, 7C, 9A A9 C33	
c3	• recognising and understanding simple percentages.	9C B16	
d1	• reading calculator displays to the nearest whole number and knowing how to interpret results which have rounding errors.	5A, 9B, 9C, 12A, 13B A1, A3 18A, 18B, 18C	(d) Solve number problems with the aid of a calculator, interpreting the display.

8

d2	• solving addition, subtraction, multiplication and division problems using numbers with no more than two decimal places.	5B, 7A, 7C *A9* 18A, 18B, 18C, 21A, 21B, 25A, 25B *C33*		
e1	• making sensible estimates of a range of measures in relation to everyday objects.	5IT, 5A, 5B, 9IT, 9A, 12IT, 12A *B15* 20IT, 20A, 25IT	(e)	Make sensible estimates of a range of measures in relation to everyday objects.
e2	• understanding the relationship between the units of length/ 'weight'/capacity/time.	5A, 5B, 9IT, 9B, 12A, 12C *A8, B15, B19* 18B		

Level 5

a1	• understanding and using non-calculator methods by which a three-digit number is multiplied by a two-digit number and a three-digit number is divided by a two-digit number.	3A, 3B *A1*	(a)	Use an appropriate non-calculator method to multiply or divide two numbers.
a2	• multiplying and dividing mentally single-digit numbers of powers of 10 with whole number answers.	3IT, 3C		
b1	• calculating fractions and percentages of quantities using a calculator where necessary.	5A, 5B, 9C, 13IT, 13A, 13D *B16* 16A, 17A, 23B *C27*	(b)	Find fractions or percentages of quantities.
b2	• using unitary ratios.	5IT, 5A, 12IT, 12B *A7, B23* 17A, 22IT, 22A, 23C *C35*		
b3	• understanding the notion of scale in maps and drawings.	5IT, 5A, 12IT, 12A, 12B *A7, B23* 22IT, 22A, 23C *D44*		
c1	• using 'trial and improvement' methods.	1B, 11D 18A, 18B, 18C, 19B, 25A	(c)	Refine estimations by 'trial and improvements' methods.
c2	• approximating, using significant figures or decimal paces.	2C, 5A, 9A, 9B, 9C, 10C, 10E, 12A, 12B, 12C *A3* 18A, 18B, 18C, 21A		
d1	• using Imperial units still in daily use and knowing their rough metric equivalents.	9IT, 9A, 12A, 12B *A8, B15, B19* 18B *D42*	(d)	Use units in context.
d2	• converting one metric unit to another.	5IT, 5A, 9A, 9B *B15, B19* 23C		
d3	• using negative numbers in context, including ordering, addition, subtraction and simple multiplication and division.	12B *B24* 16B, 24B		
e	• using index notation to express powers of whole numbers.	3B *A4, B24* *C36*		Assessed at a higher levels (8a)

Level 6

a1	• ordering decimals and appreciating place values.	7IT, 7A, 7C, 9A, 11A 23C *C27*	(a)	Calculate with fractions, decimals, percentages or ratio, as appropriate.

a2	• understanding and using equivalent fractions and equivalent ratios and relating these to decimals and percentages.	5A, 6C, 8C, 13B *B16* 14A, 14B, 15C, 16IT, 16A, 17A, 21A *C27, C34*		
a3	• working out fractional and percentage changes.	5B, 9C, 12A *B16* 17A *C36*		
a4	• converting fractions to decimals and percentages and finding one number as a percentage of another.	5A, 7C, 13B *B16* 15C, 21A, 23C *C27*		
a5	• calculating, using ratios in a variety of situations.	5A, 9C *B15* 17A, 21A, 22A *C34*		
b	• using estimation and approximation to check that answers to multiplication and division problems involving whole numbers are of the right order.	5A, 5B 17A, 17B, 25A	(b)	Use estimation to check to calculations.

Level 7

a	• multiplying and dividing mentally single-digit multiples of any power of 10, realising that with a number less than one multiplication has a decreasing effect and division has an increasing effect.	3IT, 3A, 9A, 9B, 11D 25B	(a)	Multiply and divide mentally single-digit multiples of any power of 10.
b1	• solving problems and using multiplication and division with numbers of any size.	5A, 5B, 7B, 7C, 13C *B16* 17A, 17B, 18A, 18B, 18C, 19B, 23C, 25A	(b)	Use a calculator efficiently when solving problems.
b2	• expressing positive integers as a product of primes.	3B *A4* 25B		
b3	• using the memory and bracket facilities of a calculator to plan a calculation and evaluate expressions.	11D 17B *C32*		
c1	• recognising that measurement is approximate; and choosing the degree of accuracy appropriate for a particular purpose.	5IT, 5A, 7IT, 7B, 7C, 9IT, 9A, 12C *B15* 17A, 17B, 18B, 23C, 25IT	(c)	Recognise that measurement is approximate and choose the degree of accuracy appropriate for a particular purpose.
c2	• recognising that a measurement expressed to a given unit is in possible error of half a unit.	7A		
c3	• understanding and using compound measures, eg speed, density.	9B, 9C, 12IT, 12A, 12B, 12C *A8, B19, B20* 17A, 17B *C35, D42*		

Level 8

a1	• expressing and using numbers in standard index form, with positive and negative integer powers of 10.	13C *B24* 17B, 23C *C36*	(a)	Calculate with numbers expressed in standard form.
a2	• using index notations to represent powers and roots.	3A 17B *C36*		

		Programme of Study	Task Maths		Statement of Attainment
b1	•	substituting negative numbers into formulae involving addition, subtraction, multiplication and division.	2A, 11G C43	(b)	Evaluate formulae, including the use of fractions or negative numbers.
b2	•	calculating with fractions.	13IT, 13A, 13D 14A, 14B, 16A, 23A C27		
c	•	estimating and approximating to check that the results of calculations are of the right order.	9A, 9B, 12C 17A, 17B, 18A, 18B, 18C, 23C, 25A	(c)	Solve numerical problems, checking that the results are of the right order of magnitude.

Level 9

a	•	distinguishing between rational and irrational numbers.	13B B24	(a)	Distinguish between rational and irrational numbers.
b	•	understanding upper and lower bounds of numbers expressed to a given degree of accuracy.	7A, 9C 17A, 17B, 23C	(b)	Understand the significance of approximations.

Level 10

a1	•	calculating the upper and lower bounds in the addition, subtraction, multiplication and division of numbers expressed to a given degree of accuracy.	7A	(a)	Determine the possible effects of errors on calculations.
a2	•	determining the possible effects of error on calculations involving measurements.	7C 17B		

Attainment Target 3:
Algebra

Pupils should recognise and use symbolic and graphical representation to express relationships.

		Programme of Study	Task Maths		Statement of Attainment
		Level 4			
		Pupils should engage in activities which involve:			**Pupils should be able to:**
a1	•	generalising, mainly in words, patterns which arise in various situations, eg symmetry of results, 'multiple', 'factor', 'square'.	3IT, 3A, 3B, 4IT, 4A, 10A, 11A, 13B A4 15A, 15B, 15C	(a)	Make general statements about patterns.
a2	•	applying strategies such as doubling and halving to explore properties of numbers.	3IT, 3A, 3B, 3C, 8IT, 11A, 13IT, 13A 24A		
a3	•	recognising that multiplication and division are inverse operations and using this to check calculations.	11A, 11D B25		
a4	•	dealing with inputs to and outputs from simple function machines.	3C		
b	•	understanding and using simple formulae or equations expressed in words.	3C, 9B A6, B18	(b)	Use simple formulae expressed in words.
c	•	learning the conventions of the co-ordinate representation of points; working with co-ordinates in the first quadrant.	2C, 4B, 10A, 10B D42	(c)	Use co-ordinates in the first quadrant.

Level 5

a1	• generating sequences.	4IT, 4A, 13E *A5, B25*	(a)	Follow instructions to generate sequences.
a2	• recognising patterns in numbers through spatial arrangements.	3B, 4IT, 4A *A4, A5, A6* 15C, 16A		
a3	• understanding and using terms such as 'prime', 'square root' and 'cube root'.	8B, 10C, 10D, 11A *A4* 15C		
a4	• recognising patterns in equivalent fractions.	13IT, 13A, 13B		
b1	• expressing simple functions symbolically.	1IT, 1B, 2A, 2B, 4A, 6B, 11F *A6* 15A, 15B, 15C, 18A, 18B, 18C, 19B	(b)	Express a simple function symbolically.
b2	• understanding and using simple formulae or equations expressed in symbolic form.	2IT, 2A, 2B, 3C, 9B *A6, B18, B25* 18A, 18B, 18C, 19B *C32, C37, C39*		
c	• understanding and using co-ordinates in all four quadrants.	2C 24A, 25B *D43*		Assessed at a higher level (6c)

Level 6

a1	• using spreadsheets or other computer facilities to explore number patterns.	11H 18A, 18B 25A, 25B	(a)	Explore number patterns using computer facilities or otherwise.
a2	• suggesting possible rules for generating sequences.	4IT, 4A *A5, A6*		
b	• solving linear equations; solving simple polynomial equations by 'trial and improvement' methods.	3C, 4A, 6B, 11E, 11G *B25* 15C, 18A, 18B, 19B *C37, C38*	(b)	Solve simple equations.
c	• drawing and interpreting simple mappings in context, recognising their general features.	4B 16B *D43*	(c)	Use and plot Cartesian co-ordinates to represent mappings.

Level 7

a1	• using symbolic notation to express the rules of sequences.	4A *A6* 15C	(a)	Use symbolic notation to express the rules of the sequences.
a2	• exploring complex number patterns generated by a computer.	13B 18A, 18B, 25A, 25B		
a3	• using the rules of indices for positive integer values.	17B *C36*		
a4	• understanding the meaning of reciprocals and exploring relationships.	13B 17B *C35, C36*		
b1	• solving a range of polynomial equations by 'trial and improvement' methods.	13E *B25* 16B, 18B *C38*	(b)	Solve equations or simple inequalities.
b2	• using algebraic and graphical methods to solve simultaneous equations in two variables.	6B, 11H *B25* 16B, 18C *C37*		

b3	• drawing and interpreting the graphs of linear functions.	4B, 6A, 12C 15C, 16B, 20A *D42, D43*		
b4	• generating various types of graph on a computer or calculator and interpreting them.	4B 15C, 16B, 25B		
b5	• constructing and interpreting flow diagrams with and without loops.	3A, 13E *B17, B25* *C29*		

Level 8

a1	• manipulating algebraic expressions.	11F, 13E 15A, 15B, 16B, 18C *C32, C38, C39, D52*	(a)	Manipulate algebraic formulae, equations or expressions.
a2	• understanding and using a range of formulae and functions.	9B 18B, 22B, 25A *C32, C39*		
a3	• understanding the relationship between powers and roots.	8B 15C, 17B *C36*		
a4	• understanding direct and inverse proportions.	17B *C35*		
a5	• interpreting and using m and c in $y = mx + c$.	4B 16B *D43*		
b1	• solving a variety of linear and other inequalities	11E, 11G 22A, 23B *D48*	(b)	Solve inequalities.
b2	• using straight-line graphs to locate regions given by linear inequalities.	23B *D48*		
c1	• knowing the form of graphs of simple functions, eg quadratic, cubic, reciprocal.	6A 16B, 17B, 18A, 25B	(c)	Interpret graphs which represent particular relationships.
c2	• interpreting graphs which describe real-life situations and contexts.	12IT, 12A, 12B, 12C *B19, B20* 17B, 20IT, 20A, 20B *D42*		

Level 9

a1	• expressing general laws in symbolic form.	17B *C35*	(a)	Express general laws in symbolic form.
a2	• using rules of indices for negative and fractional values.	17B *C36*		
b1	• solving equations using graphical methods.	16B *D43*	(b)	Solve equations using graphical methods.
b2	• calculating growth and decay rates and displaying them graphically.	17A *C36*		
c	• constructing tangents to graphs to determine the gradient.	12C *B20* *D42*	(c)	Use the gradients of graphs found by constructing tangents.

Level 10

a	• using a calculator or computer to investigate whether a sequence given iteratively converges or diverges.	13E *B25* 16B *C38*	(a)	Use a calculator or computer to investigate sequences.

		Programme of Study	Task Maths		Statement of Attainment
b	•	manipulating a range of algebraic expressions in a variety of contexts.	11F, 11I, 13E 16B, 18A, 18C, 25B *C32, C38, C39, D52*	(b)	Manipulate algebraic expressions where necessary when solving problems.
c	•	finding the approximate area between a curve and the horizontal axis between two limits, and interpreting the result.	12C *B20*	(c)	Find the approximate area between a curve and the horizontal axis between two limits, and interpret the result.
d1	•	sketching the graph of functions derived from other functions, eg $y = f(x-a)$, $y = f(kx)$, $y = f(x) + a$ from the graph of $y = f(x)$ for different values of a and k.	16B	(d)	Sketch and compare the graphs of functions.
d2	•	interpreting and using co-efficients in quadratics.	16B, 25B		

Attainment Target 4:
Shapes and space

Pupils should recognise and use the properties of two-dimensional (2-D) and three-dimensional (3-D) shapes and use measurement, location and transformation in the study of space.

		Programme of Study	Task Maths		Statement of Attainment
		Pupils should engage in activities which involve:	**Level 4**		**Pupils should be able to:**
a1	•	constructing simple 2-D and 3-D shapes from given information and knowing associated language.	8IT, 11C, 11F *A7* 19IT, 19A, 22IT, 22A, 22B, 24IT, 24A *C40*	(a)	Construct 2-D or 3-D shapes and know associated languages.
a2	•	reflecting simple shapes in a mirror line.	6D *A11* 24B *D49, D51*		
a3	•	understanding the congruence of simple shapes.	6C *A11* 15IT, 15B, 16IT, 16A, 19A, 22A, 24IT *C31, C40*		
a4	•	understanding and using language associated with angle.	6A, 6B, 6C *A7, A8, A10* 20B, 22IT, 22A, 22B, 24IT, 24A, 24B *C31*		
b	•	specifying location by means of co-ordinates in the first quadrant and by means of angle and distance.	2C, 12B *A11* 22IT, 22A *C44*	(b)	Specify location.
c	•	recognising rotational symmetry.	1A, 2B, 6IT, 6D *A2* 15IT, 15A, 15B, 16IT, 20B, 22A, 22B, 24IT *C31*	(c)	Recognise rotational symmetry.
d1	•	finding perimeters of simple shapes.	18A, 18C	(d)	Find perimeters, areas or volumes.
d2	•	finding areas by counting squares, and volumes by counting cubes.	1IT, 1B, 8IT, 8A, 10IT, 13A *A13, B26* 15C, 16IT, 16A, 18IT, 18A, 18C, 23B *C40*		

Level 5

a	•	measuring and drawing angles to the nearest degree.	12B *A7, B23* 19IT, 19A, 21A, 22A *D44*	(a)	Use accurate measurement and drawing in constructing 3-D models.
b1	•	explaining and using properties associated with intersecting and parallel lines and triangles, and knowing associated language.	6C *A10* 20B, 22A, 22B, 24A *C31*	(b)	Use properties of shape to justify explanations.
b2	•	identifying the symmetries of various shapes.	1A, 2B, 6IT, 6D, 11B, 11J, 11K, 13IT *A2* 19IT, 19A, 19B, 22B		
c1	•	using networks to solve problems.	12B 14B *C29*	(c)	Use networks to solve problems.
c2	•	specifying location by means of co-ordinates in four quadrants.	2C *A13* 24A, 24B *D49, D51*		
d1	•	finding areas of plane figures (excluding circles), using appropriate formulae.	5A, 8IT, 8A, 8D, 10IT, 10A *A13, B26* 16IT, 16A, 18A, 18B, 18C, 23B, 25A	(d)	Find areas of plane shapes or volumes of simple solids.
d2	•	finding volumes of simple solids (excluding cylinders), using appropriate formulae.	1B, 9B *A13, B26* 13B *C40*		
d3	•	finding the circumference of circles, practically, introducing the ratio π.	9B *B26* 18B, 20B		

Level 6

a	•	recognising and using common 2-D representation of 3-D objects.	1IT, 1A, 4A, 4B 15C, 19IT, 19B, 22B *C40*	(a)	Use 2-D representation of 3-D objects.
b1	•	enlarging a shape by a whole number scale factor.	8C *A11* 24B *D47, D49*	(b)	Transform shapes using a computer, or otherwise.
b2	•	classifying and defining types of quadrilaterals.	6C, 8IT, 11B, 11J, 11K 24A, 25A *C31*		
b3	•	knowing and using angle and symmetry properties of quadrilaterals and other polygons.	2IT, 2B, 6IT, 6A, 6B, 6C, 6D, 8IT, 8C, 8D, 11B, 11J, 11K, 13IT, 13A *A2, A10, A14* 15A, 15B, 16IT, 16A, 20B, 22A, 24IT, 24A, 25A *C31*		
b4	•	using computers to generate and transform 2-D shapes.	6IT, 6A, 6B 24A, 24B		
b5	•	devising instructions for a computer to produce desired shapes and paths.	6A, 13E 24A		
c	•	understanding and using bearings to define directions.	12B *B23* *C44*	(c)	Understand and use bearings to define direction.

d	•	finding areas of circles using the formulae.	9B *B26* 16A, 18B, 18C, 23B	(d)	Demonstrate that they know and can use the formulae for finding the areas and circumferences of circles.

Level 7

a	•	using co-ordinates to locate position in 3-D	10FCT6 *D51*	(a)	Use co-ordinates (x, y, z) to locate position in 3-D.
b	•	determining the locus of an object moving subject to a rule.	20B, 22IT, 22A, 22B *C44*	(b)	Determine the locus of an object which is moving subject to a rule.
c	•	understanding and applying Pythagoras' theorem.	10IT, 10A, 10B, 10C, 10D *B21, B23* 16A, 18B, 18C, 19B, 20B, 24A, 25A, 25B *C40, C41, D46, D50*	(c)	Use Pythagoras' theorem.
d	•	using knowledge and skills in length, area and volume to carry out calculations in plane and solid shapes.	8D, 9B, 10IT, 10A *A13, A14* 16IT, 16A, 18A, 18B, 18C, 19B, 20B, 22B, 23B, 25A *C40, D44*	(d)	Carry out calculations in plane and solid shapes.
e	•	enlarging a shape by a fractional scale factor.	8C *A11* *D47, D49*		Assessed at a higher level (8a)

Level 8

a	•	understanding and using mathematical similarity; knowing that angles remain unchanged and corresponding sides are in the same ratio.	8C, 8E, 12B *A11* 16A, 23B *C31, D46, D47*	(a)	Use mathematical similarity to solve problems.
b	•	using sine, cosine and tangent in right-angled triangles, in 2-D.	2C, 10E, 12B *A14, B21, B23* 20A, 20B, 24A, 25A, 25B *C40, C41, D50*	(b)	Use sine, cosine or tangent in right-angled triangles.
c	•	distinguishing between formulae for perimeter, area and volume by considering dimensions.	18B *D52*	(c)	Distinguish between formulae by considering dimensions.
d	•	understanding and using vector notation, including its use in describing translations.	8E, 10D *B22* 24A, 24B *D49, D51*		Assessed at a higher level (9b)

Level 9

a1	•	calculating distances and angles in solids using plane sections and trigonometric ratios.	19B, 22B *C40, C41*	(a)	Carry out more complex calculations in plane or solid shapes.
a2	•	understanding the conditions for congruent triangles.	24A, 24FCT6 *C31, C40*		
a3	•	understanding and using the relationship between surface areas of similar figures and volumes of similar 3-D solids.	16A, 23B *D47*		
a4	•	calculating lengths of circular arcs and areas of shapes whose perimeters include circular arcs; calculating the surface area of cylinders and volumes of cones and spheres.	9B *B26* 16A, 18B, 20B, 22B, 25A *D46*		

b	•	understanding and using the laws of addition and subtraction of vectors.	8E B22 24B D51	(b)	Use vector methods to solve problems.
c1	•	finding sine, cosine and tangent of angles of any size.	20A, 20B C43	(c)	Use sine, cosine or tangent with angles of any size.
c2	•	sketching the graphs of sine, cosine and tangent functions for all angles.	16B, 20A, 20B C43		
c3	•	generating trigonometric functions using a calculator or computer and interpreting them.	16B, 20A, 20B C43		

Level 10

a1	•	knowing and using angle and tangent properties of circles.	16A, 20B, 22A, 24A C44, D46	(a)	Solve problems in 2-D or 3-D.
a2	•	using sine and cosine rules to solve problems including simple cases in 3-D.	10A 24A D50		
a3	•	understanding how transformations are related by combinations and inverses.	24B D49		
a4	•	using matrices to define transformations in 2-D.	24B D49		

Attainment Target 5:
Handling data

Pupils should collect, process and interpret data and should understand, estimate and use probabilities.

	Programme of Study	Task Maths	Statement of Attainment

Level 4

		Pupils should engage in activities which involve:			**Pupils should be able to:**
a	•	inserting, interrogating and interpreting data in a computer database.	7C 21FCT, 23FCT2	(a)	Interrogate and interpret data in a computer database.
b1	•	specifying an issue for which data are needed.	21B	(b)	Conduct a survey on an issue of their choice.
b2	•	collecting, grouping and ordering discrete data using tallying methods and creating a frequency table for grouped data.	7IT, 7B, 7C 21IT, 21B		
b3	•	understanding and using the median and mode in everyday contexts.	7A, 7B, 7C A12 21B D45		
b4	•	constructing and interpreting bar-line and line graphs and frequency diagrams with suitable class intervals for discrete variables.	7A, 7B A12 17A, 20A, 21IT C42		

b5	• creating a decision tree diagram with questions to sort and identify a collection of objects.	14B *C29*		
c	• understanding, calculating and using the mean and range of a set of data.	7A, 7C *A12* 21B *D45*	(c)	Use the mean and range of a set of data.
d1	• giving and justifying subjective estimates of probabilities.	11IT 14IT, 17IT, 23A	(d)	Estimate and justify the probability of an event.
d2	• understanding and using the probability scale from 0 to 1.	11IT 14A, 14B, 23A *C28*		
d3	• listing all the possible outcomes of an event.	14A, 14B, 23A *C28, C30*		

Level 5

a	• inserting and interrogating data in a computer database; drawing conclusions.	7C 21FCT, 23FCT2	(a)	Use a computer database to draw conclusions.
b1	• designing and using an observation sheet to collect data; collating and analysing results.	21B, 23IT	(b)	Design and use an observation sheet to collect data.
b2	• collecting, ordering and grouping continuous data using equal class intervals and creating frequency tables.	7A, 7B *A12* 21IT, 21A		
c1	• constructing and interpreting pie charts from a collection of data with a few variables.	17A, 17B, 21A *D45*	(c)	Interpret statistical diagrams.
c2	• constructing and interpreting conversion graphs.	12A, 12B *B19* *D42*		
c3	• constructing and interpreting frequency diagrams and choosing class intervals for a continuous variable.	7A *A12* 21A *D45*		
d1	• understanding that different outcomes may result from repeating an experiment.	11IT 14IT, 14A, 23IT, 23A	(d)	Use an appropriate method for estimating probabilities.
d2	• recognising situations where estimates of probability can be based on equally likely outcomes, and others where estimates must be based on statistical evidence.	14A, 23A, 23B, 23C		
d3	• knowing that if each of n events is assumed to be equally likely; the probability of one occurring is $1/n$.	14A, 14B, 23A *C28*		

Level 6

a1	• specifying an issue for which data are needed; designing and using observation sheets to collect data; collating and analysing results.	7FCT 1, 2, 3, 4 21B	(a)	Design and use a questionnaire to survey opinion.
a2	• designing and using a questionnaire to survey opinion (taking account of bias); collating and analysing results.	21B, 21FCT, 23FCT2		

b1	• creating scatter graphs for discrete and continuous variables and having a basic understanding of correlation.	7B *A12*	(b)	Understand and use the basic ideas of correlation.
b2	• constructing and interpreting information through two-way tables and network diagrams.	12B *B17* 23C *C29, C30*		
c	• identifying all the outcomes when dealing with two combined events which are independent, using diagrammatic, tabular or other forms.	14A, 14B, 23A, 23B *C28, C30*	(c)	Identify all the outcomes of combining two independent events.
d	• appreciating that the total sum of the probabilities of mutually exclusive events is 1 and that the probability of something happening is 1 minus the probability of it not happening.	7B 14A, 14B, 23A, 23B *C28*	(d)	Know that the total probability of all the mutually exclusive outcomes of an event is 1.

Level 7

a1	• specifying a simple hypothesis; designing and using an appropriate questionnaire or method to test it; collecting and analysing results to see whether a hypothesis is valid.	7IT, 7B, 21B	(a)	Organise and analyse data.
a2	• using and recording grouped data with class intervals suitably defined; producing a frequency table; calculating the mean using a calculator.	7A, 7B 23C *D45*		
a3	• comparing the mean, median, mode and range of a frequency distribution, where appropriate, for given sets of data, and interpreting the results.	7A, 7B 21B *D45*		
a4	• drawing a frequency polygon as a line graph from a frequency distribution for grouped data; making comparisons between two frequency distributions.	21A		
a5	• constructing and interpreting flow diagrams with and without loops.	B17 *C29*		
a6	• drawing a line of 'best fit' by inspection on a scatter diagram.	7B *A12*		
b1	• understanding and using relative frequency as an estimate of probability.	7B 14A, 17IT, 23C	(b)	Understand and use relative frequency as an estimate of probability.
b2	• appreciating, when assigning probabilities, that relative frequency and equally likely considerations may not be appropriate and 'subjective' estimates of probability have to be made.	14IT		
c	• understanding and applying addition of probabilities for mutually exclusive events.	14B, 23A, 23B *C28*	(c)	Given the probability of exclusive events, calculate the probability of a combined event.

Level 8

a	• designing and using a questionnaire with multiple responses or an experiment with several variables, collating and analysing results to test a hypothesis.	7FCT 1, 2, 3, 4 21B, 21FCT, 23FCT2	(a)	Design and use a questionnaire or experiment to test a hypothesis.

b1	• constructing a cumulative frequency table.	7B *A12*	(b)	Construct and interpret a cumulative frequency curve.
b2	• constructing a cumulative frequency curve using the upper boundary of the class interval, finding the median, upper-quartile, lower-quartile and inter-quartile range, and interpreting the results.	7B *A12* *D45*		
c1	• calculating the probability of a combined event given the probability of two independent events, and illustrating the combined probabilities of several events using tabulation or tree diagrams.	14B, 23A	(c)	Calculate the probability of a combined event given the probabilities of independent events.
c2	• understanding that when dealing with two independent events, the probability of them both happening is less than the probability of either of them happening (unless the probability is 0 or 1).	14A, 14B, 23A *C28*		

Level 9

a1	• constructing and interpreting a histogram with understanding of the connection between area and frequency.	21A	(a)	Use diagrams, graphs or computer packages to analyse a set of complex data.
a2	• presenting a set of complex data in a simplified form using a variety of diagrams and graphs and computer statistical packages.	21IT		
b	• using sampling to investigate a 'population' and recognising the reliability of different methods in relation to different sizes of population.	21B, 23C	(b)	Use sampling to investigate a 'population'.
c	• producing a tree diagram to illustrate the combined probability of several events which are not independent.	14B, 23A *C28*	(c)	Use conditional probabilities.

Level 10

a1	• describing the dispersion of a set of data; calculating the standard deviation of a set of data.	7A 21A	(a)	Describe the dispersion of a set of data.
a2	• considering different shapes of histograms representing distributions, with special reference to mean and dispersion, including the normal distribution.	21A		
b	• interpreting various types of diagram, such as those used in critical-path and linear programming.	23B *C29, D48*	(b)	Interpret diagrams such as those used in critical-path analysis or linear programming.
c	• understanding the probability for any two events happening.	23A *C28*	(c)	Calculate the probability of any two events happening.

9 EQUIPMENT AND RESOURCES

We are assuming that the following items of equipment are always available to all students:

rulers	scientific calculator
protractors	lined paper
compasses	centimetre squared paper
scissors	7 millimetre squared paper
glue	graph paper

From time to time students require access to a computer. A disk of programs that can be run on the makes of computer commonly found in classrooms is available from the publisher (see the following section).

When other equipment is needed for a chapter, this will be clearly indicated in the guide for that chapter.

10 COMPUTERS AND GRAPHICAL CALCULATORS

The use of computer programs is suggested in many places in the student's books.

Many of these references are to one of five computer programs on a disk specially prepared for Task Maths. This disk is available from the publishers and runs on several different types of computer (see order form). The five programs are *'Recurring decimals'*, *'Circle patterns'*, *'Spread'*, *'Tilekit'* and *'Estimating time'*. Notes on running these five programs are provided in the section called *'Running the computer programs'* on page 156.

There are also references in the course to other programs. Graph-plotting programs are mentioned several times. New graph-plotting programs are constantly being published; many teachers already have their favourites. Our suggestions are *'FGP'* for the BBC. *'FGP'* or *'Omnigraph'* for the Nimbus and *'Mouse plotter'* for the Archimedes (see below for addresses). The use of databases and spreadsheets are suggested on several occasions. We suggest the use of the database program, *'Pinpoint'* (see below for address). Ask your IT specialist for advice about the software used in your school. *'Spread'* is a small spreadsheet, suitable for use on most of the occasions in this course when a spreadsheet is suggested. The program *'Digame'* is suggested for Chapter 14 and the *'ATM Logo microworlds'* disk is suggested for a Further Coursework Task in Chapter 22. *'Geomat'* or *'Moves'* is useful for Chapter 24.

Logo is mentioned on several occasions in the book and some familiarity with the language is assumed. It would be helpful if students have access to a computer with *Logo*, while undertaking work on questions involving *Logo*. There are a few instances where it is suggested that writing and using a short program in *Logo* or *BASIC* might help students to complete the task. Examples of suitable programs are provided either in the student's book or in this teacher's resource book.

Throughout the book graphical calculators are suggested as an alternative to graph-plotting programs. It is worth remembering that graphical calculators are useful for a lot more than just drawing graphs. For example, they are often far more convenient than 'ordinary' calculators for a variety of situations concerned with trial and improvement.

'FGP' and *'Moves'* are available as part of *'SLIMWAM 1'* from ATM, 7 Shaftesbury Street, Derby DE3 8YB.

'Digame' is available as part of *'SLIMWAM 2'* from ATM.

'ATM Logo microworlds' is published by ATM.

'Omnigraph' and *'Geomat'* are marketed by SPA, PO Box 59, Leamington Spa, Warwicks CV21 3QA.

'Mouse plotter' is published by Shell Centre, University of Nottingham, University Park, Nottingham.

'Pinpoint' is published by Logotron, 124 Cambridge Science Park, Milton Road, Cambridge CB4 4ZS.

TASK MATHS

Guide to Chapter 14: **TABLE GAMES**

Outline

The task for this chapter is to develop useful strategies for playing dice and domino games.

The activity which introduces the task is to play Digame, a dice game for two or more players. Students are asked to write about the strategies they use when playing the game.

In Section A Digame is used to introduce the concept of probability as a fraction between 0 and 1. Intuitive ideas of combined probabilities are also introduced.

In Section B dominoes are used to develop probability ideas further and tree diagrams help with the solution of some of the problems. Network diagrams are introduced as a method of solving problems about chains of dominoes.

There are six Further Coursework Tasks. Two are about darts (analysing strategies and redesigning the board), two are about dominoes (designing a game for a larger domino set and exploring domino rings). One task is about designing a board game and the final task invites students to choose any game they know and write about some aspects of it.

Strategies

One way of introducing this task is for the class to watch two people (one perhaps being the teacher) play Digame on the computer. Students can then play the game in small groups (of between 2 and 4) using dice or the computer game. This activity is best not rushed: a lesson is needed to help students to develop appropriate strategies.

Sections A and B are intended to be worked through individually by each student. Some students might find it helpful to make their own set of dominoes for Section B.

Equipment and Resources

For introduction to the task and Section A:
 computer program Digame
 dice

For Section B:
 set(s) of dominoes

For FCTs 1 and 4:
 dartboard

For FCT 5:
 dominoes

Relevant Review Exercises

C27	*Fractions and decimals*	page 93
C28	*Probability*	page 95
C29	*Networks and flow charts*	page 100
C30	*Combinatorics*	page 103

TABLE GAMES

National Curriculum Statements

Introduction to the task
5/4d1; 5/5d1; 5/7b2

Section A
2/6a2; 2/8b2; 5/4d2; 5/4d3; 5/5d1; 5/5d2; 5/5d3; 5/6c; 5/6d; 5/7b1; 5/8c2

Section B
2/6a2; 2/8b2; 4/5c1; 5/4b5; 5/4d2; 5/4d3; 5/5d3; 5/6c; 5/6d; 5/7c; 5/8c1; 5/8c2; 5/9c

Questions in Sections

Accessible to all students (no bars)	Somewhat harder (one bar)	More difficult (two bars)
Section A, 1–5	Section A, 6	Section A, 7–8
Section B, 1–9	Section B, 10–13	Section B, 14–15

Further Coursework Tasks

neutral: 2, 3, 4, 5
easier: 1
more difficult: 6

INTRODUCTION TO THE TASK: HINTS

This activity helps to challenge some common misunderstandings or superstitions: for example, if you have just thrown a 6 it will probably be followed by a 1.

Encourage students to think about, and explain, their strategies. On the other hand, it is probably unwise to force 'correct' strategies onto students. One of the problems with probability as a topic is that students are taught the theory but it means nothing to them because they do not believe it! For this reason it is worth spending time on this activity; this will set the scene for Section A.

If the computer is used, some students might not believe that the computer is 'throwing' the die fairly. This is an understandable, and perhaps justified, disbelief: after all, what evidence is there that the computer really is producing numbers 'at random'?

We are not sure about the optimal strategy for Digame. But, because the die has no memory (is this assumption believed by students? Is it believed by anyone?) a logical strategy should involve deciding **what score for the turn** to stop at, rather than **how many throws** to make.

For an optimal strategy, your behaviour should also be influenced by the stage of the game. If you are a long way behind you presumably need to take greater risks so that you have a chance of catching up. If you are a long way ahead, you can afford to be cautious and to consolidate your position.

SECTION A: ANSWERS

1 (a) 0   (b) 2   (c) 3 ways: 2, 3; 3, 2; 5   (d) 1 way   (e) yes; 17

2 C and F are probably helpful and B, D and E are probably not helpful. People argue about A.

3 (a) $\frac{1}{6}$ (b) $\frac{5}{6}$ (c) $\frac{1}{2}$ (d) 1   (e) 0   (f) 10

4 (a) There are 36 outcomes.   (b) 11   (c) $\frac{11}{36}$ (d) $\frac{25}{36}$ (e) 22

5 (a) This is the theoretical result, unlikely to happen in practice!   (b) and (c) Dice have no memories.   (d) If you are a long way behind take risks.

6 About 20

7 (a) $\frac{1}{6}$ (b) $\frac{17}{36}$ (c) $\frac{15}{216}$ or $\frac{5}{72}$ (d) 0   (e) $\frac{153}{216}$

8 Assuming you **don't** get a 1, the average score on one throw of the die is $\frac{1}{5}(2 + 3 + 4 + 5 + 6) = 4$. Hence you need 25 throws on average, assuming no 1s. Pr(25 not 1s) = $(\frac{5}{6})^{25}$ = 0.01.

SECTION B: ANSWERS

1 (a) There are 28 dominoes.   (b) 7   (c) 7   (d) 13
2 (a) $\frac{7}{28}$ or $\frac{1}{4}$ (b) $\frac{7}{28}$ or $\frac{1}{4}$ (c) $\frac{2}{28}$ or $\frac{1}{14}$ (d) $\frac{3}{28}$ (e) 0
3 (a) 6   (b) 12   (c) 11   (d) 2
4 (a)

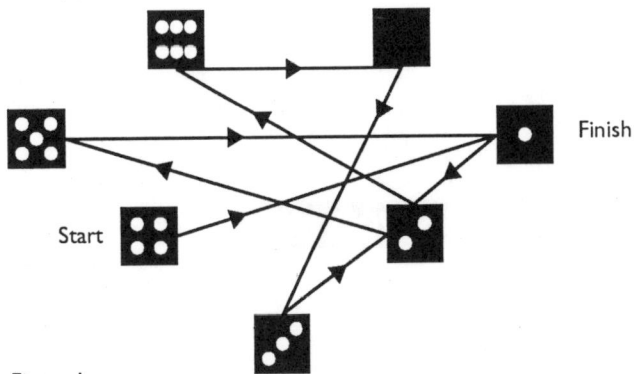

Figure I

TASK MATHS

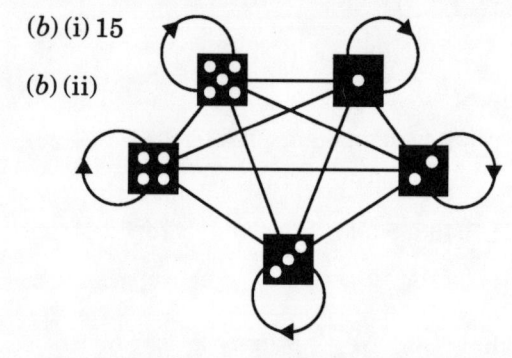

(b) (i) 15

(b) (ii)

(c) Matching the numbers is the same as not lifting your pen; each line represents one domino, so there are no repeats.
(d) No

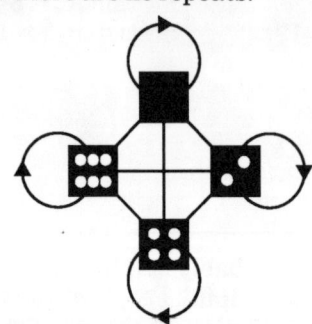

This network cannot be drawn without taking your pen off the paper (there are five lines – an odd number – coming out of each point).

5 (a) 2   (b) 1   (c) 3   (d) 0   (e) 4
6 (a) 2   (b) 0   (c) 4   (d) 2
7 Double-five and five
8 (a) 2; (1,4) scores 3   (b) 2; (6,6) scores 4   (c) 3; (4,1) or (5,2) or (5,6) scores 2   (d) 3; (6,6) scores 8   (e) 2; (3,6) scores 4
9 (a) See case (c) above; you score more than the next player.   (b) See case (d) above.   (c) The first player may also have the double-six domino.   (d) $\frac{7}{28}$ or $\frac{1}{4}$
10 (a) You need to get a total of 6 or 10; there are many ways to do this.   (b) You need to get 12 or 20. The ends can be: 6 and 6; double-3 and 6; double-4 and 4; double-5 and 2; double-6 and blank; double-2 and double-4; double-1 and double-5; double-blank and double-6; double-4 and double-6.
11 (a) 8   (b) $\frac{8}{17}$
12 (b) $\frac{1}{4} + \frac{1}{4} = \frac{1}{2}$
13 (a) $\frac{1}{2}$
14 (b) $\frac{1}{6} + \frac{5}{36} = \frac{11}{36}$
15 (a) $\frac{42}{756}, \frac{147}{756}, \frac{147}{756}, \frac{420}{756}$ (b) $\frac{42}{756}$ (c) $\frac{420}{756}$ (d) $\frac{21}{28} \times \frac{20}{27} \times \frac{19}{26} = \frac{7980}{19656}$

FURTHER COURSEWORK TASKS

1) Write about some aspects of darts. For example, write about possible finishing scores for a game of 501 Down. Or write about the way the numbers are arranged on a dartboard.

The main qualities students require for this task are being systematic and considering all possibilities.
  The possible finishing scores with three darts, given that you must finish with a double (including 50, which is double 25); are: all numbers from 2 to 158, 160, 161, 164, 167 and 170.
  Alternatively, the possible scores with three darts (when you do not need to throw a double to finish) are those above together with 159, 162, 165, 168, 171, 174, 177 and 180.
  One way of encouraging students to think about *why* certain scores are impossible is to change the dartboard in some way. Suppose, for example, the dartboard had numbers only up to 10 instead of up to 20. Or suppose it had only odd numbers (say 1, 3, 5, 7, ..., 39).
  Generally, the numbers are arranged on the dartboard in such a way that high numbers and low numbers are separated. One way of investigating this might be to do a 'moving average' of three numbers (or four numbers, or five numbers) around the dartboard. For example, $5 + 20 + 1 = 26$; $20 + 1 + 18 = 39$. One measure of the 'evenness' of the spread of numbers is the **range** of these moving averages. Having decided what criterion to use, students might explore modifications which would improve the evenness of the spread of numbers according to that criterion.

2) Design a board game.

You might want to get some ideas by looking at board games you know.

You might want to test your game by playing it. This might help you to think of improvements to your game.

The mathematical elements of this task include:
  devising the game;
  making decisions which might involve intuitive notions of probability (e.g. in a game based on letters, why do you have more Es than Xs?);
  devising, possibly through experiment, sensible scoring systems which produce a game that is interesting to play and finishes within a reasonable period of time;
  writing down the rules clearly, so that someone else can work out how to play the game.
Some students might want to choose a context which interests them as the setting for their game (e.g. football, or a game for very young children to play). Some students might need encouraging to concentrate on the (mathematical) essentials of the game, rather than on creating beautiful boards or developing an elaborate story line.
  One possibility, which makes the mathematics more explicit, is to develop variants of games such as dominoes and Scrabble, which involve numbers and operations on numbers.
  Students' accounts need to include an explanation of where their idea came from. For example, they might have brought together ideas from several commercial games. They can show they are working

at a higher level if they can explain how their ideas developed, rather than simply presenting the end product. Why have they included particular elements in their game? Have they thought through all possible eventualities, or might their game reach stalemate under certain circumstances?

Students who can write about **strategies** for playing their game are likely to be working at an even higher level. This might not be easy for them to do in general terms, but one approach is to give examples of moves from their game, accompanied by the strategic decisions which would be made and why.

> 3) Some sets of dominoes contain more dominoes than the standard sets in Britain. For example, one set has all possible dominoes from double-blank to double-nine.
>
> Design a version of Threes and Fives which could be played with such a set.

One possibility is that the game of Threes and Fives with the enlarged set would have exactly the same rules as the game of Threes and Fives with the normal set. Students could investigate the scoring possibilities with the large set. For example, a double-nine on one end and a double-six on the other would give 30 (scoring 16 points). The previous stage to this is either a double-nine on one end and a six on the other to give 24 (scoring 8 points), or a double-six on one end and a nine on the other to give 21 (scoring 7 points). There is one other way of getting 30, but the previous stage to that scores zero. What is the highest score you can make following a 30 (and a score of 16)? With the ordinary set of dominoes the best opening move is (4,5), because it scores 3 and no more than 2 can be scored on the next move. What is the best opening move with the larger set?

An alternative approach is to change the rules. Students might, for example, explore the possibilities of 'Threes and Sevens' or 'Fives and Sevens' or 'Threes, Fives and Sevens'. Students might want to consider 'safe moves' and 'risky moves' and 'moves worth the gamble' in any of these situations. Probability theory could be used here.

> 4) This is how the numbers are arranged round a dartboard. Is this a good arrangement? How do you think they should be arranged?
>
> The area in which you score 20 on a dartboard is the same size as the area in which you score 1. Some people think that it should be harder to score 20 on a dartboard than it is to score 1.
>
> You might want to redesign a dartboard so that it is harder to score some numbers than others.

One way of designing a dartboard is so that the area for a number is inversely proportional to its score. Students could redesign a dartboard along these lines, either by keeping the usual division into sectors or by changing it in some other way (for example, by having two numbers in one sector, one on the inside and one on the outside). Students might also wish to give consideration to the arrangement of numbers, as in FCT 2.

There are a variety of aspects of redesigned dartboards which might be explored. One is to find the average score if darts land 'at random' within the scoring area. One way of seeing if numbers are appropriately arranged might be to see whether darts landing at random in 'one half' of the dartboard score the same on average as darts landing at random in 'the other half'. There are obviously many ways of 'halving' the dartboard for this purpose.

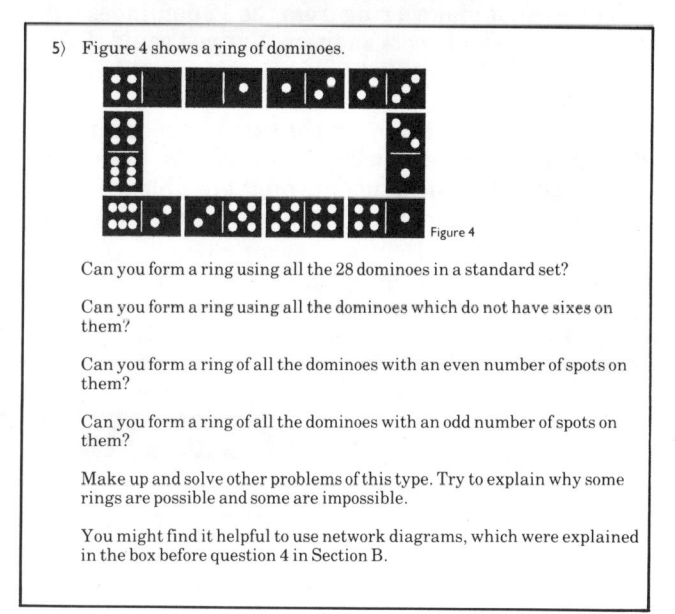

> 5) Figure 4 shows a ring of dominoes.
>
> *Figure 4*
>
> Can you form a ring using all the 28 dominoes in a standard set?
>
> Can you form a ring using all the dominoes which do not have sixes on them?
>
> Can you form a ring of all the dominoes with an even number of spots on them?
>
> Can you form a ring of all the dominoes with an odd number of spots on them?
>
> Make up and solve other problems of this type. Try to explain why some rings are possible and some are impossible.
>
> You might find it helpful to use network diagrams, which were explained in the box before question 4 in Section B.

The 28 dominoes in the standard set can be represented by the network diagram shown below.

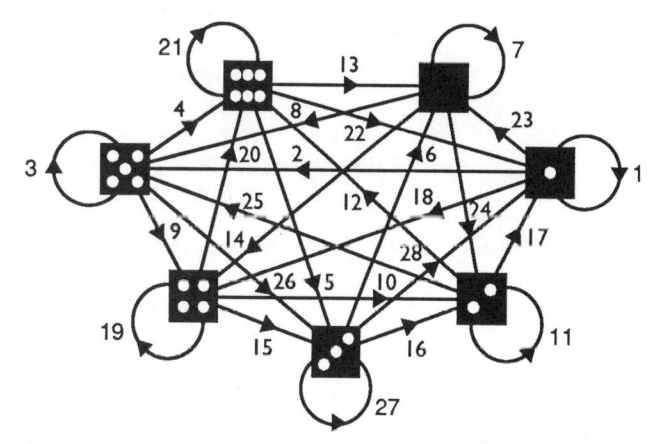

Making a closed ring of dominoes is equivalent to being able to draw the network, starting and finishing at the same place and without taking your pen off the paper or going over any line twice. There is a theorem which says that this is possible provided that there is an even number of lines meeting at each vertex. This is the case in the diagram above and so a ring is possible. There are in fact very many different ways of arranging the 28 dominoes in a ring.

TASK MATHS

It is not possible to make a ring from the 21 dominoes which do not have sixes on them. It is possible to make a ring from the 15 dominoes which do not have sixes or fives on them.

You certainly cannot make a ring from the 16 dominoes with an even number of spots on them. The network diagram for these dominoes is not even connected. (Students might be able to explain why.) Some (6) of these 16 dominoes have two odd numbers on them. A ring can be made from these. Some (10) have two even numbers on them. A ring cannot be made from these.

You cannot make a ring from the 12 dominoes with an odd number of spots on them. But you could if, for example, you left out the 4 such dominoes which contain a one.

It is interesting to look at the same problems for domino sets of different sizes (for example, the set described in FCT 3). Students might be able to find, and prove, theorems which apply to domino sets of *any* size.

> 6) Choose a game. It could be a card game, such as Chase the Ace or Crib. It could be a dice game, such as Yahtzee. It could be a board game such as Monopoly or Sorry.
>
> Write about some aspects of the game.

This is a difficult task to organise. There is usually a great deal of mathematics in a card game or a board game. Some of it is trivial or very dificult, particularly if you start considering probabilities. If students make mistakes in their work (for example, in connection with difficult ideas like independence of events) they should be given due credit for the probability ideas they **are** able to use intelligently.

Students will need to describe the game they are investigating, although more will be expected of them than a mere description. However, they need to be rewarded for a clear description, because this is usually by no means easy to do. Students also need to be rewarded for making imaginative choices about what is worth considering and what should be left out, and for organising and communicating their findings in a clear way.

ASSESSING STUDENTS' COURSEWORK TASKS

Further Coursework Task 2

It is not a trivial task to design a game which actually works! Unless students test their games out by playing them several times they are likely to overlook some eventualities, with the consequence that players might not know what to do or the games might grind to a halt. Writing down the rules so that they are understandable is also a challenge.

Many students design board games based on throwing dice and moving counters round boards, which have reward or penalty squares related to the story lines for the games. Such students might be producing cross-curricular coursework containing little mathematics!

Creating games based on mathematical ideas is one way of demonstrating statements of attainment from several of the mathematics attainment targets. The following extract is from the work of a student who designed a calculation game using the numbers on the dominoes. She could have improved her work by thinking more carefully about her choice of numbers on the dominoes and by describing in more detail problems that might arise when the game is played. Nevertheless, this extract shows that she can design a task in a given context (Ma1/6a).

How to play the Game

We made up a set of dominoes consisting of 30 different kinds, below is all of them.

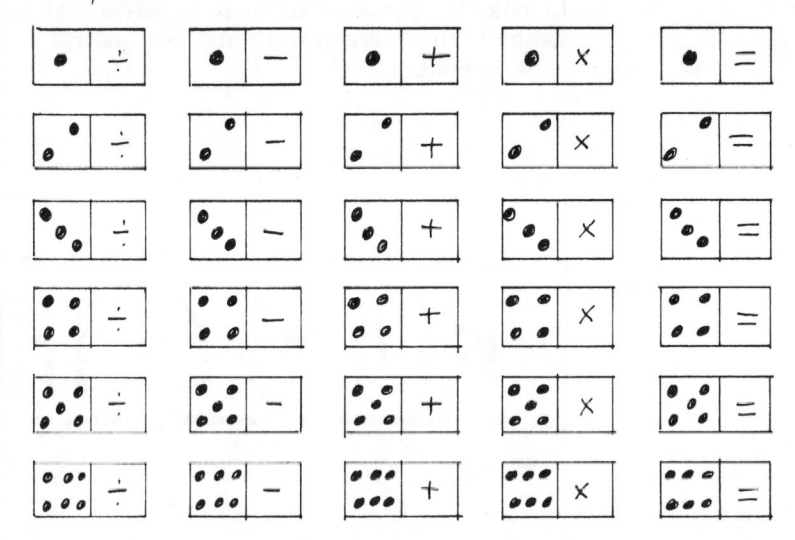

[A 6×5 grid of domino cards showing dots (1 to 6) paired with operators ÷, −, +, ×, =]

Then we made up a set of answer cards with the numbers from 10 to 20 on them....

I will now try and explain how to play our game in 3 easy stages.

Stage one
Shuffle all the dominoes except the answers and deal them out evenly between the two players. (You should have 15 each.)

Stage two
One of the players picks out one of the answer cards and puts it down on the table (for all to see).

Stage three
Decide who will start and put down your cards one at a time taking it in turn, you have to acheive a line of dominoes to form a sum with the answer (one of the players chose) at the end.

The aim of the game.

The aim of the game is to acheive the answer on the answer card. The person who completes the sum is the winner....

Some examples of our game.

① The answer to acheive = 17
$4 \times 2 + 6 + 5 - 2 = 17$

TABLE GAMES

TASK MATHS

Games based on sporting activities seem to help students to produce games not based on moving counters round a board. One student, who is a keen football player, invented a game in which the moves along and across the pitch are determined by the scores on two 20-sided dice. The game has 'danger areas' and a number of other special cards and events to make the game model more closely a real game of football. This piece of work also demonstrates achievement of Ma1/6a.

RULES OF THE GAME

Shuffle the blue and pink cards and place face down.

1 You have two 20 sided dice one of them is for going forward for example if you throw the dice and it lands on a 12 you go up the pitch 12 squares to the left or right *across the pitch* you throw the other dice, the even numbers mean go right and the odd numbers go left.

2 If you throw a 1 or 6 on the forward dice you lose the ball. If you throw a 2 or 5 on the left and right dice you lose the ball

3 If you land on the red zones on the pitch you have to take a pink card, the card will say whether you lose the ball or not. If you land in the red when you are in the box you get a penitey. The red zones are all over the pitch the card will say. Freekick for you, Freekick against you (you lose the ball) miss 2 goes carry on

4 You can only score when over the line on the pitch (you will see it). So if you are behind the line you have to pass the ball (throw the dice so the ball goes in front of the line) Then you can shoot (By just throwing the dice normal)

5 When you get the ball in the goal you pick up a blue card to see if the goalie has saved it or let it in. The card will say: (goal/saved)

6 With a freekick you throw *one of* the dice once and go in any direction   ↑↓ ↖↙ ↓→ ←↓

Another student based his game on motor racing. He developed a complex set of rules, which he amended in response to the problems he met when playing the game with other people. His heartfelt comments below show the struggle he had to develop a successful game and demonstrates that he is beginning to 'examine critically' (Ma1/6b).

> I got the idea for my game from quite a few other board games and I am thinking of going into production. I redesigned it twice after my Dad had played it and made more problems than there originally were and now it is so complicated that I am having problems understanding it. A bad aspect of the game is that it would be hard to understand and the game might get boring. But a good aspect of the game is that I've done it and it looks good.

Further Coursework Task 6

A good way to start the write-up for this task is to describe how to play the game and to explain which aspects of the game are to be explored and why. This is not trivial, because some aspects of the game might be almost impossibly difficult to analyse, while others yield little of mathematical interest. Working out general strategies for games, and justifying them by using probability theory, is often very difficult. However, students can demonstrate their ability to use and apply their understanding of probability by considering particular examples of play.

In the following extract the student is writing about Yahtzee. She is trying to work out the probability of throwing '3 of a kind' by considering the probability of throwing three 3s, a 5 and a 6 in one throw. She lists the twenty rearrangements and then writes the following:

> Next I shall place 20, the amount of ways possible of rearranging a 3 of a kind over 6×6×6×6×6 because there are 6 ways of throwing a number on each dice and there are 5 dice
>
> So the probability of throwing a three of a kind is $\frac{20}{7776} = \frac{5}{1944}$ I shall now show it in a decimals and percentage. The decimal is = 0.002572. The percentage is 0.25%
>
> No matter what the 3 of a kind is it will always be $\frac{5}{1944}$ ways of throwing it. This is because rearranging 3 of one kind and two different numbers will always be 20 different ways.

Her last two sentences hint that she realises that there are many other ways of getting '3 of a kind', which she does not deal with. Nevertheless, her work shows that she can comment constructively on solutions (Ma1/7b).

Another student works out the probability of 'straights'. He has forgotten to exclude the possibility of getting a 'large straight' from his consideration of the 'small straight' case. But nevertheless he is working at a high level. He can co-ordinate a number of features in solving problems (Ma1/9a) and justify the solution (Ma1/9b).

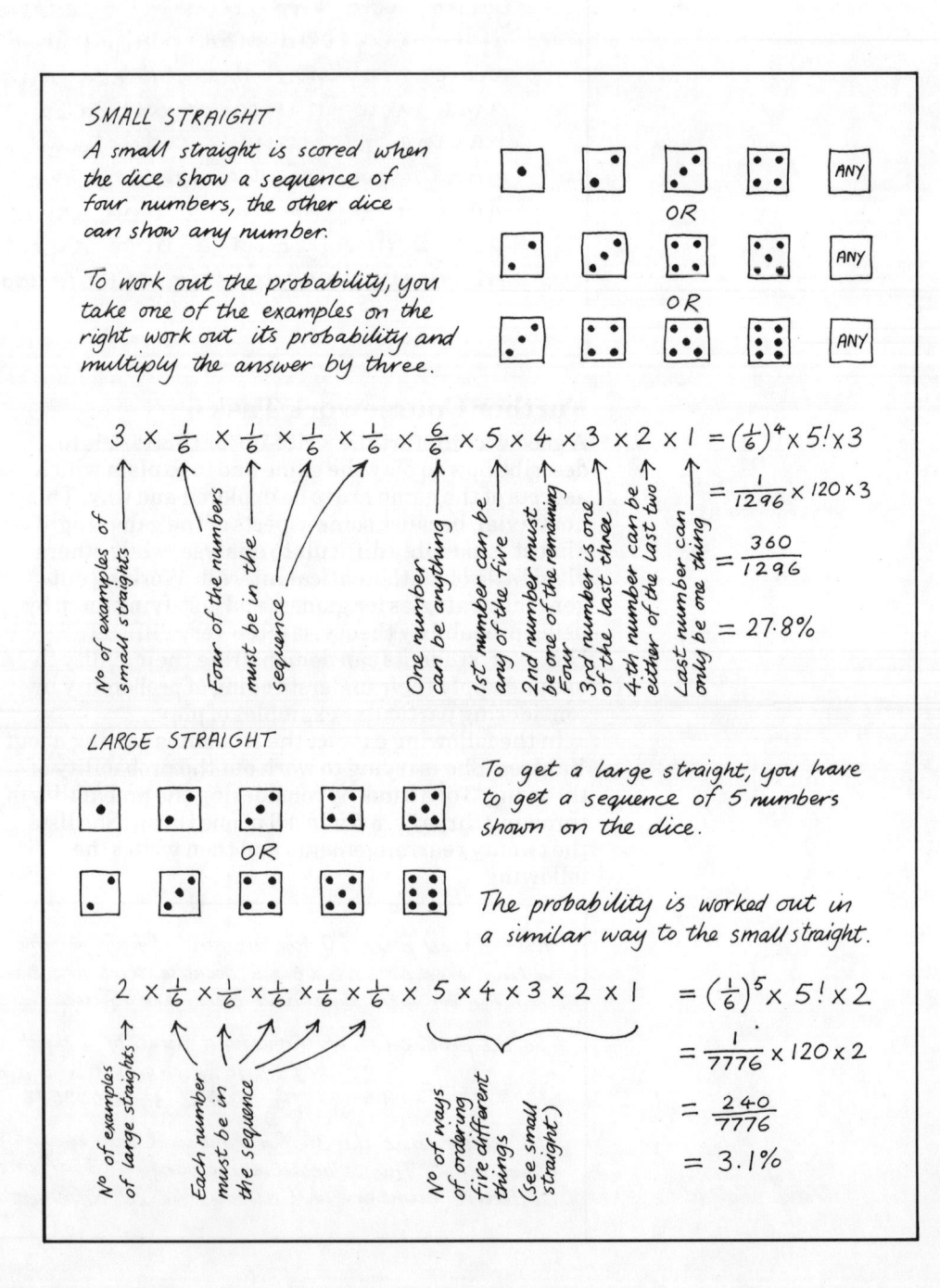

SMALL STRAIGHT

A small straight is scored when the dice show a sequence of four numbers, the other dice can show any number.

To work out the probability, you take one of the examples on the right work out its probability and multiply the answer by three.

$$3 \times \frac{1}{6} \times \frac{1}{6} \times \frac{1}{6} \times \frac{1}{6} \times \frac{6}{6} \times 5 \times 4 \times 3 \times 2 \times 1 = \left(\frac{1}{6}\right)^4 \times 5! \times 3$$

$$= \frac{1}{1296} \times 120 \times 3$$

$$= \frac{360}{1296}$$

$$= 27.8\%$$

- N° of examples of small straights
- Four of the numbers must be in the sequence
- One number can be anything
- 1st number can be any of the five
- 2nd number must be one of the remaining four
- 3rd number is one of the last three
- 4th number can be either of the last two
- Last number can only be one thing

LARGE STRAIGHT

To get a large straight, you have to get a sequence of 5 numbers shown on the dice.

The probability is worked out in a similar way to the small straight.

$$2 \times \frac{1}{6} \times \frac{1}{6} \times \frac{1}{6} \times \frac{1}{6} \times \frac{1}{6} \times 5 \times 4 \times 3 \times 2 \times 1 = \left(\frac{1}{6}\right)^5 \times 5! \times 2$$

$$= \frac{1}{7776} \times 120 \times 2$$

$$= \frac{240}{7776}$$

$$= 3.1\%$$

- N° of examples of large straights
- Each number must be in the sequence
- N° of ways of ordering five different things (see small straight)

In fact the actual game of Yahtzee is more complicated than these accounts indicate, because you can have second and third throws of any number of your five dice. One way students can tackle this extra dimension is by considering particular examples, as the student is doing the following extract. She is working out the chances of getting three sixes on the second and third throws. She is making good use of her knowledge of probability, even though she cannot complete the analysis of the problem.

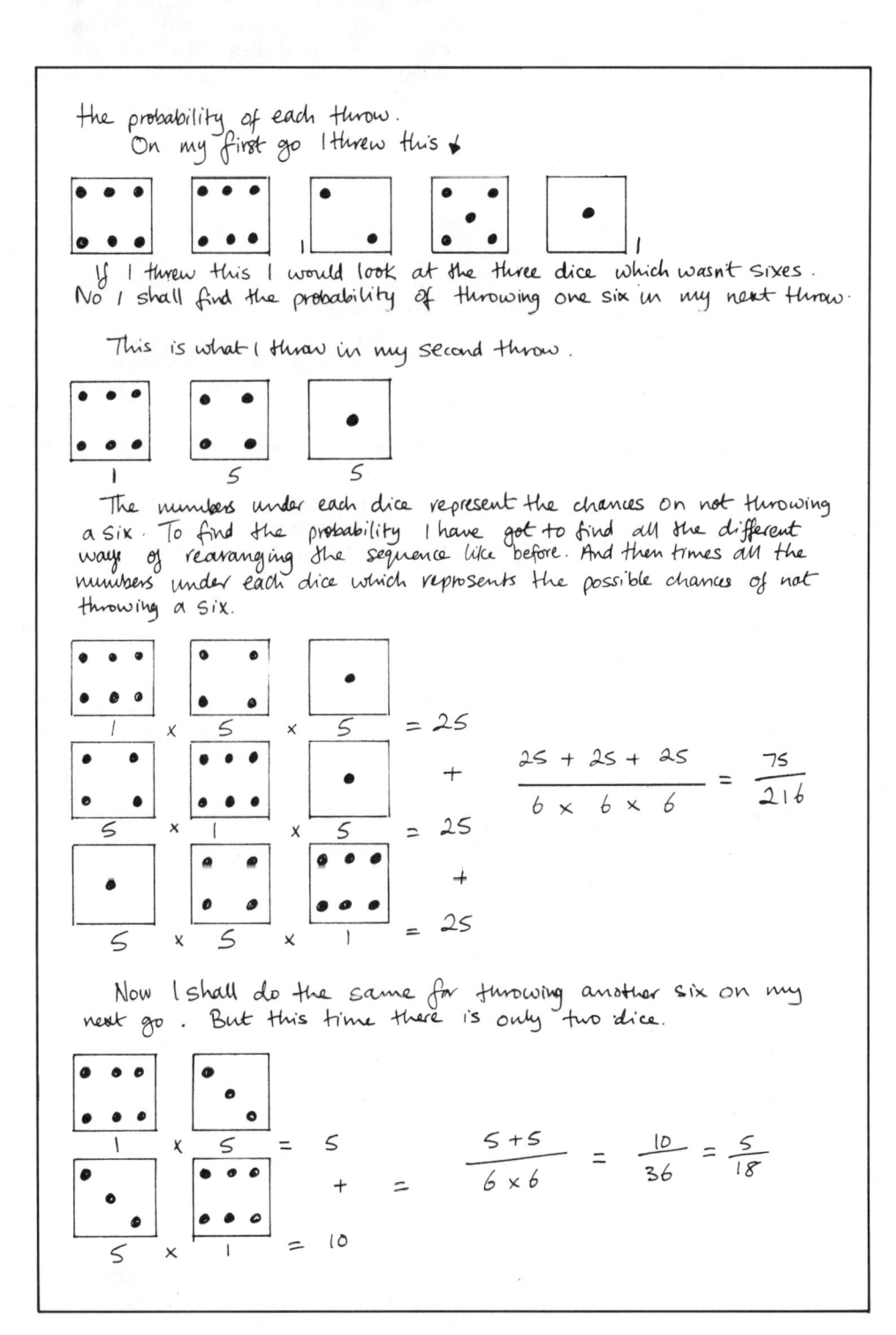

---

the probability of each throw.
On my first go I threw this ↓

[dice: 6] [dice: 6] [dice: 3] [dice: 5] [dice: 1]

If I threw this I would look at the three dice which wasn't sixes. No I shall find the probability of throwing one six in my next throw.

This is what I throw in my second throw.

[dice: 3] [dice: 4] [dice: 1]
  1   5   5

The numbers under each dice represent the chances on not throwing a six. To find the probability I have got to find all the different ways of rearranging the sequence like before. And then times all the numbers under each dice which represents the possible chances of not throwing a six.

[dice: 6] × [dice: 6] × [dice: •] = 25
  1   5   5

[dice: 6] × [dice: •] × [dice: 6] = 25 $\dfrac{25 + 25 + 25}{6 \times 6 \times 6} = \dfrac{75}{216}$
  5   1   5   +

[dice: •] × [dice: 6] × [dice: 6] = 25
  5   5   1

Now I shall do the same for throwing another six on my next go. But this time there is only two dice.

[dice: 6] × [dice: 5] = 5
  1   5

[dice: 5] × [dice: 6] = 10 $\dfrac{5 + 5}{6 \times 6} = \dfrac{10}{36} = \dfrac{5}{18}$
  5   1

Guide to Chapter 15: COLOURINGS

Outline

The task for this chapter is colouring plane and solid shapes according to certain rules.

In the introductory activity students find all the ways of colouring a particular type of tile using three colours. Convincing themselves that they have found them all involves understanding the concepts of symmetry, congruence, right-handedness and rotation.

In Section A coloured tiles of different designs are used to pose some questions about rotations. Other questions involve finding all the possible ways of colouring different tiles, and a strategy for this is explained. The more difficult questions invite students to find general rules which apply for any number of colours.

In Section B the concept of congruence is reinforced and Venn diagrams are used to solve more problems about coloured tiles.

Section C begins with the well-known 'painted cubes' problem and develops it to involve the use of fractions, decimals, algebra and graphs.

There are five Further Coursework Tasks. Two of them involve designing and colouring your own tiles, one is about painted cuboids, one invites students to devise their own sequence of cube models to paint, and one is about painting cubes using more than one colour.

Strategies

Much of the work in this chapter will simply be an exercise in colouring unless students approach the tasks systematically and use combinatoric arguments to convince themselves that they have found all the possibilities. With some questions (e.g. question 1 from Section A) some students might need to be discouraged from copying all the drawings from the text book.

Most of the chapter is probably best tackled by students working individually or in small groups. However, Section C can be introduced through class discussion. It might be worth painting a set of polystyrene cubes (obtainable from E.J. Arnold) to help you demonstrate the problem. Note that questions 1 and 2 in Section C are often set as a coursework task; some students could profitably spend a week of lessons answering them.

Equipment and Resources

For all parts:
coloured pencils

For introduction to the task
resource sheet 23, *Square tiles*

For Sections A and B:
resource sheet 24, *Triangle tiles*

For Section B:
resource sheet 25, *Hexagon tiles*

For Section C and FCTs 3, 4 and 5:
interlocking cubes
resource sheet 1, *Isometric dot*

Relevant Review Exercises

C27	*Fractions and decimals*	page 93
C28	*Probability*	page 95
C30	*Combinatorics*	page 103
C31	*Properties of shapes*	page 107

COLOURINGS

National Curriculum Statements

Introduction to the task
4/4a3; 4/4c

Section A
3/4a1; 3/5b1; 3/8a1; 4/4c; 4/6b3

Section B
3/4a1; 3/5b1; 3/8a1; 4/4a3; 4/4c; 4/6b3

Section C
2/6a2, 2/6a4, 3/4a1, 3/5a2, 3/5a3, 3/5b1, 3/6b, 3/7a1, 3/7b3, 3/7b4, 3/8a3, 4/4d2, 4/6a

Questions in Sections

Accessible to all students (no bars)	Somewhat harder (one bar)	More difficult (two bars)
Section A, 1–4		Section A, 5,6
Section B, 1,2,4,5	Section B, 3,6	Section B, 7–9
Section C, 1–5	Section C, 7–9	Section C, 10–13

Further Coursework Tasks

neutral: 1, 3, 4
easier:
more difficult: 2, 5

INTRODUCTION TO THE TASK: HINTS

This is a worthwhile activity for all students and sets the scene for the task. It need only take one or two lessons. It is worth discouraging students from colouring at random, and forcing them to adopt a systematic approach before they have spent too much time on the activity.

A key stumbling block is deciding that

[tile image] is different from [tile image]

Some students will find the task easier if they cut the tiles out. This helps them to check for repeats and to sort their tiles logically. Encourage students to explain *why* they know they have all possible tiles (see results below).

There are six possible 'types' of tile. The number of each type is shown below

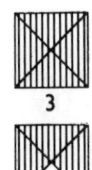

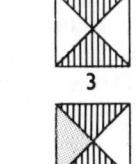

3 3 3
6 3 6   Total 24

Explaining why there is only this number of each type involves the use of symmetry.

SECTION A: ANSWERS

1. (a) Anticlockwise 90° (b) 180° (c) Clockwise 90°
   (d) Clockwise 90° (e) 180° (f) Clockwise 60°
   (g) Anticlockwise 120°
2. 11 (3 with one colour, 6 with two colours, 2 with 3 colours)
3. (a) 7 (add r,r; b,b; y,y; r,b; r,y; b,y; y,b)
   (b) 6 (add r,r; b,b; y,y; r,b; r,y; b,y)
   (c) 7 (add r,r; b,b; y,y; r,b; r,y; b,y; y,b)
   (d) 8 (add r,r; b,b; y,y; r,b; r,y; y,r; b,y; y,b)
   (e) 6 (add r,r; b,b; y,y; r,b; r,y; b,y)
   (f) 11 (add r,r,r; b,b,b; y,y,y; r,r,b; b,b,r; r,r,y; y,y,r; b,b,y; y,y,b; y,b,r; y,r,b) (Compare (f) with answer to question 2.)
4. 6 (3 with one colour, 3 with two colours)
5. (a) $5 + \frac{1}{2} \times 5 \times 4 = 15$ (b) $N + \frac{1}{2}N(N-1) = \frac{1}{2}N(N+1)$
6.

No. of colours	Type A	Type B	Type C	Total
(a) 4	4	$4 \times 3 = 12$	$\frac{4 \times 3 \times 2}{4} = 6$	22
(b) 5	5	$5 \times 4 = 20$	$\frac{5 \times 4 \times 3}{5} = 12$	37
(c) N	N	$N(N-1)$	$\frac{N(N-1)(N-2)}{N} = (N-1)(N-2)$	$2N^2 - 3N + 2$

SECTION B: ANSWERS

1. There are 10 types: A,J; B,P; C,L,R; D,K; E,I,O; F,N; G; H; M; Q.
2. 3 types, using 3 colours (see question 6 in Section A)
3. 7 types, using 4 colours

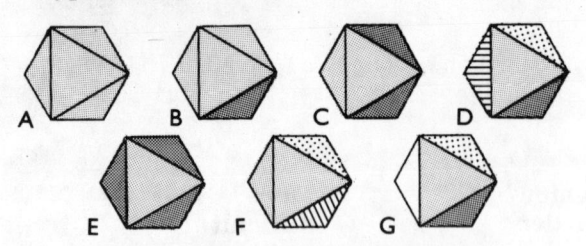

4. (a) 3 (b) 12 (c) 9 (d) 18 (e) 13 or 4
5. It depends whether you include tiles which also have blue on them or not.
6. 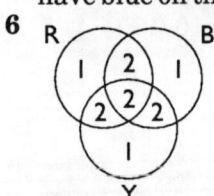 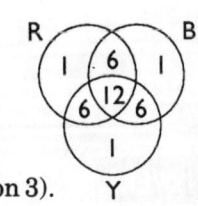
7. There are 33 tiles. 3 of type A and 6 each of B, C, D, E, F, G (see question 3).
8. (a) 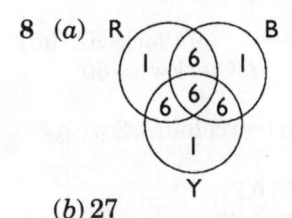
   (b) 27
9. Any tile with three non-symmetrical regions. These are two examples:

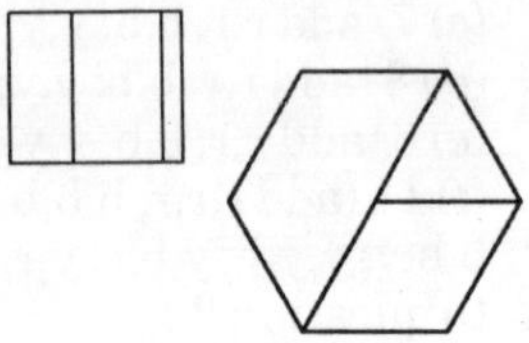

SECTION C: ANSWERS

1. (a) 8 (b) 12 (c) 6 (d) 1
2.

Size	Number of faces painted 0	1	2	3	Total number
2×2×2	0	0	0	8	8
3×3×3	1	6	12	8	27
4×4×4	8	24	24	8	64
5×5×5	27	54	36	8	125
6×6×6	64	96	48	8	216
7×7×7	125	150	60	8	343
8×8×8	216	216	72	8	512
9×9×9	343	294	84	8	729
10×10×10	512	384	96	8	1000

3. (a) No. $11^3 = 1331$; $12^3 = 1728$
   (b) Yes. $97336 = 46^3$ (c) 272 ($2000 - 12^3$)
4. (a) 54 (b) 108
5. (a) 150 (b) 600
6. (a) 48 (b) 50%
7.

Total	Painted faces	Total faces	Fraction	Percent.
8	24	48	$\frac{1}{2}$	50
27	54	162	$\frac{1}{3}$	33
64	96	384	$\frac{1}{4}$	25
125	150	750	$\frac{1}{5}$	20

8. (a) 1000 (b) 125 000
10. (a) 8 (the corners of the large cube)
    (b) $12(N-2)$ ($N-2$ along each of 12 edges)
    (c) $6(N-2)^2$ (there is a square of side $N-2$ on each face)
    (d) $(N-2)^3$ (there is a cube of edge $N-2$ left inside once outer layer is removed).
12. (a) 2197 (b) 64 (c) 1000 (d) 216 (e) 8000
    (f) Yes, for a cube of edge 1898.
13. (a) (2,24), (3,108), (4,288), (5,600), (6,1080) and (7,1764) are points on the graph.
    (b) $y = 6x^2(x-1)$

FURTHER COURSEWORK TASKS

1) Here are some tile designs.

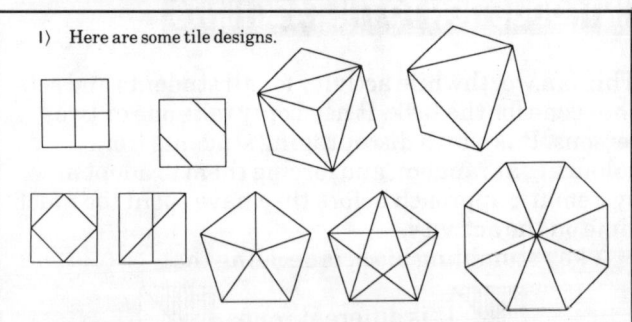

Choose one of these designs or make up a design of your own.

How many different tiles of your chosen design can you make using 3 colours?

How many tiles of your chosen design can you make using 4 colours?

You might want to discover how many you can make using N colours.

For most (if not all) students it is best that this is *not* just an exercise in colouring. Students need to be systematic and look for 'types' of tiles.

Some students might be able to consider relationships between different tile designs. For example, why is the number of tiles obtained by colouring

with N colours, N times the number obtained by colouring

COLOURINGS

with N colours?

Why is the number of squares obtained by colouring

with 3 colours a square number (11^2)? (See question 2 in Section A.) And does this generalise to N colours?

> 2) Find two different tile designs both of which produce the same number of tiles when three colours are used.
>
> You might want to use the designs of Task 1, or to make up your own designs.
>
> You can, of course, do the same task using a different number of colours.

This task is all about symmetry. Two designs will have the same number of tiles when 3 colours are used if they have the same number of regions and these regions have the same symmetry. Here are some examples:

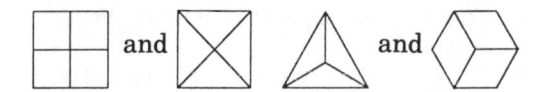

and   and

There might be occasions when tile designs with different symmetries happen to produce the same number of tiles when coloured with three colours.

There are many related questions which students could work on. Here are some of them.

Given that you know the number of tiles with three colours, can you predict the number of tiles with four colours?

If you are given a number, can you find a tile design which produces this number of tiles, when coloured using three colours? Can you find a tile design, which produces this number of tiles, when coloured using any number of colours?

Another possible activity is ordering designs according to the number of tiles they produce. The simplest design is this:

It has one region. Does it matter what shape it is?
Is the second simplest design this?

Is any design with two regions as simple as this? And so on.

> 3) Section C was about painting the outside of cubes made out of smaller cubes.
>
> Figure 12 shows other sequences of models made out of cubes.

Figure 12

Choose one of these sequences or make up a sequence of your own. If the outsides of your sequence of models are painted red, how many of each of the small cubes of each model have no faces painted? 1 face painted? And so on.

You might want to find formulae which give the answers for the Nth model in your sequence.

Whether students choose one of the sequences suggested, or whether they make up a sequence of their own, the task is about visualising, and is an excellent way of exploring some of the relationships between algebra and geometry. Students will probably need to build their models from interlocking cubes.

Counting is no easy matter and counting 'systematically', so that the count can be generalised, is even more difficult.

Students might find it useful to shade isometric drawings of their models in a way which shows which cubes are painted on one side, which on two sides, which on three sides, etc. (see students' work in the following section). This helps them to see the patterns formed by such cubes and might make it easier for them to use the geometry of their models to obtain, and justify, number patterns or algebraic formulae.

Students should be encouraged to tackle a sequence of models, which *they* will find demanding. The sequence of 'pyramid' models is more difficult than the other two suggested in the student's book. It might prove difficult to use isometric drawings to help record results for this sequence, because of the complexity of the models. Alternative methods can be invented, such as this one.

35

The circles round some of the 3s are used to indicate that there are two different ways in which cubes can be coloured on three sides.

Here is a table of results for the first seven models in the sequence of pyramids.

Model number	Number of faces painted						Total number of cubes
	0	1	2	3	4	5	
1	0	0	0	1	3	1	5
2	0	1	3	6	3	1	14
3	1	6	8	11	3	1	30
4	5	15	15	16	3	1	55
5	14	28	24	21	3	1	91
6	30	45	35	26	3	1	140
7	55	66	48	31	3	1	204

Students might be able to use the geometry of the models to explain, for example, why the numbers in the 5 Column are all 1 or why the numbers in the 0 Column have differences which are square numbers (relatively straightforward); or why the numbers in the 3 Column have a constant difference of 5 or why the numbers in the 2 Column have differences which increase by 2 (much harder).

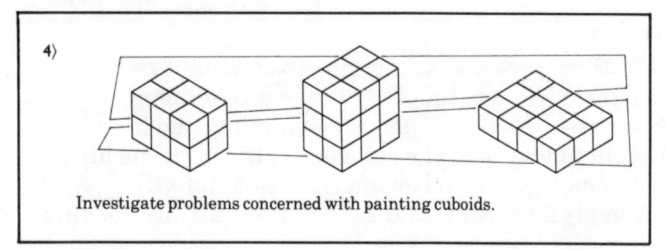

4) Investigate problems concerned with painting cuboids.

The results for painted cuboids are most noticeably different from those for painted cubes when one (or two) of the dimensions of the cuboids are 1. For a 1 by 1 by N cuboid all cubes are painted on four faces except for the 2 at the ends, which are painted on five. For a 1 by M by N cuboid 4 of the cubes are painted on four faces, and many of the cubes are painted on two **opposite** faces, or on three faces which do not **all** meet at a common vertex.

Again, students might find it useful to shade pictures of their models in a way which shows which cubes are painted on two sides, which on three sides, which on four and which on five.

The patterns for larger cuboids are more similar to those for cubes. Students can use methods similar to those suggested in Section C and some students will be able to obtain formulae by generalising those in question 10 of that section.

5) 27 small cubes are put together to make a large cube as in question 1 of Section C. The outside is painted red. The cubes are then separated.

Is it possible to paint each of the other faces of the small cubes blue or yellow, in such a way that the cubes can be put together to show a completely blue large cube, and can also be put together to show a completely yellow large cube?

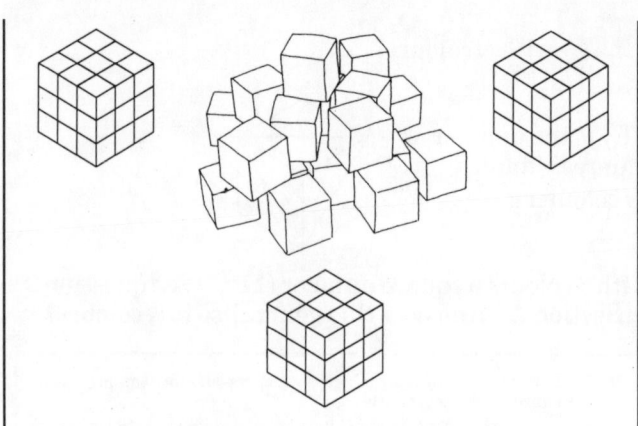

If it is possible, you might want to discover in how many different ways it can be done. You will need to decide what you mean by 'different'.

You might want to try solving a similar problem for a large cube which is made from 8 small cubes. Or 64 small cubes. Or 125 small cubes. Or N^3 small cubes.

One interesting aspect of this task is that students will need to find a way of recording their results; this is not trivial, but we strongly recommend that you leave it to your students to devise an appropriate method of recording. (See examples of students' work in the following section.)

The solution for the $3 \times 3 \times 3$ cube is outlined in the next paragraph. We have met both students and teachers who 'can prove' that there isn't a solution!

The main principle which guides the solution is that there are no faces to waste. 27 cubes have 27×6 faces altogether. A $3 \times 3 \times 3$ cube has 9×6 faces exposed. So a third of the available faces must be painted red. The same applies also to blue and yellow. You can then reason as follows:

One cube is at the centre. When the outside is red this cube must be entirely blue and yellow (3 faces of each). Similarly there is a blue and red cube, and a red and yellow cube. That accounts for 3 cubes.

The large cube has eight corners which mean 8 cubes painted red on three faces. We have already accounted for two of them. There are to be 6 more. Likewise 6 blue on three faces, and 6 yellow on three faces. 18 altogether.

This leaves 6 cubes to be painted red on two faces, yellow on two faces and blue on two faces.

The only flexibility is in how you colour the 18 cubes. How many cubes do you have with three red, two blue and one yellow face(s); and how many with three red, two yellow and one blue face(s)? It is up to you. You might consider some choices more 'elegant' than others; what you mean by 'elegant' is something else to explain.

It is not a trivial task matching a student's solution to your solution, particularly if the student has used a completely different method of recording the results!

An interesting twist is to fit the cubes together so that, as well as giving all one colour on the outside, faces which touch each other inside the cube have the same colours. The problem given in the coursework task generalises. If you have N^3 cubes, you can colour them using N colours in such a way that they can be assembled into a cube in different ways to show in turn each of the N colours entirely covering the surface of the cube. This is even true when $N = 1$! If students can solve the problem when $N = 3$ they should be able to manage it when $N = 1$ or 2. They might also be able to tackle $N = 4$ (see examples of students' work in the next section). The method outlined above for solving the solution when $N = 3$ generalises to some extent. One or two students might even obtain the general solution for all N.

ASSESSING STUDENTS' COURSEWORK TASKS

Further Coursework Task 3

This task is suitable for students of all abilities, because its difficulty depends largely on the complexity of the models chosen. In the extracts given below the student has chosen a fairly simple sequence of models. She collects her data accurately and derives and verifies formulae for her results. She can pose her own questions in a given context (Ma1/6a).

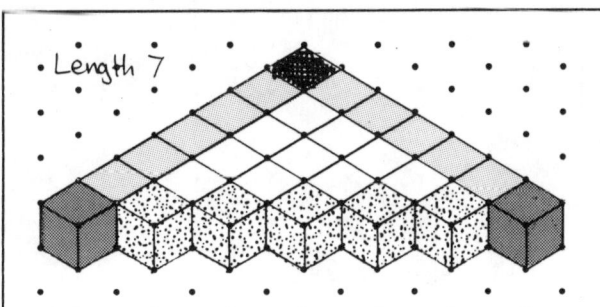

Length 7

TOTAL CUBES = 28
10 cubes have 2 painted
10 cubes have 3 painted
6 cubes have 4 painted
2 cubes have 5 painted

Length or width	No. of cubes	2 faces painted	3 faces	4 faces	5 faces
2	3	0	0	1	2
3	6	0	2	2	2
4	10	1	4	3	2
5	15	3	6	4	2
6	21	6	8	5	2
7	28	10	10	6	2
8	36	15	12	7	2
9	45	21	14	8	2

The rule for cubes with 3 faces painted is slightly more complicated.

x = length or width T = No. of cubes with 3 faces painted.

$$T = (x-4) + x$$

My rule tested
$(2-4) + 2 = -2 + 2$ $(7-4) + 7 = 3 + 7$ IT WORKS !!!
$ = 0$ $ = 10$

In the following extracts a student is applying the same ideas to a considerably more complicated sequence of models. Her level of achievement is likely to be higher.

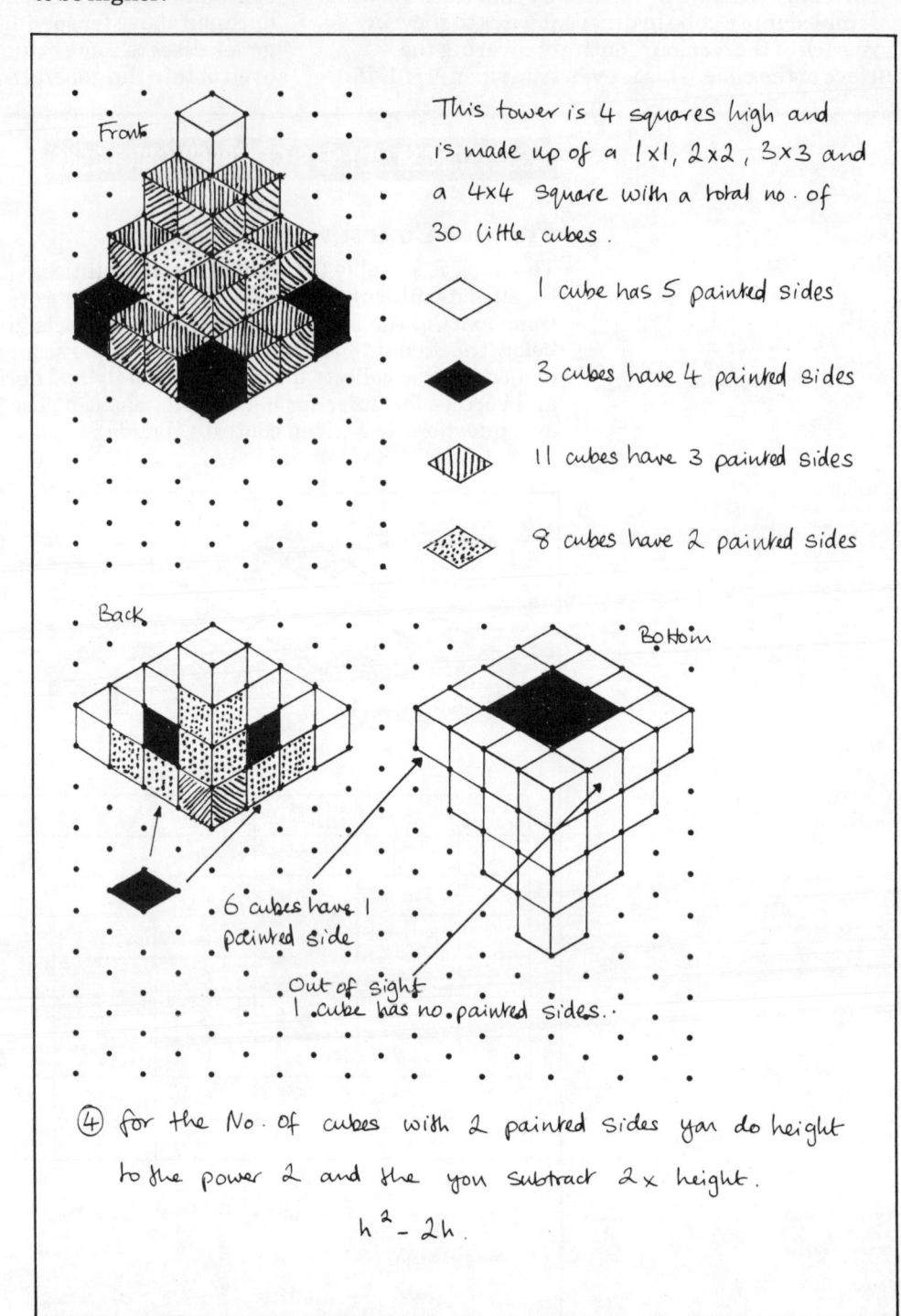

> This tower is 4 squares high and is made up of a 1x1, 2x2, 3x3 and a 4x4 square with a total no. of 30 little cubes.
>
> ◇ 1 cube has 5 painted sides
>
> ◆ 3 cubes have 4 painted sides
>
> ▦ 11 cubes have 3 painted sides
>
> ▨ 8 cubes have 2 painted sides
>
> 6 cubes have 1 painted side
>
> Out of sight
> 1 cube has no painted sides.
>
> ④ For the No. of cubes with 2 painted sides you do height to the power 2 and then you subtract 2× height.
>
> $h^2 - 2h$.

In this final extract another student has taken her work a stage further than the other students, because she has explained how her formulae relate to the models. She can co-ordinate a number of variables when solving problems (Ma1/9a) and justify the solution (Ma1/9b).

COLOURINGS

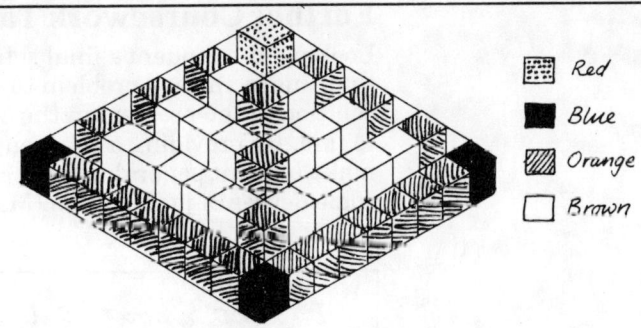

Here is a table of the ones that have tried out already.

	N⁰ of cubes with sides painted					
	5 sides	4 sides	3 sides	2 sides	1 sides	0 sides
2 layers	1	4	4	–	–	–
3 layers	1	4	16	4	9	1
4 layers	1	4	28	16	25	10
5 layers	1	4	40	36	49	28

Now I shall try to work out some formulars.

For 5 sides painted.
This will always be the N⁰ 1 (the cube on the top)

For 4 sides painted
This will always be the N⁰ 4 (the 4 cubes on the corners of the bottom layer

For 3 sides painted
These are the ones coloured in with orange, and they are along the edges (not the corners) of the bottom layer, and on the corners) of the other layers. So the ones on the bottom layer could be worked out by going :- (Asuming the bottom layer is 11 x 11)

$(11-2)4$ or $(x-2)4$ $x = 11$

and the rest would be
4×4 or $(Y-2)4$ y = N⁰ of layers

This comes from the N⁰ of layers minus 2 because there aren't any 3 sided cubes on the top, and we have already counted up the ones on the bottom layer, so that isn't needed either. It is then times by 4 because on each layer the only cubes with 3 sides painted are on each of the 4 corners.

The answers to these 2 would then be added together to make the answer. so, $(x-2)4 + (Y-2)4$ = N⁰ of cubes with 3 sides painted.

x = N⁰ of cubes on one side of the bottom layer
Y = N⁰ of layers.

For 2 sides painted
To start with you would need to do $x-2$ to get the side of the next layer up. This N⁰ would then need to be timzed by itself. This is to get the total N⁰ of cubes that have any N⁰ of sides painted from this layer up ⟶ (or the 2nd layer up.) The next thing to do is to take off one (the total) for the 5 sided cube on top. Next you do $(Y-2)4$ and take this off the N⁰ which you have already got. This is to get rid of all the 3 sided cubes on those layers!!! So this is long way of working out for 2 sides painted. ① $(x-2)^2$
② -1
③ $-(Y-2)4$

39

TASK MATHS

Further Coursework Task 5

Looking at a student's final solution might suggest that this is an easy problem to solve. But even the solution to the problem in the 3 × 3 × 3 case is not easy to find. By providing a solution the student has to make implicit generalisations and this account gives some degree of justification (Ma1/6c).

> I went about this by getting 27 small cubes and fitting them together to make a large cube.
>
> I have found out that 8 cubes need 3 painted faces
> 12 cubes need 2 painted faces
> 6 cubes need 1 painted face
> 1 cube needs 0 painted faces
>
> I wrote the equivalent R's on the cubes I then tried to fit in the B's and Y's but found a special sequence is required and easier to work out on paper.
>
> I wrote the R's down first and then made the B's and Y's fit in.
>
> I have made up this table to sort out the sides.
>
> I then tried out my cubes, first all red sides, then blue sides, then yellow, and I successfully got it to work.

R	R	R	Y	Y	Y
R	R	R	B	B	B
R	R	R	B	Y	Y
R	R	R	B	Y	Y
R	R	R	B	Y	Y
R	R	R	B	Y	Y
R	R	R	B	B	Y
R	R	R	B	B	Y
R	R	R	B	B	Y

R	R	B	B	B	Y
R	R	B	B	B	Y
R	R	B	B	B	Y
R	R	B	B	Y	Y
R	R	B	B	Y	Y
R	R	B	B	Y	Y
R	R	B	B	Y	Y
R	R	B	B	Y	Y
R	R	B	B	Y	Y

R	R	B	Y	Y	Y
R	R	B	Y	Y	Y
R	B	B	Y	Y	Y
R	B	B	Y	Y	Y
R	B	B	Y	Y	Y
R	B	B	Y	Y	Y
R	B	B	B	Y	Y
R	B	B	B	Y	Y
B	B	B	Y	Y	Y

Students will tackle bigger cubes in different ways. In the extracts below the student first counts how many faces of each colour are needed for a 4 × 4 × 4 cube and then uses this to show how all 64 cubes should be coloured. The second extract shows part of this list.

		N° of them
3 sides of small cubes painted Yellow	=	8
2 sides of " " " "	=	24
1 sides of " " " "	=	24
0 sides of " " " "	=	8

		N° of them
3 sides of " " " Blue	=	8
2 sides of " " " "	=	24
1 sides of " " " "	=	24
0 sides of " " " "	=	8

		N° of them
3 sides of " " " Red	=	8
2 sides of " " " "	=	24
1 sides of " " " "	=	24
0 sides of " " " "	=	8

		N° of them
3 sides of " " " Green	=	8
2 sides of " " " "	=	24
1 sides of " " " "	=	24
0 sides of " " " "	=	8

N° of small cubes	Y	B	R	G
55	1	1	2	2
56	1	1	2	2
57	1	1	2	2
58	1	1	2	2
59	1	1	2	2
60	1	1	2	2
61	1	1	2	2
62	1	1	2	2
63	1	1	2	2
64	1	1	2	2

N° of faces painted

This was easy to do because I split the four colours into two groups. Then because there was 8 3 faces painted each and 8 0 faces painted each I could combine them easily. With Y and B colours first having 3 faces and R and G colours 0 faces then vice versa. Also because 24 2 faces are painted for all colours and 24 1 faces are painted for all colours I can do the same for them.

COLOURINGS

He uses the same idea for a 5 × 5 × 5 cube, which he apparently finds a lot more difficult.

Table (e)
						N° of them
3 sides of "	"	"	"	Orange	=	8
2 sides of "	"	"	"	"	=	36
1 sides of "	"	"	"	"	=	54
0 sides of "	"	"	"	"	=	27

N° of small cubes	\multicolumn{5}{c	}{N° of faces painted}	N° of small cubes	\multicolumn{5}{c	}{N° of faces painted}
	Y	B	R	G	O		Y	B	R	G	O
1	1	1	1	1	2	12	1	1	1	2	1
2	1	1	1	2	1	13	1	1	2	1	1
3	1	1	2	1	1	14	1	2	1	1	1
4	1	2	1	1	1	15	2	1	1	1	1
5	2	1	1	1	1	16	1	1	1	1	2
6	1	1	1	1	2	17	1	1	1	2	1
7	1	1	1	2	1	18	1	1	2	1	1
8	1	1	2	1	1	19	1	2	1	1	1
9	1	2	1	1	1	20	2	1	1	1	1
10	2	1	1	1	1	21	1	1	1	1	2
11	1	1	1	1	2	22	1	1	1	2	1

To do 5 × 5 × 5 cubes in 5 colours was very difficult indeed. Because I have found no pattern throughout it is really just trial and error. Because of this it took a very long time. Although there is no pattern there are little patterns what you use and looking how many you need of each on tables a, b, c, d, e tells what to use most. I used little patterns when I rotated the same numbers around the 5 colour columns. Also I decided to do it in blocks. First I used the biggest numbers of how many faces. These were the 1 faces and 2 faces. then after using most of the 1 faces I changed to 2 faces and 0 faces. Then I finished off with 3 faces and 0 faces with the last of the 2's and 1's faces in here somewhere.

COLOURINGS

In order to solve these problems he has needed to co-ordinate a number of features (Ma1/9a).

In the final extract another student has developed a method of solution which appears to generalise more easily than the method used by the previous student. This extract shows his solution for a $7 \times 7 \times 7$ cube.

Now for 7^3 using 7 colours

First I will get rid of the 3 faced cubes using (3,2,1)

	R	G	B	Y	P	O	W
8	3	2	1	0	0	0	0
8	0	3	2	1	0	0	0
8	0	0	3	2	1	0	0
8	0	0	0	3	2	1	0
8	0	0	0	0	3	2	1
8	1	0	0	0	0	3	2
8	2	1	0	0	0	0	3

this leaves

no 3f cubes
52 2f cubes
142 1f cubes
93 0f cubes

Now to even out the 2f + 1f cubes using (1,1,1,1,1,1)

	R	G	B	Y	P	O	W
15	1	1	1	1	1	1	0
15	0	1	1	1	1	1	1
15	1	0	1	1	1	1	1
15	1	1	0	1	1	1	1
15	1	1	1	0	1	1	1
15	1	1	1	1	0	1	1
15	1	1	1	1	1	0	1

this leaves

no 3f cubes
52 2f cubes
52 1f cubes
78 0f cubes

Now to finish off using (2,2,1,1)

	R	G	B	Y	P	O	W
26	2	2	1	1	0	0	0
26	0	2	2	1	1	0	0
26	0	0	2	2	1	1	0
26	0	0	0	2	2	1	1
26	1	0	0	0	2	2	1
26	1	1	0	0	0	2	2
26	2	1	1	0	0	0	2

The total number of cubes is 343, which is correct.

The best way to work it out is to first, get rid of all the 3 faced cubes by using (3,2,1) combinations. Then see what that leaves you. Then equal 3 and 2 faced cubes by using (2,1,1,1,1) or (1,1,1,1,1,1) if you can. Then finish of using (2,2,1,1). You don't really need to bother about the 0 faced cubes, but check it once completed because it may be wrong. If it is, just choose a different combination.

The extension was hard to work out for a start, but once you get the hang of it it's easy.

TASK MATHS

Guide to Chapter 16: EVERY PICTURE TELLS A STORY

Outline

The task for this chapter is using and devising a variety of pictures which help to explain aspects of mathematics.

The pictures used for the introductory activity are different shapes which always have the same fraction of their area shaded. Students are asked to comment on the pictures and to create a similar set of pictures.

Section A is a development of the introductory activity. Questions involve the areas of rectangles, parallelograms and triangles, symmetry, congruence, fractions, circles and spheres. There is also work on chord and tangent properties of circles and other geometrical results.

Section B begins with the use of dotty pictures to explain various results, such as why *even + odd = odd*. There is a question about negative numbers. The middle part of this section uses pictures to establish rules for multiplying out two brackets, and for factorising quadratic expressions. There is also work on the forms of graphs of linear, quadratic, cubic and trigonometric functions, which suggests the use of a graphical calculator or a graph plotter on a computer. The last few questions return to the topic of solving equations using iterative methods (previously met in Book 4, Chapter 13) and use cobweb diagrams to illustrate why the methods work.

There is one Further Coursework Task. Students are asked to design a poster which tells a story about some mathematics.

Strategies

This is a rather rich chapter, and it might be appropriate for some students to tackle it in stages. Students will probably do most of the work individually or in small groups.

A discussion with the whole class about the introduction to the task is likely to be worthwhile.

Students might need to be discouraged from copying the pictures in Section A.

A discussion of the pictures for multiplying out brackets (Section B, questions 7 to 13) might help to explain the methods. It is strongly recommended that either a graphical calculator or a graph plotter on a computer **is** used for questions 16 to 23 in Section B. The last few questions of Section B should challenge, and interest, the most able students.

The Further Coursework Task provides an opportunity to create mathematical posters for display.

Equipment and Resources

For introduction to the task:
coloured pencils
resource sheet 1, *Isometric dot*

For Section A:
resource sheet 26, *Circle pictures*

For Section B:
resource sheet 27 (A–D), *Graph pictures*
graphical calculator or graph-drawing program on a computer

For FCT 1:
coloured pencils   large marker pens   coloured gummed paper
large sheets of plain, squared or coloured paper

EVERY PICTURE TELLS A STORY

Relevant Review Exercises

C27	Fractions and decimals	page 93
C31	Properties of shapes	page 107
C32	Algebraic manipulation	page 112
C34	Ratio	page 116
C38	Polynomial equations	page 128
D43	Graphs of functions	page 249
D46	Properties of circles	page 261
D47	Enlargement and similarity	page 262
D52	Algebraic fractions and dimensional analysis	page 277

National Curriculum Statements

Introduction to the task
2/6a2; 4/4a3; 4/4c; 4/4d2; 4/5d1; 4/6b3; 4/7d

Section A
2/5b1; 2/6a2; 2/8b2; 3/5a2; 4/4a3; 4/4d2; 4/5d1; 4/6b3; 4/6d; 4/7c; 4/7d; 4/8a; 4/9a3; 4/9a4; 4/10a1

Section B
2/5d3; 3/6c; 3/7b1; 3/7b2; 3/7b3; 3/7b; 3/8a1; 3/8a5; 3/8c1; 3/9b1; 3/10a; 3/10b; 3/10d1; 3/10d2; 4/9c2; 4/9c3

Questions in Sections

Accessible to all students (no bars)	Somewhat harder (one bar)	More difficult (two bars)
Section A, 1–9	Section A, 10–11, 14–17	Section A, 12–13, 18–20
Section B, 1–3, 5–6	Section B, 7–10, 15–19	Section B, 4, 11–14, 20–25

Further Coursework Tasks

neutral: 1
easier:
more difficult:

INTRODUCTION TO THE TASK: HINTS

A third of the area of each of the pictures is coloured.

But it is worth encouraging students to look for further connections. The blue pictures all have rotational symmetry of order 3 (and this is how you can demonstrate that the blue piece is one third). Each red piece can be seen to be one third because the shape can be divided into three congruent pieces. The yellow pictures all have a line of symmetry (although this does not usually help you to see that the yellow piece is one third). The purple pictures all have rotational symmetry of order 2 (although this does not usually help you to see that the purple piece is one third). The green pictures are the rest: no symmetry, and no congruence.

Students might have other ingenious, and plausible, theories about the colour coding. These should be encouraged.

Students can make up their own pictures in which a third of the area is coloured. They can try to colour their pictures in line with the colour coding, or their interpretation of it. (They might even want to introduce a fifth colour!) Squared paper or isometric paper is likely to be useful for this activity.

The most obvious 'slightly different story' is to change the fraction which is shaded.

SECTION A: ANSWERS

1 (a) $\frac{1}{2}$ (b) $\frac{1}{4}$ (c) $\frac{1}{2}$ (d) Lack of symmetry
2 (a) $\frac{1}{3}$ (b) $\frac{1}{2}$ (c) $\frac{1}{8}$ (d) $\frac{2}{3}$
4 (a) $\frac{1}{2}$ (b) $\frac{1}{2}$ (c) $\frac{1}{2}$
5 (a) $\frac{1}{9}$ (b) $\frac{1}{2}$ (c) $\frac{1}{9} + (\frac{1}{2} \text{ of } \frac{8}{9}) = \frac{5}{9}$ (d) $\frac{5}{9}$
6 (a) $\frac{5}{8}$ (b) $\frac{5}{8}$
7 (a) $\frac{1}{9}$ (b) $\frac{1}{3}$
8 (a) All sides built so they are twice length of sides of smaller octagon (therefore equal). All angles $90° + 45° = 135°$ (therefore equal)   (b) 4:1

45

TASK MATHS

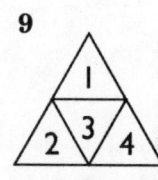

9 Ratio of the areas is 3:2
10 (a) $\frac{1}{3}$ (b) Rhombus (c) $\frac{2}{3}$ (d)(i) Total area of dotted hexagons is $\frac{3}{4}$ of area of whole hexagon. So total area of shaded parts is $\frac{2}{3}$ of $\frac{3}{4}$ which is $\frac{1}{2}$.
(ii) Total area of hexagons surrounding each shaded part is $\frac{13}{16}$. So total area of shaded parts is $\frac{2}{3}$ of $\frac{13}{16}$ which is $\frac{13}{24}$.
11 (a) 79% (b) 79% (c) 21%
12 (a) 60% (b) 60% (c) 60%
13 (a) 52% (b) 52% (c) 52%
14 (b) 90°. By symmetry the angles on the straight line are equal.
15 (b) Equal (c) 13 cm
16 (b) At midpoint of chord (c) 8 cm
17 (b) Isosceles (c) Equal (e) Equilateral, because its sides are all the radii of equal circles
18 (a) Kite (b) AD
19 (a)(i) $\frac{1}{3}$ (ii) 2:1 (iii) CG:GN = 2:1; BG:GM = 2:1
(b) 2:1; shear preserves ratios of parallel distances
20 (a) Square, because whole diagram has 4-fold symmetry (b) Because each have a right angle and angle D (c)(i) 2 (ii) $\sqrt{13}$ (d) 4:13 (e) $\frac{1}{3}$
(f) Area of shaded triangle is $\frac{4}{13}$ of $\frac{1}{3} = \frac{4}{39}$. Centre square is whole square – 4 triangles AMD + 4 shaded triangles = $1 - \frac{4}{3} + 4 \times \frac{4}{39} = \frac{1}{13}$.

SECTION B: ANSWERS

3 (a) Any even square of dots can be split into smaller squares of 4 dots. (b) Take off even square which is a multiple of 4. This leaves two even lines of dots (together a multiple of 4) and one dot left over.
4 (a) $(2N+1) + (2P+1) = 2(N+P+1)$
(b) $2N + (2P+1) = 2(N+P) + 1$
(c) $2N(2P+1) = 2(2NP + N)$
(d) $(2N+1)(2P+1) = 2(2NP + N + P) + 1$
(e) $(2N+1)^2 = 4(N^2 + N) + 1$
(f) $N + (N+1) + (N+2) = 3(N+1)$
(g) $2N + (2N+1) + (2N+2) + (2N+3) + (2N+4) = 10(N+1)$
5 (g) Positive
6 (b) E.g. two identical staircases with N layers fit together to make a rectangle with sides N and $N+1$.
8 (a)

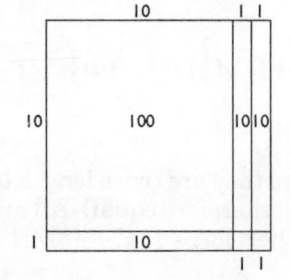

(b) $a^2 + 3a + 2$; $(e+2f)(e+f)$
9 (b) $a^2 + 5a + 6$ (c) $(x+4y)(x+y)$ (d) $900 + 30 + 30 + 1 = 961$
10 (a) 21×19 (b) $(x-1)(x+1)$ (c) $(a-b)(a+b)$
(d) 33×27 (e) $25^2 - 2^2$ (f) $p^2 - 4q^2$
(g) $7(p-3)(p+3)$
11 (a) $p^2 - 2p - 3$ (b) $(a-2)(a-1)$ (c) $(p-2)(p+1)$
(d) $(x+3)(x-2)$
12 (a) $a^2 - ab - 12b^2$ (b) $p^2 - 5pq + 6q^2$
(c) $(x+4y)(x-2y)$ (d) $(x-4y)(x-2y)$
13 (a) $(2N+3)(N+1)$ (b) $2p^2 + 9p + 4$
(c) $(3a-b)(a-3b)$ (d) $(3x+2)(x-3)$
14 (a)

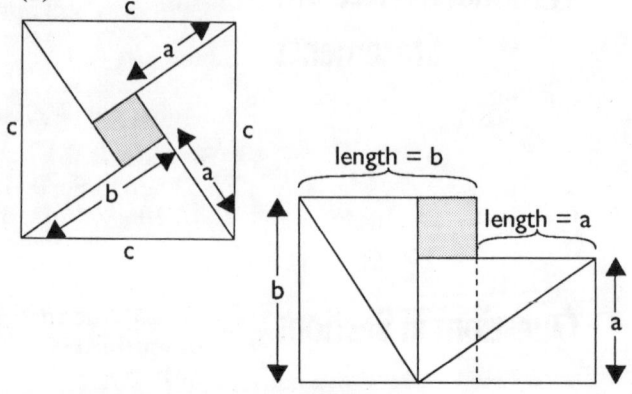

Total area = c^2 – shaded square
Total area = $a^2 + b^2$ – shaded square
Hence $c^2 = a^2 + b^2$
(b)(i) $M^2 + N^2$ (ii) $4(MN/2) + (M-N)^2 = 2MN + (M-N)^2$ (iii) $M^2 + N^2 = 2MN + (M-N)^2$
15 (b) One line is when x is twice y; the other is when y is twice x. (c) $y = x$ and $y = -x$ (d) $x + y = 5$ (or $2x + 2y = 10$) (e) They give dimensions of rectangles with perimeter 10 and sides in the ratio 2:1.
16 (a) Any equation of the form $y = 2x + c$ (b) Any equation of the form $y = mx - 3$ (c) Any line through the point (1.5, 0) (d) $y = -2x - 3$
18 (a)(i) $x = 0$ (ii) The origin; order 2 (b)(i), (ii), (iii) and (iv) Line of symmetry is $x = 0$ (v) Rotational symmetry of order 2 about $(0,-4)$ (vi) Rotational symmetry of order 2 about $(0,4)$ (vii) Lines of symmetry $y = x$ and $y = -x$; rotational symmetry of order 2 about the origin (viii) Lines of symmetry $y = x - 4$ and $y = -x - 4$; rotational symmetry of order 2 about $(0,-4)$ (ix) Lines of symmetry at $x = 0, x = 180, x = -180, x = 360 \ldots$; half-turn symmetry about $(90,1), (-90,1), (270,1) \ldots$; and translation symmetry with vector $(360,0)$
(x) Lines of symmetry at $x = 90, x = -90, x = 270, x = -270 \ldots$; half-turn symmetry about $(0,-1), (180,-1), (-180,-1) \ldots$; and translation symmetry with vector $(360,0)$ (xi) Line of symmetry $x = -2$ (xii) Half-turn symmetry about the origin (xiii) Lines of symmetry $y = x - 4$ and $y = -x + 4$; rotational symmetry of order 2 about $(4,0)$
19 (a) A (b) B (c) B (d) C (e) B (f) C
20 Alternative answers are possible (a) $y = x^3 + 2$

(b) $y = -x^2 + 2$ (c) $y = x^3 - x + 2$ (d) $y = -x^3 - 3$
(e) $y = x^2 + 2x - 2$
21 (0.4, 2.6)
22 $x = 1.57; y = 2.64$
23 (a) 1 and -3 (b)(i) $y = 4; -3.8$ and 1.8 (ii) $y = 1$; 1.2 and -3.2 (iii) $y = -x; 0.8$ and -3.8 (iv) $y = x$; 1.3 and -2.3
24 (a) 4.37 (b) You get 4.37 again
25 (a) 0.64 (b) The sequence is alternately attracted towards two limit points 0.799 and 0.513 (c) The sequence is attracted in turn towards four limit points 0.827, 0.501, 0.875 and 0.383 (d) Sequence is chaotic.

FURTHER COURSEWORK TASKS

Make a poster to tell a story about some mathematics. Design the poster carefully so that it communicates its message clearly.

Write an account to go with your poster.

- Your account should clearly state the mathematical purpose of your poster.
- The account should explain the decisions you made when you designed your poster.
- Describe how you collected any information you needed to make your poster. If you obtained information from books, say which books. If you obtained information from talking to people, explain this.
- The account should explain any geometrical constructions you needed to use.
- If you needed to calculate any lengths before you could draw your poster your account should explain your calculations.

There are several different posters you could choose to make.

1) You could make an artistic poster.

This provides a wonderful opportunity for students with artistic talents to demonstrate what they can do. The tessellations and Rangoli patterns in Chapter 6 of Book 4 might provide some useful suggestions. Modern constructivist art is a rich source, and there are seven useful articles by Ulrich Grevsmuhl in Mathematics Teaching, issues 122 to 128.

It is fairly easy to obtain books on the mathematics involved in Islamic art.

Tarquin Publications (Diss, Norfolk) publish a book called Geometrical Patterns from Roman Mosaics.

ATM publish a poster about Celtic Knots and several books are available which reproduce Celtic designs.

The many other ways of creating interesting images include: designs from lines (curve stitching and also Chapter 2 of Book 4); optical illusions; impossible objects; and designs based on modulo arithmetic tables.

2) You could make a poster which provides a puzzle for other people to solve.

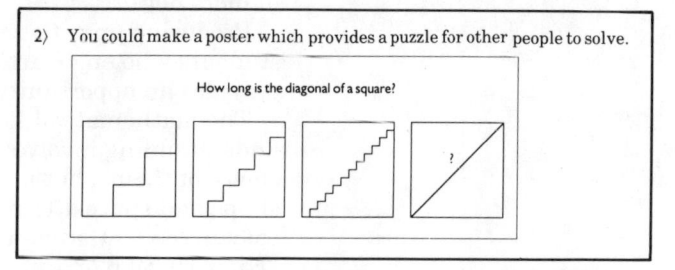

  How long is the diagonal of a square?

This is one of many possible ideas for posters which might appeal to less artistic students. Hopefully the puzzle chosen is visually attractive. Students can either make up their own puzzle, or reproduce a puzzle they have come across. In either case it is probably appropriate that their coursework includes notes which give the solution to the puzzle. Students might need to be reminded of the importance of providing references to their sources.

3) You could make a poster which explains some mathematics.

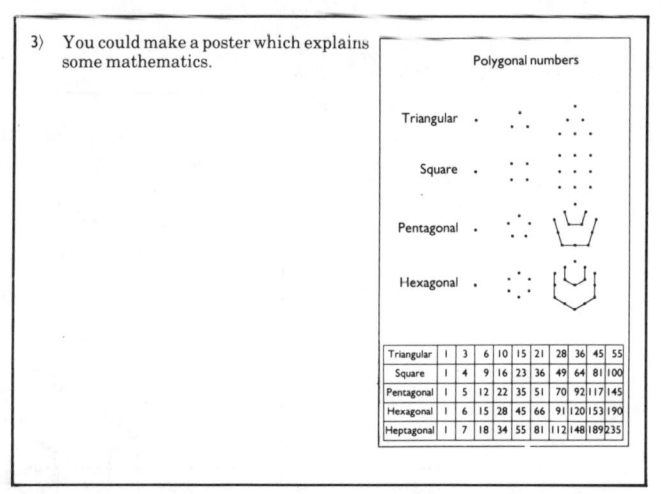

Polygonal numbers

Triangular
Square
Pentagonal
Hexagonal

Triangular	1	3	6	10	15	21	28	36	45	55
Square	1	4	9	16	23	36	49	64	81	100
Pentagonal	1	5	12	22	35	51	70	92	117	145
Hexagonal	1	6	15	28	45	66	91	120	153	190
Heptagonal	1	7	18	34	55	81	112	148	189	235

There are plenty of posters of this kind which can be shown to students. Many of these are rather dull and students might well be able to improve on them.

If students have to sort out their ideas about concepts (such as place value) before they can produce their posters the task will be very worthwhile. It is likely that the coursework should include notes about the poster, and perhaps also suggest follow-up activities and questions.

ASSESSING STUDENTS' COURSEWORK TASKS

Students who design a puzzle poster or a poster to explain some mathematics have plenty of opportunity to demonstrate their mathematical knowledge or skills. They do this by choosing an appropriate puzzle or topic, and writing a commentary on the mathematics to accompany their poster. Work on artistic posters is more difficult to assess against attainment targets concerned with knowledge, skills and understanding; this issue will now be considered in more detail.

Producing an artistic poster provides a task for students who enjoy art and feel successful at it. It also provides an opportunity for cross-curricular work.

The mathematical knowledge, skills and understanding involved will depend on the students' choice of theme, but is likely to include work from the shape and space attainment targets. It is relatively easy to see how students could produce work to achieve level 6 or 7 in strand (i), but the task is unlikely to offer students much opportunity in strand (iii).

Students who choose to base their work on Islamic art can use grid papers and ruler and compass constructions to good effect, because Islamic drawing is based on construction rules and is not arbitrary. In the following extract a student is explaining how she used a triangular grid to develop her design.

> These are my first rough drawings of my design. I started by drawing shapes using the lines on the paper and eventually came up with this design. This was just the first design that came into my head so it is really just the basic research for this investigation.

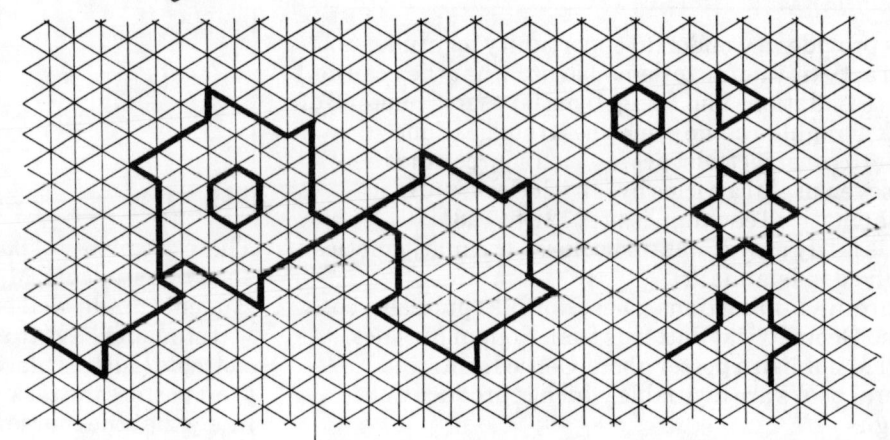

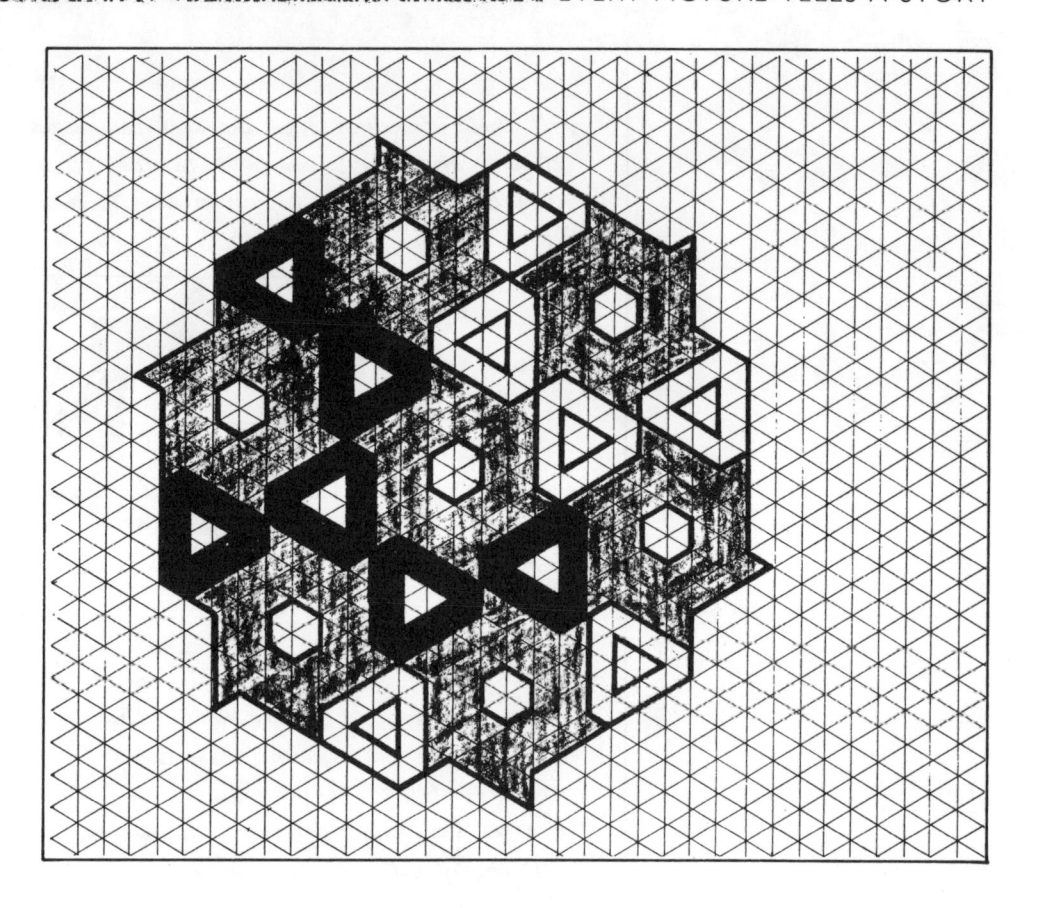

EVERY PICTURE TELLS A STORY

This work demonstrates Ma1/6a. Another student uses a square and octagon construction as her starting point. Such a construction often appears in books about Islamic art. She explains how the design is drawn on the grid, and she colours it in two different ways.

> To make my designs based on squares and octagons I have to start off with a grid like this. 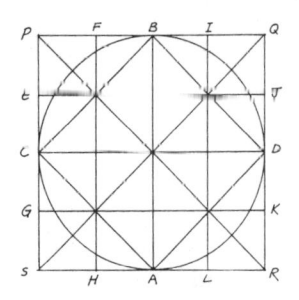
>
> I drew this by drawing the circle first and then drawing the square PQRS around it.
> I then drew in the diagonal lines PR and QS and the horizontal and vertical line AB and CD. I then drew in the square ABCD.
> I then drew in the other four construction lines FH, IL, EJ and GK.
> The grid has many lines of symmetry.

49

TASK MATHS

All these drawings over the next few pages use the squares and octagons grid. First you have to start off with the same grid on every design. I have explained how to draw this grid on page 3.

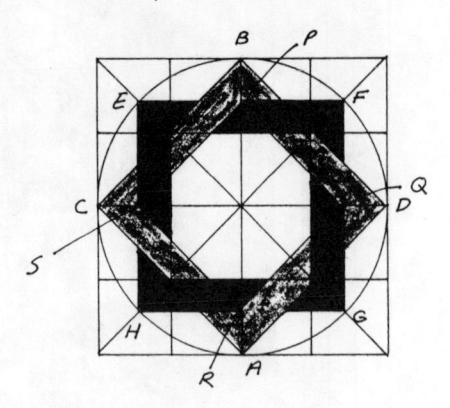

After I had drawn the grid I started on the design.
Firstly I drew the square ABCD. Then I drew an inner square PQRS. From that square (the outside) I drew a line from E to H, from H to G etc forming the square EFGH.
I drew the inner square a centimetre in although the measurements all comply with the construction lines.
The design consists of rotational symmetry.
(The circle is drawn with a compass and the other lines are all drawn with a ruler on all designs)

This design is just like the one on page 7 but because it is coloured differently the design looks different

This student is working at a higher level than the previous student, because she has developed a new line of enquiry from that suggested by the teacher (Ma1/7a).

The student from whose work the following extract is taken has researched how to construct Celtic knot designs, using the techniques suggested in the ATM poster. She explores the number of different 'ribbons' she can get in square and irregular shapes, before developing her final design incorporating four ribbons and an impressive use of symmetry. This student is also working at level 7.

EVERY PICTURE TELLS A STORY

> I discovered that if I want to get a pattern with more than 1 ribbon I had to do it in a square.

This pattern has 2 ribbons. 4x4 grid

This is a 6x6 grid and has 3 ribbons

This is a 8x8 grid. it has 4 ribbons

This celtic pattern has 2 ribbon

If the celtic grids are squares they are not symmetrical.

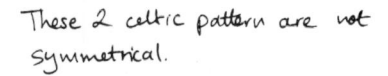

These 2 celtic pattern are not symmetrical.

This celtic pattern has 2 ribbon

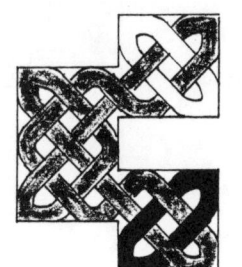

This celtic pattern has 3 ribbon. This pattern is also symmetrical

Some students researched Roman mosaic pavements. The following extract is from the work of a student who devised his own border pattern, having read about the significance of such patterns for Roman pavements. This work demonstrates Ma1/6a because it did not develop a new line of enquiry.

TASK MATHS

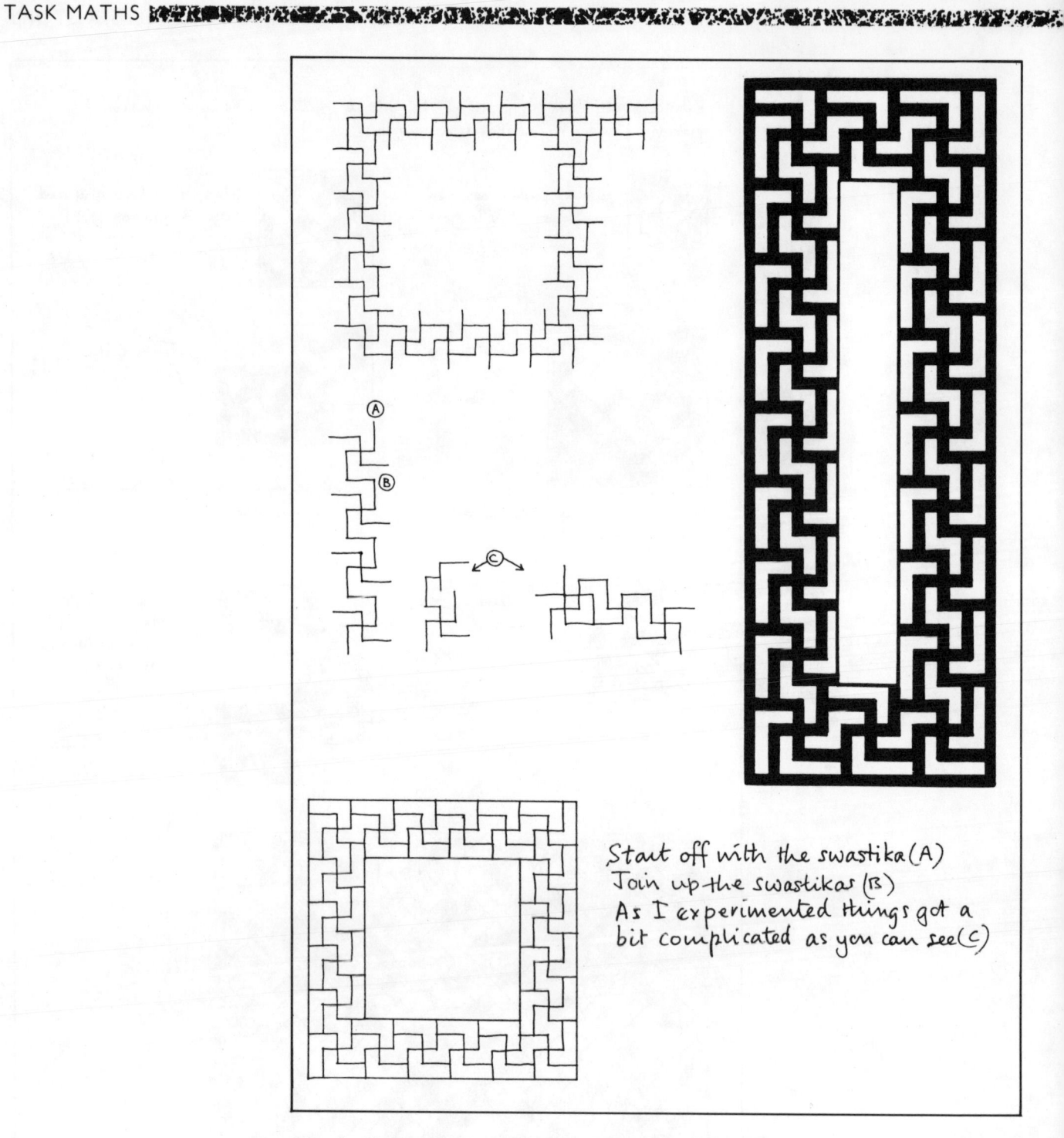

Start off with the swastika (A)
Join up the swastikas (B)
As I experimented things got a bit complicated as you can see (C)

The final extract shows how students can apply their mathematical knowledge and skills to this task. The student is developing a Roman pavement design consisting of a grid of 4 by 4 squares. She is trying out a number of designs and analysing them in terms both of their mirror and rotational symmetry and also of the proportions of black and white they contain. She then comments about how her preference for certain designs relates to these qualities. This extract indicates that she is likely to achieve Ma1/8a because she is trying to give reasons for her choice of design.

EVERY PICTURE TELLS A STORY

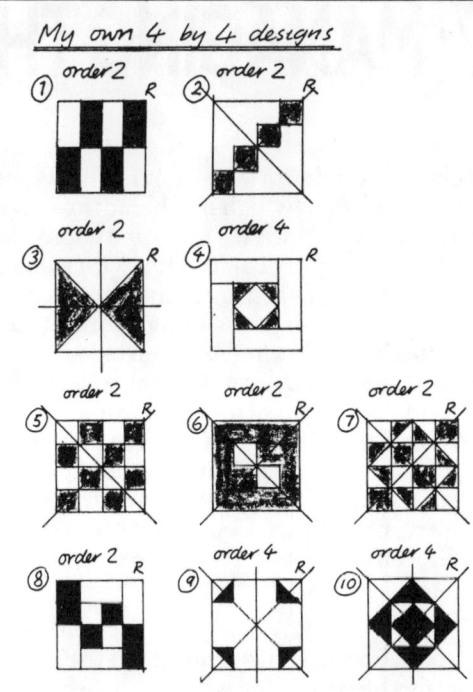

My own 4 by 4 designs

① order 2 ② order 2 R
③ order 2 R ④ order 4 R
⑤ order 2 R ⑥ order 2 R ⑦ order 2 R
⑧ order 2 R ⑨ order 4 R ⑩ order 4 R

Pattern No.	Mirror symmetry No. of lines	Rotational symmetry order?	AREA Black	White	Do I like the pattern?
1	X	✓2	8	8	X
2	✓2	✓2	4	12	✓
3	✓2	✓2	8	8	X
4	X	✓4	2	14	X
5	✓2	✓2	8	8	X
6	✓2	✓2	14	2	✓
7	✓2	✓2	8	8	X
8	X	✓2	6	10	X
9	✓4	✓4	2	14	✓
10	✓4	✓4	6	10	✓

The patterns I have noticed in this table are that every 4 by 4 design has rotational symmetry.
I have also proved in these results that designs with 2 lines are mirror symetry have order 2 rotational symetry and designs with 4 lines of mirror symetry have order 4 rotational symetry. This fact is true because mirror symetry is where you can draw a line down the pattern and have two exact copies of the pattern, so if you put the pattern together with the two patterns at opposite ends, when you turn the whole pattern round 180° the pattern will be exactly the same.

If you put your finger on the * and turn the pattern round you will be able to see rotational symetry.

My favourite design is No. 6. All my favourite designs have both types of symetry.

53

TASK MATHS

Guide to Chapter 17: **MANAGING THE FUTURE**

Outline

In this chapter students look into the future, both personally and globally, and consider ways in which mathematics can help them make sense of it.

The introductory activity invites students to discuss what facts about their lives in 2010 they can predict with some accuracy.

Section A is about earning money and budgeting how to spend it. The work involves rates of pay, saving, simple interest, compound interest and interpreting barcharts and pie charts.

Section B is about the world resources needed by individuals and families, and about ways in which the world population is changing. Work involves the use of direct and inverse proportion, making sensible approximations, using percentages and interpreting graphs. The last few questions are about exponential growth, and fractional indices are used.

There are six Further Coursework Tasks, inviting students to find out about different aspects of the future.

Strategies

The introductory activity lends itself to class discussion. Students will probably do the rest of the work in this chapter individually or in small groups.

Some students find ideas about rate intuitively easy; others find them very hard and will require individual support. It might be appropriate to discuss some questions with the whole class to develop the necessary techniques.

Some students could leave out some of the earlier questions in both Sections A and B.

Equipment and Resources

None specifically, although students will need access to a range of books and magazines to research their FCT.

Relevant Review Exercises

C33	*Money 2*	page 115
C34	*Ratio*	page 116
C35	*Rate and proportion*	page 118
C36	*Indices and exponential growth*	page 123
D42	*Everyday graphs*	page 244
D45	*Statistics 2*	page 257

National Curriculum Statements

Introduction to the task
2/5b1; 5/4d1; 5/7b1

Section A
2/5b2; 2/6a2; 2/6a3; 2/6a5; 2/6b; 2/7b1; 2/7c1; 2/7c3; 2/8c; 2/9b; 5/4b4; 5/5c1

Section B
2/6b; 2/7b1; 2/7b3; 2/7c1; 2/7c3; 2/8a1; 2/8a2; 2/8c; 2/9b; 2/10a2; 3/7a3; 3/7a4; 3/8a3; 3/8a4; 3/8c1; 3/8c2; 3/9a1; 3/9a2; 3/9b2; 5/5c1

MANAGING THE FUTURE

Questions in Sections	Accessible to all students (no bars)	Somewhat harder (one bar)	More difficult (two bars)
	Section A, 1–6	Section A, 7–9	Section A, 10–13
	Section B, 1–4a, 6–10	Section B, 4b–5, 11–12	Section B, 13–19

Further Coursework Tasks

neutral: 1, 3, 4, 6
easier: 2
more difficult: 5

INTRODUCTION TO THE TASK: HINTS

This activity sets the scene and fosters interest in the FCTs.
  Class discussion might be more appropriate than a written response. It is worth emphasising the questions posed at the start. In other words, focus attention on which of the students' answers are accurate, which it is difficult for them to be sure about, and which questions are simply 'impossible' to answer? These considerations are more important than the answers themselves.

SECTION A: ANSWERS

1. (a) £120   (b) £111
2. (a)(i) £105.63   (ii) £2.03   (b) £3.01
3. (a) 20 months   (b) Both factors make it longer
4. (a) £60   (b) £45   (c) £70
5. (a) £22.50   (b) £17.63   (c) £56
6. (a) £18   (b) £54
7. (a) £9   (b)(i) £27   (ii) £63   (iii) £9x
   (c) £129.50   (d) £41.16
8. (a) £116.64   (b) £124.80
9. £1024
10. (a) £204   (b)(i) £208.08   (ii) £220.82
    (iii) £253.65
    (c) $(1.02)^{12} = 1.268$
11. (a)(i) About 70%   (ii) Non-manual under 18
    (iii) Non-manual 40–49   (b) Difficult to say (arguments either way)
12. (a)(i) (25) 7%   (ii) (200) 56%   (b)(i) (155) 43%
    (ii) (63) 18%   (c) These figures are totals; not all North Americans and Asians are typical.
    (d) About 20 times
13. (a) About 10:1   (b) About 25 times

SECTION B: ANSWERS

1. (a)(i) 3.5 kg   (ii) About 180 kg   (b) About 300 kg
   (c) 9 million kg   (d) Some people eat no potatoes (rice, etc. instead)
2. (a) 15   (b) 36   (c) 156
3. (a)(i) 6   (ii) 8   (iii) 12   (c)(i) 16   (ii) 28
   (iii) 730   (d)(i) 5 days   (ii) 13 days   (iii) 8 weeks
4. (a)(i) 320 million   (ii) 180 million
   (iii) 7 million   (b)(i) 75 million   (ii) 85 million
   (c)(i) 220 000   (ii) 230 000; 210 000
5. (a) 330 g   (b) Directly could be things you see (writing paper, packaging, etc.); indirectly paper used e.g. in business to produce the goods you buy (e.g. records, bills).   (c) 700 000 tonnes
   (d) 140 g per day   (e) 58%
6. (a)(i) 30 days   (ii) 40 days   (iii) 240 days
   (iv) 16 days
7. (a)(i) £3   (ii) £12   (iii) £4
8. (a) 240 miles   (b) 8 hours   (c) 2.4 hours
   (d) 1 hour   (e) Not as good as it looks, because of getting to and from airport, checking in, etc.
9. (a) A is weight; B is height   (b) 70 years
10. (a) Records change suddenly, not gradually
    (b) About 3.4 mins (but extrapolation obviously isn't valid for ever).
11. (a)(i) To nearest £25   (ii) Because second-hand prices have to be sampled   (b) 53%, 57%, 59%, 62%, 64%, 67%, 67%, 71%, 74%, 77%, 85%
    (c) Prices drop quite a lot in first two years and then fairly steadily (at least for 5 years).
    (d) Between £4000 and £4500
12. (a) 130 000   (b) Between 12 and 13 days
13. (a)(i) 240 000   (ii) 2.3×10^{13} (b) 1700
14. (a)(i) 2.64   (ii) 3.16   (iii) 1.59   (iv) 2.11
    (b)(i) 129.6   (ii) 129.6
15. (a)(i) 10 billion   (ii) 20 billion   (iii) 7 billion
    (iv) 14 billion   (d) 12 billion
16. (a)(i) £121   (ii) £146.41   (iii) £177.16
    (iv) £214.36   (v) £259.37   (c) About £186
17. (a) (118) 33%   (b) (10) 3%
18. (a)(i) 12.5 g   (ii) 6.25 g   (c) 9 g
    (d)(i) 9.5×10^{-5} g   (ii) 7.7 g
19. 31 g of A; 997 g of B; 84 g of C; virtually nothing of D.

FURTHER COURSEWORK TASKS

1) How much interest is there in 'green' issues? Which 'green' issues interest or worry people the most?

   Conduct a survey among students in your school. You might also want to ask parents, teachers, other adults or younger children.

This provides an opportunity to do a statistical survey. Students might find it useful to work as a group.

The suggestions provided in Chapter 21 (Section B and FCT), about designing a successful statistical survey, are relevant here. Students need to be clear what they want to find out; to design a suitable questionnaire; to choose a suitable sample; to display relevant results clearly and meaningfully; to analyse results for a purpose; to draw realistic conclusions.

Most students will be wise to decide in advance exactly what they mean by 'green issues'. Leaving those who respond to the survey to make this decision will provide a more chaotic set of information which will be more difficult to analyse and interpret.

> 2) How much does it cost you to live for a year?
>
> Describe the budget you need to live for a year. Include your share of the cost of the home in which you live, for items such as heating and lighting. Include food, clothes, holidays and all your other expenses.
>
> If you prefer you can work out how much it will cost you to live for a year after you have left home.
>
> Remember to take account of *all* your expenses.

This is a popular task. Encourage, and give credit for, appropriate research and for displaying and writing about results in ways which are clear and easy to understand. Keeping the purpose in mind and communicating that purpose in the finished work is more relevant than doing a lot of 'hard sums' for the sake of it.

Appropriate use of pie charts might help students to communicate their findings dramatically.

Students can make the task more challenging by comparing current data with data from a few years ago, or by predicting what is likely to change most in the next few years.

> 3) Is there equal opportunity for men and women, and/or for people from different ethnic groups, in terms of pay and employment prospects in the area where you live? Do people want there to be equal opportunities?
>
> You can collect some evidence from within your school or from outside it. For example, you can find what jobs students in your school want to do, and whether they are optimistic about getting the jobs they want.

This also provides an opportunity to do a statistical survey, and the remarks about FCT 1 apply here also. It is especially useful with this activity for students to work as a group: they will then be aware from the outset of a variety of viewpoints, and will help each other to clarify the issues they want to explore.

How are the students going to define equal opportunities? How are they going to measure prejudice? It might be appropriate to remind students of the law in these areas: they need to avoid sexist or racist questions which might cause offence to others. Students also need to consider carefully how they are going to process the responses. What are they going to do with racist responses to the questionnaire?

> 4) Look at some of the ways in which people are trying to protect the world's environment and explain how some of these ideas might work. Try to find some statistics to use with your explanation.
>
> For example, you could find out what proportion of cars locally are using unleaded petrol. Or whether people are changing any of their living habits to be more 'environmentally friendly'.

There is a danger that this could become entirely a science or a humanities project. But conversely, here is an opportunity for a cross-curricular task. There are many diverse ways of tackling this task. The task requires individual research, and is suitable for those students who are already interested in these issues and are able to do the research.

> 5) How much energy does your family use at home during a year?
>
> You might want to compare your use of energy with that of a typical family in Britain. On average, the amount of energy used by a family in one year is as follows.
>
> | | | |
> |---|---|---|
> | Coal | 600 kg | 150 therms |
> | Oil | 150 litres | 50 therms |
> | Natural gas | | 390 therms |
> | Electricity | 4100 units | 140 therms |
> | Total | | 730 therms |
>
> (1 therm is approximately the same as 30 units of electricity. 1 unit is 1 kWh, the amount of electricity a 1 kW fire uses in an hour)

This task is quite difficult. It is not easy to understand the meaning of the units and their equivalence. Nor is it easy to collect or to organise the data. It is only appropriate if students have access to the required data, either at school or at home.

The task provides a good opportunity for students to explore and explain concepts such as percentage change and moving averages.

> 6) Houses increase in value. Cars decrease in value.
>
> Find out about the way in which different possessions increase or decrease in value and look at the reasons why this happens.

This task is suitable for all students because it can focus on just one item, e.g. house prices or can consider a range of prices, which is more challenging. It is obviously relevant to the cross-curricular theme of economic awareness. The analysis can also be straightforward or complex. Credit needs to be given for the research necessary, which is not easy to come by because you need to collect evidence dating back a number of years. Cars are a popular topic, because the prices are readily available from used car guides. Some students will be able to take into account inflation as well as the raw figures. You may need to encourage students to be fairly focused so that they can do calculations and work out percentage changes etc. Otherwise their work becomes too vague and general.

MANAGING THE FUTURE

ASSESSING STUDENTS' COURSEWORK TASKS

Further Coursework Task 2

This is a popular and accessible task for most students. Credit needs to be given for the research required. because many students at Key Stage 4 know little about the cost of living.

In the following extract the student decides to work out her boyfriend's cost of living, and they are obviously both surprised by the mismatch between his estimates and actual expenditures. She concludes by giving him good advice! She can design a task in a given context (Ma1/6a). She is also interpreting the information she collected (Ma1/5b).

Total income per month is £875
He pays out:
Board £60 a month
Car repayments £100 a month
Petrol · £80 a month
Clothes - £50 a month
Toiletries £12 a month
Going out money £50 a month
Savings £80 a month.
Bills that have been divided by 12 so that they can be added to each monthly bill
Road tax and insurance - £100 ÷ 12 = £8·38 a month
Poll tax £272 ÷ 12 = £22·67 a month
Leisure centre membership £13 ÷ 12 = £1·08 a month
the amount that he pays out each month amounts to £464·13 a month.

£875·00   — total wage per month
£464·13   — spenditure each month
£410·87   — amount left after spenditure

I asked my boyfriend what he spends the remaining £410·87 a month on. So he said that.
He spends a further £50 a month on clothes and saves £80 a week for holidays etc. and £80 for presents for christmas, special events and birthdays. This amounts to £210·00 a month further spenditure
The remaining £200·87 is used for eating out, snacks at work, newspapers and other items.
I think that my boyfriend's budget could have been more better as he still has £200·87 left at the end of each month so he could afford to spend some more on clothes or save more or a better idea would be to pay his car loan off.
Other than that i think that the budget is quite well worked out.

Other students enjoy inventing a fantasy life for themselves, which is appropriate provided that they base their work on realistic estimates of the cost of living. In this first extract the student outlines his plan for the task.

TASK MATHS

> How much does it cost me to live for a year?
>
> This is the project that I have chose to do. I am going to show my working out and I will explain how I got all my information.
>
> I got all my information by looking at my parents bills i.e. Electricity, Gas, Water rates etc. Then I rounded it up to the nearest five. I earn £20,000 per annum as gross pay. When all the tax's are deducted I will have much less. I have got a second hand car in which I do approximately about 8000 miles per annum I change my car abord every five years which gives me enough time to save up for a new one.
>
> I also have a 3 bedroom detached house, for £37,000. I don't really change houses because there is really no need because I am happy with the house.
>
> I have all the furniture that I need i.e. Sofa, dining table, armchairs, beds etc. I also have other household appliances like hoover, washing machine, dishwasher, cooker, TV, video, hifi, radio etc
>
> I go out about once or twice per week depending on where I go and how much I spend there.

He then works out the detailed cost of mortgage, heating, running the car, replacing household goods, as well as the items mentioned in the following extract, in which he is working out that he cannot afford to get married unless his wife works too. (His cost of living is £13 820 per annum and the £13 910 figure is his annual income after tax, national insurance and other deductions.) This student is showing evidence for Ma1/7b.

> *If I decided to get married then I would be in more difficultie than if I got injured because. Most of the bills will double e.g. poll tax, telephone, Food, Leisure So then I will not be able to afford them at all.*
>
> *e.g.*   <u>Yearly</u>.
>
> | | | |
> |---|---|---|
> | | poll tax = £405 — £810 | |
> | For just me. | telephone = £200 — £400 | For both of us |
> | | food = £1500 — £3000 | |
> | | leisure = £250 — £500 | |
> | | <u>Clothes = £1000 — £2000</u> | |
> | | Total   £3355   £6710 | |
>
> *If we were still on my salary we will be in debt because there is not much savings. Then I will need an extra few thousands to pay for my wife as well as me.*
>
> *e.g. For me to live it costs £13820 per anum. but with my wife it costs an extra £3355*
>
>   £13820
>   +   3355
>   <u>£17175</u>
>
> *I am in debt by*   13910
>   −17175
>   <u>− 3265</u>

Further Coursework Task 5

Once the students have collected the information they need for the task they still have a lot of work to do sorting it out, and converting it into therms, so that they can make comparisons between different sources of energy. This task provides students with the opportunity to apply a wide range of mathematical knowledge and skills.

In the following extract, the student begins his work by providing all the relevant information about his house and family.

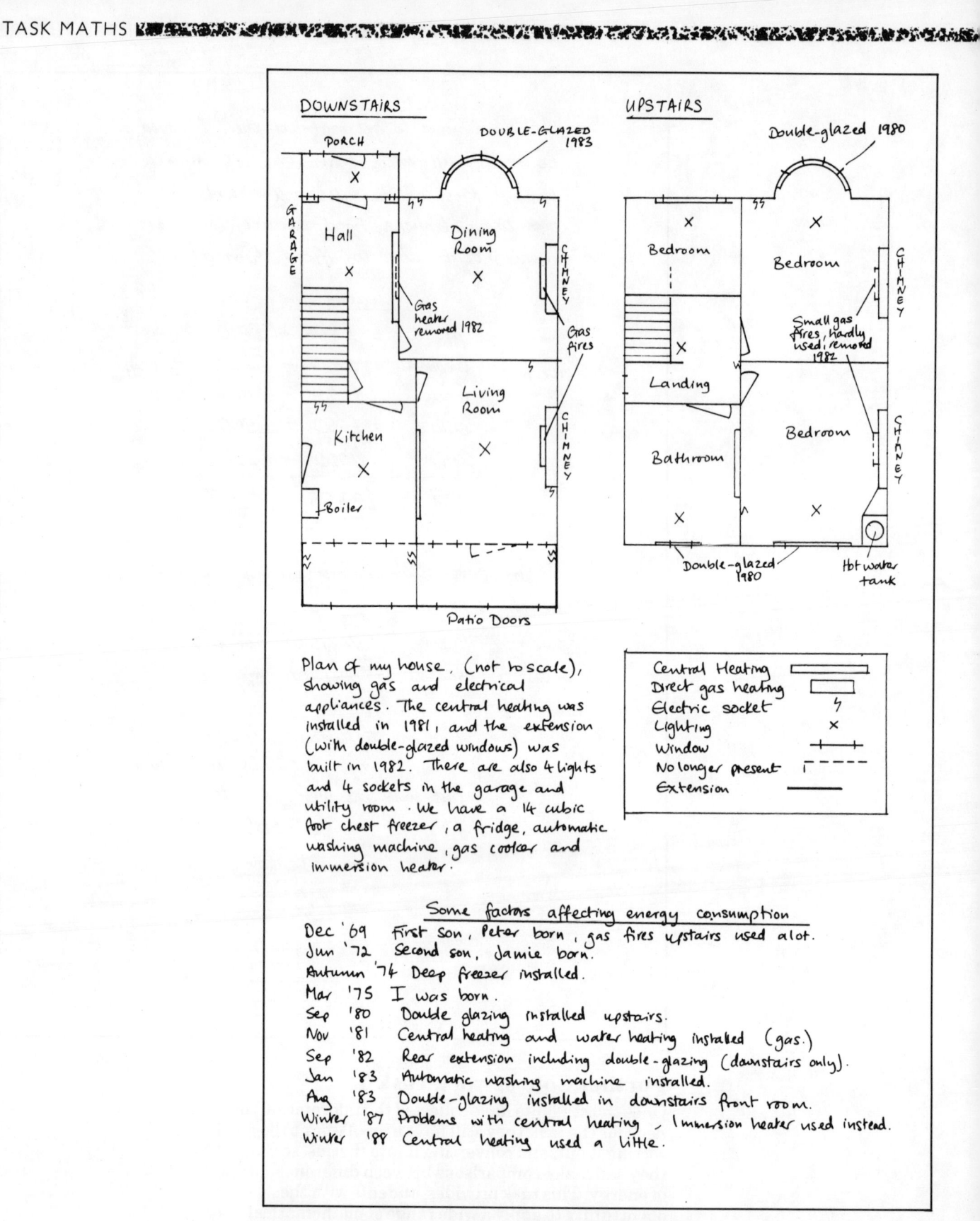

Plan of my house, (not to scale), showing gas and electrical appliances. The central heating was installed in 1981, and the extension (with double-glazed windows) was built in 1982. There are also 4 lights and 4 sockets in the garage and utility room. We have a 14 cubic foot chest freezer, a fridge, automatic washing machine, gas cooker and immersion heater.

Some factors affecting energy consumption

Dec '69   First son, Peter born, gas fires upstairs used a lot.
Jun '72   Second son, Jamie born.
Autumn '74   Deep freezer installed.
Mar '75   I was born.
Sep '80   Double glazing installed upstairs.
Nov '81   Central heating and water heating installed (gas).
Sep '82   Rear extension including double-glazing (downstairs only).
Jan '83   Automatic washing machine installed.
Aug '83   Double-glazing installed in downstairs front room.
Winter '87   Problems with central heating, Immersion heater used instead.
Winter '88   Central heating used a little.

He then records, and calculates in therms, the gas and electricity consumption for his home over a period of 20 years. He also works out the moving average of the total consumption. The following two extracts show part of this work and part of one of his graphs.

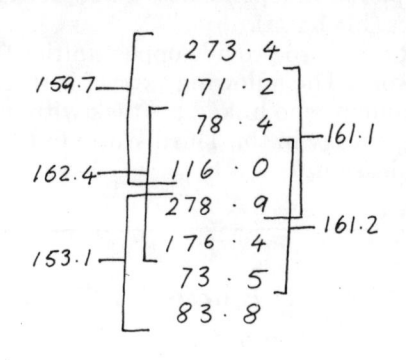

MANAGING THE FUTURE

```
          273·4
159·7 ┐ ┌ 171·2
       │ │  78·4 ┐ 161·1
162·4 ┐│ │ 116·0 ┘
       └ │ 278·9 ┐
153·1 ─ │ 176·4 ┘ 161·2
         │  73·5
         └  83·8
```

To find out what the underlying trend beneath the figures was, I calculated a moving average of the total energy consumption. This is found by taking the mean average of 4 quarters (1 year) and plotting it on the graph, in the middle of the four quarters.

The next four quarters are then averaged and plotted, and so on. (see diagram). I only showed a moving average for 1 decade (the 80's) as most things which affected the energy consumption happened during the last 10 years, and before 1980, the trend was probably a fairly steady increase. On top of this, working out the moving average was quite tedious and took a long time to write out.

Graph showing quarterly energy consumption

— ✶ — Total energy consumption   — ⊗ — Gas consumption
— ✶ — Moving average of total   ● Customer reading

[Graph showing quarterly energy consumption from Spring '86 through Autumn '89, with total energy consumption peaking around 350, moving average around 150-200, and electricity consumption near the bottom around 50.]

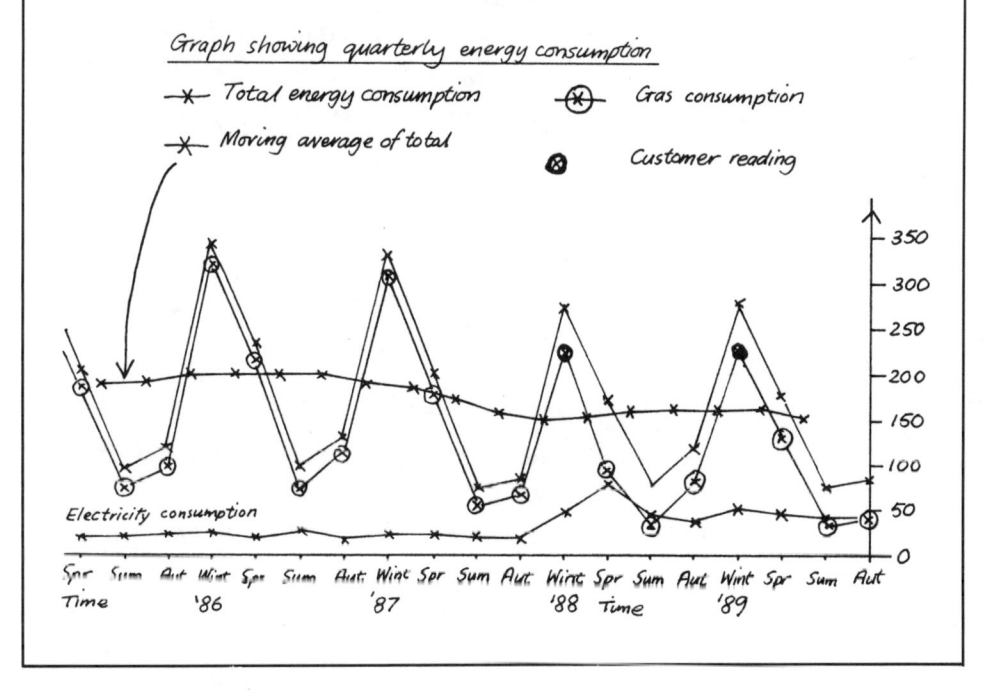

It is said by some people that everyday tasks are not suitable for students who are able at mathematics. However, this student has taken the opportunity to learn new mathematical skills (moving averages) as well as make good use of his existing knowledge. He has thus explored independently a new area of mathematics (Ma1/10a).

This task may also provide opportunities for cross-curricular work. The following extract is from the work of a student who linked his task with work he had done on energy in the Third World in his humanities lessons.

To compare my results with those of a typical family I found the average of all seven years from my data, and used that as a comparison:—

	TYPICAL FAMILY	MY FAMILY
COAL	150.00	0.00
OIL	50.00	0.00
NATURAL GAS	390.00	634.42
ELECTRICITY	140.00	122.83
TOTAL	730.00	757.25

All data is in therms. Electrical units converted in the way described on the page with the table.

From studying the graphs, it shows that our household electricity consumption has almost doubled, and the gas consumption has dropped by almost a third.

However this does not necessarily mean that the number of electricity generating stations should be doubled, as this may only apply to the fairly affluent society, and be balanced by the less affluent.

Third world countries are currently exporting fuels to developed countries such as our own, as they have fuel surplus to their current needs, but their requirement for fuel is also increasing as they become industrialised, so that eventually they may no longer have surplus fuel.

This will mean that we will either have to conserve fuel, or find alternative sources to resolve our future needs.

Moves are already being taken in Great Britain to conserve fuels. As an example, building regulations are continually being revised to require builders to install ever increasing thicknesses of insulation into new properties.

Further Coursework Task 6

In the following extracts a student is looking at car depreciation. He begins by defining what he means by depreciation, by making use of his knowledge from his work in other parts of the curriculum.

> Depreciation is the process in which an object loses it's value over a period of time. Different objects depreciate at different rates. The rate at which an object depreciates depends on a lot of things.
>
> For a start, the demand for an object is important. If nobody wants to buy second hand whatevers, their value will fall, and they will depreciate rapidly. If there is a high demand, people will want to buy them and their value usually remains relatively high.
>
> Age is also an important factor. Most things purchased start to lose their value immediately after they are bought. This is because after being bought new, if sold again it is classed as being second hand. and of course no-one would buy secondhand, when they could buy new for the same amount of money.
>
> Some objects will lose their value over a period of time, but when a very long time has elapsed they may begin to gain value.

He goes on to consider depreciation of cars and takes care to match similar or contrasting groups of cars, so that he can make comments on the reasons for differences in depreciation between different makes and types of car.

> The thing about Jaguar, BMW and Mercedes is that these cars are prestigious'. These famous names are associated with powerful well made cars, and supposedly are symbols of wealth and status.
>
> Although these companies make a lot of very expensive cars (£30,000+) BMW and Mercedes make cars in price ranges similar to that of the manufacturers mentioned earlier. The rate at which these cars depreciate is quite different.
>
> | | New Price | Second Hand Value | Saving On New |
> |---|---|---|---|
> | BMW 318i (D reg) | £9695 ('86) | £7325 | £2370 (24%) |
> | Ford Sierra 2.0i GLS (D reg) | £9618 ('86) | £5125 | £4493 (47%) |
>
> The drop in price of the Ford is twice as much as the BMW, though they both started out at the same price. The same applies to newer models, but can be a lot more extreme.

This second extract is just one part of an analysis of a wide range and variety of groups of cars. This work could have been improved if he had attempted to take into account the rate of inflation since 1986, but the piece of work as a whole provided evidence for Ma1/6a.

TASK MATHS

Guide to Chapter 18: **EQUABLE SHAPES**

Outline

The task for this chapter is to discover properties of equable shapes: shapes for which the area is numerically equal to the perimeter.

In the introductory activity students find some equable shapes using centimetre squared paper.

In Section A techniques are explained for finding equable shapes drawn on squared paper. The later questions are about equable rectangles with non-integral sides. Students can use *Spread* or algebra. The last few questions involve rearranging formulae and the graph of the function $y = \frac{2x}{x-2}$.

Section B starts with diagrams which students measure. This helps them see the significance of the unit used when deciding whether or not a shape is equable. Later questions are about a variety of equable shapes and involve the use of Pythagoras' theorem, trial and improvement methods, and *Spread* or algebra.

Section C is about equable shapes with holes. The first few questions are straightforward, while the later questions provide applications for multiplying out brackets, factorising, difference of two squares, simultaneous equations, and quadratic equations solved by factorising or using the formula.

There are four Further Coursework Tasks. One is about designing your own equable shapes, and another about using techniques for generating equable shapes. The other two tasks are more difficult. They are about: equable solids and the relationship between the equable circle and other equable shapes.

Strategies

Most students will work on their own or in small groups. But it might be appropriate to pick out key questions to discuss with the whole class. Examples of such questions are question 9 in Section A (for focusing on spreadsheets or *Spread*, perhaps in preparation for their use in connection with a FCT) and question 13 of Section A (for focusing on rearranging a formula).

This chapter involves the use of a large amount of algebra. You might find it sensible to map out different routes through the chapter for different students to follow. If you want to introduce students to a spreadsheet or to *Spread*, question 9 of Section A is suitable for this purpose for most students. More able students might want to use algebra for question 9 (as suggested in questions 10 and 11). They can make use of spreadsheets or *Spread* in Section B, starting at question 8.

Measuring the shapes in questions 1, 2 and 3 of Section B might appear to be a low-level activity. But these questions draw attention to the fact that deciding whether a shape is equable or not depends on the units being used to measure perimeter and area.

Review Exercises provide further practice for the important techniques required for this task. It might be appropriate for students to alternate work on the chapter with work on relevant Review Exercises.

Equipment and Resources

For Sections A and B and FCT 3:
  computer, with spreadsheet or *Spread*
  graphical calculator or computer with graph-drawing program

For Section B:
  resource sheet 28, *Measuring in decimals of an inch*

Relevant Review Exercises

C32	*Algebraic manipulation*	page 117
C37	*Equations 2*	page 125
C38	*Polynomial equations*	page 128
C39	*Rearranging formulae*	page 132
D52	*Algebraic fractions and dimensional analysis*	page 277

National Curriculum Statements

Introduction to the task
2/4a2; 2/4a8; 4/4d2

Section A
2/4a2; 2/4a8; 2/4d1; 2/4d2; 2/5c1; 2/5c2; 2/7b1; 2/8c; 3/5b1; 3/5b2; 3/6b; 3/7a2; 3/8c1; 3/10b; 4/4d1; 4/4d2; 4/5d1; 4/7d

Section B
2/4a8; 2/4d1; 2/4d2; 2/4e2; 2/5c1; 2/5c2; 2/5d1; 2/7b1; 2/7c1; 2/8c; 3/5b1; 3/5b2; 3/6b; 3/7a2; 3/7b1; 3/8a2; 4/4d1; 4/4d2; 4/5d1; 4/5d3; 4/6d; 4/7c; 4/7d; 4/8c; 4/9a4

Section C
2/4a2; 2/4a8; 2/4d1; 2/4d2; 2/5c1; 2/5c2; 2/7b1; 2/8c; 3/5b1; 3/5b2; 3/7b2; 3/8a1; 3/10b; 4/4d1; 4/4d2; 4/5d1; 4/6d; 4/7c; 4/7d

Questions in Sections

Accessible to all students (no bars)	**Somewhat harder** (one bar)	**More difficult** (two bars)
Section A, 1–9	Section A, 10–12	Section A, 13
Section B, 1–5	Section B, 6–7	Section B, 8–14
Section C, 1–4	Section C, 5–7	Section C, 8–16

Further Coursework Tasks

neutral: 2
easier: 1
more difficult: 3, 4

INTRODUCTION TO THE TASK: HINTS

This activity sets the scene for the task and, incidentally, provides consolidation and practice of work on area and perimeter. It is appropriate for the whole class to work at the activity for one lesson and to share results. It might be wise to restrict the time allowed to one lesson, because some students can waste time drawing random shapes and never finding an equable one! So students will benefit from considering the techniques developed in Section A.

We suggest restricting attention to shapes which can be drawn on squared paper. Some students can be encouraged to justify such hypotheses as that there is only one equable square. Instead of solving $x^2 = 4x$ for this, it might provide greater insight to argue about how area is changing compared to the perimeter (the idea of the area graph and the perimeter graph crossing once, apart from at the origin).

SECTION A: ANSWERS

1. (*a*) 1 (the 4 by 4)   (*b*) 1 (the 6 × 3)
2. No, because perimeter is *twice* the length plus breadth.
4. (*a*) Only the sides of the bump are extra.   (*b*) Because area and perimeter are increased by 2.
5. (*a*) No   (*b*) Because the bumps touch each other.
6. In order to get back to your starting point you have to go down the amount you went up, and left the amount you went right.
7. (*a*) P = 21.2; A = 20.8 No   (*b*) P = 32.6; A = 32.2 No   (*c*) P = 25; A = 25 Yes   (*d*) P = 28.8; A = 28.8 Yes
8. 3.33
10. (*a*) 10 + 2*a*   (*b*) 5*a*   (*d*) *a* = 3.33   (*e*) 16.67
12. (*c*)(i) 4.67   (ii) 3.14
13. (*b*) $y = \dfrac{2x}{x-2}$ (*d*) It goes off to infinity
    (*e*) Lengths of 2 or less   (*f*) The graph suggests

TASK MATHS

they are big and getting bigger quickly (actual values are 42, 402 and 4002).

SECTION B: ANSWERS

1. (a) 2 cm, 4 cm, 8 cm (b) 6.3 cm, 12.6 cm, 25.1 cm (c) 3.1 cm², 12.6 cm², 50.3 cm² (d) Circle 2
2. (a) 6 cm by 3 cm, 7 cm by 2.8 cm, 10 cm by 10 cm, 7.6 cm by 5.7 cm, 11.4 cm by 9.1 cm (b) 18 cm, 19.6 cm, 40 cm, 26.6 cm, 41 cm (c) 18 cm², 19.6 cm², 100 cm², 43.3 cm², 103.7 cm² (d) Rectangles 1 and 2
3. (a) 2.3 ins. by 1.2 ins., 2.8 ins. by 1.1 ins., 4 ins. by 4 ins., 3 ins. by 2.3 ins., 4.5 ins. by 3.6 ins. (b) 7 ins., 7.8 ins., 16 ins., 10.6 ins., 16.2 ins. (c) 2.76 sq ins., 3.08 sq ins., 16 sq ins., 6.9 sq ins., 16.2 sq ins. (d) Rectangles 3 and 5.
4. (a) For 1, P = 24 cm, A = 24 cm². For 2, P = 24 cm, A = 24 cm². For 3, P = 31.4 cm, A = 78.5 cm². (b) For 1, P = 9.5 ins., A = 3.7 sq ins. For 2, P = 9.5 ins., A = 3.7 sq ins. For 3, P = 12.6 ins., A = 12.6 sq ins. (c) 1 and 2 are equable for centimetres, and 3 for inches.
5. For A, A = 20, P = 18. For B, A = 18, P = 18. For C, A = 19.6, P = 19.6. B and C are equable.
6. (a) 30, 33.75, 33.6 (b) 30, 30, 33.6 (c) A and C
7. 2
8. (a) P = 10.28, A = 6.28 (b) 3.27
9. (a) P = 25.8, A = 27 (b) P = 24.3, A = 22.5 (c) 5.60
10. 6.67
11. (a) $P = 4\sqrt{x^2 + 16}$, A = 8x (b) $4\sqrt{x^2 + 16} = 8x$ (c) 2.31 (d) 18.5
12. (a) $P = 6 + 2\sqrt{h^2 + 9}$, A = 3h (b) $6 + 2\sqrt{h^2 + 9} = 3h$ (c) Equation simplifies to $5h^2 - 36h = 0$; h = 7.2 (d) 21.6 (e) $P = 6 + 2x$, $A = 3\sqrt{x^2 - 9}$, equation simplifies to $5x^2 - 24x - 117 = 0$, giving x = 7.8
13. (a) 5,12,13; 6,8,10; 6,25,29 (b) 7,15,20; 9,10,17
14. 6.2

SECTION C: ANSWERS

1. (a) P = 38, A = 26, No (b) P = 32, A = 33, No (c) P = 42, A = 48, No (d) P = 48, A = 48, Yes
2. (a) Remove a 1 by 1 square (P = A = 24) (b) Remove a 3 by 3 square (P = A = 40)
3. (a) Remove a 2 by 2 square (P = A = 36) (b) Remove a 4 by 4 square (P = A = 50)
4. (a) P = 32, A = 32 (b) P = 40, A = 43 (c) A 9 by 5 rectangle (P = A = 40)
5. (a) P = A = 16π or 50.3, Yes (b) P = A = 12π or 37.7, Yes (c) P = 9π or 28.3, A = 11.25π or 35.3, No
6. For A, P = 42, A = 24, No. For B, P = 52, A = 52, Yes
7. (a) and (b) 20 + 8π or 45.1 (c) Yes
8. (a) $64 - x^2$ (c) 4
9. (c) x + y = 17; x = 9.5, y = 7.5
10. (b) All values of x

11. (c) $\frac{1}{3}$
12. (a) A = 24, P = 20 (c) $\frac{1}{6}$
13. x = 0.83
14. $2x^2 - 6x - 21 = 0$; 5.07 by 10.14
15. (a) $x^2 - y^2$ (b) $4x + 4y$
16. (a) $\pi(r^2 - s^2)$ (b) $2\pi(r + s)$ (c) 2

FURTHER COURSEWORK TASKS

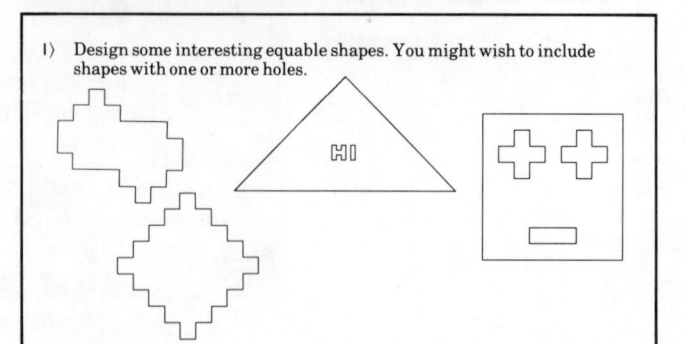

1) Design some interesting equable shapes. You might wish to include shapes with one or more holes.

We wondered whether this task should be considered 'neutral' rather than 'easier'. Students could do advanced work from this very open starting point, but they are likely to find a more focused task helpful (see FCT 3).

If squared paper is used, this task offers students a fairly straightforward opportunity to show originality. Encourage students to include 'failures' produced on the way to developing final designs. The task provides an opportunity to make, and communicate, decisions about the *definition* of perimeter. For example, can you have 'whiskers' or lines inside shapes counting as part of the perimeter (and do they count once or twice)?

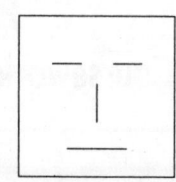

It will help students to design equable shapes if they are aware (having tackled questions in Section C) that shapes with holes are equable if the 'border' width is 2.

Isometric paper can be used instead of, or as well as, squared paper. If it is used, take the unit of area to be the area of the smallest equilateral triangle.

2) Question 3 of Section A was about adding a bump to an equable shape so that the new shape obtained was still equable.

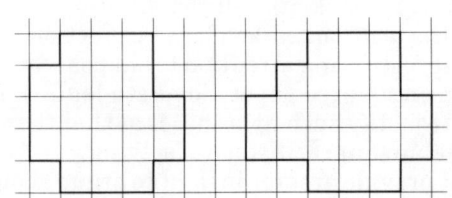

The bump suggested for that question is not the only shape of bump that can be used for this purpose.

Here are some other bumps that could be used, and there are many more.

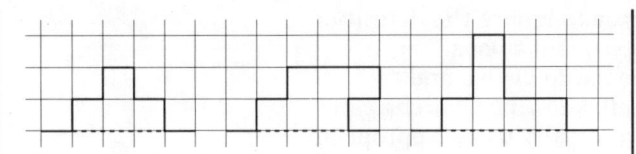

Find other bumps which could be used. Explain how you know that your bumps will work.

Classify your bumps according to the length of the join. You might like to try to find all the possible bumps for a given length of join. How do you know when you have found them all?

It is fairly easy to get started on this task. But knowing that you have found *all* the bumps of a particular type (e.g. of a particular size) is harder. There are many ways of working at this task and students might need help to focus their work rather than producing a large number of valid bumps at random. There is an opportunity for students to justify why their bumps work, perhaps using arguments similar to that of question 4 in Section A.

Some students might want to explore what happens when bumps interfere with each other, as in question 5 of Section A.

3) A solid shape could be called equable if its surface area is numerically equal to its volume.

Find some equable solids.

Explore equable solids of a particular type in more detail. For example, you might want to write a computer program to find equable cuboids with edges which are integers.

This task provides the opportunity for the use of any of the following: *Spread* or a spreadsheet; computer programming; hard algebra. There are very many avenues to explore: students will need to focus their work and look at some aspects in depth.

The equable cube is perhaps an obvious starting point. Trial and improvement, or solving $x^3 = 6x^2$, quickly leads to an edge of 6. The equable sphere (radius 3) fits exactly into the equable cube (compare with the two-dimensional result in FCT 4).

Hollow cylinders are equable if they have a radius of 2 and *any* height. Solid cylinders, on the other hand, are equable if $h = \dfrac{2r}{(r-2)}$. There is an interesting link here with equable rectangles.

Finding *all* the (finite number) of equable cuboids with integral edges is hard, but not impossible if you have programming skills. (Proving you have all the solutions is considerably harder.) A suitable *BASIC* program for generating cuboids with edges of integral length is the following:

```
10 FOR M = 1 TO 50
20 FOR N = 1 TO M
30 FOR P = 1 TO N
40 IF 2*(M*N+N*P+M*P) = M*N*P THEN PRINT M,N,P
50 NEXT P
60 NEXT N
70 NEXT M
80 END
```

An alternative approach is to find particular equable cuboids (e.g. with dimensions 4 by 5 by x or 8 by 11 by x). These will not necessarily have edges of integral length.

A twist to this exploration is to find equable lidless boxes with (or without) edges of integral length.

One line of exploration is to take two cuboids made (conceptually, perhaps) of interlocking cubes, e.g. 6 by 7 by 6 and 2 by 3 by 4, and work out how to join them together to make an equable model. In the case suggested, you join them by a 4 × 2 overlap.

Students can also investigate adding bumps to equable solids which leave them equable. Possible bumps are 4 × 4 × 1 and 6 × 3 × 1 cuboids; but many other possibilities are worth exploring. The key is that the cross-section of the bump is itself equable (although this restriction can be removed if the bump is not of uniform thickness).

Equable cones, pyramids and hemispheres can be explored using algebra or using *Spread* or a spreadsheet.

4) Explore the relationship between the equable circle and other equable shapes.

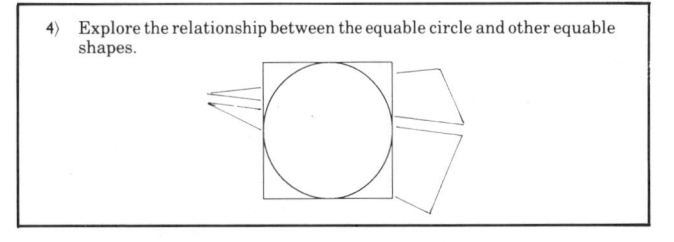

Any polygon which circumscribes the equable circle is equable. This is fairly straightforward to prove (see the examples of students' work on page 70). However, students are likely to do some interesting exploration before they come up with this general result.

The converse of this result is not true. There are equable polygons which do not circumscribe the equable circle. Rectangles are examples. The equable circle can never fit entirely inside an equable polygon unless that polygon circumscribes it. Students might be able to justify this result too.

ASSESSING STUDENTS' COURSEWORK TASKS

Further Coursework Task 2

Students can use the idea of bumps to generate further examples of equable shapes. The student quoted below

TASK MATHS

either misunderstood or chose to ignore the definition of 'bumps' suggested in the student's book. Nevertheless, she has managed to devise and investigate shapes for herself, showing that she can interpret situations mathematically using appropriate diagrams (Ma1/4b).

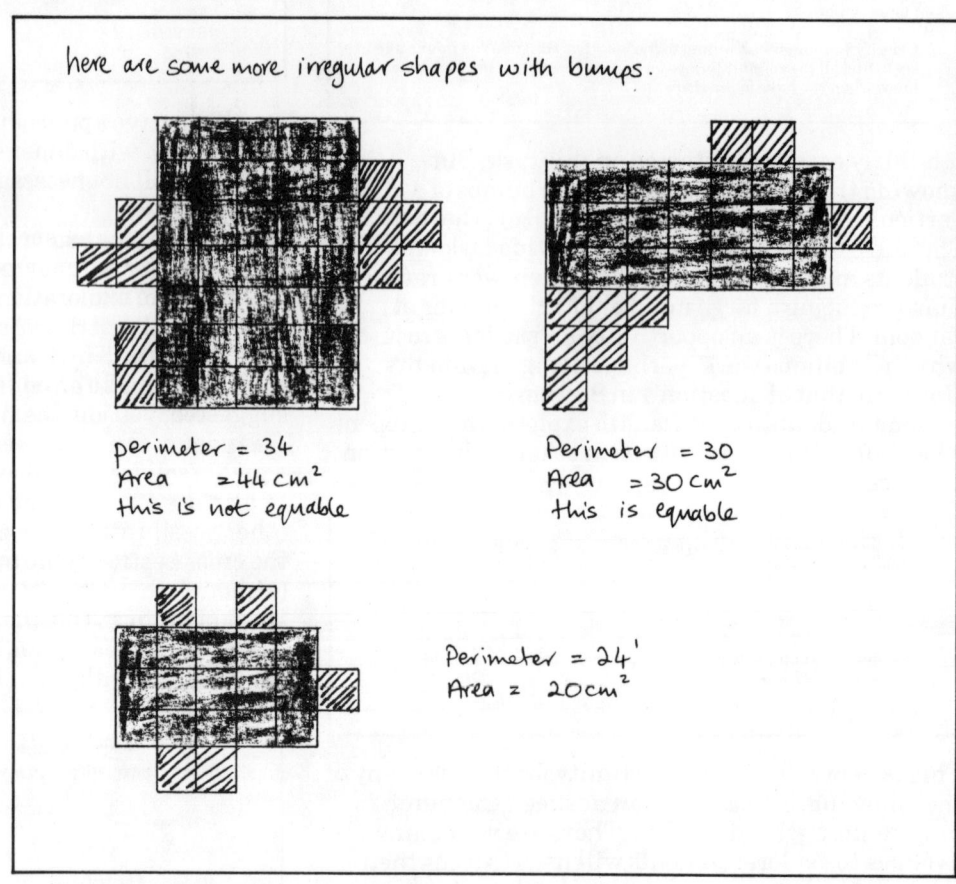

> here are some more irregular shapes with bumps.
>
> perimeter = 34
> Area = 44 cm²
> this is not equable
>
> Perimeter = 30
> Area = 30 cm²
> this is equable
>
> Perimeter = 24
> Area = 20 cm²

In the following extract a student is looking at bumps of different shapes and working out how to find which bumps will preserve the 'area = perimeter' property. She can make generalisations with some degree of justification (Ma1/6c).

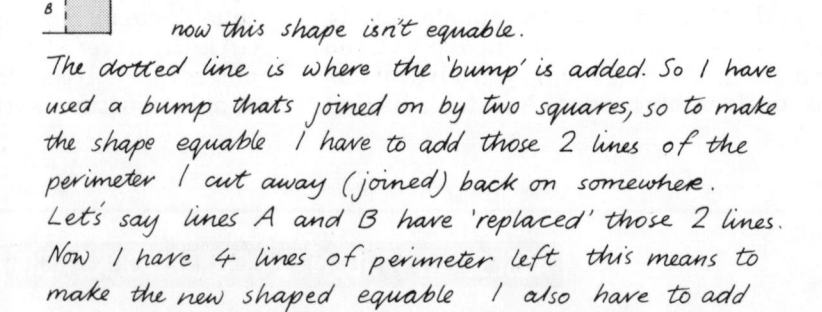

> A
> B
> now this shape isn't equable.
> The dotted line is where the 'bump' is added. So I have used a bump that's joined on by two squares, so to make the shape equable I have to add those 2 lines of the perimeter I cut away (joined) back on somewhere. Let's say lines A and B have 'replaced' those 2 lines. Now I have 4 lines of perimeter left this means to make the new shaped equable I also have to add 4 squares. But I haven't, I've only added 3. (If you understand all of that you're doing well!)

EQUABLE SHAPES

> Now, I'll try to explain why the following shape is equable....
>
> The bump is attached by 2 lines A and B. again replace these lines so altogether I have 10 lines left I have also added 10 bumps. so that shape stays equable. I have added 10 lines and 10 squares. This balances it all out. Really I have added 12 lines but 2 have to replace the ones that were used for the join.

Another student found a rule for generating bumps which preserved the equable property. Here she is considering bumps consisting of two identical rectangles which overlap by two squares, which (judging by her concluding remark) she probably developed from the original 2 by 1 bump suggested in the text. This work also provides evidence for Ma1/6c.

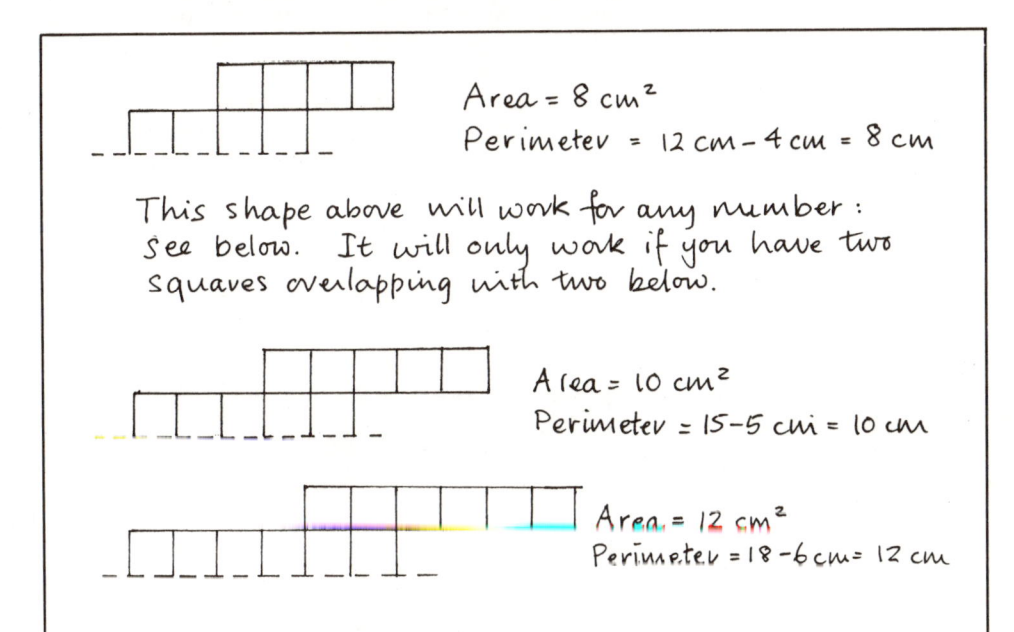

> Area = 8 cm²
> Perimeter = 12 cm - 4 cm = 8 cm
>
> This shape above will work for any number: see below. It will only work if you have two squares overlapping with two below.
>
> Area = 10 cm²
> Perimeter = 15 - 5 cm = 10 cm
>
> Area = 12 cm²
> Perimeter = 18 - 6 cm = 12 cm
>
> This table shows my results for that bump:
>
> | Amount of squares attached to equable shapes | Perimeter (P) | Area (A) |
> |---|---|---|
> | 3 cm square | 6 cm (9-3) | 6 cm |
> | 4 cm squares | 8 cm (12-4) | 8 cm² |
> | 5 cm squares | 10 cm (15-5) | 10 cm² |

6 cm squares	12 cm (18−6)	12 cm²
7 cm squares	14 cm (21−7)	14 cm²
8 cm squares	16 cm (24−8)	16 cm²
9 cm squares	18 cm (27−9)	18 cm²
10 cm squares	20 cm (30−10)	20 cm²

Following on with this you may have noticed that in the table I started at three this was because the shape before three didn't apply because it's shape isn't the same but it Area and perimeter are the same (see below)

Area = 4 cm²
Perimeter = 6−2 cm = 4 cm

Further Coursework Task 4

This task might seem quite easy once you have sorted the ideas out, but considerable research is likely to be needed to spot what is happening. This student started his work by looking back at the various equable shapes he had found, and used accurate drawings to show that some of them circumscribed the equable circle.

These drawings helped him see the proof of the general result that any polygon circumscribing a circle is equable (see the extract below). In this extract he also demonstrates that the converse of the theorem is not true, showing that he understands the role of counter-examples (Ma1/8b).

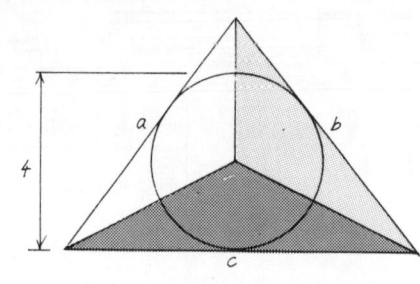

The triangle can be split into 3 triangles, if the centre of the equable triangle is used as can be seen.

As with each of the individual triangles the height is 2 (the radius of the equable circle) then the base must be the area of the triangle as proved below:—

area = 0.5 × base × height
area = 0.5 × base × 2
area = base

Therefore any shape which can be divided into triangles with a height of 2 each must be equable, and circumscribe the equable circle with all of its sides a tangent to the equable circle.

However, not all equable shapes will circumscribe the circle, with all of the sides being tangents to the equable circle as shown below...

Example 1. — the equable rectangle.

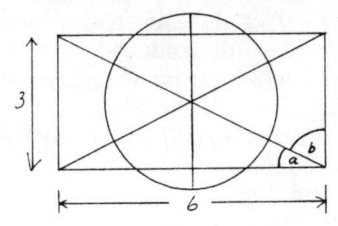

Reasons why there is no relationship:
a) the height of the triangles are not 2
b) the triangle does not bisect the angle of the corner, in any of the 4 (a does not equal b)

The above reasons also apply for other shapes. which are usually irregular, these being the only exceptions to the relationships previously shown.

TASK MATHS

Guide to Chapter 19: DISSECTING CUBES

Outline

The task for this chapter is to dissect cubes and other solids in a number of different ways, to explore methods of constructing the dissections, and the properties of the solids produced.

In the introductory activity students construct their chosen dissection of a cube out of paper.

Section A is about nets. It starts with different nets and simple dissections of cubes and cuboids. Later questions involve more difficult dissections, and there is one question about dissecting a tetrahedron.

Section B poses questions about the surface area and volume of the solids obtained by making various dissections of cubes, cuboids, tetrahedrons and pyramids. Use is made of Pythagoras' theorem and algebra. Later questions develop the use of trigonometry to find the angles between edges and planes.

There are four Further Coursework Tasks. Two involve making a cardboard model of a cube or some other shape, one develops the idea, introduced in Section B, of considering the total surface area obtained from a dissection, and one is about sections of a cube.

Strategies

It is worth spending time on the introductory activity, because it helps students to develop an appreciation of three-dimensional space and also of how nets are constructed. There is a lot of work in this chapter: several of the questions in Sections A and B could be used as coursework tasks in themselves. When students are working on Sections A and B encourage them to draw only rough sketches of nets; the introductory activity and the FCTs are the appropriate places for accurate constructions. Similarly, encourage students to use the diagrams in the book to help their thinking; it might be a waste of their efforts copying them.

Students benefit from discussing ideas in small groups. Much of the work depends on visualising. The teacher cannot 'teach' this: students need time to develop ideas for themselves. If students are going to tackle the questions involving the use of 3-D trigonometry (Section B, question 9 onwards) this could be introduced through class discussion and it might be helpful to make use of some models to illustrate the concepts of angles between lines and angles between planes.

All students should find one of the FCTs well worth doing. Most students enjoy the challenge of making their own models as suggested in FCTs 1, 3 and 4. For those who do not, FCT 2 invites students to focus on some of the ideas behind a particular type of dissection, and FCTs 3 and 4 can also be interpreted in this way.

Equipment and Resources

For introduction to the task and FCTs 1, 3 and 4:
   adhesive tape
   polythene bags (one for each student to store all the bits!)
   thick paper or card (for FCT models)

Relevant Review Exercises

C37	*Equations 2*	page 125
C40	*Nets and polyhedra*	page 137
C41	*Pythagoras' theorem and trigonometry in three dimensions*	page 141

DISSECTING CUBES

National Curriculum Statements	Introduction to the task 4/4a1; 4/5a; 4/5b2; 4/6a Section A 4/4a1; 4/4a3; 4/5a; 4/5b2; 4/6a Section B 2/5c1; 2/7b1; 3/5b1; 3/5b2; 3/6b; 4/5b2; 4/5d2; 4/6a; 4/7c; 4/7d; 4/9a1
Questions in Sections	**Accessible to all students** (no bars) Section A, 1–6(c) Section B, 1–3 **Somewhat harder** (one bar) Section A, 6(d)–7 Section B, 4–6 **More difficult** (two bars) Section A, 8–9 Section B, 7–14
Further Coursework Tasks	neutral: 1 easier: more difficult: 2, 3, 4

INTRODUCTION TO THE TASK: HINTS

A good way of introducing this task is to do it yourself first, and then to show students each stage: the cube with the lines drawn on it; what happens when you cut it; how you flatten it out; and how you think about the missing faces. It takes several lessons for many students to develop facility with this. Once students have made a good start their models can be put on one side (perhaps in an uncompleted state) and perhaps return to it when the FCTs are tackled. Through working on questions in Sections A and B students will improve their understanding and be helped to construct more complex models than they originally thought of.

At first students tend to use a lot of trial and error in producing their nets, but gradually they adopt a more systematic and mathematical approach to the problem. Don't rush them! It helps most students if they work in small groups. Although doing their own nets, they all have similar problems to solve and by helping to sort out other students' problems students learn how to sort out their own.

SECTION A: ANSWERS

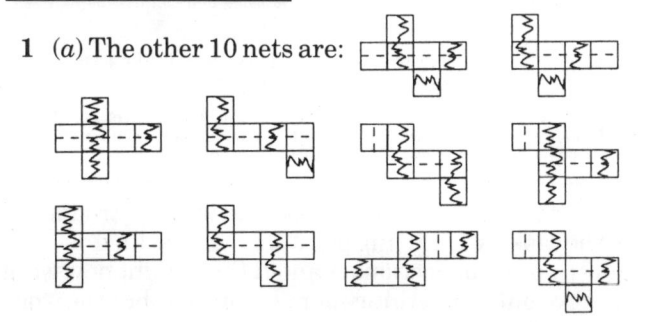

1 (a) The other 10 nets are:

(b) See above (– – – one cut/∿∿ second cut/third cut is not shown)
(c)(i) One face missing   (ii) Five faces in a row
(iii) Two tops

2 (a)(i) Yes   (ii) No   (iii) Yes   (iv) Yes   (v) No
(vi) No   (b)(i) No (*pairs* of opposite faces are the same)   (ii) No (once you have four square faces the other two have to be square)   (iii) No (see (i))   (iv) Yes (see (a)(iii)   (v) No (see (i))
(vi) Yes (see (a)(iv))

4

73

There are other possible nets.
    You could also have any plane cut which passes through the centre of the cuboid (but students are *likely* to choose the four shown above).

5 (*a*) (A75)

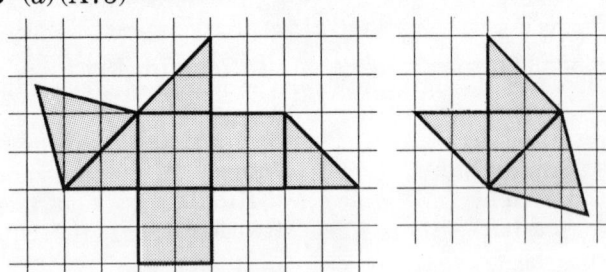

There are other possible nets.
(*b*)

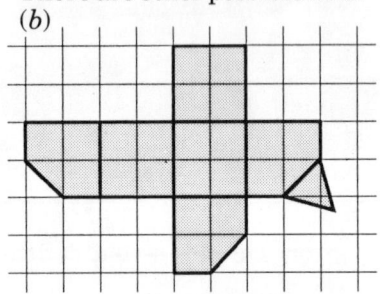

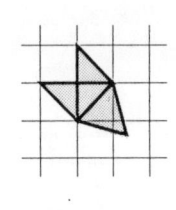

There are other possible nets.

6 (*a*) $\frac{1}{3}$ (of a $3 \times 3 \times 3$ cube) (*b*) $\frac{1}{8}$ (of a $4 \times 4 \times 4$ cube) (*c*) $\frac{1}{6}$ (of a $3 \times 3 \times 3$ cube) (*d*) $\frac{1}{18}$ (of a $6 \times 6 \times 6$ cube)
7 There are other possible nets.
8 (*a*) There are other possible nets.

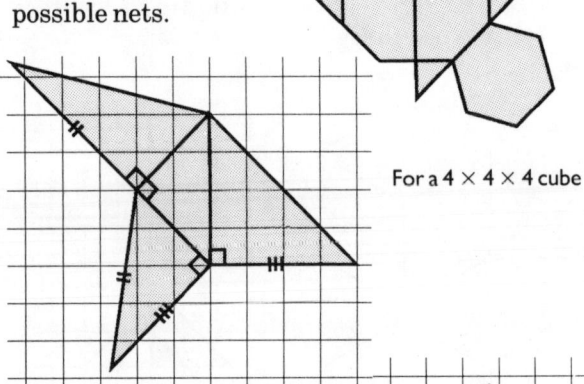

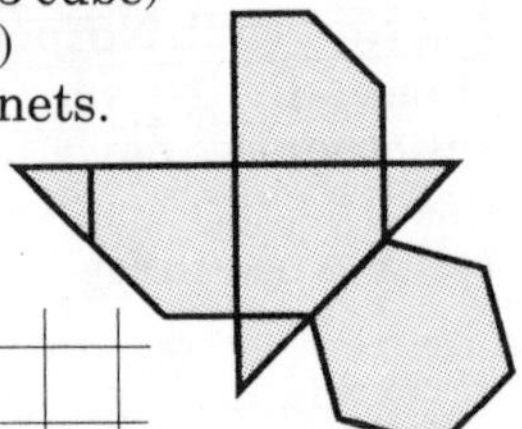

For a $4 \times 4 \times 4$ cube

(*b*) There are other possible nets.

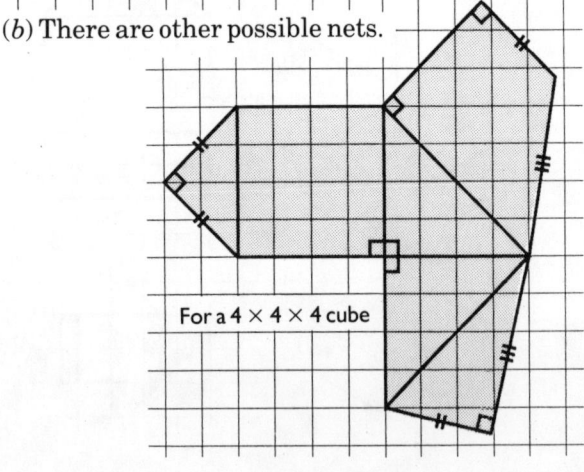

For a $4 \times 4 \times 4$ cube

9 For a tetrahedron of edge 2 units. There are other possible nets.

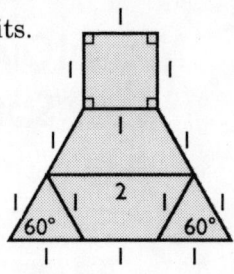

10 Yes. It has point symmetry about its centre.

SECTION B: ANSWERS

1 (*a*) 500 cm^3 (*b*) 400 cm^2
2 (*a*) 576 cm^3, 1152 cm^3 (*b*) 480 cm^2, 672 cm^2
3 (*a*) 125 cm^3 (*b*) 600 cm^2 (*c*) 150 cm^2
    (*d*) 1200 cm^2 (*e*) Answer to (*d*) is twice answer to (*b*), because each little cube has half its faces new.
4 (*a*)(i) 7 (ii) 4 (iii) 28 (*b*) No, because you create the same additional surface area with each cut wherever the cut is.
5 (*a*) 171.5 cm^3 (*b*) 216 cm^2
6 (*a*) 2 (*b*) 384 cm^2, 768 cm^2 (*c*) 288 cm^3, 1440 cm^3
7 (*a*) 121.5 cm^3, 607.5 cm^3 (*b*) 192 cm^2, 435 cm^2
8 (*a*) 14, 24, 12 (*b*) 21 cm^3 (*c*) 833 cm^3
    (*d*) 473 cm^2
9 (*a*) 62 cm^3 (*b*) 27° (*c*) 34° (*d*) 108 cm^3, 0
10 (*a*) Centre of cube (*b*) $\frac{1}{2}\sqrt{3} = 0.87$ (*c*) $\frac{1}{6}$ (*d*) $\frac{1}{2}$
    (*e*) 35° (*f*) 45°
11 (*a*) 0.87 (*b*) 1.73 (*d*) 0.58 (*e*) 0.82 (*f*) 0.12
12 (*a*) 0.06 (*b*) 1.22
13 (*a*) 1.12 (*b*) Smaller
14 (*a*) 0.87 (*b*) 0 (*c*) $\sqrt{2} = 1.41$ (*d*) 0 (*e*)(i) 1.22 (diagonals are $\sqrt{3}$ and $\sqrt{2}$) (ii) 78° and 102°
    (*f*) 1.30 (*g*) 1.41 (rectangle) (*h*) 1 (square)

FURTHER COURSEWORK TASKS

1) Make a cardboard model of a dissection of a cube. You can dissect the cube into as many pieces as you wish.

Here are some ideas you might want to think about when choosing what dissection to make.

- You might want to dissect the cube into shapes that you think are attractive.
- You might want to dissect the cube into several identical pieces.
- You might want your dissection to be symmetrical in some way, or to produce pieces which are symmetrical.
- You might want the pieces to all have the same volume, but to be different shapes.
- You might want to create a kind of 3-D jigsaw puzzle, in which it is difficult for someone else to know how to fit the pieces together.

Write about how you chose your dissection, and about how you made it. Include nets for the pieces. Also include failures, and try to exlain in what ways you went wrong, and what you did to correct your mistakes.

Students can use the work they did in the introduction to the task as a starting point. Having tackled questions from Sections A and B they might now want to move onto something more ambitious, but the work on the introduction to the task can be included to show how their ideas developed. If students are encouraged to use their initiative they can produce amazingly complex dissections. As the work progresses it becomes increasingly difficult for the teacher to help, because students have a much better grip of what is going on, having developed their ideas for themselves. The teacher has a useful role to play in encouraging some students to be more ambitious, persuading students to keep their 'failed attempts' so that they can write about how they overcame their problems, and persuading some students to calculate (perhaps using Pythagoras' theorem or trigonometry) rather than measuring everything. More mundanely, but equally importantly, teachers need to provide students with polythene bags and boxes, so that work can be stored between one lesson and the next.

Some students will prefer thick paper to card for their final model. Thick paper is flimsier, but easier to work with. Students can be encouraged to make an 'outer cube' into which all the pieces of the dissection will fit.

When working on this task there are times, particularly near the beginning, where progress appears slow. But students seem suddenly to gain inspiration and confidence, and then they take off!

The task refers to questions from Section B. These questions help students to get started. Some students might be able to obtain general results (see below). The ideas provide scope for the use of algebra, trigonometry, and area and volume results. Only some students will be able to produce generalisations expressed algebraically. Other students will move towards them through a series of numerical examples (see students' work in the next section).

Question 4 is about slicing up a cube so that the total surface area is k times that of the original cube. If one face of the original cube has an area of 1, each cut adds 2 to the total surface area. So if there are N cuts the total surface area is $6 + 2N$. Thus $6 + 2N = 6k$, which gives $N = 3(k - 1)$.

Question 6 is about cutting a cube into two cuboids so that the surface area of one is p (which can be assumed to be greater than 1) times that of the other. When an edge of the cube is of unit length,
$4(1 - x) + 2 = p(4x + 2)$
(see diagram). This leads to
$$x = \frac{3-p}{2(p+1)}$$

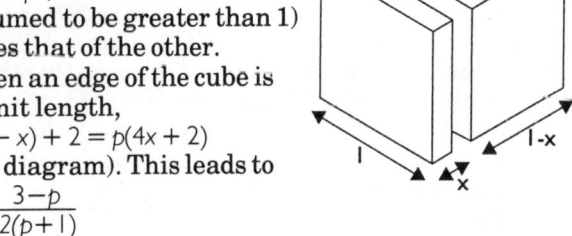

which demonstrates that p must be less than 3. When $p = 2$ the ratio of the volumes is 5, which might surprise many students. This might encourage some to obtain the ratio of the volumes q in terms of p. In fact,
$$q = \frac{3-p}{3(p-1)}$$

and students could include the graph of this function in their explanations. (See also students' work in the next section.)

Sloping cuts as suggested at the end of the FCT and in question 9 of Section B, prove more demanding, in terms both of volume and of surface area.

---

2) Questions 2, 3, 4 and 6 of Section B are all about slicing a cube into cuboids.

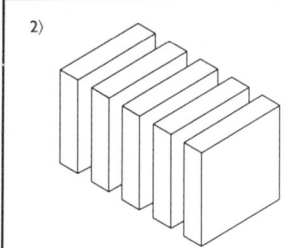

Explore this situation further.

If you cut a cuboid into two cuboids, you might want to consider how to make the surface area of one of the cuboids p times the surface area of the other.

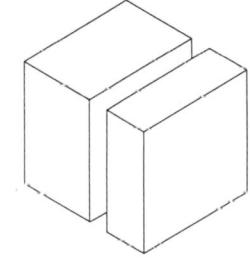

You might want to consider several different ways of cutting a cube into two pieces so that one piece has twice the volume of the other.

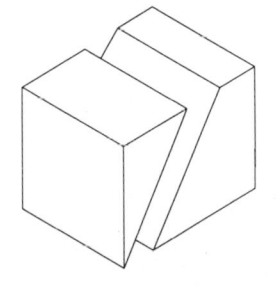

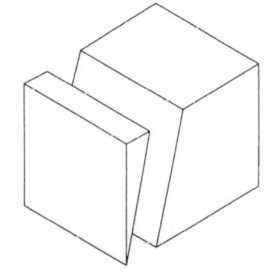

or three times the surface area of the other.

---

3) Investigate the different sections of a cube (the shapes you create when you cut a cube with a plane cut).

Here are some of the questions you might want to explore.

- What are the ways of getting a triangular section?
- Is it possible to get all types of triangle: equilateral, isosceles, scalene, acute-angled, right-angled, obtuse-angled? 
- How do you get a section which is a rectangle? Or a rhombus? Or a parallelogram? Or a trapezium? What types of quadrilateral section are possible?
- What type of pentagonal or hexagonal sections are possible?

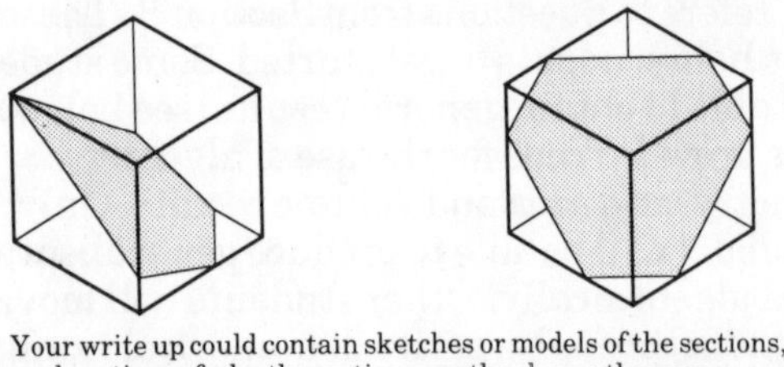

Your write up could contain sketches or models of the sections, and also explanations of why the sections are the shapes they are.

Focusing from the outset on the shape of the section (the missing face of the introduction to the task) is probably more difficult than focusing on the pieces obtained from a dissection. The task is most likely to appeal to students who like thinking about geometry in their heads.

A section is always a polygon. The number of sides of the section depends on which edges are intersected by the cut. If three edges are intersected you get a triangle. (The only way this can happen is if the three edges meet at a common vertex). If the plane of the cut is perpendicular to a pair of faces of the cube (in other words, if it is vertical when the cube is placed on a horizontal table) the section is a rectangle. If the cut is parallel to a face then the section is a square. But there are also other ways of getting a square.

Is *any* rectangle a section of a cube of suitable size? This suggests another line of enquiry. Given a rectangle (say a 3 by 2 rectangle) what are the largest and smallest cubes which have this rectangle as a section?

You can also get a parallelogram or a rhombus (see question 14(*e*) in Section A).

Pentagons and hexagons can also be obtained and, in particular, the regular hexagon but not the regular pentagon.

Specifying the shape of triangle you want and then finding out how to cut the cube is a tough assignment, involving the use of Pythagoras' theorem (and perhaps also the sine and cosine rule if angles are specified). Symmetry can be used to see how to get an equilateral triangle. Symmetry arguments also explain how to cut the cube so that an isosceles triangle is produced. If you want to get a triangle with particular side lengths *a*, *b* and *c* (say 4, 5 and 6) you can proceed as follows.

$u^2 + v^2 = a^2 = 16$
$v^2 + w^2 = b^2 = 25$
$u^2 + w^2 = c^2 = 36$

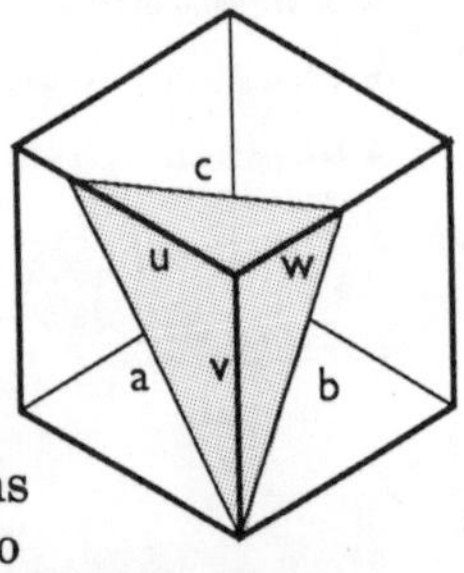

This gives $u^2 = \frac{27}{2}$, $v^2 = \frac{5}{2}$ and $w^2 = \frac{45}{2}$.

Using the same three equations it can be shown that $a^2 + b^2 > c^2$, so that only acute-angled triangles can be obtained.

These are just some of the avenues which could be explored. Encourage students to present their work as a combination of intuitive insights (supported by appropriate sketches) and logical, perhaps algebraic, reasoning.

4) Make a cardboard model of a dissection of some shape other than a cube. Or alternatively, write about the different ways of dissecting some other shape.

You could, for example, choose to look at dissections of a tetrahedron, or a cylinder.

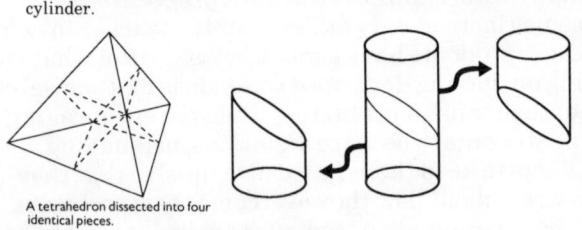

A tetrahedron dissected into four identical pieces.

The approach of the introductory activity can be used for this task. Students are likely, because of unfamiliarity, to find it harder to visualise dissections of solid shapes other than the cube.

A regular tetrahedron can be dissected into two identical pieces in many different ways. The most obvious way is, perhaps, to use a plane of symmetry. An alternative, which is indicated in the drawing in the student's book, is to use a plane which passes through the midpoints of four edges (this produces a square cross-section). The second method has the advantage that a second such plane will cut the tetrahedron into four identical pieces. (Actually **any** plane passing through the midpoint of one pair of opposite edges cuts the tetrahedron into two identical pieces. This is because the tetrahedron has half-turn symmetry about the line joining midpoints of opposite edges.)

An oblique cut of a cylinder produces a cross-section which is an ellipse. But the top edge of the net for this cut is a sine curve.

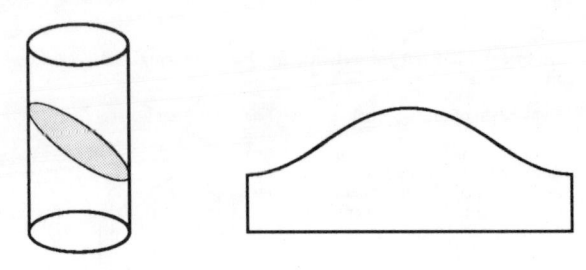

Height is proportional to the *x*-coordinate, which is $r \sin \theta$. When the cylinder is unwrapped the distance across the net is proportional to θ.

DISSECTING CUBES

ASSESSING STUDENTS' COURSEWORK TASKS

Further Coursework Task 1

Students can include the nets they use to make each piece of their dissection, together with a sketch of that piece. This extract shows some of the pieces a student had to make for her dissection. Her work is correct, if not very detailed, She can design a task in a given context (Ma1/6a).

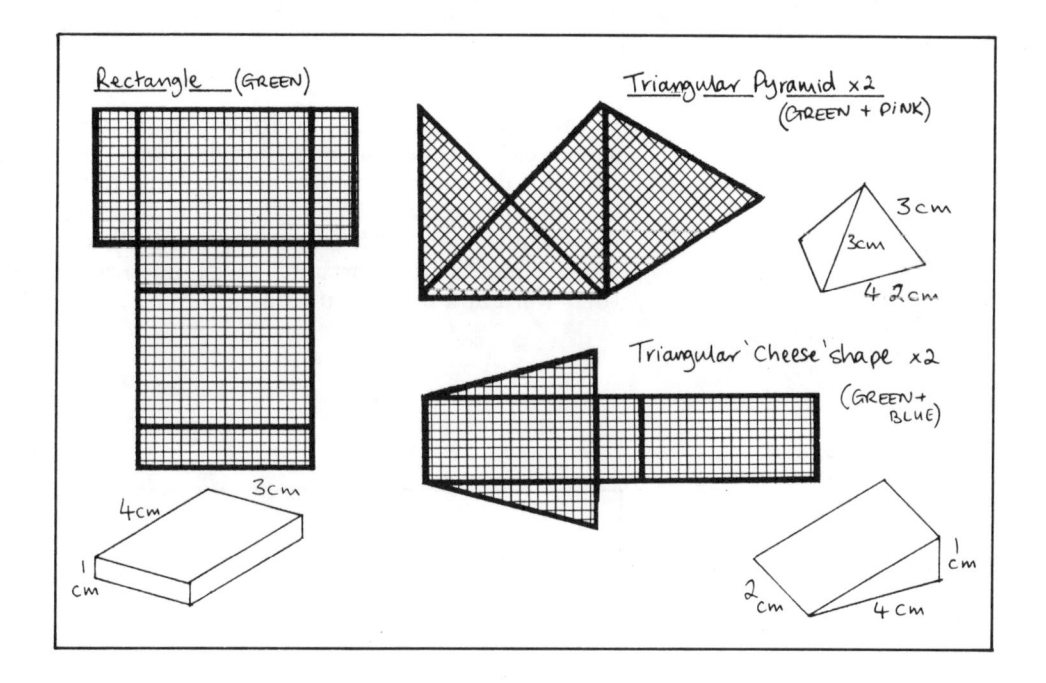

Students who have chosen a complicated dissection with a large number of pieces can use 3-D sketches to show how all the pieces fit together. This will provide strong evidence for Ma1/5b.

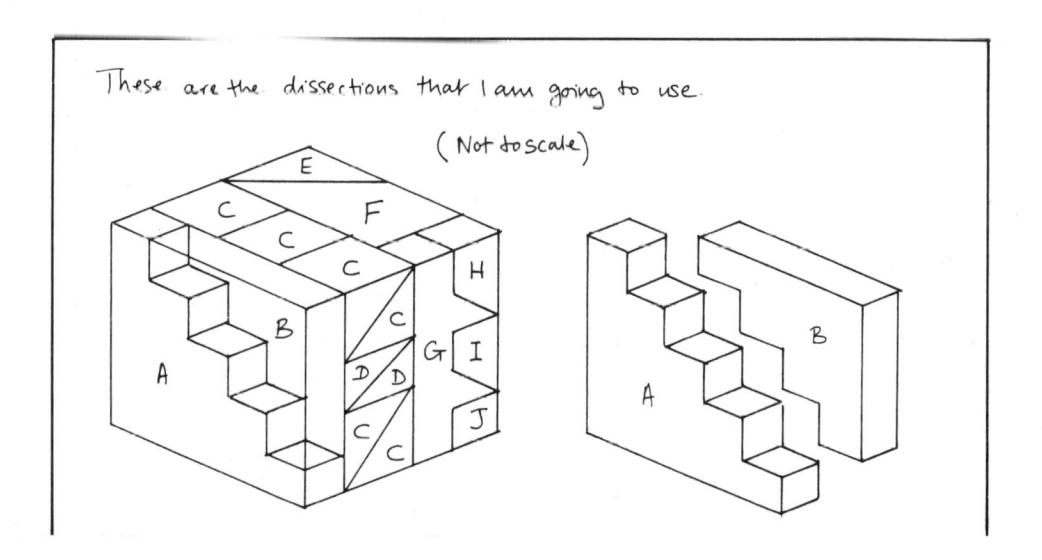

TASK MATHS

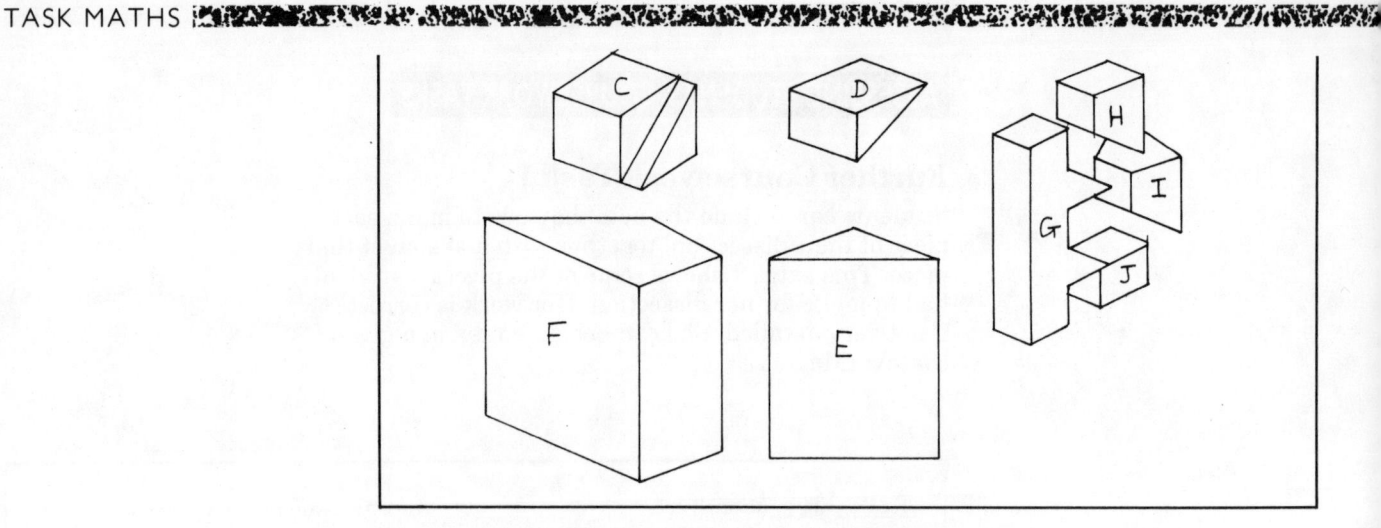

In the following extract the student starts with a 3-D sketch of her dissection and then develops the net from the lines drawn on the cube, as suggested in the introductory activity. Her explanation is somewhat flawed, although her final net is correct. This task gives students an opportunity to 'examine critically' their work and improve it (Ma1/6b).

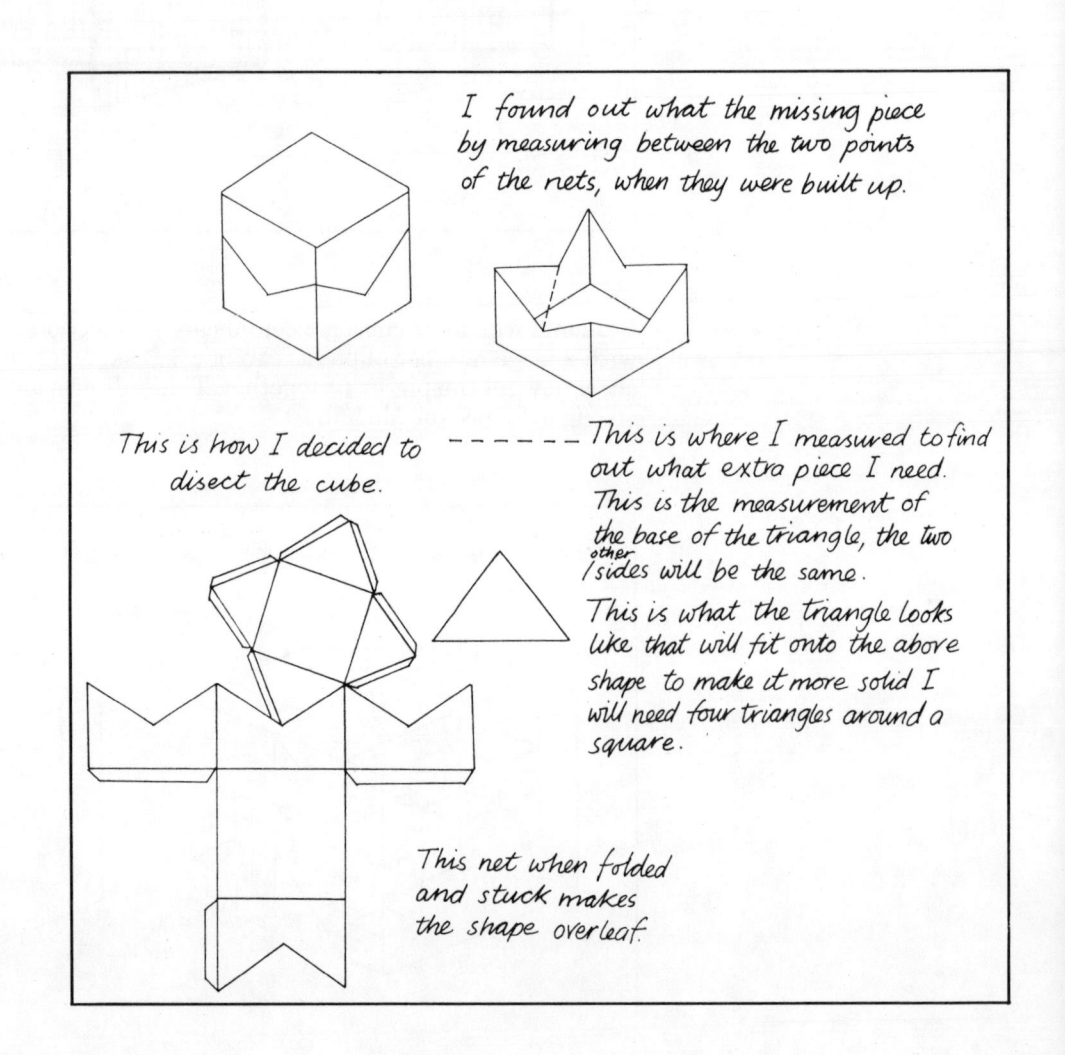

I found out what the missing piece by measuring between the two points of the nets, when they were built up.

This is how I decided to disect the cube.

This is where I measured to find out what extra piece I need. This is the measurement of the base of the triangle, the two other sides will be the same.

This is what the triangle looks like that will fit onto the above shape to make it more solid I will need four triangles around a square.

This net when folded and stuck makes the shape overleaf.

DISSECTING CUBES

This extract is part of an account which clearly explains how a number of nets for pieces forming a complex dissection are developed. Complex dissections involve students in co-ordinating a number of features (Ma1/9a).

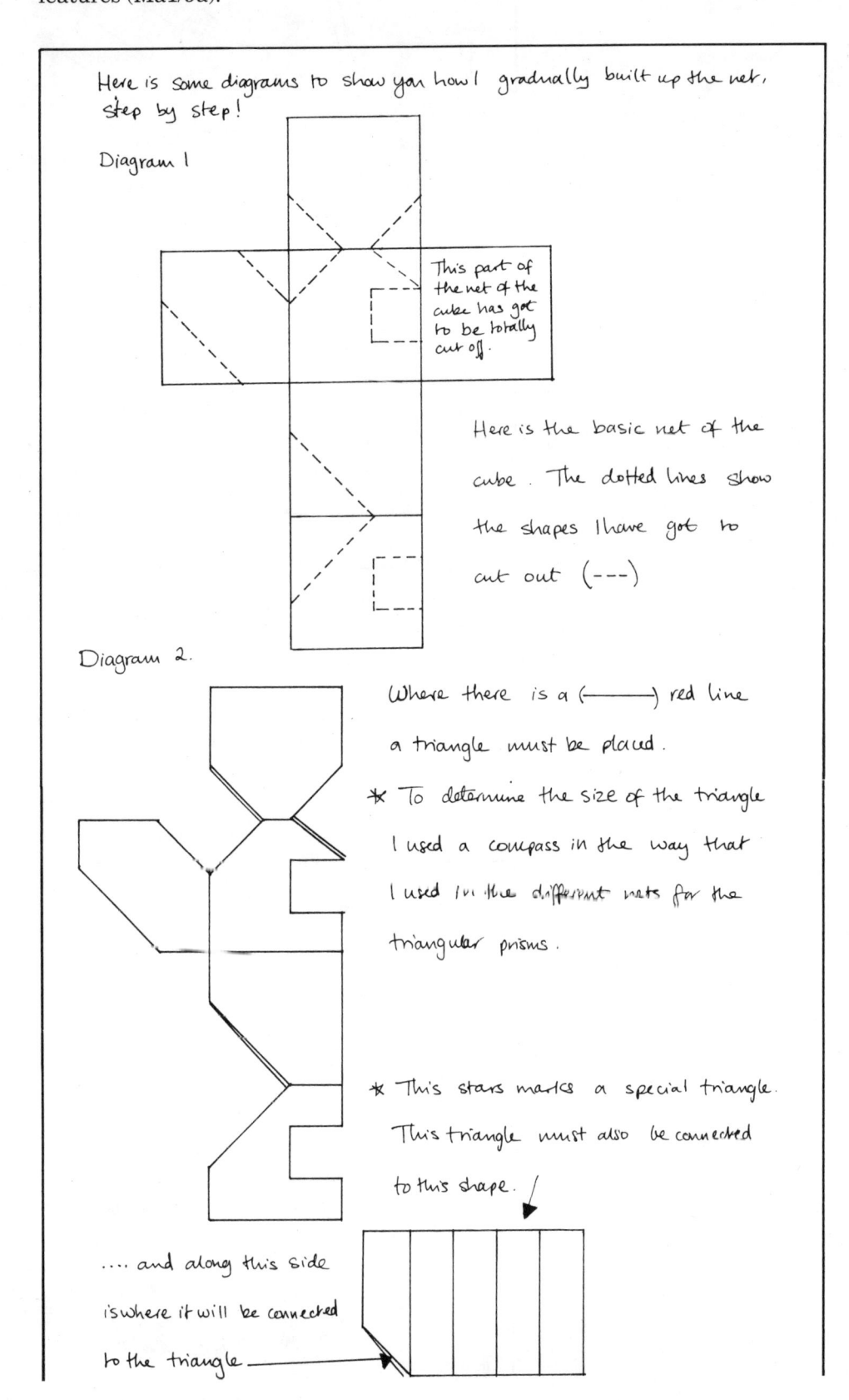

Here is some diagrams to show you how I gradually built up the net, step by step!

Diagram 1

This part of the net of the cube has got to be totally cut off.

Here is the basic net of the cube. The dotted lines show the shapes I have got to cut out (- - -)

Diagram 2.

Where there is a (———) red line a triangle must be placed.

* To determine the size of the triangle I used a compass in the way that I used in the different nets for the triangular prisms.

* This stars marks a special triangle. This triangle must also be connected to this shape.

.... and along this side is where it will be connected to the triangle

TASK MATHS

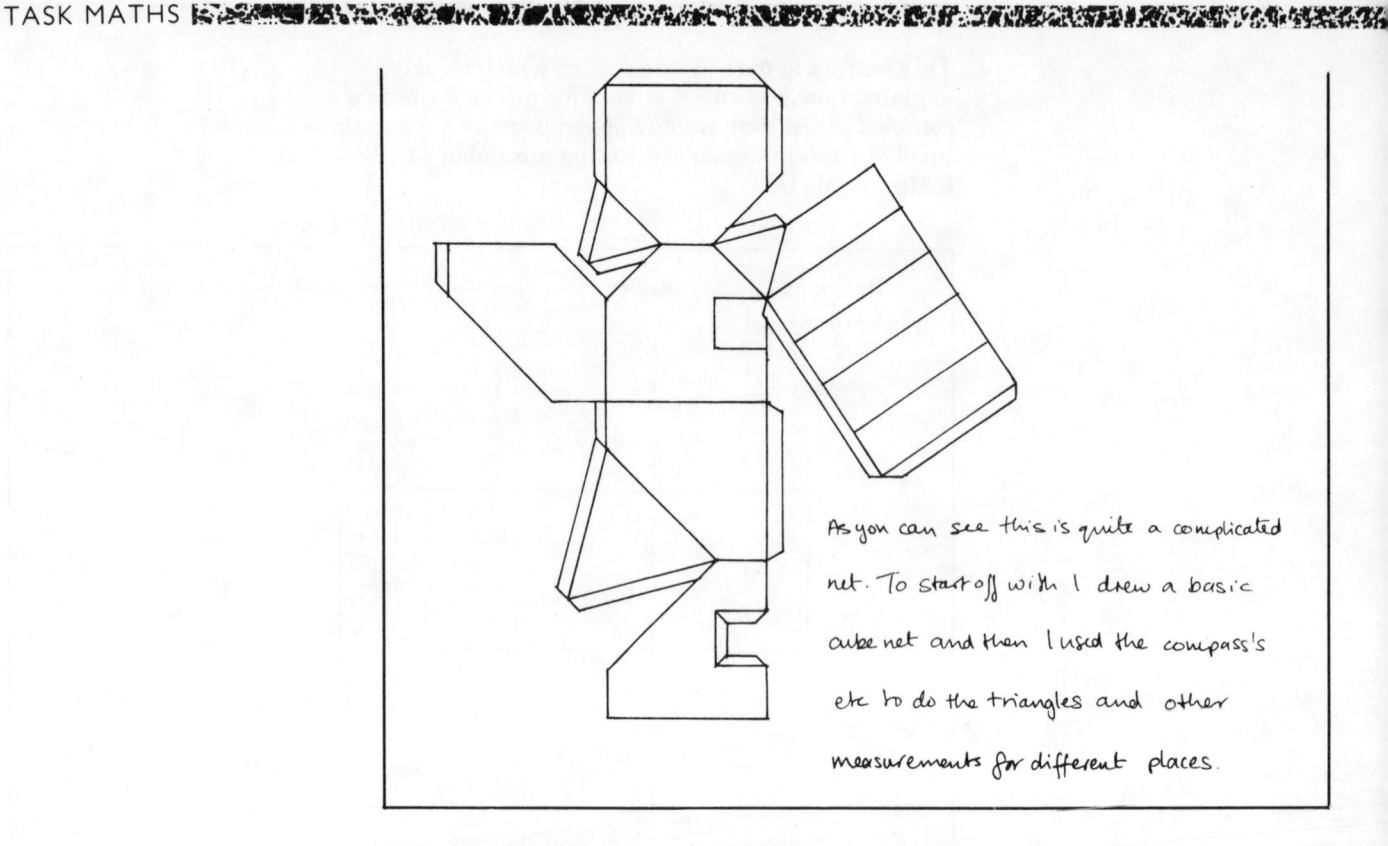

As you can see this is quite a complicated net. To start off with I drew a basic cube net and then I used the compass's etc to do the triangles and other measurements for different places.

Further Coursework Task 2

Probably the easiest way for students to get started on this task is to consider a series of special cases. In the following extract the student is considering how to divide cubes of different sizes into two cuboids so that the surface area of one is twice that of the other. She is also looking at the volume of each cuboid. The extract is one of a series of similar examples. She can give some degree of justification to her solution (Ma1/6c).

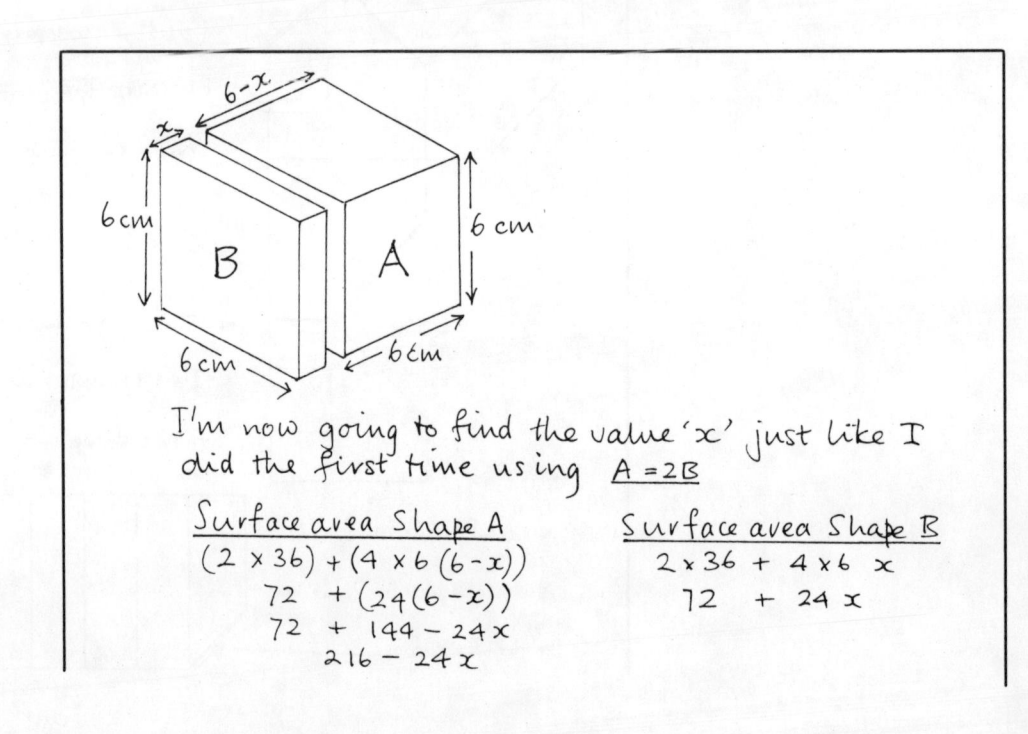

I'm now going to find the value 'x' just like I did the first time using A = 2B

Surface area Shape A
$(2 \times 36) + (4 \times 6(6-x))$
$72 + (24(6-x))$
$72 + 144 - 24x$
$216 - 24x$

Surface area Shape B
$2 \times 36 + 4 \times 6 x$
$72 + 24x$

> $216 - 24x = 2(72 + 24x)$
> $216 - 24x = 144 + 48x$
> $216 - 144 = 24x + 48x$
> $72 = 72x$
> $x = 1$
>
> I will now on and find the volumes of the shapes
>
> **Volume of Shape A** **Volume of Shape B**
> $5 \times 6 \times 6$ $6 \times 6 \times 1$
> $= 180 \text{ cm}^3$ $= 36 \text{ cm}^3$
>
> I will now find the ratio by dividing the two numbers
> $180 \div 36 = 5$ $5:1$
> The ratio is the same as last time.

In the following extract another student has gone a stage further and noticed that you always need to cut off $\frac{1}{6}$ of an edge to make one surface area twice the other, and that then one volume is five times the other. She proves this using algebra which involves more than one variable in a fairly complex equation (Ma1/9a and Ma1/9b).

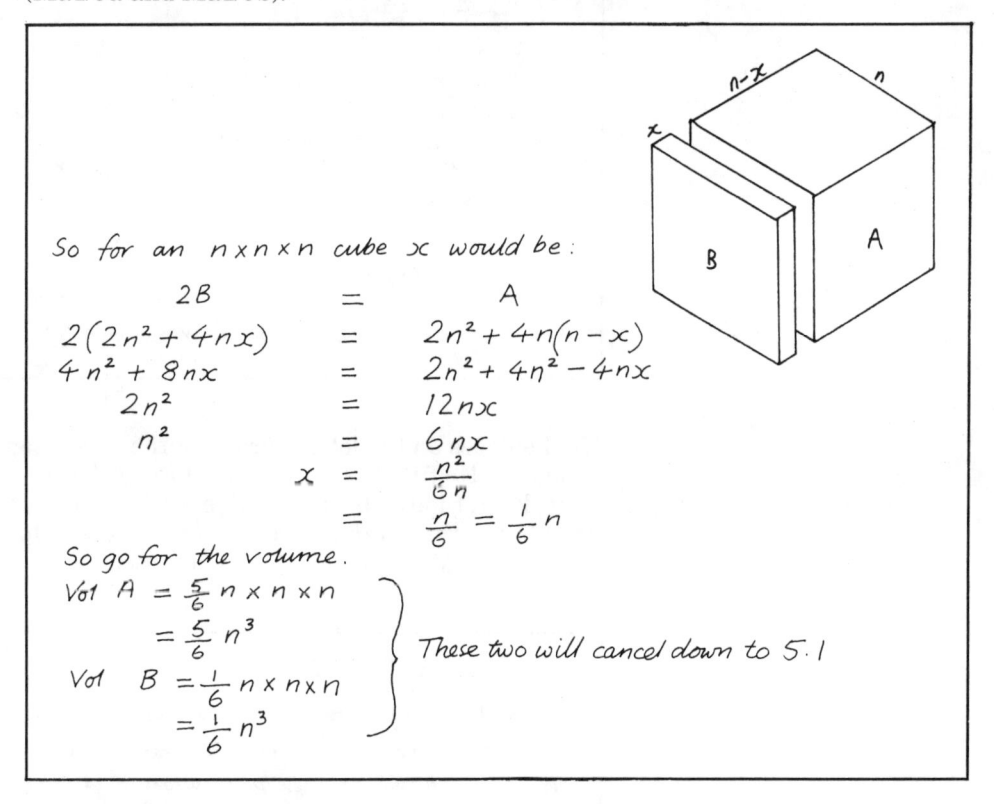

> So for an $n \times n \times n$ cube x would be:
>
> $2B = A$
> $2(2n^2 + 4nx) = 2n^2 + 4n(n-x)$
> $4n^2 + 8nx = 2n^2 + 4n^2 - 4nx$
> $2n^2 = 12nx$
> $n^2 = 6nx$
> $x = \frac{n^2}{6n}$
> $ = \frac{n}{6} = \frac{1}{6}n$
>
> So go for the volume.
> Vol $A = \frac{5}{6} n \times n \times n$
> $ = \frac{5}{6} n^3$
> Vol $B = \frac{1}{6} n \times n \times n$
> $ = \frac{1}{6} n^3$
>
> These two will cancel down to 5·1

A different student extended the problem further and considered different ratios for the surface areas of the two cuboids. He realized that it was only sensible to consider ratios $p:1$ for which $p < 3$. In this extract he is working out one surface area as a percentage of the other for values of p between 1 and 3 in steps of 0.1. His cube has edge length Y and a piece of length X is cut off.

> I shall now show the working for each equation from
> 1.1 all the way through to 2.9.
>
> ratios of surface areas = 1 : 1.1
> Piece where Y−X is the width   Piece where X is the width
> $4Y(Y-X) + 2Y^2$ $= 1.1 \times 4XY + 2Y^2$
> Remove the brackets
> $6Y^2 - 4XY$ $= 4.4XY + 2.2Y^2$
> Add 4XY to both sides
> $6Y^2$ $= 8.4XY + 2.2Y^2$
> Take $2.2Y^2$ from both sides
> $3.8Y^2$ $= 8.4XY$
> Divide both sides by Y
> $3.8Y$ $= 8.4X$
> Divide both sides by 3.8
> Y $= 2.21X$
> X as a percentage of Y = **45.2%**
>
> ratios of surface areas = 1 : 1.2
> Piece where Y−X is the width   Piece where X is the width
> $4Y(Y-X) + 2Y^2$ $= 1.2 \times 4XY + 2Y^2$
> Remove the brackets
> $6Y^2 - 4XY$ $= 4.8XY + 2.4Y^2$
> Add 4XY to both sides
> $6Y^2$ $= 8.8XY + 2.4Y^2$
> Take $2.4Y^2$ from both sides
> $3.6Y^2$ $= 8.8XY$
> Divide both sides by Y
> $3.6Y$ $= 8.8X$
> Divide both sides by 3.6
> Y $= 2.444X$
> X as a percentage of Y = **40.9%**

He then goes on to plot the graph of the percentages against ρ. He finally gets a general result for any ratio. Even though his use of algebra is somewhat unorthodox this work shows stronger evidence for Ma1/9a and Ma1/9b than the last extract.

> **FINDING THE FORMULA**
>
> I shall now try to find a formula so I can work out the "X as a percentage of Y" from the "ratios of surface areas" when the "ratios of surface areas is" R. I shall take the piece where X is the width to be A and the piece where Y−X is the width to be B. So the ratio is A:B.
>
> A = 1 for B to be 1.5, 2.0, 2.5 etc
> $B = 4Y^2 - 4XY + 2Y^2$
> Divided by the area of A which is : − $4XY + 2Y^2$
>
> $$\frac{4Y^2 - 4XY + 2Y^2 \; (B)}{4XY + 2Y^2 \; (A)}$$
>
> simplify this

$$\frac{6Y^2 - 4XY}{4XY + 2Y^2} \frac{(B)}{(A)}$$

If I simplify this equation further so as to make it easier to solve, I am left with this:—

$$\frac{2Y(3Y - 2X)}{2Y(2X + Y)} \frac{(B)}{(A)}$$

Divide top and bottom by 2Y and that gives the completed formula.

$$\frac{3Y - 2X}{2X + Y} \frac{(B)}{(A)}$$

I shall now try this on an example then work it out using algebra to see if it is correct.

Example if B = 1.75 (i.e. 1.75:1)

$$1.75 = \frac{3Y - 2X}{2X + Y}$$

Multiply both sides by 2X + Y

$$1.75 \times (2X+Y) = \frac{3Y-2X}{2X+Y} \times 2X+Y$$

Cancel the 2X + Y off from top and bottom

$1.75 \times (2X + Y) = 3Y - 2X$
$3.5X + 1.75Y = 3Y - 2X$

Add 2X to both sides
$5.5X + 1.75Y = 3Y$

Take 1.75Y from both sides
$5.5X = 1.25Y$
$X = 22.7\%$ of Y

VERIFYING THE FORMULA USING ALGEBRA

I shall now verify the formula $\frac{3Y - 2X}{2X + Y}$

Ratios of surface areas = 1 : 1.75

Piece where Y−X is the width   Piece where X is the width

$4Y(Y-X) + 2Y^2$ $= 1.75 \times 4XY + 2Y^2$

Remove the brackets
$6Y^2 - 4XY$ $= 7XY + 3.5Y^2$

Add 4XY to both sides
$6Y^2$ $= 11XY + 3.5Y^2$

Take $3.5Y^2$ from both sides
$2.5Y^2$ $= 11XY$

Divide both sides by Y
$2.5Y$ $= 11XY$

Divide both sides by 2.5
Y $= 4.4X$

X as a percentage of Y = 22.7%

So the formula was right. But just as an extra verification I shall now draw on the previous graph plotting the point 1.75 along the X axis to see if it is 22.7% (refer to graph)

TASK MATHS

ANSWERS TO REVIEW EXERCISES C

EXERCISE 27 FRACTIONS AND DECIMALS

Relevant chapters

- 14 Table games
- 15 Colourings
- 16 Every picture tells a story
- 25 Getting the most out of life

National Curriculum statements

2/4c1; 2/5b1; 2/6a1; 2/6a2; 2/6a4; 2/8b2

Levels of difficulty of questions

Accessible to all students (no bars)	Somewhat harder (one bar)	More difficult (two bars)
1–16	17–20	

Answers

1. (a) $\frac{1}{2}$ (b) $\frac{3}{4}$ (c) $\frac{2}{3}$ (d) $\frac{3}{8}$
3. (a)(i) $\frac{1}{4}$ (ii) 25% (b)(i) $\frac{5}{8}$ (ii) 62.5%
4. (a) 45 (b) 25%
5. 160
6. £7500
7. (a) £40 000 (b) £10 000
8. 0.25, 0.36, 0.4, 0.52, 0.6
9. 4.9, 4.86
10. 0.4, $\frac{3}{5}$, $\frac{2}{3}$, 0.7, 0.73, $\frac{3}{4}$, 1.2
11. (a) $\frac{3}{5}$ (b) First week
12. (a) $2 \div 5$ or $4 \div 10$, etc. (b) $7 \div 2$ or $14 \div 4$, etc. (c) $19 \div 4$ or $38 \div 8$ (d) $21 \div 8$ or $42 \div 16$ (e) $47 \div 32$ (f) $47 \div 40$
13. (a) $\frac{5}{8}$ (b) $\frac{3}{8}$ (c) 6
14. (a)(i) $\frac{3}{8}$ (ii) $\frac{1}{8}, \frac{1}{4}, \frac{3}{8}, \frac{1}{2}$ (b) $\frac{1}{8}, \frac{3}{16}, \frac{1}{4}, \frac{5}{16}, \frac{3}{8}, \frac{7}{16}, \frac{1}{2}$
15. (a) $\frac{5}{8}$ (b) $\frac{1}{8}$
16. $1\frac{3}{16}$
17. $\frac{1}{4}$
18. $\frac{1}{2}$
19. (a) 2 (b) 2.4 (c) 4 (d) $R_1 = R_2 = 16$
20. (a)(i) $\frac{29}{41}, \frac{70}{99}, \frac{169}{239}$ (ii) 0.6666666667, 0.7142857142, 0.7058823529, 0.7073170732, 0.7070707071, 0.7071129707 (iii) Getting close to 0.707 (b)(i) $\frac{2}{3}, \frac{1}{5}, \frac{2}{3}, \frac{1}{5}, \frac{2}{3}, \frac{1}{5}$ (ii) Alternately $\frac{2}{3}$ and $\frac{1}{5}$

EXERCISE 28 PROBABILITY

Relevant chapters

- 14 Table games
- 15 Colourings
- 23 What do you believe?

National Curriculum statements

5/4d2; 5/4d3; 5/5d3; 5/6c; 5/6d; 5/7c; 5/8c1; 5/8c2; 5/9c; 5/10c

Levels of difficulty of questions

Accessible to all students (no bars)	Somewhat harder (one bar)	More difficult (two bars)
1–6	7–14	15–29

Answers

1. (a) $\frac{1}{2}$ (b) 50%
2. (a) $\frac{1}{2}$ (b) $\frac{1}{6}$
3. $\frac{11}{100}$
4. (a) $\frac{1}{5}$ (b) $\frac{1}{10}$ (c) $\frac{2}{5}$
5. (a) 1, 2, 3, 4, 6, 8, 12, 24 (b) $\frac{1}{2}$
6. (a)(i) $\frac{1}{3}$ (ii) $\frac{1}{2}$ (c) $\frac{1}{6}$
7. (a)(i) $\frac{13}{30}$ (ii) $\frac{8}{15}$ (b) $\frac{1}{2}$
8. (a) $\frac{7}{15}, \frac{7}{30}, \frac{7}{30}, \frac{1}{15}$ (b) $\frac{8}{15}$
9. (a) $\frac{3}{10}, \frac{3}{10}, \frac{3}{10}, \frac{1}{10}$ (b) $\frac{3}{10}$ (c) $\frac{3}{5}$
10. (a) $\frac{25}{102}$ (b) $\frac{1}{221}$
11. (a) $\frac{1}{9}$ (b) Daily weather is not independent.
12. (b) 92%
13. $\frac{3}{5}$
14. $\frac{1}{14}$
15. (a) Some people are counted more than once.
    (b) [Venn diagram: M, G, C with values 15, 35, 40, 45, 25, 10, 0, 30]
    (c) 35, 45 (d) $\frac{7}{22}$ (e)(i) 90 (ii) $\frac{1}{2}$ (f) Wrong
16. (a) 7 (b) $\frac{13}{28}$
17. (a) $\frac{3}{10}$ (b) $\frac{9}{100}$ (c) 6 days
18. (a)(i) $\frac{1}{12}$ (ii) $\frac{1}{2}$ (b) Both more likely to bus if it rains.
19. (a) $\frac{1}{6}$ (b) $\frac{1}{12}$ (c) $\frac{1}{9}$ (d) $\frac{1}{4}$
20. (a)(i) $\frac{2}{3}$ (ii) $\frac{1}{3}$ (iii) $\frac{2}{9}$ (b) $\frac{1}{9}$
21. (b)(i) $\frac{2}{9}$ (ii) 0 (iii) $\frac{16}{45}$ (iv) $\frac{29}{45}$

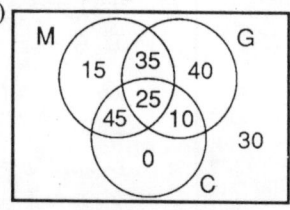

22 (a) $\frac{1}{5}$ (b) $\frac{1}{5}$ (c) $\frac{2}{5}$
23 (a) $\frac{1}{10}$ (b) $\frac{2}{5}$ (c) $\frac{3}{5}$
24 (a) 14.95 (b) $\frac{29}{95}$ (c) $\frac{66}{95}$
25 (a) $\frac{3}{20}$ (b) $\frac{3}{40}$ (c) $\frac{7}{20}$
26 (a)(i) 0.58 (ii) 0.42 (b) No idea how many cigarettes heavy smokers smoke. (c) 40.3 (d) 0.15
27 Ann or Bill $\frac{11}{36}$, draw $\frac{7}{18}$. Ann and Bill still equal, $\frac{13}{36}$, draw $\frac{5}{18}$. Paint all faces blue. Ann $\frac{1}{6}$, you $\frac{1}{2}$, draw $\frac{1}{3}$.
28 (a) $\frac{37}{72}$ (b) $\frac{13}{72}$
29 (a) 0.37 (b) 0.33 (c) 0.04

EXERCISE 29 NETWORKS AND FLOW CHARTS

Relevant chapters

14 Table games

National Curriculum statements

3/7b5; 4/5c1; 5/4b5; 5/6b2; 5/7a5; 5/10b

Levels of difficulty of questions

Accessible to all students (no bars)	Somewhat harder (one bar)	More difficult (two bars)
1–7	8–12	13–14

Answers

1 (a) (1,2), (2,3), (3,1), (3,4) (b) Night
2 £2.50
3 (a)(i) EVEN (ii) ODD (b) Any EVEN number (c) No
4 (a) 3 (b) 7 (c) 6, 16, 26, ... or −4, −14, ... (d) Greater than 0 and less than 10.
5 (a) 3 (b) 58 (c) 10 (d) 8
6 (a) Missing triangle has sides 6, 5, 5 (b) 8 (c) FBA, 8 cm (d) Straight line FA, 7.6 cm.
7 (a)(ii) Parallelogram (c) DCE, DCBAE, DAE, DABE, DABCE
8 (a)(i) Llangollen, Betws-y-Coed (ii) 39 miles (b) DLWShSLChCHBPD, 364 miles
11 (a) 6.05 p.m.
12 (a)(i) 3 (ii) 4 (iii) 4 (b) 30, 31, 32, 33, 34, 35 (c)(i) 50 (ii) 66
13 (a) $y = 1.5, x = 1, y = 1.75, x = 1.5, y = 1.625, x = 1.25$ (b)(i) 1.33 (ii) 1.67
14 (a) $\frac{\sqrt{3}}{2}$ (c) $(\frac{5}{4}, \frac{\sqrt{3}}{4})$

EXERCISE 30 COMBINATORICS

Relevant chapters

14 Table games
15 Colourings

National Curriculum statements

5/4d3; 5/6b2; 5/6c

Levels of difficulty of questions

Accessible to all students (no bars)	Somewhat harder (one bar)	More difficult (two bars)
1–13	14–18	19–20

Answers

1 12
2 (a) 20, 25, 29 (b) (2,6), (4,4), (3,5)
3 3, double 3; 5, double 2; treble 1, double 3
4 (a) 12 (b) 10
5 20p, 10p, 10p, 10p, 10p; 50p, 5p, 2p, 2p, 1p; 20p, 20p, 10p, 5p, 5p
6 (a)(i) 1 large and 1 small (ii) 1 large, 2 medium and 1 small (b) 84
7
W	D	L	P
7	0	1	21
4	2	2	14
3	1	4	10
2	1	5	7
1	2	5	5

8 20 (5 rows of 4)
9 (3,0), (3,1), (2,0)
10 (a)(i) £1.20 (ii) 2100 ml (b)(i) (12,0), (10,1), (8,2), (6,3), (4,4), (2,5), (0,6) (ii) 8 small and 2 large
11 Manchester United, Liverpool, Arsenal, Luton Town, Tottenham Hotspur, Nottingham Forest
12 (a) 24 (b) 14 mammals, 7 birds and 0 insects
13 (a)(i) 123, 231, 312, 132, 213, 321 (ii) 132 or 312 (b) Yes; there are 24 choices.
14 (a) 5 (b) 15 (c) 4 (d) 4
15 (a) C = 4, E = 16, M = 16, D = 12 (b) 36 (c) 28 (d) 60 (e) C = 4, E = 392, M = 9604, D = 200
16 63
17 (a) None (b) 237
18 294; three 70-seater coaches and two 42-seater coaches
19 216
20 (a) 7 (b) For N people required number of matches is $\frac{N(N-1)}{6}$. This is not an integer when N = 8

TASK MATHS

EXERCISE 31 PROPERTIES OF SHAPES

Relevant chapters

15 Colourings
16 Every picture tells a story
24 Telling the computer what to draw

National Curriculum statements

4/4a3; 4/4a4; 4/4c; 4/5b1; 4/6b2; 4/6b3; 4/8a; 4/9a2

Levels of difficulty of questions

Accessible to all students (no bars)	Somewhat harder (one bar)	More difficult (two bars)
1–16	17–23	24–26

Answers

1 (a) E   (b) Triangular prism   (c) F (Pyramid)
2 Isosceles, right-angled
3 (a) (−4,2)   (b) 24 cm^2 (c)(i) (4,−2)   (ii) Kite
4 (a) B   (b) A, B, E   (c) 540°   (d) 1.5 cm^2
5 (a)(i) 60°   (ii) 30°   (b) 75°
6 (a) A, C   (b) C   (c) Parallelogram
7 (a) 4   (b) Rhombus   (d) Parallelogram
   (e) None
8 (a) AEB or BEC   (b) ABC
9 40° and 100°; or 70° and 70°
10 (a)   (b)   (c)

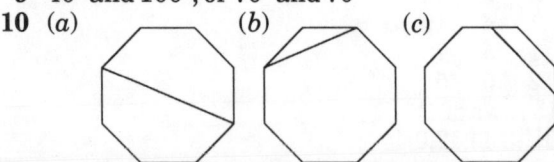

11 (a) 20 cm   (b) 15 cm   (c) 20 cm   (d) 3 cm
12 (a)   (b) Isosceles
   (c) Trapezium   (d) Two 60° and four 150° angles

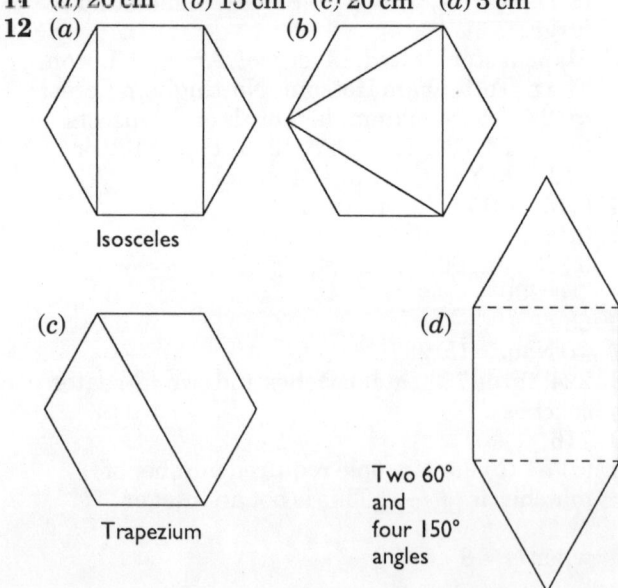

13 (a) C and E   (b) A and B
14 (a) A and D   (b) B and C
15 (a)(i) 180 − x   (ii) 180 − x   (b) EDA
16 (a) Any isosceles triangle
   (b) Any parallelogram   (c) 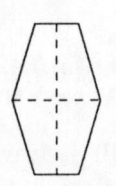
17 (a) Square or parallelogram   (b) Rhombus or arrowhead or parallelogram   (c) Kite or rectangle or parallelogram   (d) Trapezium
18 (a) A suitable kite   (b) x = 100, y = 50
19 (a) A, F   (b) B, D   (c) A, B, C, D, E, H   (d) A, C, D, E, F, H   (e) Kite or trapezium.
20 (a) 120°, 30°, 30°   (b) Reflection in AD
   (c) 
21 (a)(i) ACE, BFD   (ii) Lots of possibilities
   (b)(i) 120°   (ii) 30°   (iii) 60°
22 (a) 6   (b) Equilateral   (c) 12 cm^2
   (d)(i) Rectangle   (ii) Rhombus
   (e)(i) ACE or BFD   (ii) Lots of possibilities
23 (a)(ii) AC is diameter   (c)(ii) Rectangle
24 (a) DEF, GHI   (b)

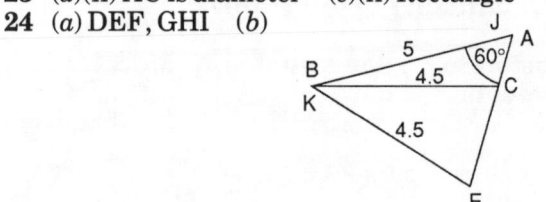

25 (a) Parallelogram   (b) 0, 1, 2, 4   (c) 2, 4
   (d) m = n = 2, rectangle; m = n = 4, square.
26 (a) Yes   (b) Yes   (c) No   (d) Yes

EXERCISE 32 ALGEBRAIC MANIPULATION

Relevant chapters

16 Every picture tells a story
18 Equable shapes
25 Getting the most out of life

National Curriculum statements

2/7b3; 3/5b2; 3/8a1; 3/8a2; 3/10b

Levels of difficulty of questions

Accessible to all students (no bars)	Somewhat harder (one bar)	More difficult (two bars)
1–4	5–9	10–21

REVIEW EXERCISES C

Answers

1. (a)(i) 1 (ii) 3 (iii) 6 (iv) 10
   (b) Triangular
   (c) $(15+16+17+18+19+20) \div 7 = 15$
   (d) 21, 28
2. (a)(i) 7600 (ii) 4900 (iii) 3600
3. (a) $6 \times (7+3)$ (b) $(4 \times 3)+(6 \times 3)$ (c) $12-(7-5)$
   (d) $(12+8) \times (12-8)$
4. (a) $5a+b$ (b) $p+10q$ (c) $3r-5s+15t$
   (d) $4a+3b$
5. (a) $3(x-2y)$ (b) $2a(2a+3b)$ (c) $3pq(2p-3)$
6. (a) -3 (b) -27 (c) 29 (d) 254
7. (a) $10q+p$ (b) $11p+11q$ (c) 9
8. (a) $9x^2-4$ (b) $9x^2-4$
9. (a) a^2-9 (b) p^2+6p+8 (c) $c^2+5cd+6d^2$
   (d) $x^2+xy-2y^2$ (e) $12a^2-10ab-12b^2$
   (f) $4x^3-9xy^2$
10. (a) $(x+1)(x+3)$ (b) $(x-4)(x-1)$ (c) $(2x+1)(x+2)$
11. (a)(i) $(x+5)(x+2)$ (ii) $(x-1)(x-10)$ (b) $-7, 11$
12. (a) $(x-5)(x+5)$ (b) $(2x-7y)(2x+7y)$
    (c) $3(2a-5b)(2a+5b)$ (d) $3pq(q-2p)(q+2p)$
13. (a) 91 800 (b) It is 102 multiplied by 900
    (c) Ten; one factor is 5×10^9, the other ends in 4.
14. (a) $x(x-1)(x+1)$ (b) One must be multiple of 2, and one a multiple of 3.
15. (a) $(n-1)(n+1)$ (b) n^2-1 has factor $n-1$.
16. (a) $\pi(R+r)(R-r)$ (b) 15 metres (c) $R=20, r=5$
17. (a) $2x^2$ (b) $7x+6$ (c) 4
18. (a) $\pi r(2h+r)$ (c) 3:2
19. (a) 12 (b) They are all 12 (c) $n+3, n+4, n+7$
    (d) $(n+3)(n+4)-n(n+7) = 12$
20. (a)(i) $u_2 = 1^2 + 2^2$ (ii) $u_3 = 1^2 + 2^2 + 3^2$
    (b) $u_2 = 5, u_3 = 14, u_4 = 30$
    (c) $S_1 = 6, S_2 = 30, S_3 = 84, S_4 = 180$
    (d) $\frac{1}{6}n(n+1)(2n+1)$
21. (ii) Difference is always 2
    (iii) $(n+1)(n+2)-n(n+3) = 2$
    (iv) Difference is always 8; $(2n+1)(2n+3)-(2n-1)(2n+5)$

EXERCISE 33 MONEY 2

Relevant chapters

17 Managing the future

National Curriculum statements

2/4a2; 2/4a8; 2/4b1; 2/4c2; 2/4d2

Levels of difficulty of questions

Accessible to all students (no bars)	Somewhat harder (one bar)	More difficult (two bars)
1–6		

Answers

1. (a)(i) £285 (ii) £312.95 (b) £33
2. £40
3. £6.60
4. £36.96
5. (a)(i) £85 (ii) 2.30 a.m. (b)(i) £8 (ii) £15
6. (a) £175 (b) 40% (c) 875 (d) £298 (e) 3375

EXERCISE 34 RATIO

Relevant chapters

16 Every picture tells a story
17 Managing the future
22 Knowing where you are

National Curriculum statements

2/6b2; 2/6a5

Levels of difficulty of questions

Accessible to all students (no bars)	Somewhat harder (one bar)	More difficult (two bars)
1–15	16	

Answers

1. £36
2. £75
3. 60
4. About 130
5. (a) Dark green (b) Mid-green
6. 200 g
7. 240 m^2
8. 200 ml
9. (a)(i) 51 (ii) 1 (b) 5:8
10. 4:1
11. 80
12. £125
13. 40
14. (a) 8, 2 (b) 21, 5 (c) 8, 2 (d) 34, 8
15. £3600, £6000, £8400
16. 195

EXERCISE 35 RATE AND PROPORTION

Relevant chapters

17 Managing the future

National Curriculum statements

2/5b2; 2/7c3; 3/7a4; 3/8a4; 3/9a1

87

Levels of difficulty of questions

Accessible to all students (no bars)	Somewhat harder (one bar)	More difficult (two bars)
1–19	20–25	26–30

Answers

1. 10 days
2. £83
3. (a) £216 (b)(i) 4 hours (ii) £33.60 (iii) £249.60
4. (a)(i) £144 (ii) £4.50 (iii) £7.20 (iv) £226.80 (b) £17.01
5. 66 miles per hour
6. (a) 24 miles per hour (b) 17.45
7. (a) 13.50 (b) 20 minutes (c) 20.50 (d) 15 miles
8. (a) 20 miles (b)(i) 0.5 miles per minute (ii) 30 miles per hour (c) 12 miles
9. 42 miles per gallon
10. (a) £323 (b) 216 miles (c) £3.46 (d)(i) 6 l (ii) £2.30
11. (a) 300 g, 180 g, 75 g, 2100 ml (b) 150 g
12. 15 minutes
13. (a) 4.5 cm (b) 0.3 mm
14. 7 hours
15. (a) £1.46, £1.49, £1.58 (b) Range of answers possible around £5.70
16. (a) 2 litre bottle
17. 500 g packet
18. 42 miles per gallon
19. (a)(i) £70 (ii) 15 days (iii) 26 days (b) £2 (c) 40, 50, 60 (e)(i) Heavy Hire
20. (a) 2 hours (b) 64 mins (c) 45 minutes per kilogram plus an extra 20 minutes.
21. (a) 163 cm (b) 14 (c)(i) 7 (ii) 5.25
22. (a) 2400 m^2 (b) 40 m^2 (c) 60 m^2 (d) 24 mins
23. (a) 36, 48, 60, 72, 84, 96 (b) 196, 147, 117.6, 98, 84, 73.5
24. D
25. B; $y = \frac{120}{x}$
26. (a) 2160 g/cm^2 (b) 10 cm
27. (a) B (b) D
28. (b) 6.32, 8.94 (d) Graph is a straight line through the origin.
29. (a) 2:3 (b) 12 cm
30. (a) $E = kx^2y$ (b) $a = 100b$ (d) $E = 0.016xy$

EXERCISE 36 INDICES AND EXPONENTIAL GROWTH

Relevant chapters

17 Managing the future

National Curriculum statements

2/5e; 2/6a3; 2/8a1; 2/8a2; 3/7a3; 3/7a4; 3/8a3; 3/9a2; 3/9b2

Levels of difficulty of questions

Accessible to all students (no bars)	Somewhat harder (one bar)	More difficult (two bars)
	1–5	6–19

Answers

1. (a) 0.18 (b) 32.77 (c) 12.33
2. 6.3×10^{-3} cm
3. (a) 5.86×10^5 (b) 5.5×10^{-5} m
4. (a) 1.515×10^5 (b) 6.2:1
5. (a)(i) 2.5 (ii) 0.4 (b) 0.34
6. (a) $\frac{1}{9}$ (b) 4
7. (a) x^8 (b) N^{-2} (c) $p^{\frac{1}{2}}$ (d) $h^{\frac{8}{3}}$
8. (a)(i) 32 (ii) 512 (b) 1.8
9. (a) 2 (b) 0.5 (c) 1.5 (d) -0.5 (e) 0
10. (a) 4^{-3} (b) 2, 4
11. 81
12. £275.40, £250.31, £224.71
13. (a) 158 g (b) 174 g
14. (a) £2800 (b) £1960 (c) £960 (d) £3347
15. (a) 3520, 3098, 2726, 2399 (b) 2001
16. (a) 9.75% (b) 6 days
17. (a) £228.98 (b) 6 years
18. 171 000
19. (a) $\sqrt{2}$ (b) 8 (c) 16 (d) 2048 (e) 2^{n+1}

EXERCISE 37 EQUATIONS 2

Relevant chapters

18 Equable shapes
19 Dissecting cubes

National Curriculum statements

3/5b2; 3/6b; 3/7b2

Levels of difficulty of questions

Accessible to all students (no bars)	Somewhat harder (one bar)	More difficult (two bars)
	1–9	10–12

Answers

1. (a) $x-2$ (b) 9 (c) 23 p
2. (a) 4 (b) 1.5 (c) -5 (d) -2.8 (e) -7

REVIEW EXERCISES C

(f) -1.5
3 (a) $100-x$ (b) $25(100+x)$ (c) 33.3
4 (b) $x = -1, y = -6$
5 (b) $x = 1.5, y = 2$
6 (a) $F + 10r$ (b) $11, 17, 23, 29, 35; 22.40, 24.80, 27.20, 29.60, 32$ (d)(i) About 830 (ii) For more than 830 copies
7 (a) $x + y = 12$ (b) $15x + 20y = 205$ (c) 7 Twirls and 5 Twizzles
8 (a)(i) $5x + 14y$ (ii) $5x + 14y = 53$ (b) $4x + 6y = 32$ (c) 5 cars, 2 minibuses
9 $x = 10, y = 8$
10 (c) $R = 3.68, r = 2.68$
11 (a) 37 (b) $a = 3, b = -3$ (c) $127, 217, 271, 721$
12 (a) $6, 10, 15; 15, 27, 42, 60$ (b) $h = 0.5n(n+1)$ (c) $a = 1.5, b = 4.5$

EXERCISE 38 POLYNOMIAL EQUATIONS

Relevant chapters

16 Every picture tells a story
18 Equable shapes
25 Getting the most out of life

National Curriculum statements

3/6b; 3/7b; 3/8a1; 3/10a; 3/10b

Levels of difficulty of questions

Accessible to all students (no bars)	Somewhat harder (one bar)	More difficult (two bars)
	1–10	11–20

Answers

1 (a) $0, -5$ (b) $0, 0.25$ (c) $0, 0.5, -0.5$
2 (a) $-4, 3$ (b) $7, -4$ (c) $-2, 11$ (d) $0.33, 3$
3 $95, -\frac{19}{3}$
4 -8
5 (a) $-1, 5$ (d) $x = 2$
6 (a) $2.73, -0.73$ (b) $6.41, 3.59$ (c) $4, -3$
7 (a) $x^2 + 2x = 15$ (b) $-5, 3$
8 (a) $5 - x$ (b) $(5-x)(10-2x)(12-2x)$ (d) 1 and 2
9 (b) 6.18 (c) 44.7 m
10 (b) $(h-8)(h-2)$ (c) 8
11 (a) $0, -2, -3$ (b) $0, -0.5, 3$
12 (a) 36 m (b)(ii) 30 km/h
13 (b) $3.72, 9.28$
14 (a) $1, 3, 6, 210$ (b) $0.5n(n+1) - 0.5n(n-1) = n$ (d) 27
15 (b) -4.81 (c) 12 and 13
16 (b) 1.92
17 (a) 2.4 (b) 2.32
18 (a) $y = x - 12$ (b) $(24, 12)$
19 (a) 0.5 (c) 0.55 (d)(i) $1.732051, 2.718879, 3.648736, 4.346541$
20 Can deduce (b); $x = 0, y = 1; x = 0, y = 0; x = 1, y = 1$

EXERCISE 39 REARRANGING FORMULAE

Relevant chapters

18 Equable shapes
25 Getting the most out of life

National Curriculum statements

3/5b2; 3/8a1; 3/8a2; 3/10b

Levels of difficulty of questions

Accessible to all students (no bars)	Somewhat harder (one bar)	More difficult (two bars)
	1–9	10–16

Answers

1 (a) 105 (b) -15 (c) -30 (d) $\frac{1}{3}(P - 60)$
2 (a) $A = 10 + 2N$ (b) $\frac{1}{2}(A - 10)$
3 (a) $t = \frac{v - u}{a}$ (b) $\sqrt{\frac{2s}{a}}$
4 (a) $R = \frac{V^2}{P}$ (b) $V = \sqrt{RP}$
5 (a) $12\,°C$ (b) 3550 m (c) $H = \frac{(24.5 - T)}{0.69}$
6 (a) $s = n(13 + t)$ (b) $n = \frac{s}{(13 + t)}$ (c) 17th May
7 (a) 689 days (b)(i) $3\,330\,625$ (c) $R^3 = 25T^2$
8 (a)(i) 16 (ii) 19 (iii) 46 (b) $r = 3s + 1$ (c) 23 (d) $s = \frac{1}{3}(r - 1)$ (e) 39 squares, 2 left over
9 (a) 300 (b) '94 box', 388 (c)(i) $n, n+1, n+5, n+6$ (ii) $t = 4n + 12$ (d) $n = \frac{1}{4}(t - 12)$ (e) 36
10 (a) $h = \frac{A}{2\pi r} - r$ (b) 3.8
11 (b) $b = \frac{2l}{l - 2}$ (b) $r = \sqrt{\frac{9l_1}{h - 6}}$
12 (a)(i) $v = \frac{uf}{u - F}$ (ii) 120 cm (b)(i) $R^2 = \frac{R_1 R}{R_1 - R}$ (ii) 120 ohms
13 (a) $\frac{2}{3}, \frac{5}{7}, \frac{12}{17}, \frac{29}{41}, \frac{70}{99}, \frac{169}{239}$ (b) $0.444444, 0.510204, 0.498269, 0.500297, 0.499948, 0.500008$ (c) $\frac{985}{1393}$ (d) $\frac{q - p}{2p - q}$
14 (a)(i) $t = \frac{x}{250}$ (ii) $y = \frac{x^2}{12500}$ (b) 20 cm
15 (a)(i) 7.428571 (ii) 7.42857 (iii) $7.416208, 7.41621$ (iv) $7.416198, 7.41620$ (b) $x = \sqrt{A}$ (c) $\sqrt{55}$
16 (a) BE (b)(i) $\frac{d}{x} = \frac{x}{h}$ (ii) $d = \frac{x^2}{h}$ (c) 11.25

89

TASK MATHS

EXERCISE 40 NETS AND POLYHEDRA

Relevant chapters

19 Dissecting cubes
22 Knowing where you are
25 Getting the most out of life

National Curriculum statements

4/4a1; 4/4a3; 4/4d2; 4/5d2; 4/6a; 4/7c; 4/7d;
4/8b; 4/9a1; 4/9a2

Levels of difficulty of questions

Accessible to all students (no bars)	Somewhat harder (one bar)	More difficult (two bars)
1–12	13–17	18–24

Answers

1 (a) Triangular prism   (b) 5   (c) 6
2 (a) A
4 (a) 10 cm³   (c) 33 cm²
5

6 (a)

7 (a) 50 000 cm³   (b)(i) 3   (ii) 18   (iii) 25 500 cm²
8 (a) 64   (b) 24
9 (a) Square-based pyramid   (c) About 53 cm²
   (d)(i) About 9 cm   (ii) About 34 cm²
10 (a) 12   (b) 8   (c) 16   (d) 36
11 (a) 6   (b) 8   (c) 10   (d) 40
12 (a) 7, 15, 10   (b) 8, 18, 12   (c) N+2, 3N, 2N
13 (a) 5 cm   (b) 108 cm²   (c) 48 cm³
14 (b) DEC and BEC, or ADE and ABE
16 (b) 48 cm²   (c) 1440 cm³
18 11.7 cm
19 (a) 8.7 cm   (b) 11.2 cm
20 (a) 12.5 cm   (b) 10.4 cm
21 (a) 13 cm
22 (a) 5.39 cm   (b) 14.77 cm
23 (a) 14.1 cm   (b) 12.0 cm   (c) 6.69 cm
    (d) 190 cm²
24 (i) 4 hexagonal, 4 triangular faces   (ii) 12
    (iii) 18; 23:27   (iv) 4 dodecagonal,
    12 triangular, 4 hexagonal faces   (v) 36
    (vi) 54

EXERCISE 41 PYTHAGORAS' THEOREM AND TRIGONOMETRY IN THREE DIMENSIONS

Relevant chapters

19 Dissecting cubes
20 Repeating patterns
22 Knowing where you are
25 Getting the most out of life

National Curriculum statements

4/7c; 4/8b; 4/9a1

Levels of difficulty of questions

Accessible to all students (no bars)	Somewhat harder (one bar)	More difficult (two bars)
		1–12

Answers

1 (a) 1   (b)(i) 25 cm³   (ii) 500 cm³   (c) 21.5 cm
2 (a)(i) 8.5 cm   (ii) 7.3 cm
3 (a) 1.4 cm   (b) 55°
4 (a) 18 m   (b) 90 m
5 1 in 6.1
6 (a)(ii) $\dfrac{h}{\tan 10}$ (iii) $\dfrac{h}{\tan 10 \cos 42}$ (b) 0.13
7 (b) 39°
8 (a)(i) 1.1 m   (ii) 40°   (b)(i) 17°   (ii) 1.6 m
9 (a) 31   (b) 43 m
10 (i) [diagram: 10 m × with 4 tan 30 = 2.3 m]
    (ii) [parallelogram diagram: 45°, 10 m, 4 m]

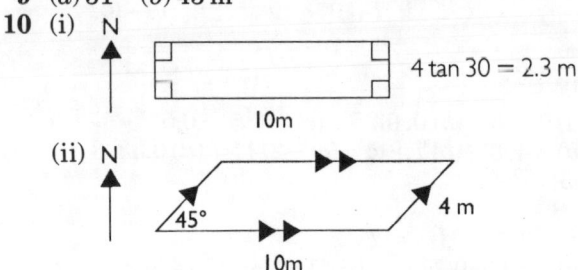

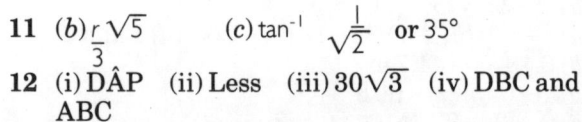

11 (b) $\dfrac{r}{3}\sqrt{5}$ (c) $\tan^{-1}\dfrac{1}{\sqrt{2}}$ or 35°
12 (i) DÂP   (ii) Less   (iii) $30\sqrt{3}$ (iv) DBC and ABC
    (v) AP = DP = $30\sqrt{3}$ (vi) 60°   (vii) 45 inches

TASK MATHS

Guide to Chapter 20: REPEATING PATTERNS

Outline

The task for this chapter is to analyse the repeating patterns that may occur in relation to time or to movement.

The introductory activity draws attention to aspects of human behaviour or our environment which have a repeating pattern.

In Section A this idea is explored further. Graphs are used to describe the repeating patterns. The second half of the section uses the movement of a big wheel to explore the sine function for angles of any size.

The first part of Section B is about toppling squares, rectangles and triangles along lines, and around squares and rectangles. Work involves angles of rotation and loci of various points of toppling shapes. Later questions are about finding the lengths of these loci, using Pythagoras' theorem and lengths of arcs of circles. The section closes with a consideration of a rolling circle and the cosine and tangent functions for angles of any size.

There are four Further Coursework Tasks. Two of them are about different aspects of toppling shapes and another is about toppling a cube. The other task is about sine waves and sound waves and provides the opportunity for students to explore graphs of the form $\sin kx$ and $k \sin x$.

Strategies

Students might find it useful to discuss the introductory task as a whole class or in groups. Students will probably work on the questions in Section A individually or in small groups.

The first thirteen questions of Section B could be used as a starting point for FCT 1. There is a lot of work in Section B. You might want to select different sets of questions for different students, depending on the level at which they are working and on the syllabus items to be covered.

Equipment and Resources

For Section B and FCTs 1 and 2:
  cardboard shapes or plastic shapes to topple (e.g. ATM MATs)

For the end of Sections A and B, and for FCT 4:
  graphical calculator or computer with graph-drawing program

For FCT 3:
  a cube or a die

Relevant Review Exercises

C41	Pythagoras' theorem and trigonometry in three dimensions	page 141
D42	Everyday graphs	page 244
D43	Graphs of functions	page 249
D44	Bearings and loci	page 253
D50	Trigonometry and triangles	page 272
D46	Properties of circles	page 261

REPEATING PATTERNS

National Curriculum Statements

Introduction to the task
2/4e1; 3/8c2

Section A
2/4e1; 3/7b3; 3/8c2; 4/8b; 4/9c1; 4/9c2; 4/9c3; 5/4b4

Section B
3/8c2; 4/4a4; 4/4c; 4/5b1; 4/5d3; 4/6b3; 4/7b; 4/7c; 4/7d; 4/8b; 4/9a4; 4/9c1; 4/9c2; 4/9c3; 4/10a1

Questions in Sections

Accessible to all students (no bars)	Somewhat harder (one bar)	More difficult (two bars)
Section A, 1–2	Section A, 3–5	Section A, 6–7
Section B, 1–6	Section B, 7–10	Section B, 11–17

Further Coursework Tasks

neutral: 1, 2, 3
easier:
more difficult: 4

INTRODUCTION TO THE TASK: HINTS

Perhaps start the work in small groups and then get students to feed their ideas into a general class discussion. It is important to clarify the notions of regular, nearly regular and irregular repeating patterns. It is not always easy to decide which category a happening belongs to.

Some results

Graph	Happening
1	C
2	L or O
3	E or K
4	M
5	A
6	I
7	K or O
8	N

The graph for happening B is:

The graph for happening D is:

The graph for happening H is:

The graphs for the other happenings will vary.

SECTION A: ANSWERS

1 (a) 84 (b) 84
2 1 is B, 2 is D, 3 is A, 4 is E, 5 is C
3 (a) Variable
   (b)
   (c)
   (e)
   (d)

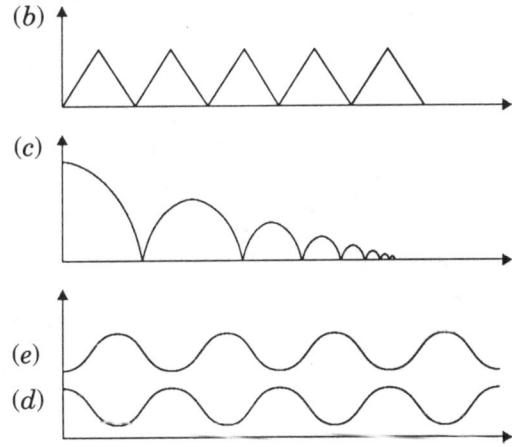

4 (a) Every day, every year (b) Day is right, because each day more or less repeats the last, though very different between June and December; year is right, because this is when the cycle repeats exactly (more or less).

5 (a) 4380 (4392 in a leap year) (b) It is daylight for half the year (c) Yes; long and short days balance out.

6 (a) 1 is height, 2 is angle. Because the angle changes uniformly, whereas height changes fastest when basket is half way up (b) At the bottom (c) Level with C on the right on the way up; level with C on the left on the way down; because this is where the height is changing fastest.

7 (a) (i) 5 m (ii) 8.7 m (iii) −8.7 m (minus sign means below the centre) (iv) 6.4 m (b) 180° (sin 180° = 0) (c) (i) 10 m (ii) After 90° (10 × sin 90° = 10) (iii) Greatest value is 1.

SECTION B: ANSWERS

1 (a) *[diagram]*

(b) 90° (c) If the dot is ignored the square looks the same after every topple; if the dot is not ignored the square looks the same after every four topples.

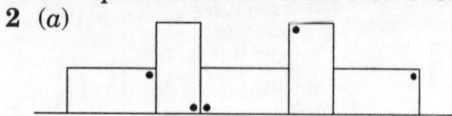

2 (a) *[diagram]*

(b) 90° (c) Every two topples if dot is ignored; otherwise every four topples.

3 (a) *[diagram]*

(b) 120° (c) Every topple if dot is ignored; otherwise every three topples.

4 (a) *[diagram]* (b) 90° or 180°

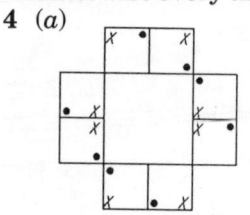

5 (a) *[diagram]* (b) 1320° (c) 24 (if you take account of the dot)

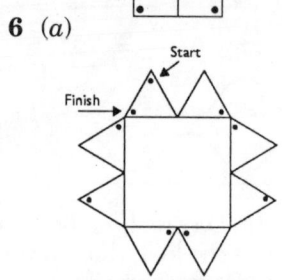

6 (a) *[diagram]* (b) 900° (c) 12 (if you take account of the dot)

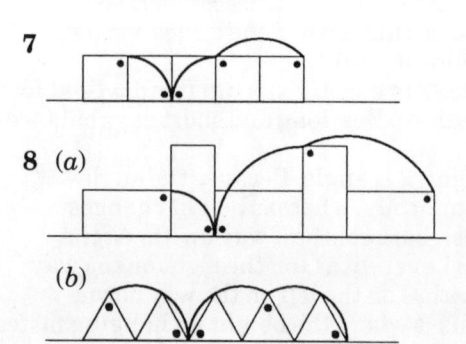

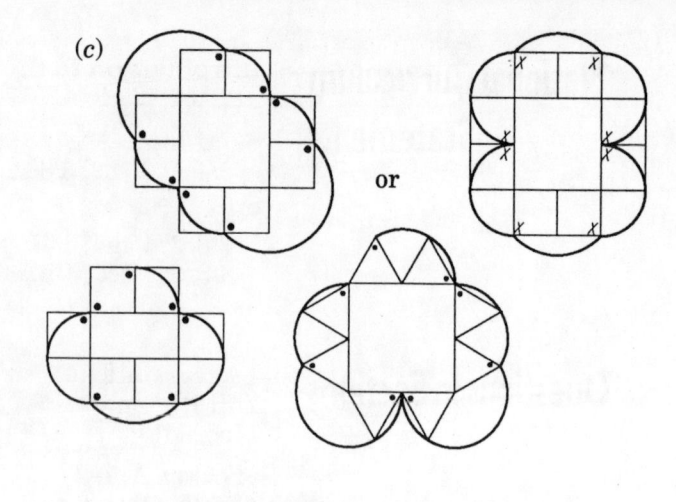

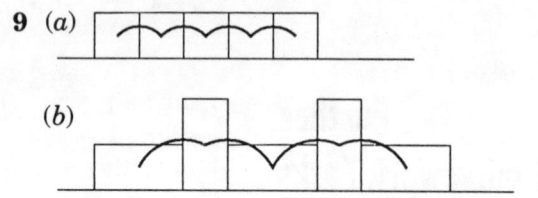

7 *[diagram]*

8 (a) *[diagram]*

(b) *[diagram]*

(c) *[diagrams]* or *[diagrams]*

9 (a) *[diagram]*

(b) *[diagram]*

10 (a) 8 cm (b) 8.9 cm (c) 10.7 cm (d) Yes, because the cycle repeats after four topples and the path includes each corner.

11 (a) 12 cm (b) 14.0 cm (c) 16.4 cm (d) Yes; there are two possible loci: one is the mirror image of the other.

12 30.3 cm for two corners and 34.0 cm for the other two corners.

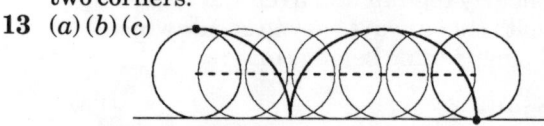

13 (a) (b) (c) *[diagram]*

(d) 12.6 cm (e) 16 cm

14 (a) Circle has turned round once, and so rolling pattern repeats (b) (i) Rolling to the *right* through 50° (ii) If P starts to the right of O it is the same distance to the right of O after rotating x clockwise as it is after rotating x anticlockwise (iii) P is the same distance above O after rotating x anticlockwise as it is below O after rotating x clockwise. (c) The graph of $y = \cos x$ is the graph of $y = \sin x$ translated 90° to the left.

15 (a) 0.34 (b) 0.71

16 (a) At the same point as P (where the tangent meets the circle) (b) A very long way up the tangent (c) A very long way down the tangent (d) Back at the starting point (e) 2.7 (f) 1 (g) Negative means below the level of O.

REPEATING PATTERNS

FURTHER COURSEWORK TASKS

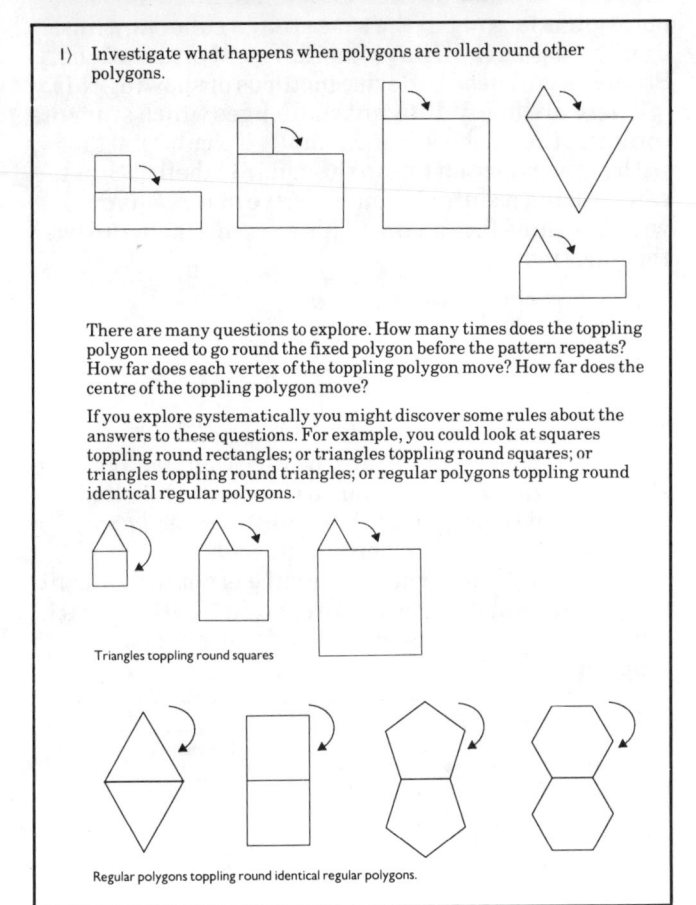

> 1) Investigate what happens when polygons are rolled round other polygons.
>
> There are many questions to explore. How many times does the toppling polygon need to go round the fixed polygon before the pattern repeats? How far does each vertex of the toppling polygon move? How far does the centre of the toppling polygon move?
>
> If you explore systematically you might discover some rules about the answers to these questions. For example, you could look at squares toppling round rectangles; or triangles toppling round squares; or triangles toppling round triangles; or regular polygons toppling round identical regular polygons.
>
> Triangles toppling round squares
>
> Regular polygons toppling round identical regular polygons.

The first thirteen questions of Section B are a good preparation for this task and for FCT 2.

This is a very rich task, which is suitable for students at any level: its difficulty depends on the chosen focus. Students will need to focus on one thing to look at in detail; otherwise they might produce a lot of pretty drawings but few patterns or generalisations.

The results which follow took a lot of research to discover. Students need to be rewarded for the work they put in to their own research.

Here are some possible lines of exploration.

After how many circuits does a shape, rolling round another shape, get back to its exact starting position?

A 1×1 square rolling round an $n \times n$ square always takes just one circuit. The total number of topples in one circuit is $4n$. 4 of these are through 180° and the rest are through 90°. So the total angle of topple is $360(n + 1)°$.

A 1×1 square rolling round an $m \times n$ rectangle does not necessarily get back to its starting point after one circuit. The total number of topples is $2(m + n)$. 4 of these are through 180° and the rest are through 90°. So the total angle of topple in one circuit is $180(m + n + 2)°$. The square will be back at its exact starting position if this is a multiple of 360, or in other words if $m + n$ is even. If $m + n$ is odd it takes the square two circuits to return to its exact starting point.

An equilateral triangle with side of length 1 toppling round an equilateral triangle with side of length n has $3n$ topples for each circuit. 3 of these topples are through 240°; the rest are through 120°. The total angle of topple is $360(n - 3)°$. So the triangle always returns to its exact starting point after one circuit.

An equilateral triangle toppling round an $n \times n$ square has $4n$ topples and the total angle of topple is $120(4n - 4) + 840 = 120(4n + 3)°$. The triangle will take one or three circuits depending on whether n is, or is not, a multiple of 3.

Regular polygons with n sides toppling round identical regular polygons topple n times. Each topple is through twice the exterior angle. So the total angle of topple is 720°.

What is the length of the locus of the top left-hand corner of a toppling shape starting in the position shown?

For a 1×1 square toppling round an $n \times n$ square the length of the locus is:

$(n + 1)\pi + \frac{1}{2}(n + 1)\pi\sqrt{2}$: if n is odd

$n\pi + \frac{1}{2}(n + 2)\pi\sqrt{2}$: if n is even but not a multiple of 4

$n\pi + \frac{1}{2}(n + 4)\pi\sqrt{2}$: if n is a multiple of 4

The length of the locus is sometimes different for a different corner.

The locus of an n-sided polygon consists of arcs of different radii. The number of different radii involved is $\frac{1}{2}n$ if n is even and $\frac{1}{2}(n - 1)$ if n is odd.

> 2) Explore what happens when different shapes are toppled along a line. 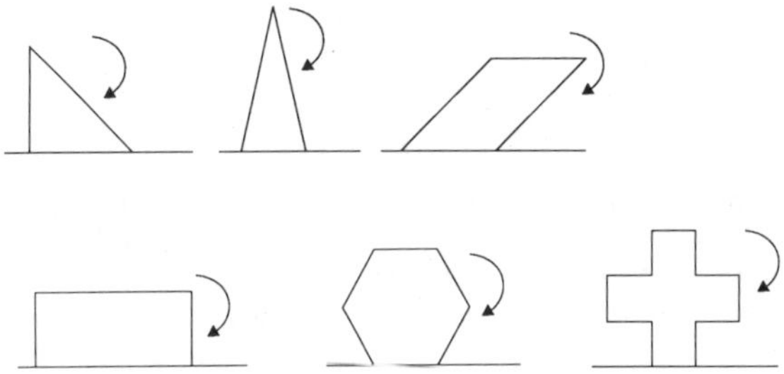
>
> How many topples are needed before the pattern repeats? What is the locus of the different corners of the shape? What is the locus of other points of the shape?
>
> Which point of the shape has the longest locus? Which has the shortest?

There are obvious links between this task and FCT 1 and the possible avenues of exploration are similar. Some students might want to incorporate elements of both tasks in their work.

The total angle of topple when a regular polygon rolls along a line until it has made one revolution is 360°. This is what one revolution means. A regular polygon with n sides has n topples, each through $\frac{360°}{n}$.

95

This is the exterior angle of the shape. The total angle of topple when a regular polygon rotates round an identical regular polygon (see FCT 1) is twice this, 720°. This is because each topple is through **twice** the exterior angle.

All this also applies to **convex** irregular polygons. Students might want to explore what happens for non-convex polygons, such as the cross shape.

Question 13 of Exercise A was about the cycloid: the locus of a point of a circle rolling along a line. Students were asked to estimate the length of this curve. There are more links here with FCT 1. The locus of a circle rolling round an identical circle is a cardioid.

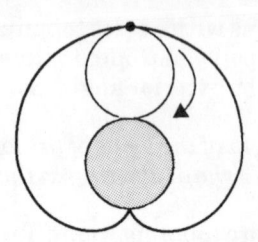

The locus of one vertex of an n-sided polygon rolling along a line approximates to a cycloid as n increases. The locus of one vertex of an n-sided polygon rolling round an identical polygon approximates to a cardioid as n increases. Some pretty drawings can be produced to illustrate this. The lengths of these loci can all be found using 'straightforward' trigonometry and a lot of ingenuity. Students working at a high level might find this an attractive and ambitious piece of work.

---

3) Imagine a tea chest in the shape of a cube repeatedly being toppled about one of its edges in a large room.

Suppose it moves from the position labelled *Start* to the position labelled *Finish* in figure 13.

Figure 13

Which way up will the cube be when it arrives at *Finish*? Will it depend on the 'route' it took?

You will need to invent a notation to describe this.

Are there repeating patterns involved in the movement of the cube?

You can, of course, look at different starting and finishing points to see what happens.

You might want to consider the locus of a corner of the cube as it topples from *Start* to *Finish*.

A die is useful for this task, because it provides a good way of keeping track of the orientation of the cube.

One way of representing two routes from start to finish is to show the numbers on the top face of the die.

		Finish	
1	5	6	2
3			
6			

Start

		Finish	
			5
			3
6	5	1	2

Start

This demonstrates that the orientation of the cube at the finish depends on the route taken. But this notation is lacking in the sense that a cube showing a 6 on the top can still have four different orientations. Students will need to devise methods of showing this.

There are many different challenges which students could set themselves. For example, if a cube starts with a given face on top on the square labelled **Start**, can it (using a suitable route) arrive at *any* square with the same face on top? This sequence helps answer the question.

3	5
6	6

Start Finish

A stronger condition can also be investigated. If a cube starts in a given orientation on the square labelled **Start**, can it (using a suitable route) arrive at *any* square with the same orientation?

The locus of one corner of the cube is not too difficult to find, but probably harder to explain clearly (at each topple it is the same as the locus of a corner of a toppling square).

---

4) Sounds are produced by sound waves. The shapes of waves for musical notes are simpler than shapes of waves for noises. The shape of the wave of a very 'pure' note is a sine graph.

$y = \sin x$

Notes of different pitches have waves of different lengths.

$y = \sin x$
$y = \sin 2x$

Notes of different loudness have waves of different height.

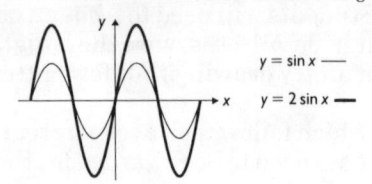

$y = \sin x$
$y = 2 \sin x$

Graphs of interesting shapes can be made by combining sine graphs,

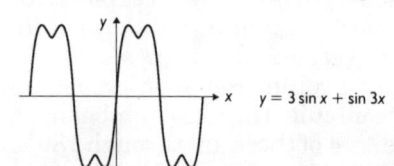

$y = 3 \sin x + \sin 3x$

or by combining sine graph with cosine graphs.

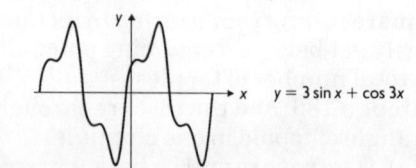

$y = 3 \sin x + \cos 3x$

Investigate graphs of this kind. You will probably want to use either a graphical calculator or a graph-drawing program on a computer.

This task can provide students with greater insight into the behaviour of trigonometric functions. Students might find it helpful to use a graph plotter which allows them to type in such things as $y = a\sin(bx) + c\sin(dx)$ and then to specify, and vary, a, b, c and d. The graph plotters *FGP* and *Mouse plotter* both allow this.

Students can investigate the effect of varying k in $y = k\sin x$, and also of varying k in $y = \sin(kx)$.

They can move on to more ambitious projects such as studying graphs of the form $y = 3\sin x + k\sin 3x$, or $y = 3\sin kx + \sin 3x$. A fundamental question which can be asked of all these graphs is 'what is the period?'

Students can also investigate graphs of the form $y = a\sin(bx) + c\cos(dx)$. When $b = d$ these simplify dramatically. How do the values chosen for a and c determine the amplitude of the graph, and also the amount by which it is translated?

ASSESSING STUDENTS' COURSEWORK TASKS

Further Coursework Task 1

There are many things which students can explore in this task and they can focus on an idea which sets them a suitable challenge. In the following extract the student is exploring unit squares toppling round rectangles and seeing how many topples are needed to bring the square back to its original position. She starts by considering $1 \times n$ rectangles. The extract shows that she can make and test generalisations (Ma1/5c).

I am now going to look back and investigate the squares that have to go around the rectangle more than once to reach the starting position.

I have so far done a 1 × 2 rectangle and a 1 × 3 rectangle so I am now going to do a 1 × 4

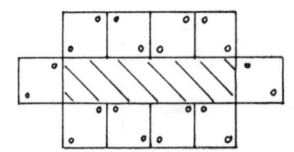

1 × 4 rectangle
1 × 1 square

This goes around twice before returning to its origin position. This means that 20 squares go around the rectangle (2 × 10) to reach the beginning.

I have already used a 1 × 5 fixed rectangle, & I found out that the square only has to go around once, before reaching the starting position.

So now I will do a 1 × 6 fixed rectangle

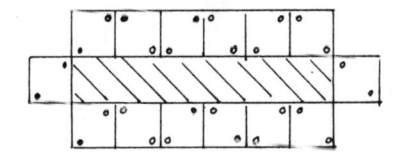

This also goes around twice before returning to the starting position
28 squares go around the rectangle (2 × 14)

TASK MATHS

> If I was to do the 1 × 7 rectangle it would go around once returning to its starting position because the number of squares that could go around it would be 16 and this is a multiple of 4
>
> | Fixed rectangle (cm) | No of topples until it returns |
> |---|---|
> | 1 × 2 | 12 |
> | 1 × 3 | 8 |
> | 1 × 4 | 20 |
> | 1 × 5 | 12 |
> | 1 × 6 | 28 |
> | 1 × 7 | 16 |
> | 1 × n | ?? |

In the following extract a student is finding the length of the locus of one corner as it topples round rectangles whose sides differ by one unit. Two circuits of the rectangle are needed to get the square back to its original position, which complicates the calculation of the length because some portions of the locus coincide. Later in his work he considers rectangles of other shapes and attempts further generalisations. The way he has tackled the problem shows that he can co-ordinate a number of variables when solving problems (Ma1/9a).

> I will find out how far the vertex moves when a square topples round a rectangle. I will start with a 1cm × 1cm toppling square and a 1cm × 2cm fixed rectangle. 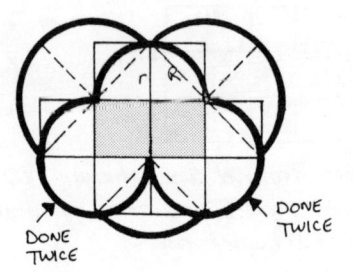
>
> $10 \times \frac{1}{4} \times 2\pi r = 5\pi r$
>
> $5 \times \frac{1}{4} \times 2\pi R = 2\frac{1}{2} \pi R$
>
> $L = 5\pi r + 2\frac{1}{2} \pi R$
>
> DONE TWICE   DONE TWICE
>
> I will draw a 2cm × 3cm fixed rectangle 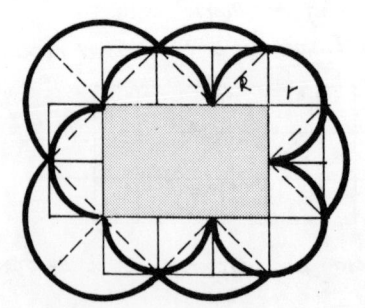
>
> $14 \times \frac{1}{4} \times 2\pi r = 7\pi r$
>
> $7 \times \frac{1}{4} \times 2\pi R = 3\frac{1}{2} \pi R$
>
> $L = 7\pi r + 3\frac{1}{2} \pi R$

REPEATING PATTERNS

I have found a pattern that r is twice the number as R.
I will draw a 3cm × 4cm fixed rectangle.

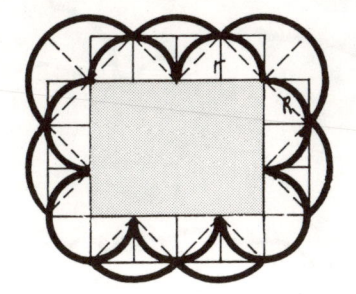

$18 \times \frac{1}{4} \times 2\pi r = 9\pi r$

$9 \times \frac{1}{4} \times 2\pi R = 4\frac{1}{2}\pi R$

$L = 9\pi r + 4\frac{1}{2}\pi R$

I predict that a 4cm × 5cm fixed rectangle will be

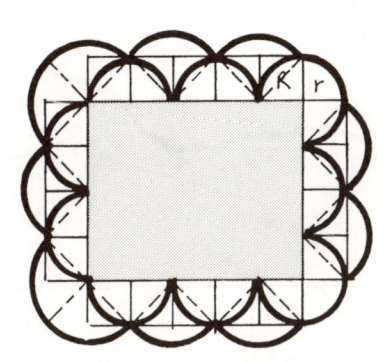

$(4+5+2)\pi r + (4+1.5)\pi R$

$= 11\pi r + 5\frac{1}{2}\pi R$

$22 \times \frac{1}{4} \times 2\pi r = 11\pi r$

$11 \times \frac{1}{4} \times 2\pi R = 5\frac{1}{2}\pi R$

$L = 11\pi r + 5\frac{1}{2}\pi R$

I am correct.

Further Coursework Task 2

Students might need encouragement to focus their work and not get carried away exploring patterns with no clear aim in mind. In the following extract the student has drawn accurately the locus of different points on a hexagon rolling over a 'bridge'. However, because she deals with so many complications (different points, difficult shape, not a flat surface) she can do no more than draw the pictures and make comments about 'humpy' patterns. So, although it is not trivial to produce the drawings, she is only demonstrating achievement of Ma1/4b.

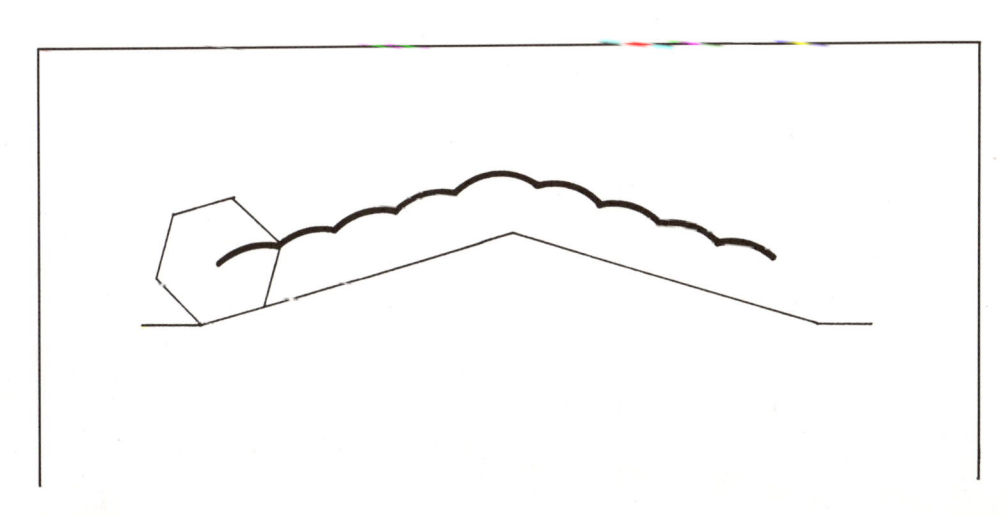

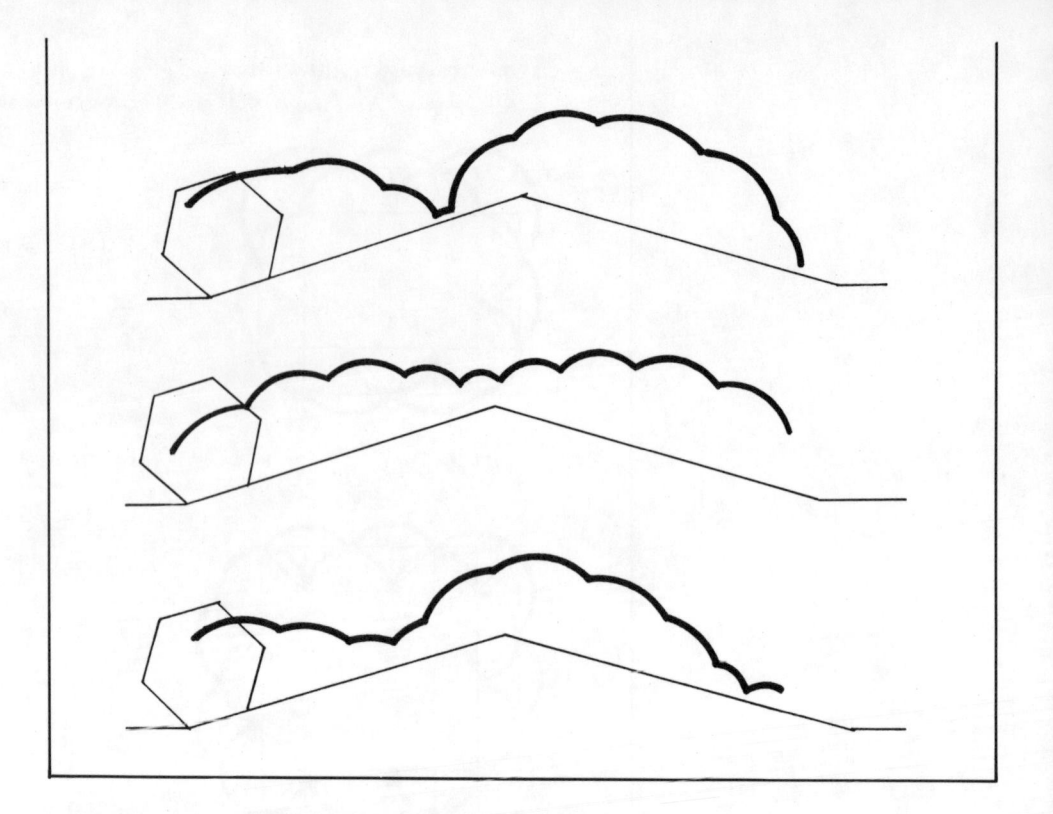

The following extract is from a piece of work in which a student is finding the length of the locus of a corner when you topple a triangle, square, pentagon and hexagon along a line. Having done all these calculations she is then able to deduce some general statements, providing strong evidence for level 9.

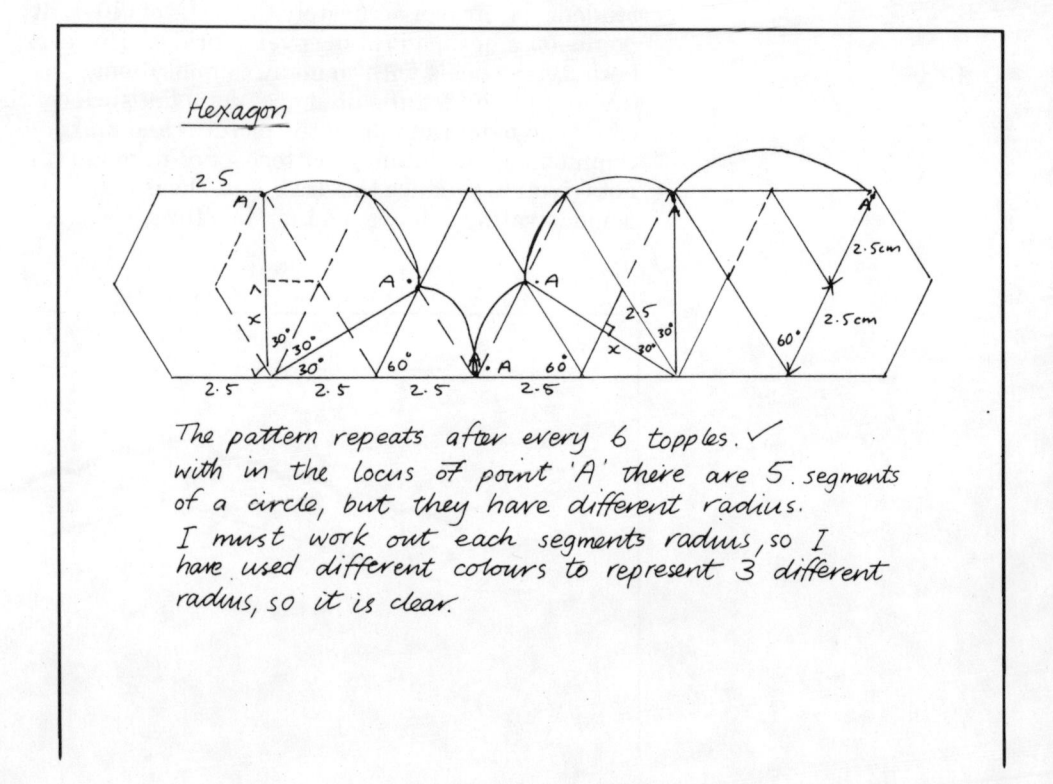

Hexagon

The pattern repeats after every 6 topples. ✓
with in the locus of point 'A' there are 5 segments of a circle, but they have different radius.
I must work out each segments radius, so I have used different colours to represent 3 different radius, so it is clear.

REPEATING PATTERNS

RADIUS OF BLUE SEGMENT:—
I am going to have to use trigonometry to work out the radius.

$$2.5 \times \left(\cos 30° = \frac{a}{h} \right) = \frac{x}{2.5} \times 2.5$$

$$2.5 \times \cos 30° = x$$
$$x = 2.16$$

I must then multiply by two because the radius goes from dot to dot. The adjacent side of the angle 30° is only half the radius
$$x = 2.16$$
$$r = 2.16 \times 2 = 4.32$$
$$4.32 = radius$$

I am now ready to find out what the circumference is on that 1/6 of the circle
$$c = 2 \pi r \cdot \tfrac{1}{6}$$
$$c = 2 \times \pi \times 4.32 \times \tfrac{1}{6} = 4.53 \text{ cm}$$

I must also multiply by 2 again because there are 2 1/6 of a circle in the locus.
$$4.53 \times 2 = 9.06 \text{ cm}$$
locus length of blue segments = 9.06 cm.

RADIUS OF BLACK SEGMENTS:—
Radius 2.5 cm
$$c = 2\pi r \times \tfrac{1}{6}$$
$$c = 2 \times \pi \times 2.5 \times \tfrac{1}{16} = 2.6 \text{ cm}$$

I must again multiply by 2 because there are 2 segments of that size.

Conclusions
* The number of topples equals the number of sides.
* The angles through which the points turned in the locus are the shapes exterior angles.
* The number of sides is the ~~num~~ fraction of a circle which is a point turned through minus 1
  e.g. Pentagon = 5 sides = 4

TASK MATHS

Guide to Chapter 21: HOW DO YOU DECIDE?

Outline

The task for this chapter is to find out how to conduct a statistical survey and communicate your results so that sensible decisions can be made.

In the introductory activity dates of birth for the whole class are collected with a view to answering the question: are the same number of babies born in the Winter as in the Summer?

Section A is about different ways of displaying data. The work involves the use of percentages and the construction and interpretation of pictograms, barcharts, frequency distributions, pie charts, frequency polygons, strip charts, and histograms with unequal class intervals. The section ends with an introduction to the normal distribution.

Section B is about designing a sensible questionnaire and choosing an appropriate sample. There are calculations using percentages, mean, median and mode.

The Further Coursework Task is to conduct a statistical survey and write a report. Nine different topics are suggested, or students can choose their own topic.

Strategies

The introductory activity requires classroom discussion. It raises issues about displaying information which are taken up in Section A. Students will probably work on Section A individually or in small groups, and will do as much of it as they can. Section B is about questionnaires and provides good material for class discussion. One way of organising this is for small groups to prepare their ideas and report them back to the whole class.

Work on the introductory activity, Section A and Section B is designed to improve the quality of the survey work undertaken in connection with the FCT.

Equipment and Resources

For FCT:
  computer database or statistical display package (preferably *Pinpoint*)

Relevant Review Exercises

D42 *Everyday graphs* page 244
D45 *Statistics 2*   page 257

National Curriculum Statements

Introduction to the task
  5/4b2; 5/4b4; 5/5b2; 5/9a2

Section A
  2/4a1; 2/4d2; 2/5c2; 2/6a2; 2/6a4; 2/6a5; 4/5a; 5/5b2; 5/5c1; 5/5c3; 5/7a4; 5/9a1; 5/10a1; 5/10a2

Section B
  2/4d2; 5/4b1; 5/4b2; 5/4b3; 5/4c; 5/5b1; 5/6a1; 5/6a2; 5/7a1; 5/7a3; 5/8a; 5/9b

Further coursework tasks
  5/4a; 5/5a; 5/8a; 5/9a

HOW DO YOU DECIDE?

Questions in Sections	Accessible to all students (no bars)	Somewhat harder (one bar)	More difficult (two bars)
	Section A, 1–12 Section B, 1–9	Section A, 13–15 Section B, 10	Section A, 16–19

| Further Coursework Tasks | neutral: 1
easier:
more difficult: | | |

INTRODUCTION TO THE TASK: HINTS

This activity is probably best as a class discussion for one lesson.

The teacher can focus on the following issues:
- the advantage of grouping data, and the different criteria which can be used for this;
- the advantages and disadvantages of different types of display;
- the place of calculations, only when they help to answer the question posed;
- the reliability of the data (the extent to which the people 'sampled' were representative).

SECTION A: ANSWERS

1. (a) 10 (b) Records, 35 (c) Dancing (d) The proportional answer is 45, but unlikely to get exactly this.
2. (a) So you can compare the quantities easily.
3. (a) 11 000 (b) No gas available (c) 6000
5. (a) Frequencies: 1, 3, 4, 10, 7, 8, 3, 1, 3 (b) Below
6. (a) (i) 1 p.m. to 3 p.m. (ii) 130 (b) (i) Monday (ii) Saturday (iii) Friday (iv) Mornings (c) **B** and **D** are sensible suggestions, **A** and **E** are debatable, **C** and **F** are less sensible (d) (i) Low use on Mondays and Friday mornings; high use on Saturdays (ii) Librarians
7. (a) Walking (b) $\frac{1}{4}$ (c) 8
8. Angles: tennis 72°, football 96°, snooker 120°, badminton 36°, basketball 36°
9. Angles: men 205°, women 155°
10. (a) About 13% (b) About 69%
12. (a) About 18 million (b) About 17% (c) By starting at 5 on the vertical scale (d) About 37%
13. (a) England (b) About 35% (c) About 20 000 km^2
14. (a) Different numbers of males and females (b) About 80% (c) About 14% (d) 28 million
15. (a) 2.5 million (b) 2.1 million (c) 48% (d) Mail (51%) (e) Men
16. (a) Frequencies: 3, 12, 15, 6, 1, 0, 0, 2, 0, 1 (b) Frequency densities: 1, 4, 5, 2, 0.11, 0.33
17. Frequency densities: 0.74, 0.71, 0.90, 0.77, 0.61, 0.60, 0.50, 0.30, last one depends on length of interval chosen.
18. (a) 16% (b) 1000 (2%)
19. (a) 600 (2%) (b) About 183 cm (mean + 1 s.d.)

SECTION B: ANSWERS

8. (b) 33% (c) 30%
9. (b) (i) Probably the median, because not influenced by extreme values (ii) Girls: median 5.5, mean 5.8; boys: median 3, mean 6
10. (a) 4 for both (b) 3.8 for both (c) (interquartile) range or standard deviation.

FURTHER COURSEWORK TASKS

1) When exploring one of the suggestions given below you might find it helpful to follow the advice given in Section B.

- First choose an appropriate set of starting questions to investigate. Word the questions so that you are clear about how you can collect data to help you answer them, and so that they help you to produce an interesting and worthwhile piece of work.
- If you need to collect a sample of information choose your sample carefully.
- If you use a questionnaire take care over the way you word questions. Decide what kind of answers you want.
- Display the information you collect clearly, and in a way which helps you, and other people, to draw conclusions from it. Do not mislead anyone. (You might want to include scattergrams, cumulative frequency graphs and other ideas from Chapter 7 in Book 4.)
- Calculate percentages, means, medians, modes, ranges, interquartile ranges, or standard deviations if these help you to draw conclusions from the results you collect.
- Look at newspapers, magazines, or books which provide similar information, so that you can compare what you find with what other people have found. You might find useful information on Teletext or Viewdata.
- Use a database or a statistical package on a computer if you think this will help you to organise your information, calculate results or display what you discover more clearly or more attractively.
- Draw conclusions which are justified by the results you have produced. Ensure that the conclusions you draw really are justified by your results.

It might be worth encouraging students to carry out the investigative work in small groups, and then to do their own individual write-ups. It is strongly recommended that some or all of Sections A and particularly B are tackled before embarking on this task. Section B will help students to collect reliable and usable data.

It is important that students choose a topic which they are interested in. They need a surprising amount of time to decide what they want to survey, but are good at coming up with their own ideas, given space and encouragement. You need to check the questionnaire before students have gone too far with the process. Encourage students to ask questions which provide numerical data to analyse. You also need to check students' methods of *sampling*. If students are working in small groups they should be able to handle 100 questionnaires or interviews, and a sample of this sort of size makes the results of the research more meaningful. Processing the results obtained from a large number of people is not a trivial task and is a good opportunity for students to practise the skills of working as a team.

Students can display their results by means of posters, which they can also use to illustrate the individual write-ups. They could also be asked to make group presentations to the rest of the class.

Use of a computer might be helpful in connection with this task. This is particularly true if students have access to an Archimedes or a Nimbus, because the program *Pinpoint* does just what is required. It helps students to design and print a questionnaire, to record and process the results and to display these results in appropriate ways.

The subjects of Chapters 17 and 23 also offer opportunities for surveys.

ASSESSING STUDENTS' COURSEWORK TASKS

Most students enjoy choosing their own topic to survey. The advantage of this is that they are interested in what they are doing and so are motivated. Teachers might want to ensure that the topics chosen lend themselves to mathematical analysis.

The students' work quoted here is all at levels 4, 5 and 6. For examples of survey work at a higher level see the corresponding section in the Guide to Chapter 23 (on page 125).

In the first extract a student is researching 'skiving'. This is an interesting topic, but the work would have been better if the student had clarified what she meant by skiving. It is not clear how she selected her sample, which is probably biased. However, her work shows that she can identify and obtain information (Ma1/4a) and use appropriate diagrams (Ma1/4b).

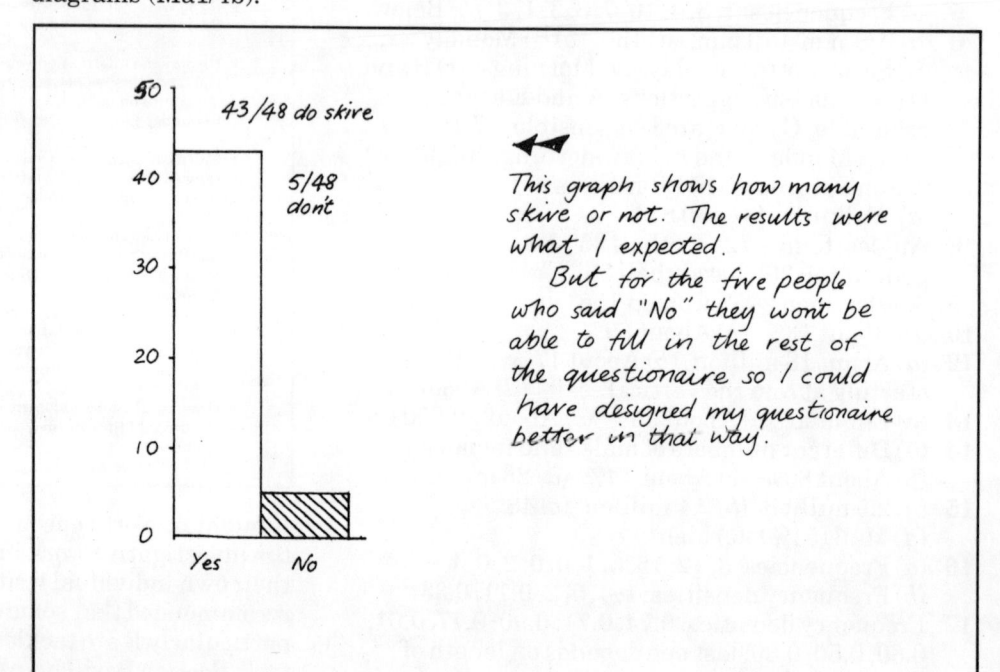

This graph shows how many skive or not. The results were what I expected.

But for the five people who said "No" they won't be able to fill in the rest of the questionnaire so I could have designed my questionaire better in that way.

HOW DO YOU DECIDE?

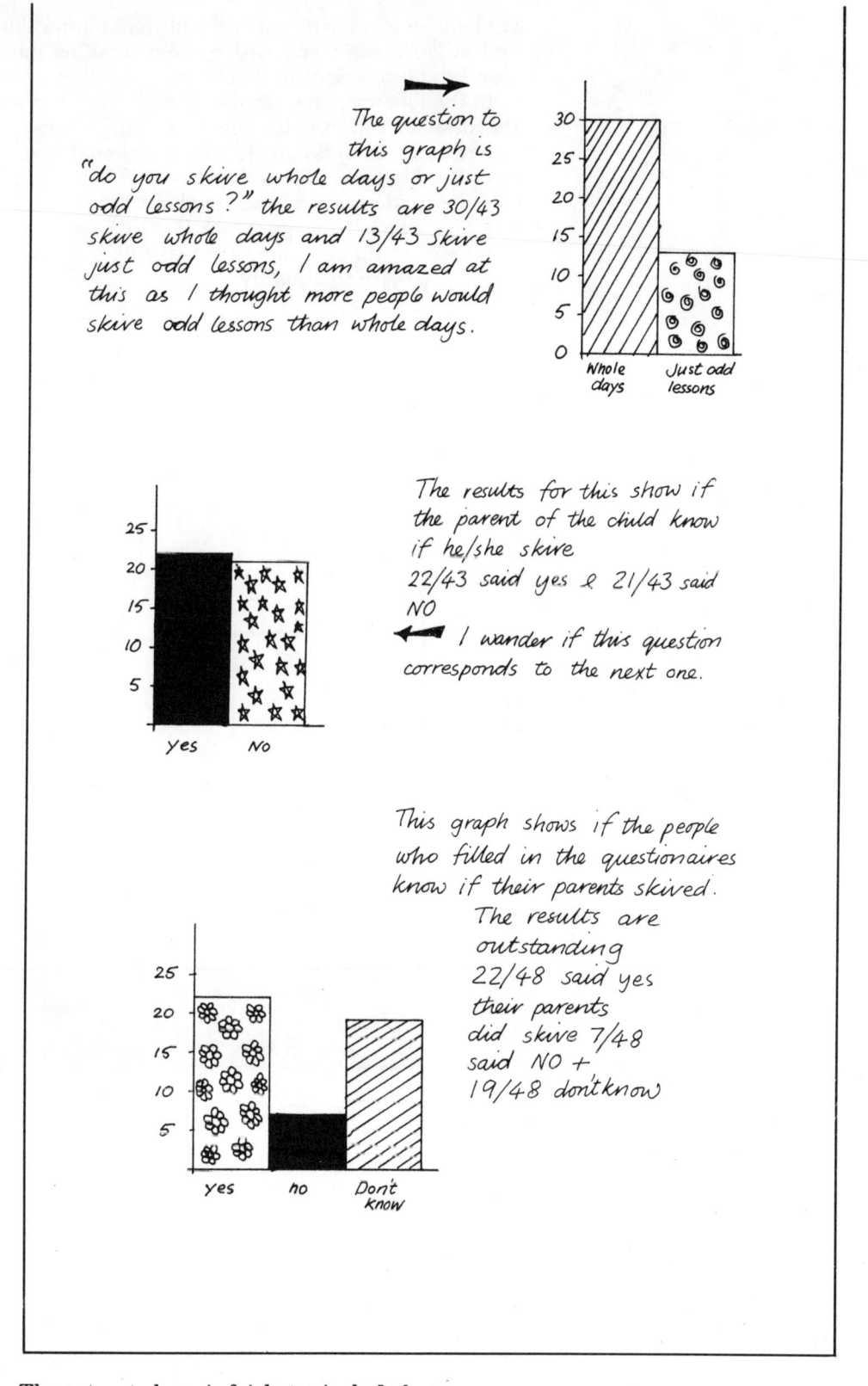

> The question to this graph is "do you skive whole days or just odd lessons?" the results are 30/43 skive whole days and 13/43 skive just odd lessons, I am amazed at this as I thought more people would skive odd lessons than whole days.

> The results for this show if the parent of the child know if he/she skive
> 22/43 said yes & 21/43 said NO
>
> ← I wander if this question corresponds to the next one.

> This graph shows if the people who filled in the questionaires know if their parents skived. The results are outstanding 22/48 said yes their parents did skive 7/48 said NO + 19/48 don't know

The extract above is fairly typical of what many students produce in response to this task. The questions are simple with a limited number of responses, the results of which are presented by means of barcharts. There is not much commentary and no statistical analysis. For work at a higher level students need to demonstrate additional knowledge and skills, or comment, with more insight, on the scope and limitations of their survey.

In the following extract the student has grouped the data she collected to show how many hours in a week people listen to music. She has then drawn a compound barchart for both males and females. She has also made some comments about her reactions to the data. She can design a task (Ma1/6a) and her comments could be evidence for Ma1/6b if it was developed more thoroughly.

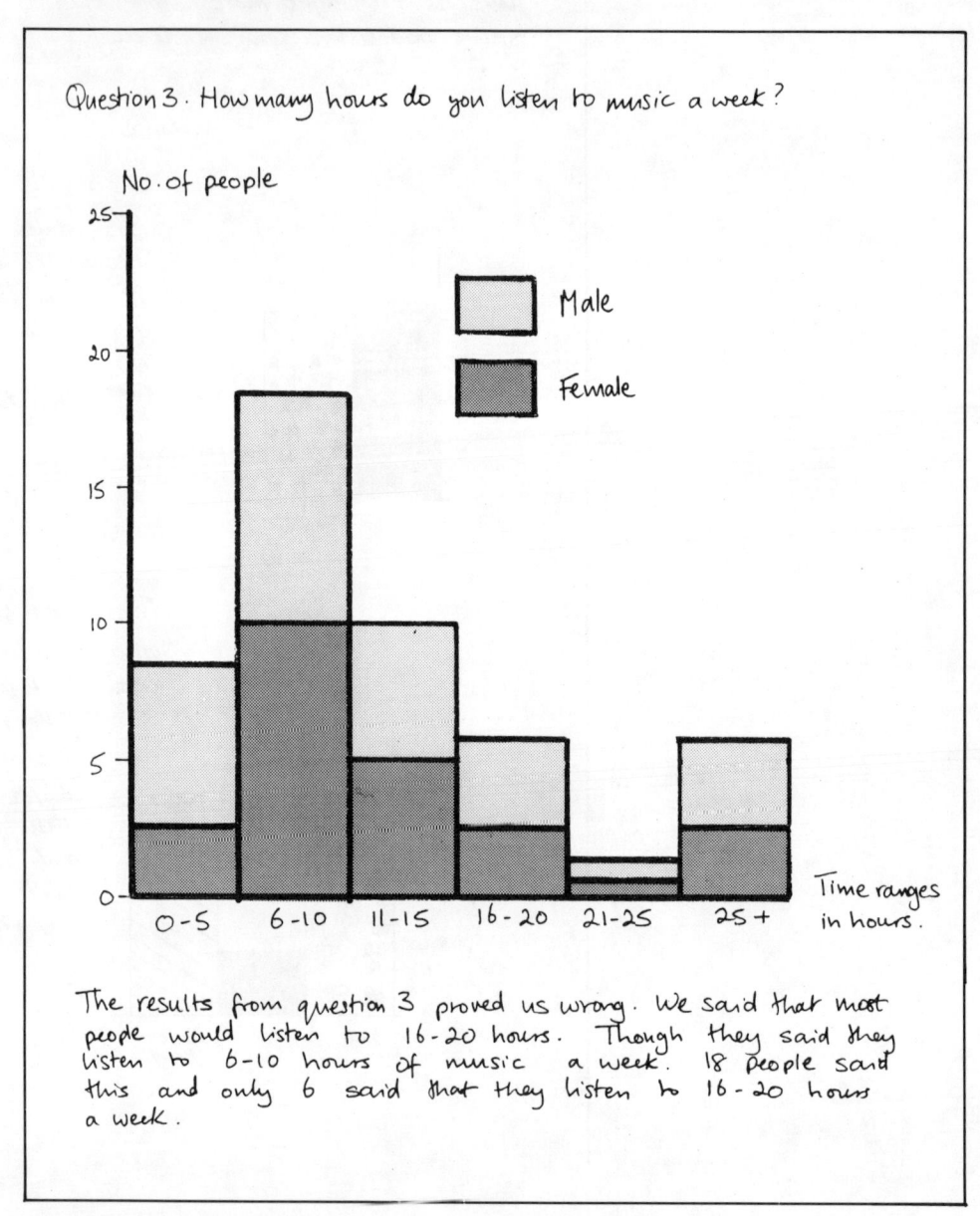

> Question 3. How many hours do you listen to music a week?
>
> [Compound bar chart showing No. of people (y-axis, 0-25) against Time ranges in hours (x-axis: 0-5, 6-10, 11-15, 16-20, 21-25, 25+) for Male and Female]
>
> The results from question 3 proved us wrong. We said that most people would listen to 16-20 hours. Though they said they listen to 6-10 hours of music a week. 18 people said this and only 6 said that they listen to 16-20 hours a week.

The final extract demonstrates Ma1/5b as the student used a variety of statistical graphs in his report.

WHEN DID YOU FIRST TRY SMOKING?

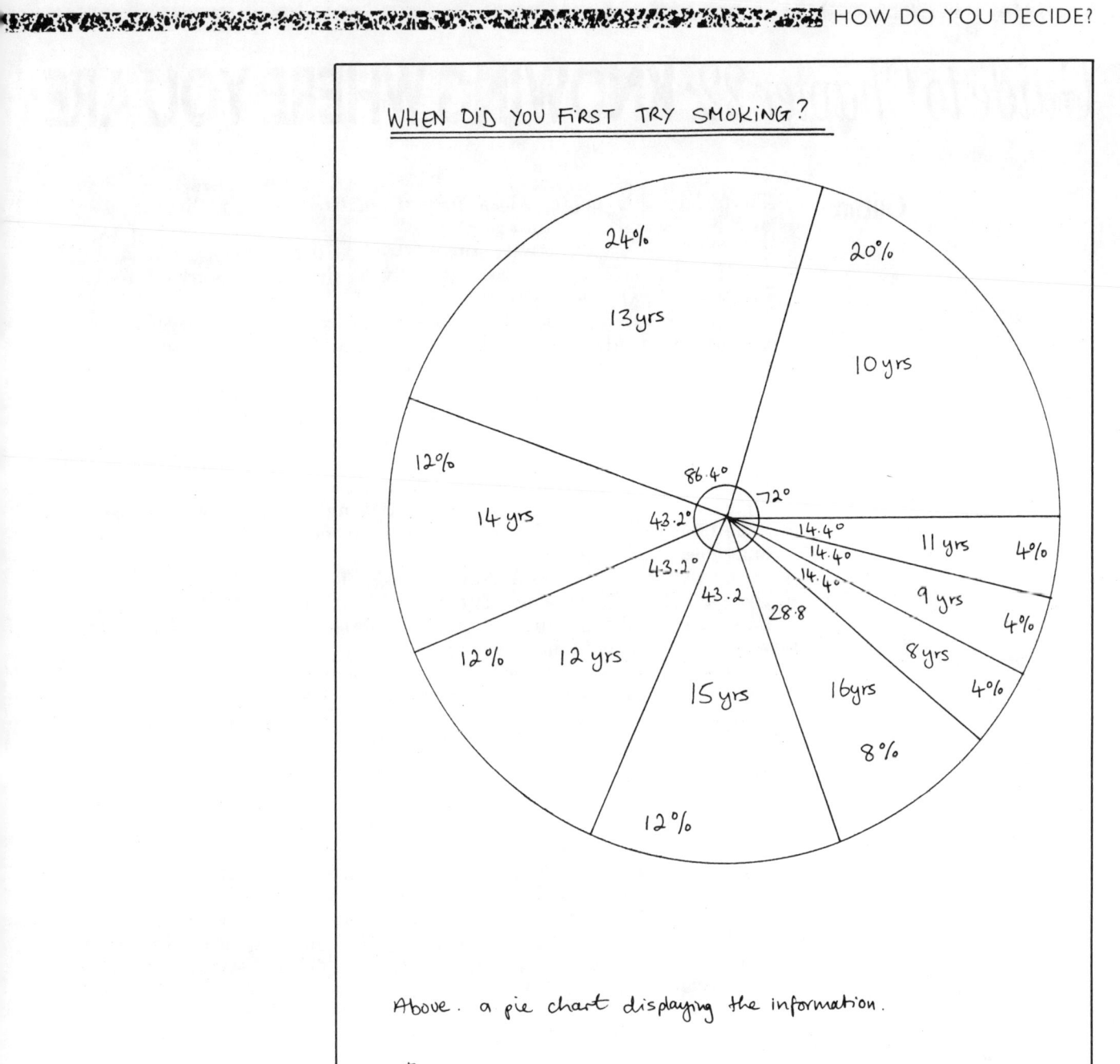

- 24% 13 yrs
- 20% 10 yrs
- 12% 14 yrs
- 4% 11 yrs
- 4% 9 yrs
- 4% 8 yrs
- 8% 16 yrs
- 12% 15 yrs
- 12% 12 yrs

Angles: 86.4°, 72°, 43.2°, 14.4°, 14.4°, 14.4°, 28.8, 43.2, 43.2°

Above: a pie chart displaying the information.

The mean is 10.8 yrs

The mode is 13 yrs

The median is 13 yrs

The range is 8 yrs

The interquartile range is 4

TASK MATHS

Guide to Chapter 22: **KNOWING WHERE YOU ARE**

Outline

The task for this chapter is locating position in both two and three dimensions, and determining loci.

In the introductory activity students work with a plan of a garden and locate positions of objects according to given rules. Students are invited to invent their own rules.

Section A applies some of the ideas of the introductory activity to goats tethered in a field. There are also questions about the circles or squares that can be drawn through one, two or three given points. Other questions are about 'ripples' of shapes and about dividing a line in a given ratio. The section ends with questions about the angle properties of circles.

Section B is about locating position in three dimensions. There are questions about the different ways in which lines, planes and solids can intersect. Other questions are about what is produced when two-dimensional shapes (squares, circles and triangles) are rotated in space. Some questions involve Pythagoras' theorem and the volume of cylinders and cones.

There are five Further Coursework Tasks. The first is about tethered goats and the second is a further exploration of 'ripples'. The third, which is most easily explored using *Logo*, is about the shape traced out by a point, which moves so that it is always half way between two other points, that move according to given rules. The fourth is about the intersection of spheres with cubes and cuboids, and the last concerns squares drawn so that their perimeters pass through a number of fixed points.

Strategies

Class discussion is an appropriate way of working on the questions set in the introductory activity. Students can work in groups to make up their own rules and then share these with the whole class.

Section A involves a lot of accurate drawing and students can do this individually. Questions 17 to 21 are about angles in circles and you might want to develop the ideas by means of activities with groups or with the whole class. The three-dimensional loci in Section B are easier to describe than they are to draw and consequently group or class discussion is appropriate.

Equipment and Resources

For all parts:
    coloured pencils
For introduction to the task:
    resource sheet 29, *Garden*
For Section A:
    resource sheet 30, *Goats*
    cardboard or plastic circles and squares (to draw round)
    Logo
    cardboard (to make angles)
For FCT 3:
    Logo with multiple turtles (*ATM Logo Microworlds* for BBC or Nimbus)
    Logo code for Archimedes or Nimbus is provided on page 112).

KNOWING WHERE YOU ARE

Relevant Review Exercises

C34	Ratio	page 116
C40	Nets and polyhedra	page 137
C41	Pythagoras' theorem and trigonometry in three dimensions	page 141
D44	Bearings and loci	page 253
D46	Properties of circles	page 261

National Curriculum Statements

Introduction to the task
2/5b2; 2/5b3; 4/4a1; 4/4a4; 4/4b; 4/7b

Section A
2/5b2; 2/5b3; 2/6a5; 3/8b1; 4/4a1; 4/4a3; 4/4a4; 4/4b; 4/4c; 4/5a; 4/5b1; 4/6b3; 4/7b; 4/10a1

Section B
3/8a2; 4/4a1; 4/4a4; 4/4c; 4/5b1; 4/5b2; 4/6a; 4/7b; 4/7d; 4/9a1; 4/9a4

Questions in Sections

Accessible to all students (no bars)	Somewhat harder (one bar)	More difficult (two bars)
Section A, 1–9	Section A, 10–14	Section A, 15–21
Section B, 1–5	Section B, 6–8(g)	Section B, 8(h)–14

Further Coursework Tasks

neutral: 1, 2, 3
easier:
more difficult: 4, 5

INTRODUCTION TO THE TASK: HINTS

Almost all students appear to have a reasonable feel for loci; but many need reminding of more complicated aspects. A good way of introducing this activity is to make a copy of the *Garden* resource sheet as an OHP slide. Class discussion can resolve any misunderstandings about the questions posed. Students can then set questions for each other in small groups, and perhaps present these for the rest of the class to answer using a second OHP slide of the *Garden* resource sheet. One lesson is probably sufficient for the whole activity.

The following diagram provides the answers to the problems posed.

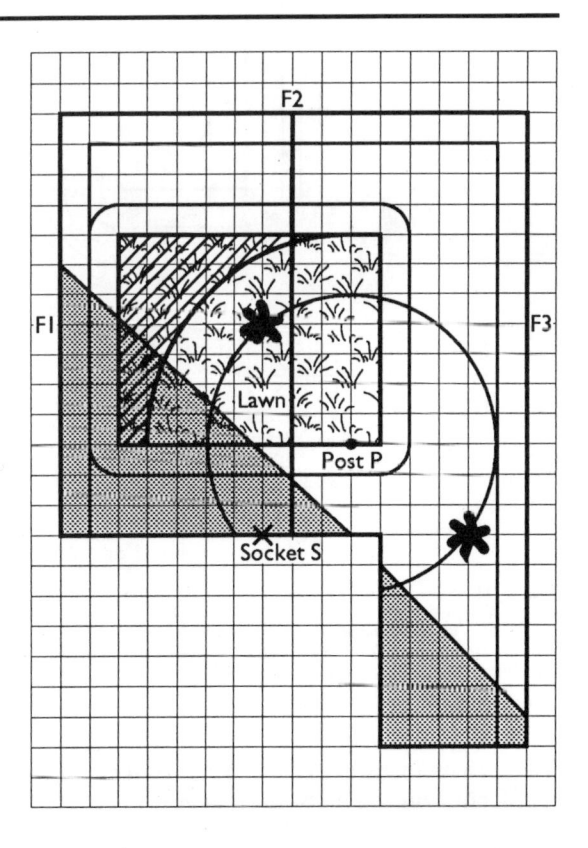

SECTION A: ANSWERS

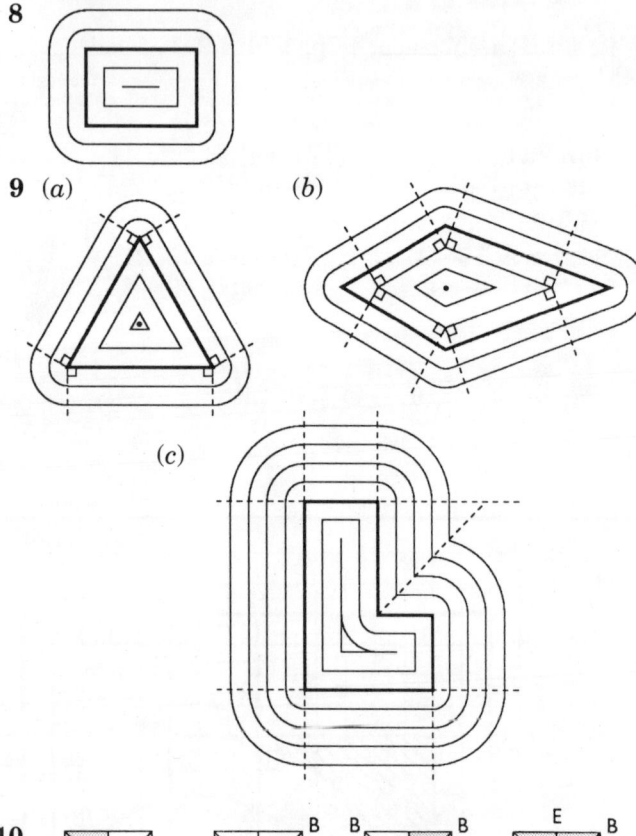

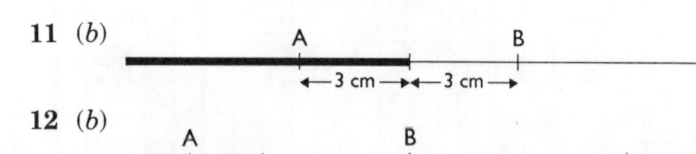

1. (a) B (b) E (c) F (d) D
2. (c) About 2.3 m
3. (b) (iv) Lie on a line (perpendicular bisector of line joining the two points) (c) (iii) None
4. (b) (iii) It depends exactly where the squares are drawn, but the complete locus is given in the notes on FCT 5. (c) (iii) Usually an infinite number, but none if two of the points are at adjacent corners of a square and the third is on the opposite side.
5. (e) 2
6. (d) 4
7. Ripples are concentric circles; last ripple is their centre.
8.
9. (a) (b) (c)
10. 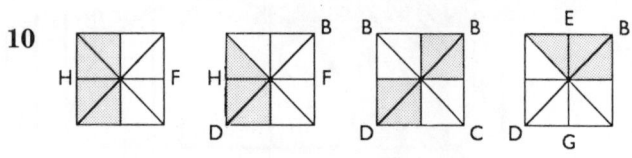
11. (b)
12. (b) 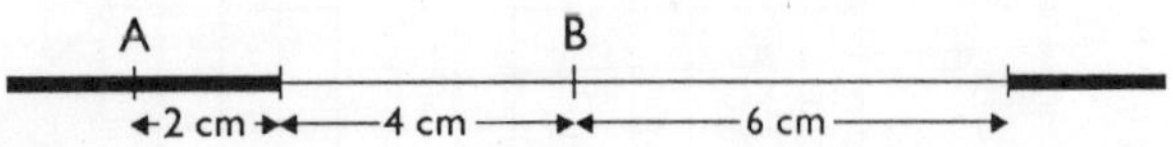
13. (b) 4 cm from A and 6 cm from B; or 20 cm from A and 30 cm from B.
14. (c) The locus is a circle of radius 4 cm and centre 2 cm from B and 8 cm from A.
15. (a) (b) (c) (d) 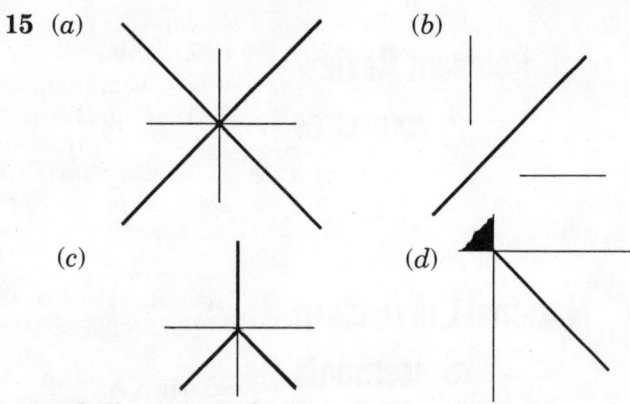
16. (d) The point is the centre of the circumcircle of the triangle (the circle through the vertices of the triangle).
17. (d) The circle with diameter AB.
18. Two major arcs of circles with common chord AB.
19. (b) Angles OPB and OBP are y (c) $2x + 2y = 180°$ (d) $x + y = 90°$ (e) This justifies the belief that the locus in 16(d) is a circle.
20. (c) $2x + 2y$ (d) 140°
21. (b) Locus is two lines parallel to AB and 3 cm away (c) Two major arcs with common chord AB (d) About 28° or 82°.

SECTION B: ANSWERS

1. Hollow sphere, radius 1 m, centre A.
2. Two planes parallel to X, either side of X, 1 m away.
3. (a) Infinite hollow cylinder with l as the axis, radius 1 m (b) Finite cylinder with a hemisphere on each end.
4. Two hollow spheres concentric with original sphere, with radii 1 m less and 1 m more.
5. A plane which bisects at right angles the line joining A and B.
6. When giving answers to question 6 it is more important that students can *describe* the intersections than that they know the *names* of all the shapes obtained.
(a) Either no meeting or an infinite line (b) No meeting, or a point, or the whole of the line (c) No meeting (if parallel or skew) or a point (d) No meeting, or one point, or two points (e) No meeting, or one point or a circle (f) No meeting, or one point, or two points, or a line (g) No meeting, or a line, or two parallel lines, or a circle, or an ellipse (h) No meeting, or a point, or two points, or three points, or six points, or a circle, or two circles, or three circles or six circles, or various arrangements of arcs of circles (see FCT 4) (i) No meeting, or a point or two points, or a line (j) No meeting (unless it is a double cone), or a point, or a line, or two lines, or a circle, or an ellipse, or a parabola or a hyperbola
7. (a) And (b) Two perpendicular planes bisecting the angles between the objects (c) Hollow cone with 90° vertical angle and axis l.

8 (a) Finite solid cylinder (b) Two identical finite cones with a common base (distance between vertices is the diagonal of the square, slant height is the side of the square) (c) Sphere (d) Torus ('rubber ring') (e) Cylinder (f) Cone (g) Two finite cones with a common base; a finite cone with a second finite cone removed from it (h) All of a plane (at right angles to the fixed line) except a circle (the circle is the envelope of the lines)

9 314 cm^2

10 Two circles of radius 8 cm, perpendicular to l, and with centres on 1 and 6 cm either side of A.

11 A circle of radius 4.8 m, perpendicular to AB and centre 6.4 m from A.

12 Hollow cylinder of area $2\pi \text{ m}^2$ (2 edges); hollow cylinder of area $2\sqrt{2}\pi \text{ m}^2$ (1 edge); circle of area $\pi \text{ m}^2$ (4 edges); annulus of area $\pi \text{ m}^2$ (4 edges).

13 If l and m are 1 unit apart, cylinder parallel to l and m, with radius $\frac{2}{3}$ and centre $\frac{1}{3}$ from m and $\frac{4}{3}$ from l.

14 Sphere, with similar dimensions to cylinder in 13.

FURTHER COURSEWORK TASKS

1) You have a field or a garden, in which you keep goats. All the goats are tethered in some way.

Make up a story about the goats which will give you some problems to solve. Here are some of the decisions you can make in your story.

What is the shape of the field or garden?

How are the goats tethered? The pictures below show some possibilities.

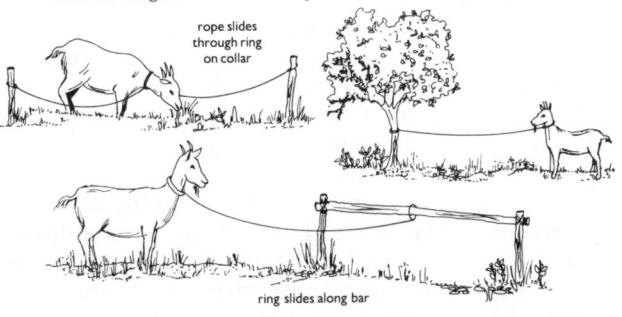

Are there buildings in the field around which the goats can move? These will affect the region of the field which the goats can reach.

How long are the tethers? Do they have to be short enough to prevent the goats eating vegetables in a vegetable plot, for example?

Are the goats replacing a lawn mower? In other words, is it important that all the grass can be reached by at least one goat?

The decisions you make will set you problems to solve. How many goats do you need? How should they be tethered?

You might want to find out what area of the field each goat can reach. And what area of grass can be eaten by two (or more) goats.

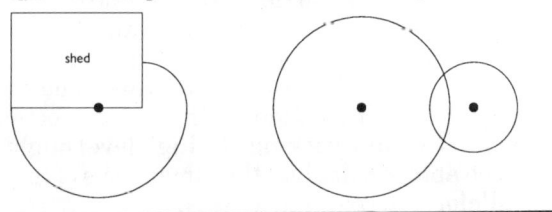

This task provides a scenario in which students can devise activities which suit their own levels of achievement. Students working at a relatively low level can tell stories about goats not eating cabbages, not fighting and so on, and demonstrate in this way that they are taking charge of the mathematics they are learning. A wide range of different loci are possible, especially if a range of shapes are used for the fixed objects which interfere with the ropes. The three methods of tying produce a circle, an ellipse and a 'running track shape', if there are no objects to interfere with the rope.

Some students will want to calculate lengths and areas, using in this way higher level knowledge of lengths and areas of arcs of circles, trigonometry, etc.

Once students are into the task they enjoy making up increasingly complex situations to solve.

2) Explore the shape of ripples obtained for different shapes. You might want to consider squares, rectangles, triangles, rhombuses, kites, semicircles, L shapes, T shapes, and so on.

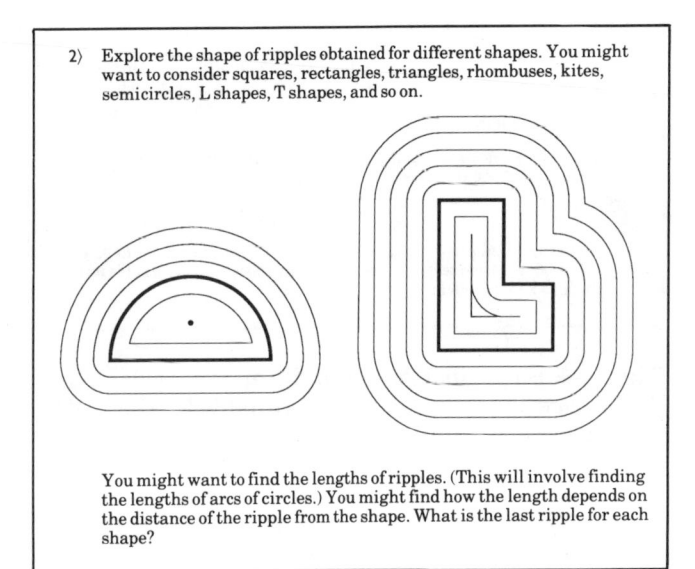

You might want to find the lengths of ripples. (This will involve finding the lengths of arcs of circles.) You might find how the length depends on the distance of the ripple from the shape. What is the last ripple for each shape?

This is another task which provides students with a context in which to set themselves challenges at an appropriate level.

Some students will concentrate on *drawing* the ripples for a range of complicated starting shapes. This is not always straightforward; many students will be challenged by the problems of sorting out the corners, and also of ripples which interfere with one another if a non-convex starting shape is used.

Some students will *calculate* lengths of ripples, a task which is considerably complicated by interference effects.

Finding the last ripples is not always as easy as it sounds. Depending on the starting shape, the last ripple can be a point or a line. What else can it be?

3) Figure 4 was drawn using three turtles.

Turtle 1 obeyed the normal *Logo* commands.

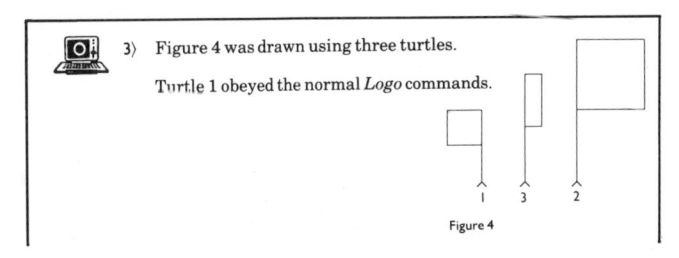

Figure 4

Turtle 2 moved at the same time as Turtle 1, but it moved *twice* the distance and it turned in the *opposite* direction (in other words, it turned *left* when Turtle 1 turned *right*).

Turtle 3 always stayed exactly half way between Turtle 1 and Turtle 2.

What does Turtle 3 draw if Turtle 1 draws a different shape?

Figure 5 shows a different arrangement. In this figure Turtle 1 and Turtle 2 follow exactly the same instructions (but Turtle 2 is not facing the same direction as Turtle 1 to start with).

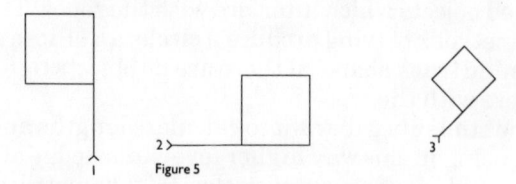

Figure 5

You can make up your own situations to explore.

    A You can change the shape that Turtle 1 draws.

    B You can change the rules which say how Turtle 2 should move.

Try to find rules that help you predict what Turtle 3 will draw when you make either change **A** or change **B**.

There is something else that can also be changed.

Turtle 3 can move so that it is a third of the way between Turtle 1 and Turtle 2. Or a quarter. Or ...

One way of exploring this idea is to use *Logo*. If you do not use *Logo* you will probably need to get people or objects to obey the turtle rules until the idea becomes clear to you.

This task is provided as one of the microworlds in the ATM *Logo Microworlds* pack, available for the BBC, Nimbus and Archimedes. If an Archimedes or Nimbus is being used you can use the following code instead.

Archimedes version:

```
TO START
CS
TELL 1 PU SETPOS [-200 0] SETH 0 PD ST
TELL 2 PU SETPOS [200 0] SETH 0 PD ST
TELL 3 PU SETPOS BISECT
END

TO F :LENGTH
TELL 1 FD :LENGTH
TELL 2 FD 2 * :LENGTH
TELL 3 PD SETPOS BISECT
END

TO R :ANGLE
TELL 1 RT :ANGLE
TELL 2 LT :ANGLE
END

TO L :ANGLE
R -1 * :ANGLE
END

TO BISECT
OP (LIST ((XCOR 1)+(XCOR 2))/2 ((YCOR 1)+(YCOR 2))/2)
END
```

Nimbus version:

```
start
cs
tell 1 setpos [-40 0] seth 0
tell 2 setpos [40 0] seth 0
tell 3 setpos bisect

f :length
tell 1 fd :length
tell 2 fd 2 * :length
tell 3 line pos bisect 1 setpos bisect

r :angle
tell 1 rt :angle
tell 2 lt :angle


l :angle
r -1 * :angle

bisect
tell 1 make 'x1 xcor make 'y1 ycor
tell 2 make 'x2 xcor make 'y2 ycor
tell 3 result ((:x1 + :x2)/2) && (((:y1 + :y2) /2)
```

Whether or not students are using a computer for this task, they will need to be encouraged to do **accurate** drawings rather than vague sketches, in order to get a grip of the situation. For some aspects of the task squared paper or isometric paper would be useful.

Students need to be encouraged not to change too many variables at the same time. Many students should be able to reason out what shape the turtle is producing, and to justify their conclusions.

This is a rich task, with plenty of ideas to explore. Here are some of the results that can be obtained.

A For the rule given in the coursework task.

If at the start, the turtles are facing in the same direction, when Turtles 1 and 2 trace out a square, Turtle 3 traces out a 1 by 3 rectangle. When Turtles 1 and 2 trace out a rectangle with sides M and N, Turtle 3 traces out a rectangle with sides $\frac{M}{2}$ and $\frac{3N}{2}$. Thus a 3 by 1 rectangle traced by Turtles 1 and 2 will produce a square traced by Turtle 3.

If at the start, the turtles are not facing in the same direction, when Turtles 1 and 2 trace out a square, Turtle 3 traces out a parallelogram. This is a rhombus when the angle between the turtles is 90° and a 3 by 1 rectangle when it is 180°. There are many different tasks students could set themselves in connection with this situation. For example, if the starting angle between the turtles is 90° a rhombus drawn by Turtles 1 and 2 will produce a parallelogram for Turtle 3. By trial and improvement students can find the angle of the rhombus, which makes the parallelogram a rectangle ($\tan^{-1}(2)$ or roughly 63°) and then go on to make Turtle 3 draw a square instead of a rectangle.

Some students working at a high level might even be able to calculate the dimensions of the parallelogram required for this.

B Turtle 2 moves the *same* distance as Turtle 1 but still turns in the *opposite* direction.

The geometry is now somewhat easier. Whatever shape Turtles 1 and 2 draw, Turtle 3 draws a straight line. The direction of this straight line bisects the angle between the two turtles at the start (and at all other times). When the angle between Turtles 1 and 2 is x, the distance moved by Turtle 3 is $\cos\left(\frac{x}{2}\right)$ times the distance moved by Turtles 1 and 2. This means that when Turtles 1 and 2 are moving parallel, Turtle 3 moves the same distance as Turtles 1 and 2. When they are moving in the opposite direction, Turtle 3 stays still, and when they are moving at 120° to each other, Turtle 3 moves half the distance of Turtles 1 and 2.

C Turtle 2 moves the **same** distance as Turtle 1 and turns in the **same** direction.

If at the start, the turtles are facing in the same direction then the path of Turtle 3 is a translation of the paths of Turtles 1 and 2.

If at the start, the turtles are not facing in the same direction, when Turtles 1 and 2 trace out a square, Turtle 3 traces out a smaller square. The direction of each side of the square for Turtle 3 bisects the directions of the corresponding sides for Turtles 1 and 2. Students can justify this by considering symmetry. If x is the angle between Turtles 1 and 2, the size of the square produced by Turtle 3 is $\cos\left(\frac{x}{2}\right)$ smaller than that produced by the other turtles. Some students working at a high level might be able to calculate this result.

D Turtle 2 moves the **same** distance as Turtle 1 but does not turn **at all**.

When Turtle 1 draws a square, Turtle 2 draws a straight line segment and Turtle 3 draws this.

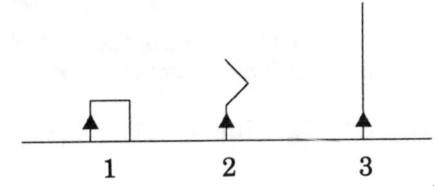

If Turtle 1 continually redraws this square Turtle 3 produces a repeating pattern.

Students can consider the different loci produced by Turtle 3, when Turtle 1 draws a variety of common shapes. When Turtle 1 draws a circle, Turtle 3 draws a cycloid.

> 4) A cube has a side of length 1 metre. Calculate the radius of a sphere which has the same volume as the cube.
>
> The sphere is placed with its centre at the centre of the cube. What is the intersection of the sphere and the cube?
>
> What happens if the centre of the sphere is not at the centre of the cube?

What happens if you use a cuboid instead of a cube?

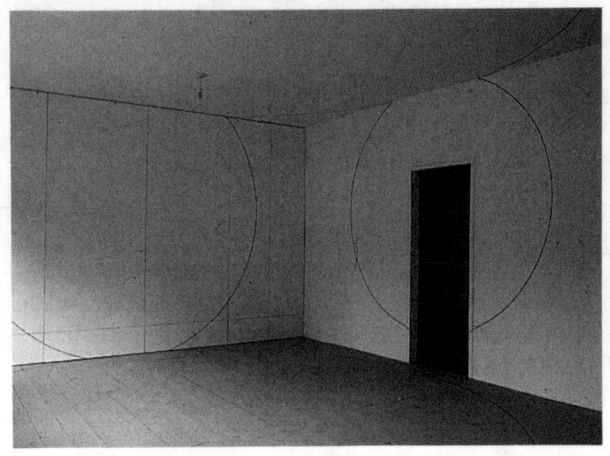

This photograph is of a work of art created by Gary Woodley, using the ideas suggested above. The cuboid is an actual room. The photograph shows a drawing of an intersection of an imaginary sphere with a room.

Some students might like to create a Gary Woodley sculpture in their minds, and draw sketches to illustrate it and to show their accurate calculations.

This task provides an opportunity for students to use coordinates and Pythagoras' theorem in three dimensions and to visualise intersections of spheres and planes.

Some results

The radius of a sphere of volume 1 m³ is 62 cm.

The distance from the centre of the cube to a corner is 87 cm. The distance of the centre of a face from a corner is 71 cm.

If the centre of the sphere is placed at the centre of the cube, the sphere intersects the six faces of the cube in identical circles with radius 37 cm.

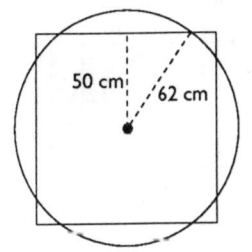

Suppose the centre of the sphere is moved towards one of the faces until the intersection with the opposite face becomes a dot. Then the radius of the circle of intersection with the face the sphere moved towards is 49 cm and consequently this circle just fits within the face.

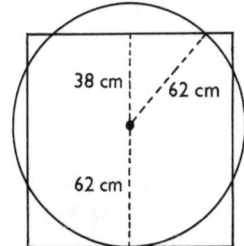

TASK MATHS

The intersection of the sphere with each of the other faces is still a circle of radius 37 cm, but its centre has been moved to a distance of 38 cm from one of the sides.

Similar methods can also be used for cuboids. Here is an example of the problems students could set themselves.

For different cuboids, what is the intersection of the cuboid with a sphere of the same volume whose centre coincides with the centre of the cuboid? If the cuboid has a volume of 1 cubic metre and dimensions 124 cm by 90 cm by 90 cm the intersection of the sphere with two of the cuboid's faces is a dot, and with the other four faces is a circle of radius 43 cm.

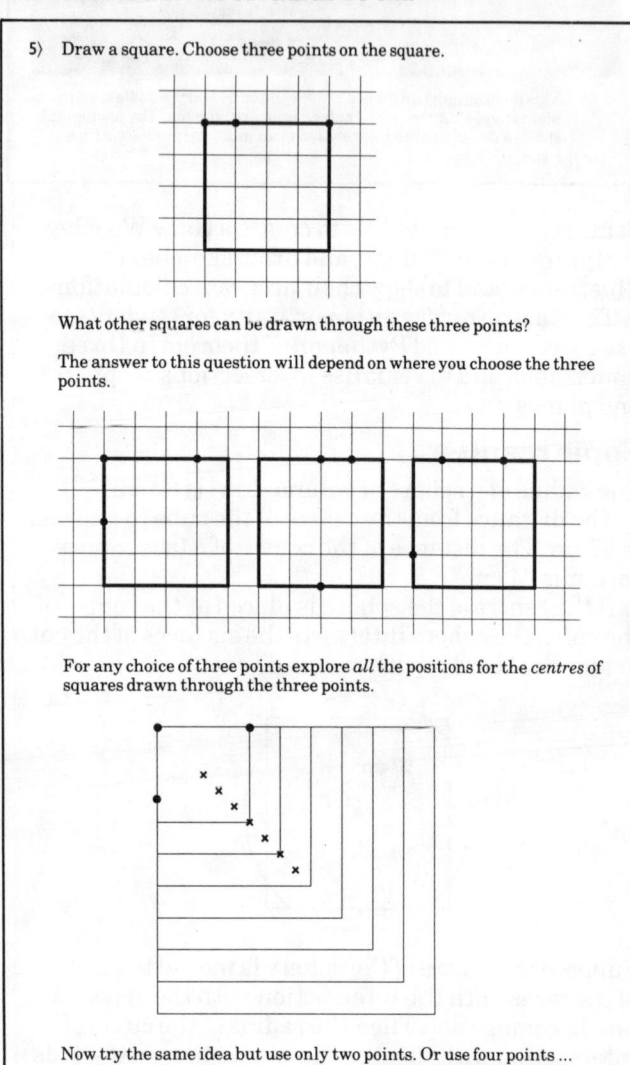

---

5) Draw a square. Choose three points on the square.

What other squares can be drawn through these three points?

The answer to this question will depend on where you choose the three points.

For any choice of three points explore *all* the positions for the *centres* of squares drawn through the three points.

Now try the same idea but use only two points. Or use four points ...

This task is difficult, not because there are complicated calculations to be performed, but because students will need to know how to experiment, through the use of accurate drawings and rough sketches, in order to obtain a clear idea of what can happen.

With three points there are several different possibilities to be considered. One way of grouping these is as follows.

Case 1: The three points are collinear.

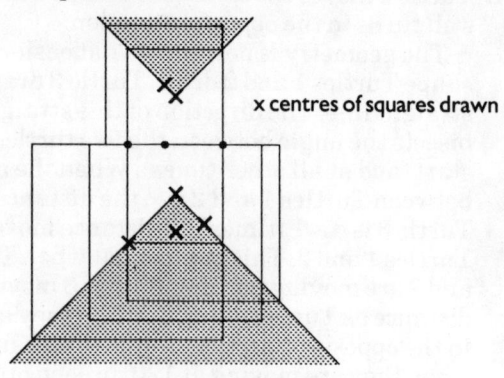

x centres of squares drawn

In this case the smallest square through the three points has side length equal to the distance between the extreme points. The longer the side length the further the square can slide sideways and still pass through the three points. The shaded region in the picture shows the locus of the centres of squares through the three points.

Case 2: The three points form a right-angled triangle.
There are two ways of getting squares to pass through these points. One set of squares have one of their corners at the right angle.

In the other set of squares the two closest points lie on one side and the third point on the opposite side.

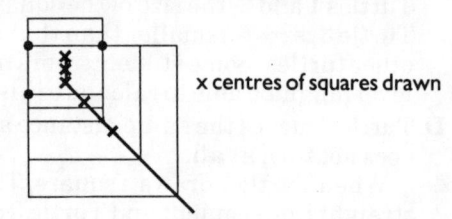

x centres of squares drawn

The heavy line indicates the locus of the centres.
Case 3: The three points form an obtuse-angled triangle.
There are two ways of getting squares to pass through the three points.

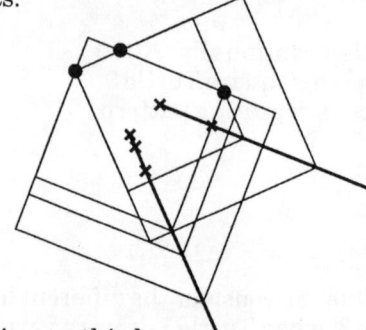

There is sometimes a third way.

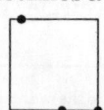

Case 4: The three points form an acute-angled triangle.
There is always a (unique) way of fitting a square round the three points so that each point lies on a different side. The locus is a single point.

114

It is sometimes possible to arrange for two points to be on one side and the third point on the opposite side. The locus is the heavy line segment shown.

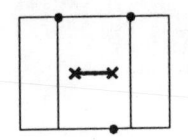

With two points there is only really one case to consider. The complete locus of the centres of squares through two points is shown below.

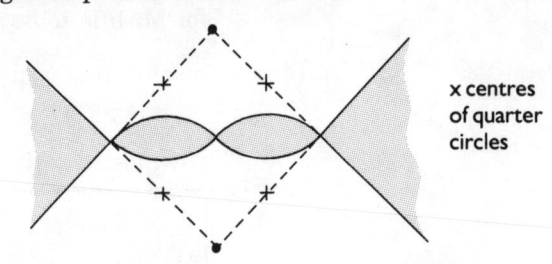

x centres of quarter circles

ASSESSING STUDENTS' COURSEWORK TASKS

Further Coursework Task 1

This task enables students to work at a wide range of levels, depending on how the task is interpreted. In the following extract a student has devised a simple situation in which he works out where to tie up three goats so that they and a man can all reach a water trough without being able to make contact with each other. He can interpret the situation and use an appropriate diagram (Ma1/4b).

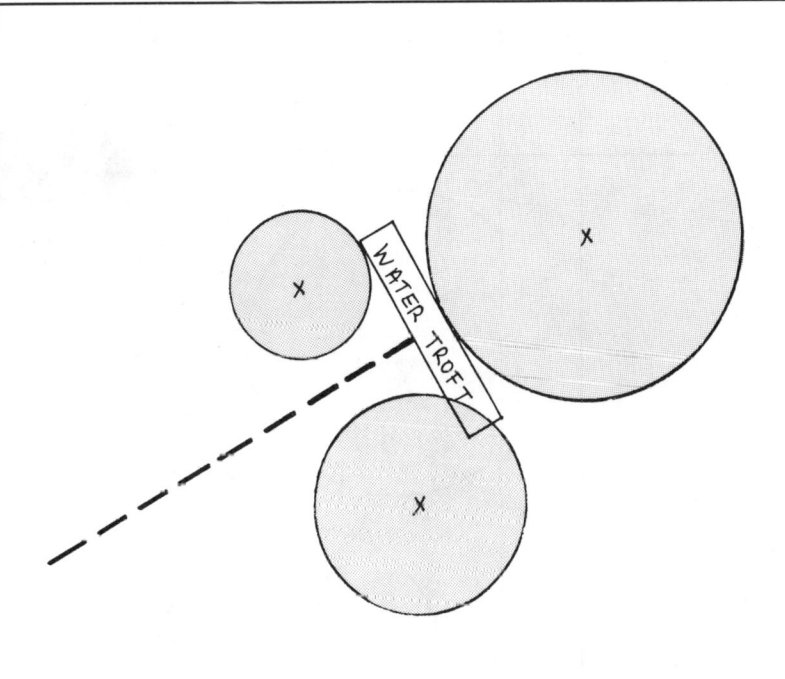

In this idea is a way in which 3 goats can reach a water troft. But they can not reach each other and there is another way which a man can fill the water troft without being hit by the goats.

TASK MATHS

In this second extract a student has made up a more complicated story but his questions are too simple for Ma1/6a to be awarded.

> Problem [1st] to stop the goat from getting on the vegetable patch, I have solved my problem by putting the goat-teid to the corner of the house, as it turns round the house it get's caught on the corners which makes it shorter.
>
> [2nd + 4th] to keep 2nd goat and 4 th goat away from each other but they only turn a certain way because of the fence.
>
> [3rd] to keep the goat of the flowers and not able to bite anyone on the pathway.

In this third extract a student creates three different objects around which the goat's rope can get caught in different ways. Here the questions she has posed are appropriate for Ma1/6a.

KNOWING WHERE YOU ARE

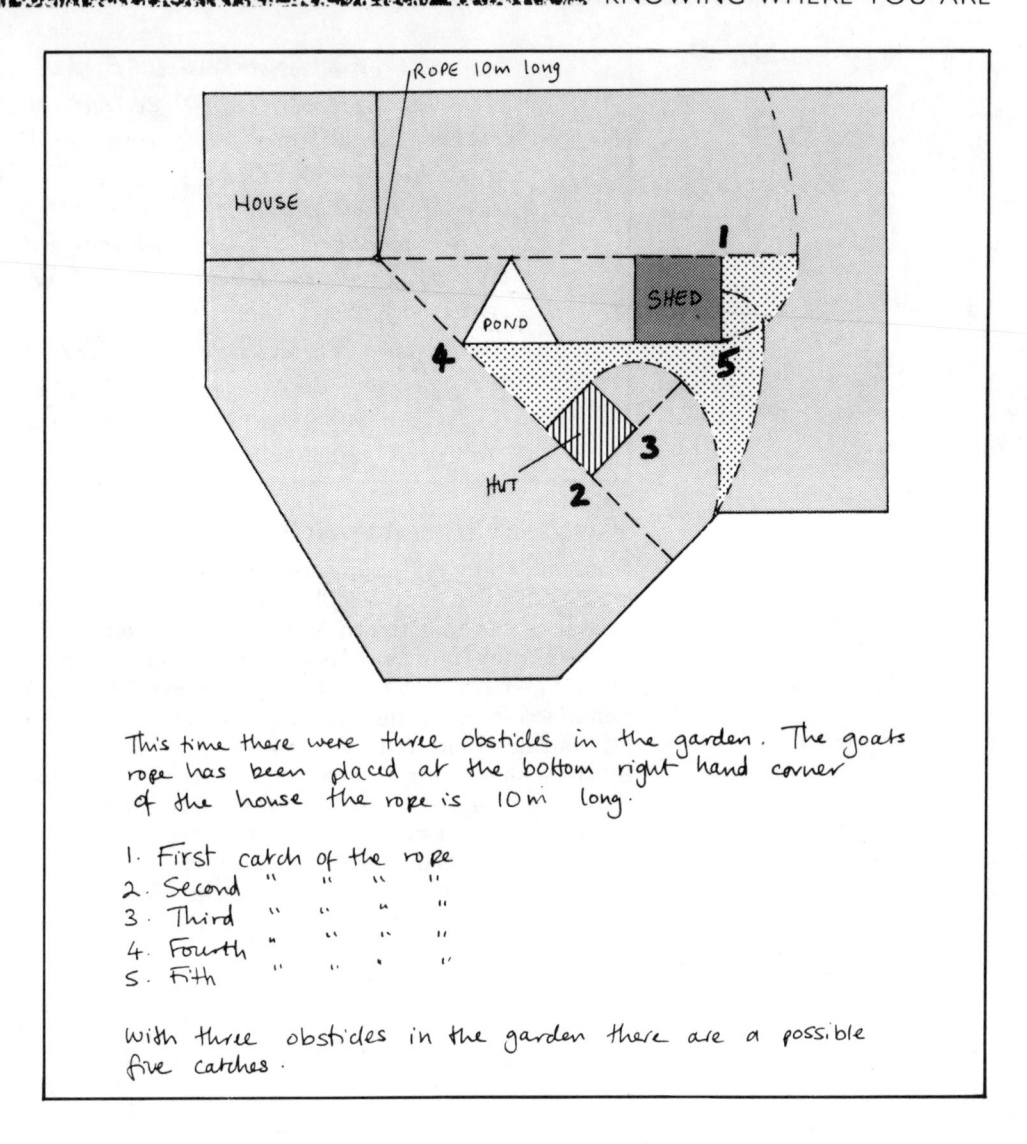

[Handwritten diagram showing a garden with House, Shed, Pond, and Hut as obstacles, with a rope 10m long attached at the bottom right hand corner of the house. Areas are numbered 1-5 showing where the rope catches.]

This time there were three obstacles in the garden. The goats rope has been placed at the bottom right hand corner of the house the rope is 10m long.

1. First catch of the rope
2. Second " " " "
3. Third " " " "
4. Fourth " " " "
5. Fifth " " " "

With three obstacles in the garden there are a possible five catches.

In the final extract a student calculates the different areas of grass eaten by her goat when it is tied up in different ways. She is also providing evidence for Ma1/6a.

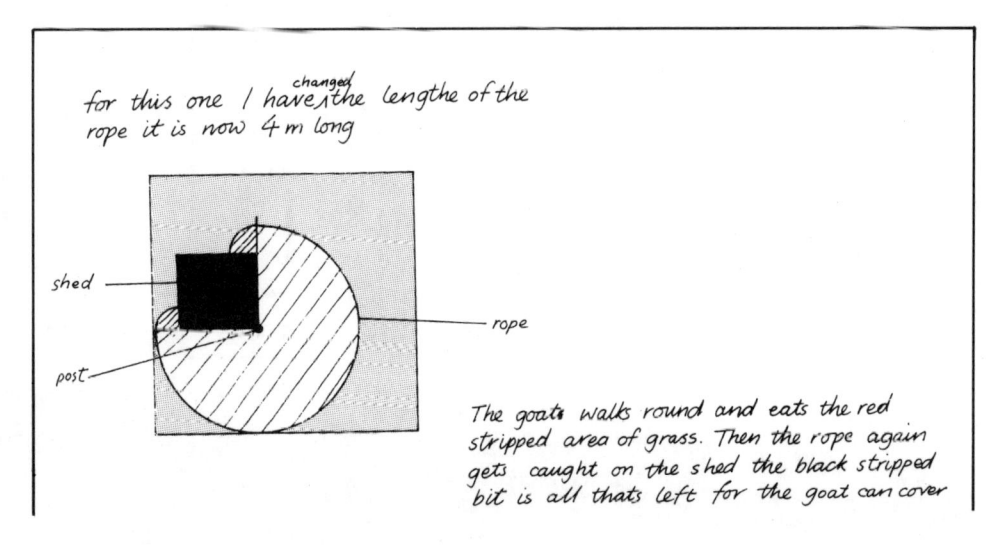

for this one I have changed the lengthe of the rope it is now 4m long

[Diagram showing shed, post, and rope with red striped and black striped areas of grass.]

The goats walks round and eats the red stripped area of grass. Then the rope again gets caught on the shed the black stripped bit is all thats left for the goat can cover

117

TASK MATHS

> The area of a whole circle if there would have been no obstacles is 50.26 but the goat only covered 3/4 without catching on to the shed so if I divide 50.26 by 4 it is 12.56 which is 1/4 then I multiplyed it by 3 which is $\boxed{37.69}$ that is the area of the red shaded bit. Then to find the area of the black stripped bit I did the same as the field before 1 × π which is pie 3.14 again I divided it by 2 because there is two quarter circles which is again 1.5 so I added 37.61 + 1.5 which is $\boxed{39.26}$ The area of land the goat ate is 39.26 m².

Further Coursework Task 2

Students enjoy making up complicated starting shapes for their ripples. This can lead them to making mistakes, because the task they set themselves might prove harder than they had anticipated. Students should be rewarded for the goals achieved and not penalised for their mistakes. In the following extract a student uses squared paper to design a series of starting shapes for his ripples. In the first diagram his inside ripples are incorrect, but once this was pointed out to him he was able to produce the second diagram successfully. His drawings are quite difficult to do, but he makes no comment on his work and does no calculations. Here it is difficult for him to achieve anything other than Ma1/4b.

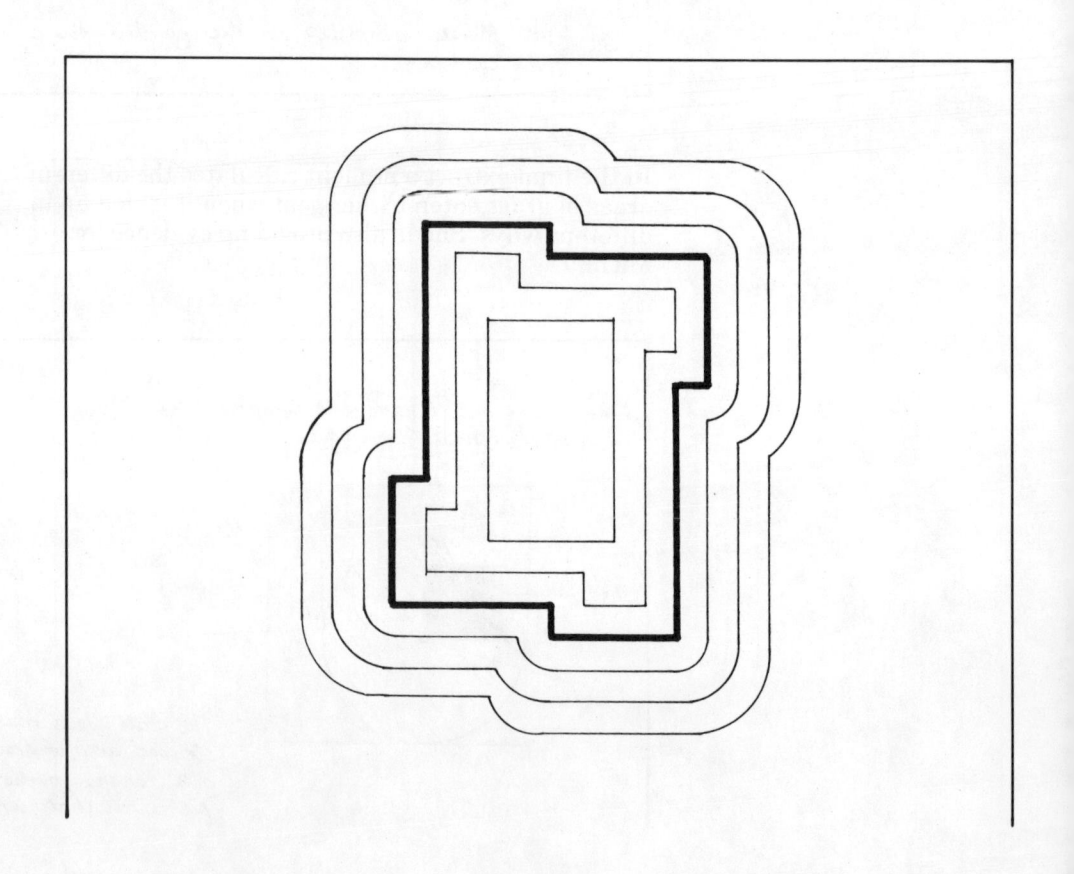

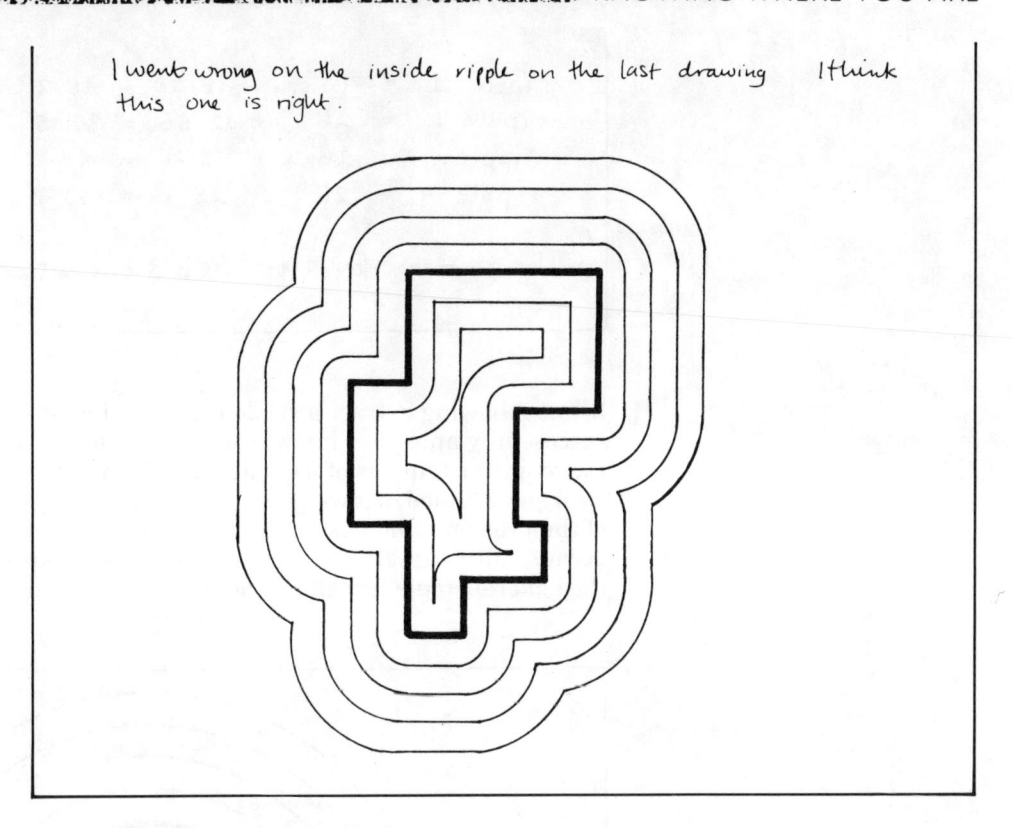

I went wrong on the inside ripple on the last drawing. I think this one is right.

In the following extract the drawing is somewhat simpler, but the student is attempting to calculate the lengths of the ripples. He does this correctly for the first two ripples, but for the next two he fails to account for the fact that some of the arcs are not quarter circles. Nevertheless, in addition to demonstrating the same achievements as the previous student, he can make and test generalisations (Ma1/5c).

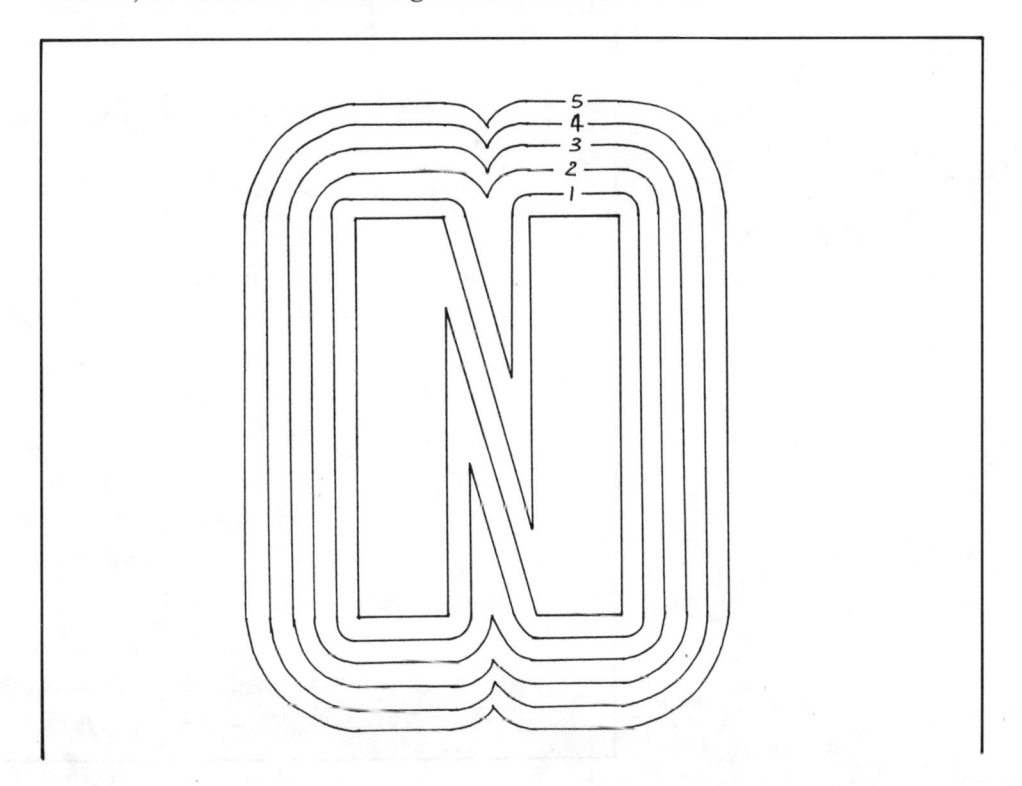

TASK MATHS

> ripple 1 = 40 cm + 6·28 = 46·28 cm
> ripple 2 = 26   + 12·56 = 38·5 cm
> ripple 3 = 26   + 18·8 = 44·8 cm
> ripple 4 = 26   + 25·1 = 51·1 cm
>
> The pattern for this is 6·3 cm between each ripple.

In the following extract a student shows that she can successfully apply her knowledge and skills to finding the lengths of ripples of a semicircle. Her work is clearly explained, showing that she has a good grasp of the problem. She has not quite achieved Ma1/6c because although this work is almost a justification of the general ripple length she never makes it explicit.

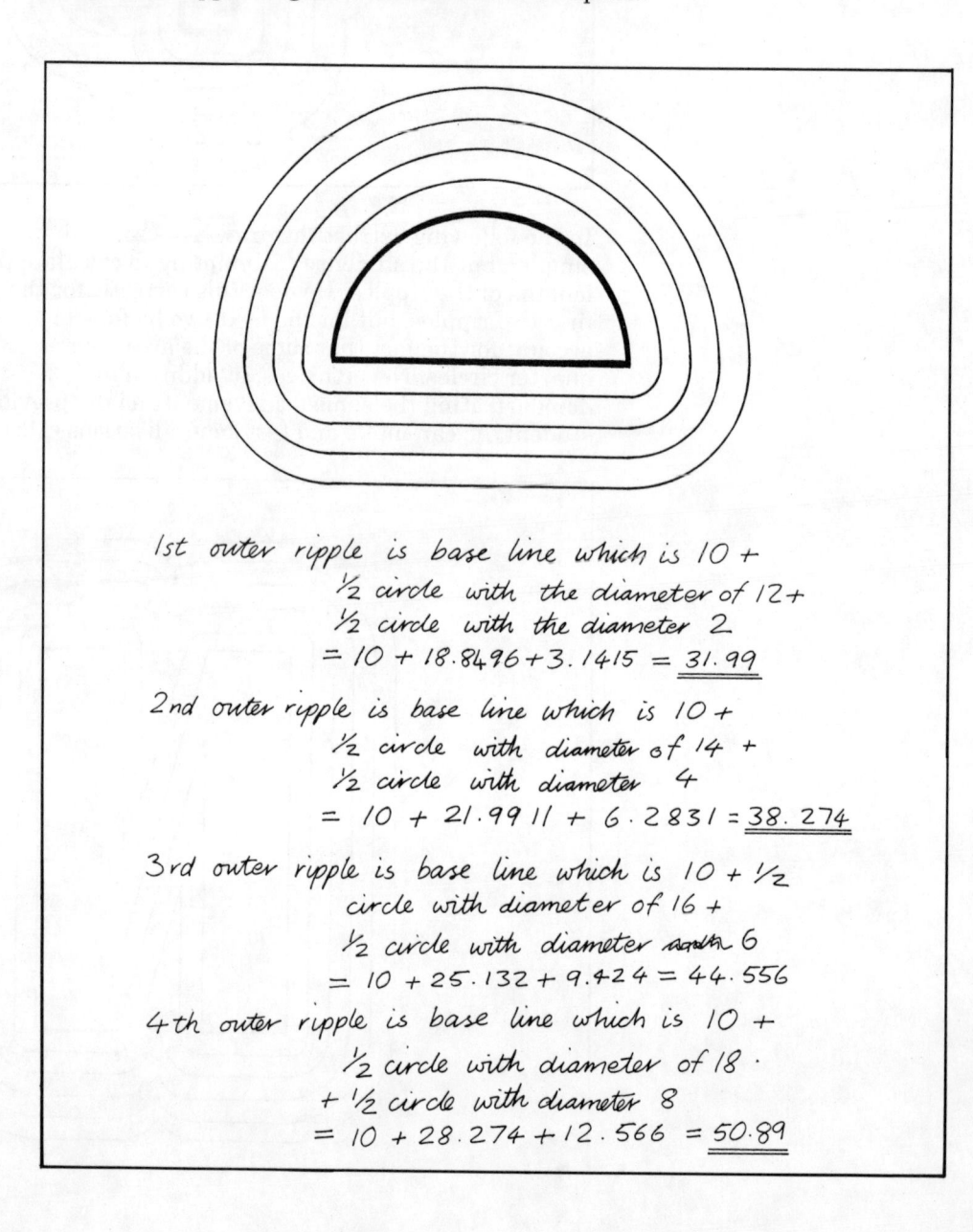

> 1st outer ripple is base line which is 10 +
>   ½ circle with the diameter of 12 +
>   ½ circle with the diameter 2
>   = 10 + 18·8496 + 3·1415 = 31·99
>
> 2nd outer ripple is base line which is 10 +
>   ½ circle with diameter of 14 +
>   ½ circle with diameter 4
>   = 10 + 21·9911 + 6·2831 = 38·274
>
> 3rd outer ripple is base line which is 10 + ½
>   circle with diameter of 16 +
>   ½ circle with diameter 6
>   = 10 + 25·132 + 9·424 = 44·556
>
> 4th outer ripple is base line which is 10 +
>   ½ circle with diameter of 18 ·
>   + ½ circle with diameter 8
>   = 10 + 28·274 + 12·566 = 50·89

KNOWING WHERE YOU ARE

In this final extract a student has realised that he has to calculate the lengths of several arcs of circles to find the lengths of his ripples. He decides to work out a large number of these first. He then uses these to calculate the lengths of ripples in a sequence of different drawings. One is given in the extract below. This work shows evidence of following a new line of enquiry (Ma1/7a).

90° turns

Radius of Arc	Length of Arc
1 cm	1.57 cm
2 cm	3.14 cm
3 cm	4.71 cm
4 cm	6.28 cm
5 cm	7.85 cm
6 cm	9.4 cm
7 cm	10.9 cm
8 cm	12.5 cm
9 cm	14.1 cm

120° turns

Radius of Arc	Length of Arc
1 cm	2.02 cm
2 cm	4.20 cm
3 cm	6.20 cm
4 cm	8.39 cm
5 cm	10.49 cm
6 cm	12.7 cm
7 cm	14.68 cm
8 cm	16.77 cm
9 cm	18.86 cm

135° turns

Radius of Arc	Length of Arc
1 cm	2.36 cm
2 cm	4.72 cm
3 cm	7.08 cm
4 cm	9.44 cm
5 cm	11.81 cm
6 cm	14.17 cm
7 cm	16.53 cm
8 cm	18.89 cm
9 cm	21.25 cm

150°

Radius of Arc	Length of Arc
1 cm	2.61 cm
2 cm	5.23 cm
3 cm	7.85 cm
4 cm	10.47 cm
5 cm	13.08 cm
6 cm	15.70 cm
7 cm	18.32 cm
8 cm	20.94 cm
9 cm	23.56 cm

This triangle has different angles of 150°, 120° and 90°

12.5 + 7.5 + 14.6 = 34.6
The length of the first ripple is :- 34.6 + 150° turn + 120° turn + 90° turn.
= 34.6 + 6.2
= 40.8
Second ripple is :- 34.6 + 12.57
= 47.17
Third ripple is :- 34.6 + 18.76
= 53.36 etc.

TASK MATHS

Guide to Chapter 23: **WHAT DO YOU BELIEVE?**

Outline

The task for this chapter is examining the truth of statements about a wide range of situations.

The introductory activity is a game which can be played by the whole class; you have to make decisions based on what you believe other people will do. Everyone chooses a number, and the winner is the person who chooses the lowest number that no-one else has chosen.

Section A begins with some questions about the introductory activity and then poses some questions about probability where the results are difficult to believe.

Section B begins with some surprising visual images and geometrical problems. There are several questions about the areas and volumes of similar shapes and solids. The last few questions are about inequalities and linear programming.

Section C points out the many ways in which statistics can be misleading and how easy it is to draw spurious conclusions. Use is made of percentages, time, the calendar, interpreting graphs, probability, maps, medians and means.

Both Further Coursework Tasks involve carrying out a statistical survey about what people believe. One uses the questionnaire that was used to collect data for Section C, so that comparisons can be made. In the other task students choose a topic about which they have strong opinions and conduct a survey to see whether or not other people agree with them.

Strategies

The three sections are independent of one another, and could be done at different times. They are linked by the emphasis on the importance of being sure or proving in mathematics, and are designed to expose some misconceptions and to challenge the basis of some beliefs.

The introductory activity is an activity for the whole class and leads into Section A. Questions 1, 2, 3 and 4 of Section B lend themselves to class discussion. Students will benefit from doing some work from Section C before tackling a FCT.

Equipment and Resources

For Section B:
  coins

For Section C:
  resource sheet 31, *Television times*

For FCT 1:
  resource sheet 32, *What do you believe?*
  computer with database program (preferably *Pinpoint*)

Relevant Review Exercises

C28	*Probability*	page 95
D45	*Statistics 2*	page 257
D47	*Enlargement and similarity*	page 262
D48	*Inequalities and linear programming*	page 265

WHAT DO YOU BELIEVE?

National Curriculum Statements

Introduction to the task
5/5b1; 5/5d1

Section A
2/8b2; 5/4d1; 5/4d2; 5/4d3; 5/5d1; 5/5d2; 5/5d3; 5/6c; 5/6d; 5/7c; 5/8c1; 5/8c2; 5/9c; 5/10c

Section B
2/5b1; 3/8b1; 3/8b2; 4/4d2; 4/5d1; 4/6d; 4/7d; 4/8a; 4/9a3; 5/5d2; 5/6c; 5/6d; 5/7c; 5/10b

Section C
2/5b2; 2/5b3; 2/5d2; 2/6a1; 2/6a4; 2/7b1; 2/7c1; 2/8a1; 2/8c; 2/9b; 5/5d2; 5/6b2; 5/7a2; 5/7b1; 5/9b

Further coursework tasks
5/4a; 5/5a; 5/8a

Questions in Sections

Accessible to all students (no bars)	Somewhat harder (one bar)	More difficult (two bars)
Section A, 1–7	Section A, 8–9	Section A, 10–11
Section B, 1–4	Section B, 5–7	Section B, 8–13
Section C, 1–8	Section C, 9–13	Section C, 14–15

Further Coursework Tasks

neutral: 1, 2
easier:
more difficult:

INTRODUCTION TO THE TASK: HINTS

This activity will probably last for one lesson. You can either work with the whole class throughout the lesson or, after an introduction with the whole class, students can work in groups (of about six).

Through discussion at the end of the lesson it is worth pointing out that, when playing this game, you base your decisions on what other people do. Can you influence or be influenced by *saying* what you are going to choose?

This activity is suitable for a very large number of people, and is a good way of raising money for charity.

SECTION A: ANSWERS

1. (a) (1,1,1), (1,1,2), (1,2,1), (1,2,2), (2,1,1), (2,1,2), (2,2,1), (2,2,2) (b) The probability is $\frac{1}{4}$ *assuming* that all possible choices are equally likely *which probably is not true!*
2. (a) (1,2), (2,1), (1,3), (3,1), (3,2), (2,3), (1,1), (2,2), (3,3) (b) It doesn't sound very sensible, but it depends what you think the other two players will do.
3. (a) 3 (b) There is no number that is chosen by only one person (c) No, we think! (d) We don't know, but whatever you think the best number is, don't tell anyone else! (Or perhaps do!)
4. (a) 3 (b) You cannot win, so it depends whether you want the person who chose 2 to win (don't choose 2) or the person who chose 4 to win (choose 2)
5. (a) 5 (b) No. Because 5 is just an average number.
6. (b) $\frac{3}{13}$ (c) $\frac{1}{6}$ (d) Picture card more likely.
7. (b) Nine possibilities (c) (i) $\frac{2}{9}$ (ii) $\frac{2}{9}$ (iii) $\frac{2}{9}$ (iv) $\frac{3}{9}$ or $\frac{1}{3}$
8. (a) (ii) Fair; 18 even totals and 18 odd totals
   (b) (ii) Not fair; 27 even products and 9 odd products
   (iii) e.g. Julie pays Thebender 30p instead of 10p.
9. (a) 1 and 4 (b) The scores that can be obtained in more than one way are 4, 6 and 12. The probability that Jason knows is $\frac{25}{36}$. (c) The (1,4) domino; probability is $\frac{15}{28}$.
10. (a) $\frac{1}{2}$ (b) (i) Put one red cube in one bag, and the other 7 cubes in the other bag (ii) $\frac{5}{7}$
11. (a) (i) $\frac{5}{12}$ (ii) $\frac{1}{6}$ (b) (ii) Probability of die 1 winning is $\frac{2}{3}$ (iii) Probability of die 2 winning is $\frac{2}{3}$ (iv) Probability of die 3 winning is $\frac{2}{3}$ (v) Probability of die 4 winning is $\frac{2}{3}$ (vi) False; the second person can have a probability of $\frac{2}{3}$ of winning by choosing appropriately.

SECTION B: ANSWERS

1. (a) $\frac{1}{4}$ (b) $\frac{1}{2}$ (c) $\frac{12}{25}$ (nearly a half)
2. Outer ring 7.1 cm²; inner ring 5.5 cm²; inner circle 7.1 cm².
3. Same way up
4. (a) 169 (b) 168 (c) Because the 'diagonal' of the large rectangle is not quite a straight line (there is a very thin gap in the middle).

TASK MATHS

6 (a) (i) *Nine times* (ii) *Forty-nine times* (b) 250 cm²
8 (a) 37 ml (b) 1350 cm²
9 500
10

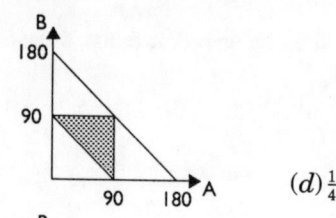

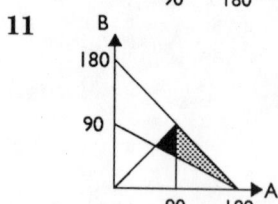

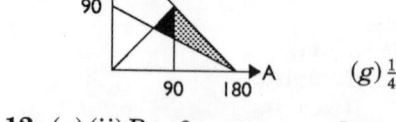

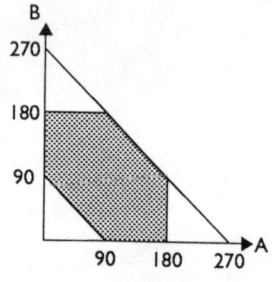

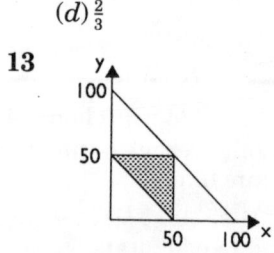

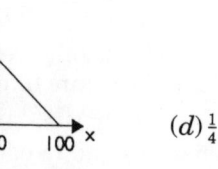

[Graph: B vs A, axes to 180, shaded square from (0,90)-(90,90)-(90,180)... region with vertices near 90] (d) ¼

11 [Graph: B vs A, axes to 180, shaded small triangle] (g) ¼

12 (a) (ii) B > 0
    (iii) A + B < 270
[Graph: B vs A, axes to 270, shaded region]
(d) ⅔

13 [Graph: y vs x, axes to 100, shaded square 0-50] (d) ¼

SECTION C: ANSWERS

1 (a) 90%
3 (a) 92% (b) 86%
6 (b) (Answers depend on use of resource sheet 31 and are approximate, depending on what you count as a programme) (i) 11% (ii) 25% (iii) 1% (iv) 5%
7 (a) Sunday (b) (i) Yes (ii) No (iii) Yes (c) 13th July 1990
8 (a) 2300 cm² (b) A4 is 624 cm²; A5 is 312 cm²; a typical exercise book is about 400 cm² (c) About 3.5 times for A4; 7 times for A5; 6 times for an exercise book.
9 (a) (i) About 20% (ii) About 70% (b) Not clear; young people are *not* dying so much of other causes (especially infectious diseases).
10 (a) Road (b) (i) 40 (ii) Yes (flu comes in epidemics) (c) 5
11 (b) **A** 0.000002 (journey distance is about 5700 km). **B** 0.00008 (distance cycled about 1120 km) **C** 0.00001 (train distance about 720 km, car distance about 2100 km). **D** 0.000002 (boat distance about 150 km, coach about 2100 km). **B** is about 40 times more dangerous than **A** or **D**.
12 (Answers depend on what you do with 'never go out' and 'when it gets dark') (a) 10 p.m. (b) 10.30 p.m. (c) Last three categories (d) Results contradict the assumption
13 (Answers depend on what you do about incomplete data) (a) (i) £1.46 (ii) £1.58 (iii) £1.60 (iv) £1.66 (v) 7.3 hours (vi) 10.8 hours (b) £1.46 (c) Assume e.g. 7 hours; £1.52 (d) Reasonably strong.
14 No; groups of friends likely to give biased sample, and sample is very small.
15 (a) 13 (b) (i) 63.6% (ii) 59.1% (c) No; one extra school makes a difference of about 2%.

FURTHER COURSEWORK TASKS

1) Some of the information used in Section C was collected from a survey of 136 fifteen-year-olds in a school in Leicestershire.

The questionnaire used is the resource sheet called *'What do you believe'*?

Use this questionnaire to find out what people in your school believe. Present your findings in the form of a report, with appropriate graphs and tables. You might want to compare some of your results with those for the Leicestershire school given in Section C.

You might find it useful to store your results in a database. You can then use the database to help you obtain your results.

This task provides students with the opportunity to use a variety of statistical techniques and also a computer database. *Pinpoint* (available for Archimedes and Nimbus only) is strongly recommended, because it deals with questionnaires and its structure mirrors the structure of this task.

2) Choose a topic about which you have strong opinions.

This topic might be to do with religion, or politics, or sport, or animal welfare, or the environment, or health, or something different.

Collect information about this topic which supports or contradicts your opinions.

This information might be the opinions of people in your school, or your family, or other people you know. To collect these opinions you can use a questionnaire.

Alternatively, this information might be obtained from books or magazines. It might be facts and figures about sporting records, or how animals are treated, or what is happening to the environment, and so on. It may include maps, diagrams and graphs.

Write a report in support of your opinions. Include in the report the statistics you have collected or the information you have discovered.

Make the best possible use of the information to support your case. On the other hand, your case will be made more strongly if you admit that some of the evidence you collect might *not* support your opinions.

You might find it useful to consider the advice given for the Further Coursework Tasks on page 177.

This task is popular with students; they usually have strong opinions! Asking them to investigate what they believe helps them to focus their work, so that they have a clear purpose in mind when they collect their information. Encourage them to start their reports with clear statements about what they believed before they started. Also encourage them to end their reports with comparisons between other people's beliefs and their own. These comparisons help to raise the level of the work, even where students have not collected much numerical data to analyse.

This task provides a good opportunity for group work. Students working in groups have to clarify and agree their beliefs before they start (or at least agree what the issues are); they can collect more information because the work can be shared; and they can also discuss what they think the results show.

This task, like the task in Chapter 21, provides a good opportunity for group presentations and for posters.

ASSESSING STUDENTS' COURSEWORK TASKS

Further Coursework Task 2

The pieces in this selection of work show what can be achieved at a higher level. In Chapter 21 there are some examples of statistical surveys done by students working at lower levels. All the extracts which follow are from pieces of work at level 8. Students were asked to choose their own topics and work in groups of three or four to collect their data. Then they each produced their own report.

The selections below show that students can give logical accounts of work with reasons for choices made (Ma1/8a).

Students who have clearly defined their goals and who state their opinions or beliefs clearly at the beginning of the report find it easier to construct an appropriate questionnaire and to draw meaningful conclusions.

> My beliefs are based upon general knowledge gained from reading and watching articles & programmes on my chosen subject. The sources of my information were
>
> T.V. programmes,
> T.V. documentaries
> Magazine Articles
> Readers Digest
>
> each of these sources gave a similar opinion on the subject of teenage smoking. These sources only helped to back up my opinions which are as follows:—
>
> THESE ARE:—
>
> Both smokers & non-smokers mix either voluntarily or by lack of choice/opportunity. This applies to both sexes.
>
> In ratio form it is evident that the female population has more smokers to non-smokers than the male population between the ages of 12 and 18 inc.
>
> The majority of adult smokers (above 16) first tried smoking cigarettes in their early teens, or prior to this age.
>
> We believe that it is the wish of the majority of both smokers & non-smokers, that smoking should be restricted in public places and totally banned on public transport.

> We believe that the majority of smokers are fully aware of the health hazards incurred through smoking e.g. cancer, many respritry diseases etc..,
>
> We believe that the majority of teenage smokers, smoke cigarettes for an image reason. We also believe that it is their opinion that smoking is a sign of maturity.
>
> We believe that smokers will generally associate with other smokers more easily than non-smokers.
>
> We believe that up to the age of 16 most people are quite capable of giving up smoking if they so wished, but due to reasons already mentioned most will take up the habit soon after.
>
> To each of these points I need to gain information so that I may prove or disprove my beliefs. The eight points I have listed have been gathered through investigation and research, some of the points are ones I would personally believe, even if I had not researched this subject, but the more statistical, & ratio beliefs were obtained from the sources I have already mentioned. To get actual statistics I needed to devise a way in which to get information from the general public. The most obvious and easy way to do this was to devise a questionnaire. The questionnaire will get me relevant information to show whether my beliefs are correct or incorrect.

A successful statistical survey needs a carefully selected sample of a reasonable size. This extract illustrates the thought that can be put into constructing an appropriate sample.

> **Who was asked**
>
> I went about this survey in a fair and unbiassed manner. I asked ten males and ten females from each of the five age groups to fill in this questionnaire. The five age groups are as follows—ten to twenty years old, twenty-one to thirty years old, thirty-one to fourty years old, forty-one to fifty years old and fifty years plus. This maybe fair due to age and sex of the people who answered it but it is unfair to say that it would be the results of a survey done in other part of Gr. Britain or the world so then it has to be said that the results are from people living within the boundaries of Leicestershire.

WHAT DO YOU BELIEVE?

Designing a successful questionnaire that elicits the responses required is not an easy task. Analysing the results of a large and complex survey requires good team work. The following extract draws attention to the difficulties experienced by a group of students.

> How we went about our survey
>
> First of all we had to be able to design a good and suitable questionnaire. The questions had to be easy to understand and easy to answer. (e.g. ticking boxes). Once we had thought of our questions we had to write them in a way, we wouldn't appear too nosey. We had 100 questionnaires printed off and they were all given out to people in this school between the ages of 14-16. This wasn't a very good way of giving them out because we didn't get any 16 year old females and we only got 4, 14 year old males so it made it very difficult to compare the answers.
>
> We did get a few problems occur. We had about 70 questionnaires returned. Some had to be thrown away because they had been defaced, the others either got lost or were thrown away.
>
> It also took a long time to collect together all the results because there were so many questions. Also one time when we were collecting results one girl lost all her questionnaires so thats what reduced us down to 64.
>
> I chose to put all my results in bar charts, pie charts and pictograms because it is a good and effective way of showing results.
>
> Another problem that occured was that we never had any questions where we could work out means, medians, averages etc so we didn't really have a lot of maths to work out apart from the pie charts and percentages.
>
> Before we could put our results into bar charts etc we had to collate all our answers. I was very pleased with some of the replies that we got back because it shows the maturity and immaturity of the people who answered the questions.

TASK MATHS

The following extract is from the work of a student who was finding out about people's attitudes to nuclear weapons. His data are difficult to deal with because of the lack of detailed knowledge among those surveyed. He has organised his results in a sensible way and has made intelligent use of the mode and the mean.

> **Q8** How long do you think it will take until anything will grow after the bomb has been dropped?
>
> Nº of people who estimated in this range
>
> | Range | Count | |
> |---|---|---|
> | 1 – 10 yrs | 12 | — Mode — I feel using this mode is |
> | 11 – 20 | 2 | the fairest average as some results |
> | 21 – 30 | 4 | were so far away from the rest |
> | 31 – 40 | 3 | — Mean   a mean would not |
> | 41 – 50 | 1 | be fair. |
> | 51 – 60 | 1 | |
> | 61 – 70 | | |
> | 71 – 80 | | |
> | 81 – 90 | | |
> | 91 – 100 | 3 | |
> | 100 – 200 | 1 | |
> | 200 – 500 | 3 | |
> | 501 + | 2 | |
> | Don't know | 18 | |
>
> What surprised me most about these results was how much they were spread out — they seem to be in two halves, 23 who thought it would take relatively little time and 9 who thought it would be a long time. On this question 22% agreed with me.
>
> **Q9** How much do you think Britain spends on nuclear missiles every year?
>
> £   No of people who estimated in this range
>
> | | |
> |---|---|
> | up to 1 million | 3 |
> | up to 10 million (more than 1 million) | 4 |
> | up to 100 million (more than 10 million) | 5 |
> | up to 1 billion (more than 100 million) | 1 |
> | 1 billion + | 11 |
> | Don't know | 26 |
>
> 12 of the 24 who answered thought it was less than 1 billion pounds but the figure is actually £2·4 billion, 10 people agreed with me in thinking this which makes it an even 50% split of people who know the actual figure or approximately how much.

A student's concluding remarks are perhaps the most significant part of this work. These remarks bring together what has been found out, provide comments on the significance of the results and how they relate to the student's opinions. The following extract is from the same piece of work as the first extract.

TELLING A COMPUTER WHAT TO DRAW

Equipment and Resources

For introduction to the task:
resource sheet 33, *Drawing shapes (Version A)*
resource sheet 34, *Drawing shapes (Version B)*

For Sections A, B and FCTs 1, 4, 5:
computer with *Logo* and/or *BASIC*

For Section B and FCT 3:
computer with *Moves* or *Geomat*

For FCT 2:
computer with *BASIC*, *Logo* or *Tilekit*

For FCT 5:
cubes (of any size)
Mathematics and Robotics (Central TV programme, 1991)

For FCT 6:
computer with *Spread* or a spreadsheet

Relevant Review Exercises

C31	*Properties of shapes*	page 107
D47	*Enlargement and similarity*	page 262
D49	*Transformations and matrices*	page 268
D50	*Trigonometry and triangles*	page 272
D51	*Coordinates and vectors*	page 274

National Curriculum Statements

Introduction to the task
4/4a1; 4/4a3; 4/4a4; 4/4c; 4/6b3

Section A
3/4a2; 4/4a1; 4/4a4; 4/5b1; 4/5c2; 4/6b2; 4/6b3; 4/6b4; 4/6b5; 4/7c; 4/8n; 4/8d

Section B
2/4a2; 2/5d3; 4/4a2; 4/4a4; 4/5c2; 4/6b1; 4/6b4; 4/8d; 4/9b; 4/10a3; 4/10a4

Further coursework tasks
4/9a2

Questions in Sections

Accessible to all students (no bars)	Somewhat harder (one bar)	More difficult (two bars)
Section A, 1–6	Section A, 7–10	Section A, 11–16
Section B, 1–7	Section B, 8–9	Section B, 10–18

Further Coursework Tasks

neutral: 1, 2, 4, 5
easier:
more difficult: 3, 6
There is also a more difficult task suggested at the end of Section B on page 228

TASK MATHS

INTRODUCTION TO THE TASK: HINTS

This is an activity for one lesson to be done in pairs. It is designed to introduce the notion that it is not easy to precisely specify a drawing in words and that telling a computer what to draw requires the development of notation and language. (Development of suitable language and notation is at the heart of many uses and applications of mathematics.) The drawings on the resource sheets have been designed to make points about this. It is insufficient to describe the first drawing on Version A as 'a square inside a circle'. Being able to talk about reflections or mirror images in connection with the second drawing on Version A helps a lot. Similarly, talking about half-turn symmetry is a help when describing the second drawing on Version B. Class discussion at the end of the activity could bring these points out: when describing a drawing look for key features, and particularly symmetry.

CODE FOR USE WITH QUESTIONS 1 TO 8 IN SECTION A

If using BBC *BASIC* on a computer students can draw the first pentagon in question 1 by typing the following:

```
MODE 1
MOVE 200,200
DRAW 600,200
DRAW 600,600
DRAW 400,800
DRAW 200,600
DRAW 200,200
```

If using Logotron *Logo* on the BBC or Archimedes computers students can draw the pentagon like this:

```
CS PU
SETPOS [20 20] PD
SETPOS [60 20]
SETPOS [60 60]
SETPOS [40 80]
SETPOS [20 60]
SETPOS [20 20]
```

If using Nimbus *Logo* students can draw the pentagon like this:

```
cs
line [20 20] [60 20] pc
line [60 20] [60 60] pc
line [60 60] [40 80] pc
line [40 80] [20 60] pc
line [20 60] [20 20] pc
```

Shapes defined by sides matrices, as in question 8, can be drawn with *BASIC* using the command PLOT. This is how the square of question 8 can be drawn:

```
MODE 1
MOVE 800,500 (to move to a suitable place to start)
PLOT 1,300,100
PLOT 1,-100,300
PLOT 1,-300,-100
PLOT 1,100,-300
```

Shapes defined by sides, matrices, as in question 8, can also be drawn with *Logo* if the following procedure is used.

For the BBC or Archimedes

```
TO VECTOR :SIDE
MAKE "X 100 * (FIRST :SIDE)
MAKE "Y 100 * (LAST :SIDE)
SETPOS (LIST XCOR + :X YCOR + :Y)
END
```

For the Nimbus

```
vector :side
make 'x 20 * (first :side)
make 'y 20 * (last :side)
line pos (xcor + :x) && (ycor + :y) pc
setpos (xcor + :x) && (ycor + :y)
```

Whatever make of machine you are using, the square of question 8 can now be drawn by typing the following:

VECTOR [3 1] VECTOR [-1 3] VECTOR [-3 -1] VECTOR [1 -3]

SECTION A: ANSWERS

1. (a) Rhombus (b) Isosceles trapezium (c) Square
2. (a) 6, 2 (b) 4, 5 (c) 3, 1
3. (a) −1 (b) 6 or −4 (c) 3 (d) 4, 9, −1 or 0
6. (a) $\begin{pmatrix} -4 & 0 & 4 & 0 \\ 0 & 4 & 0 & -4 \end{pmatrix}$ (b) $\begin{pmatrix} -2 & -2 & 2 & 2 \\ -2 & 2 & 2 & -2 \end{pmatrix}$

   (c) (i) $\begin{pmatrix} -2 & 0 & 2 & 0 \\ 0 & 2 & 0 & -2 \end{pmatrix}$ (ii) $\begin{pmatrix} -1 & -1 & 1 & 1 \\ -1 & 1 & 1 & -1 \end{pmatrix}$

   (iii) $\begin{pmatrix} -1 & 0 & 1 & 0 \\ 0 & 1 & 0 & -1 \end{pmatrix}$ (iv) $\begin{pmatrix} -0.5 & -0.5 & 0.5 & 0.5 \\ -0.5 & 0.5 & 0.5 & -0.5 \end{pmatrix}$

7. (a) $\begin{pmatrix} 4 & 7 & 10 \\ 10 & 4 & 13 \end{pmatrix}$ (b)(i) $\begin{pmatrix} 7 & 5.5 & 8.5 \\ 11.5 & 7 & 8.5 \end{pmatrix}$

   (ii) $\begin{pmatrix} 7.75 & 6.25 & 7 \\ 10 & 9.25 & 7.75 \end{pmatrix}$ (iii) $\begin{pmatrix} 7.38 & 7 & 6.63 \\ 8.88 & 9.63 & 8.5 \end{pmatrix}$

   (iv) $\begin{pmatrix} 7 & 7.19 & 6.81 \\ 8.69 & 9.25 & 9.06 \end{pmatrix}$ (v) $\begin{pmatrix} 6.91 & 7.09 & 7 \\ 8.88 & 8.97 & 9.16 \end{pmatrix}$

   (vi) $\begin{pmatrix} 6.95 & 7 & 7.05 \\ 9.01 & 8.92 & 9.06 \end{pmatrix}$

   (c) Triangle becomes a point at (7, 9).

8. (a)(i) $\sqrt{10}$ (ii) 10 (b) Isosceles (c)(i) Parallelogram (ii) Trapezium (iii) Rhombus
9. (a)(i) Equilateral triangle, side length 100
   (ii) Rectangle, side lengths 100 and 50
   (iii) Equilateral trapezium, side lengths 300, 200, 100, angle 60° (b) 200
11. (a) Make stem of T shorter or cross bits of T longer, e.g. by having FD 100 BK 200 FD 100 as fourth line
    (b) Several answers possible, but need trigonometry to do 'theoretically'.
12. Answers given assume the orientation implied on the page

Conclusions

My conclusions will be made on comparing results compiled by studying the questionnaires, with my beliefs outlined at the beginning of my project. I will be using my results to either prove or disprove my beliefs and to see if I have any evidence to back my beliefs up.

My first belief is basically an obvious one. It is obvious to all that both smokers & non-smokers will have to mix, whether they like it or not, in the community. Question 9 may brush on this subject by suggesting smokers will as a rule associate with other smokers in the community.

My second belief could be said to be more controversial. My belief was that the female population aged between 12-18 will as a percentage, have more regular smokers than the male population between the same ages. This belief was one of my own personal ones, it was not backed up by any form of national survey. My belief was somewhat supported by question 2. This question showed that 48% of the women questioned stated they smoked, compared to 46% of the men questioned. This was by no means a convincing piece of evidence to back up my belief but in my survey my belief was correct. — just!

My third belief relied on people answering the fifth question, unfortunately many people did not do this either because of its relatively obscure placement or through ignorance, so I was unable to come to a conclusion on whether my belief was true or not.

My fourth belief was that all people would accept a total ban of smoking in public. Question 4 proved to me that this was untrue. Over half the people we asked this question to, said that smoking should remain permitted in the forementioned places.

The point that all the people who answered this question were non-smokers I feel should be pointed out.

TASK MATHS

Guide to Chapter 24: **TELLING THE COMPUTER WHAT TO DRAW**

Outline

The task for this chapter is about ways of telling a computer how to draw shapes on its screen.

The introductory activity is designed to demonstrate the complexity of the task. Students work in pairs and each person tries to reproduce as accurately as possible a drawing described only in words by their partner.

Section A uses coordinate matrices to define simple shapes. These can be drawn on squared paper or a computer can be used. Use is made of the properties of triangles and quadrilaterals (including area) and of vectors. The second half of the section is about comparing the use of *Logo* and vectors for drawing a range of shapes. Questions make use of Pythagoras' theorem and basic trigonometry, and also introduce the sine and consine rules.

Section B is about how a shape can be transformed by changing its coordinates matrix. There are straightforward questions about translating, reflecting, rotating and enlarging shapes. A transformation program on a computer is useful in connection with the more difficult later questions, some of which also involve shearing. The last four questions are about the use of 2×2 matrices to define transformations, and about combining transformations.

There are six Further Coursework Tasks and students can also explore combined transformations, as suggested at the end of Section B. Three tasks are about using *Logo* or *BASIC* or software packages to draw symmetrical designs or tessellations. One task explores how robots 'see' by using matrices to determine the position of solid objects. The sixth task is about determining triangles using whole numbers.

Strategies

Students work in pairs for the Introductory Task which requires only one lesson. For questions 1 to 8 of Section A students can use either squared paper or a computer. A box before the answers to Section A provides help with the computer code to do this.

Work from question 9 onwards in Section A is greatly enhanced if *Logo* is available.

When working on Section B it is helpful for students to have a computer available for questions involving *Logo* procedures. It is also helpful to have a geometrical tranformations program such as *Geomat* or *Moves* available, particularly for questions 16 onwards. Ideally, students will work in twos or threes with such a program.

Fairly intensive use can be made of computers in this chapter. If your school has computer rooms this is a good opportunity to make use of them throughout the sections and FCTs.

matrix multiplication which are relevant to this context.

> 4) When you draw a polygon with *Logo* you usually start from a corner. This makes it hard to create patterns like these: 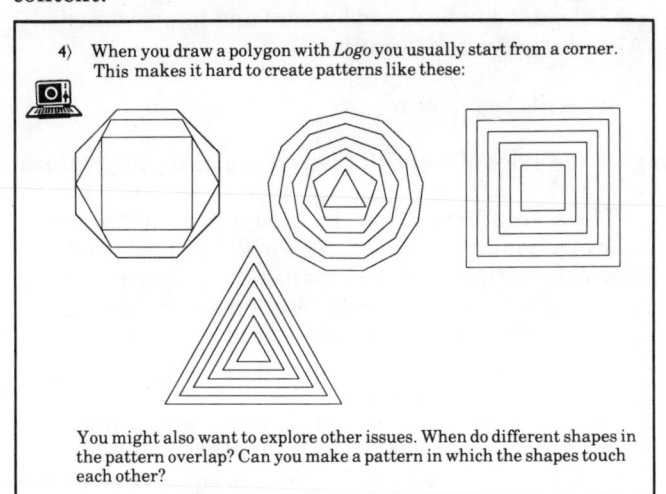
>
> You might also want to explore other issues. When do different shapes in the pattern overlap? Can you make a pattern in which the shapes touch each other?

This task is similar to FCT 1, but a particular focus has been suggested: nested polygons.

It is clearly not important that students work at the focus exactly as suggested: they might want to specify their own goals.

As with FCT 1, write-ups should describe the process students go through to produce their patterns and include the appropriate code.

> 5) Some computer robots can recognise the shapes of objects. Here is one way they can do this.
>
> Figure 3 shows a robot 'looking' at a cube 'face on'.
>
> The robot fires lasers at 1 centimetre intervals horizontally and vertically, and these tell it how far away different points on the cube's surface are 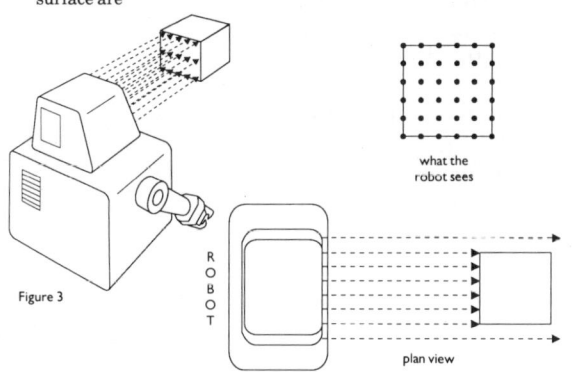
>
> Figure 3
>
> Because the cube is 'face on', all the points are the same distance (10 cm) from the robot's front. So the robot records what it sees like this.
>
> $$\begin{pmatrix} 10 & 10 & 10 & 10 & 10 & 10 \\ 10 & 10 & 10 & 10 & 10 & 10 \\ 10 & 10 & 10 & 10 & 10 & 10 \\ 10 & 10 & 10 & 10 & 10 & 10 \\ 10 & 10 & 10 & 10 & 10 & 10 \\ 10 & 10 & 10 & 10 & 10 & 10 \end{pmatrix}$$
>
> Figure 4
>
> Figure 4 shows the robot looking at the cube after it has been rotated a bit about a vertical axis.
>
> The front edge of the cube is still 10 cm from the robot. 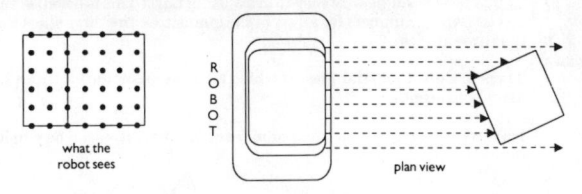
>
> This time the robot records what it sees like this.
>
> $$\begin{pmatrix} 14 & 12 & 10 & 10.5 & 11 & 11.5 & 12 \\ 14 & 12 & 10 & 10.5 & 11 & 11.5 & 12 \\ 14 & 12 & 10 & 10.5 & 11 & 11.5 & 12 \\ 14 & 12 & 10 & 10.5 & 11 & 11.5 & 12 \\ 14 & 12 & 10 & 10.5 & 11 & 11.5 & 12 \\ 14 & 12 & 10 & 10.5 & 11 & 11.5 & 12 \end{pmatrix}$$
>
> Investigate what the robot sees when the cube is rotated by different amounts.
>
> You might find it helpful to make plan views on squared paper, or to use trigonometry.
>
> Investigate what the robot sees when the cube is rotated about a vertical **and** a horizontal axis.

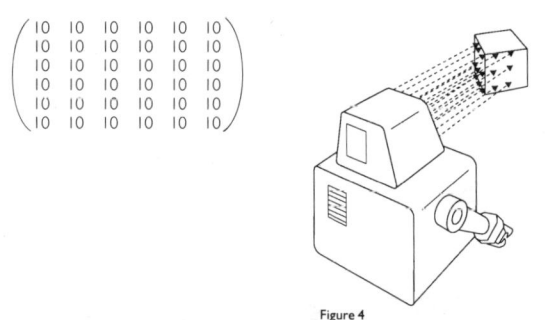

The 15-minute TV programme '*Mathematics and Robotics*' would make a good introduction to this project. Most students will probably want to work with an actual cube, at least initially.

This task suits students working at a wide range of different levels. Some students can keep their cube with one face flat on the table, and can obtain matrices by drawing and measuring. The cube can be translated as well as being rotated. Their write-ups could illustrate each position of the cube by the use of two drawings (as in the Student's Book): what the robot sees, and a plan view.

Some students will be able to calculate the matrices, using trigonometry. Turning the cube about a horizontal axis instead of a vertical axis is not too complicated if you start with the robot looking directly at a face of the cube and rotate the cube about a horizontal axis which is either perpendicular to or parallel to that face.

If, on the other hand, you start with the robot looking at a vertical edge of the cube and rotate about a horizontal axis as shown below, the situation is more complicated. It is an ambitious exercise in 3-D trigonometry to calculate the matrix for the position where what the robot sees has 3-fold symmetry. (It is not impossible if you consider the geometry of the tetrahedron whose vertices are the nearest four vertices of the cube.)

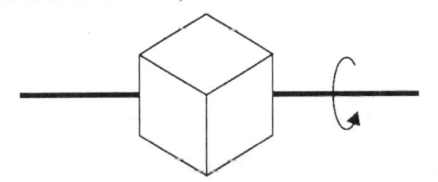

TASK MATHS

> 6) Equilateral triangles are easy to draw using *Logo*. This is because you can use whole numbers for all six of the quantities: the three sides **and** the three angles.
>
> There are **no** other triangles for which all three sides and all three angles are whole numbers.
>
> Investigate ways in which four or more of the quantities can be whole numbers. 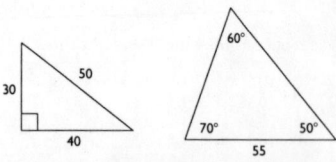
>
> One way in which this can happen is for one angle of the triangle to be 60° or 120°, and for the sides all to be integers. You could use the cosine rule with a spreadsheet to help you find triangles of this type. 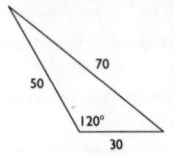
>
> You might find it helpful to refer to question 11 on page 153 of Book 4 of this series.

This task provides the opportunity to make use of Pythagoras' theorem and also trigonometry, including the sine and cosine rules.

There is an infinite number of right-angled triangles with three sides which are integers. Suitable sets of sides can be found by trial and improvement. Alternatively, the formulae

$$m^2 - n^2, 2mn, m^2 + n^2$$

give the sides of right-angled triangles for any values of m and n.

The cosine formula can be used to obtain the third side of a triangle with an angle of 60° or 120°. In the first case, if the sides next to the 60° angle are a and b, the third side is $a^2 + b^2 - ab$. Students can set up the program *Spread* or a spreadsheet to help them investigate which values of a and b give an integer value for the third side.

The **easiest** way to arrange for four of the quantities involved to be integers is to specify three angles and a side. If two of those three angles are equal it is straightforward to ensure that **five** of the quantities are integers. As stated in the question, the only way to make all six quantities integers is to make the triangle equilateral. This is because 60° is the only integer angle between 0° and 90° whose cosine is rational.

ASSESSING STUDENTS' COURSEWORK TASKS

Further Coursework Task 3

Doing this task as a piece of coursework helps students to understand more fully the difficult ideas introduced in questions 15 onwards in Section B. In the following extracts the students used *Geomat* to help them. If this topic is not taught to the students but they are asked to explore it for themselves then they can provide evidence for Ma1/10a.

In the first extract the student is working out the significance of the value of k in the matrix

$$\begin{pmatrix} 1 & k \\ 0 & 1 \end{pmatrix}.$$

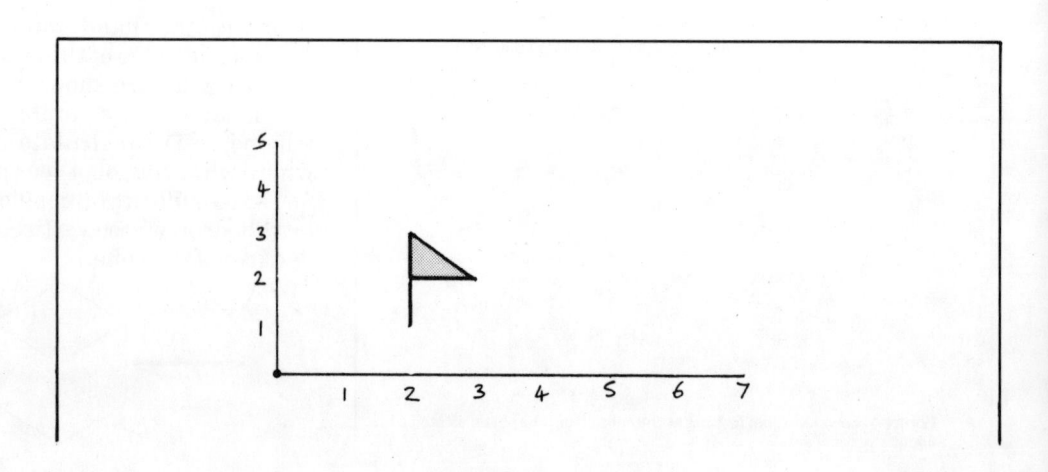

(a) (ii) $\begin{Bmatrix} 20 & 14.1 & -20 & -14.1 \\ 0 & 14.1 & 0 & -14.1 \end{Bmatrix}$

(b) (ii) $\begin{Bmatrix} 17.3 & -17.3 & 0 \\ 10 & 10 & -20 \end{Bmatrix}$

13 (a) (i) $\begin{Bmatrix} 40 & -40 & 0 \\ 0 & 30 & -30 \end{Bmatrix}$

(ii) One possible procedure is
FD 30
RT 127
FD 50
RT 143
FD 40
RT 90

(b) (i) $\begin{Bmatrix} 20 & 40 & -40 & -20 \\ 20 & -20 & -20 & 20 \end{Bmatrix}$

(ii) One possible procedure is
REPEAT 2 [FD 28.3 RT 72 FD 44.7 RT 127]

14 Possible procedures are
(a) FD 58.5   (b) FD 20
   RT 140   RT 120
   FD 58.5   FD 20
   RT 110   RT 45
   FD 40   FD 40
   RT 110   RT 151
                   FD 40
                   RT 45

15 (a) Missing side 70, angles 82, 38 (b) Missing side 127, angles 29, 21 (c) Angles 120, 32, 28 (d) Angles 78, 44, 57 (e) Angles 86, 81, 73

16 Assume side length 100. Lengths of diagonals are 162.

SECTION B: ANSWERS

1 (a) $\begin{pmatrix} 2 & 6 & 6 & 4 & 2 \\ 5 & 5 & 9 & 11 & 9 \end{pmatrix}$ (b) $\begin{pmatrix} -2 & 2 & 2 & 0 & -2 \\ 5 & 5 & 9 & 11 & 9 \end{pmatrix}$

(c) $\begin{pmatrix} 6 & 10 & 10 & 8 & 6 \\ -4 & -4 & 0 & 2 & 0 \end{pmatrix}$

2 Typical answer is $\begin{pmatrix} 1179 & 1279 & 1179 & 1079 \\ 623 & 823 & 1023 & 823 \end{pmatrix}$

3 One possible answer is $\begin{pmatrix} 200 & 800 & 600 & 200 \\ 100 & 100 & 500 & 500 \end{pmatrix}$

5 (a) $\begin{pmatrix} 1 & 5 & 3 & 1 \\ 12 & 10 & 8 & 8 \end{pmatrix}$ (b) $\begin{pmatrix} 1 & -3 & -1 & 1 \\ 4 & 6 & 8 & 8 \end{pmatrix}$

(c) $\begin{pmatrix} 7 & 5 & 3 & 3 \\ 10 & 6 & 8 & 10 \end{pmatrix}$

6 (a) $\begin{pmatrix} 1 & 13 & 7 & 1 \\ 4 & 10 & 16 & 16 \end{pmatrix}$ (b) $\begin{pmatrix} -7 & 5 & -1 & -7 \\ 0 & 6 & 12 & 12 \end{pmatrix}$

7 (a) $\begin{pmatrix} 9 & 5 & 7 & 9 \\ 8 & 6 & 4 & 4 \end{pmatrix}$ (b) $\begin{pmatrix} 1 & -1 & -3 & -3 \\ 4 & 8 & 6 & 4 \end{pmatrix}$

8 (a) $\begin{pmatrix} 7 & 3 & 5 & 7 \\ 10 & 8 & 6 & 6 \end{pmatrix}$ (b) (i) $\begin{pmatrix} 1 & 5 & 7 & 7 & 3 & 1 \\ 4 & 6 & 6 & 10 & 8 & 8 \end{pmatrix}$

(ii) Many possibilities

10 (a) Yes; change the heading of the turtle before you start (b) No (c) Yes; change the position of the turtle before you start (d) No

11 (a) $\begin{pmatrix} -4 & -4 & -4 \\ 2 & 2 & 2 \end{pmatrix}$ (b) No

(c) Yes; need more columns.

12 (a) $(x,y) \to (x,-y)$ (b) $(x,y) \to (-x,y)$ (c) $(x,y) \to (y,x)$ (d) $(x,y) \to (-y,-x)$

13 (a) $(x,y) \to (-x,-y)$ (b) $(x,y) \to (-y,x)$ (c) $(x,y) \to (y,-x)$

14 (a) $(x,y) \to (2x,2y)$ (b) $(x,y) \to (-3x,-3y)$ (c) $(x,y) \to (kx,ky)$

15 (a) $(x,y) \to (x+2y,y)$ (b) $(x,y) \to (x,2x+y)$

16 (a) Enlargement, centre origin, scale factor 3 (b) Half turn about origin (or enlargement, scale factor -1) (c) Rotation, centre origin, quarter turn anticlockwise (d) Shear, invariant line y-axis, factor 3 (e) Reflection in x-axis (f) Reflection in $y = x$ (g) Stretch, invariant line y-axis, scale factor 2.

17 (a) $\begin{pmatrix} 0 & -1 \\ -1 & 0 \end{pmatrix}$ (b) $\begin{pmatrix} 4 & 0 \\ 0 & 1 \end{pmatrix}$ (c) $\begin{pmatrix} -2 & 0 \\ 0 & -2 \end{pmatrix}$

(d) $\begin{pmatrix} 0.5 & -0.87 \\ 0.87 & 0.5 \end{pmatrix}$ (e) $\begin{pmatrix} 0 & -2 \\ 2 & 0 \end{pmatrix}$

18 (a) Reflection in line AB (b) Translation with vector $(-3\ 4)$ (c) Rotation 60° clockwise about C (d) Enlargement, centre D, scale factor -0.5 (e) Shear, factor -2, invariant line EF.

19 (a) Translation with vector $(-1\ -7)$ (b) Half-turn about B (c) Clockwise rotation of 60° about D (d) Translation, direction 45° to EF, distance 2 × length of EF (e) Reflection in line at 45° to GH (through G) (f) Enlargement with scale factor 6 through a different point.

FURTHER COURSEWORK TASKS

There are some easier questions about combined transformations in Review Exercise 49 on page 268.

A wider exploration of the effect of combining two or more transformations would make a suitable Further Coursework Task.

The suggestion above is made at the end of Section B. Some students will benefit greatly from being able to use a transformations program (such as *Geomat* or *Moves*) on a computer. Others might want to pursue the task entirely by producing accurate drawings and rough sketches. The ideas in question 19 of Section B will help students to get started. The statements made in this question are specific: students should be able to make more general statements, and to prove them in some cases. Results that might be obtained include the following.

A translation $\begin{pmatrix} a \\ b \end{pmatrix}$ followed by a translation $\begin{pmatrix} c \\ d \end{pmatrix}$ is a translation $\begin{pmatrix} a + c \\ b + d \end{pmatrix}$.

Successive reflections in two parallel lines a distance d apart produce a translation through $2d$ at right angles to the lines of reflection.

Successive reflections in lines intersecting in an angle a produce a rotation through $2a$ about the point of intersection.

Successive rotations through a and b about the same point produce a rotation through $a + b$ about that point.

Successive enlargements with the same centre and with scale factors a and b produce an enlargement with the same centre and scale factor ab.

Successive rotations about *different* points produce in general a rotation. (Exceptionally they produce a translation, if the total angle turned through is a multiple of 360. A special case of this is that two half-turn rotations about different points produce a translation through twice the distance between the points.)

Successive enlargements with two different centres produce in general an enlargement about a third centre. (Exceptionally they produce a translation, if the product of the scale factors is 1.)

Students might be able to describe constructions for finding the centres in the last two cases above. They might also consider other combinations: reflections with rotations, or translations, or enlargements; enlargements with rotations, or translations; and perhaps also stretches with stretches and shears with shears.

> 1) Use *Logo* to make some symmetrical designs on the computer screen.
>
> The *Logo* you are using might allow you to use several turtles at once. If so, you might want to use several turtles to create your design.

Write-ups of this task should contain *Logo* code and print-outs.

Students should describe the process they go through to produce the finished drawings and include code (and perhaps print-outs) demonstrating initial errors. It is easy when using *Logo* to get pleasing and apparently impressive designs by accident. So print-outs unsupported by code **and** explanations are of little value. Students need to demonstrate that they are in control of the situations: in other words, that they know how to vary their code slightly to produce other patterns of a similar type which they could specify in advance.

Multiple turtles, if available, can be used to vary the challenge.

> 2) Investigate how to draw tessellations of various kinds on the computer's screen.
>
> You can use *Logo* or *BASIC*. Alternatively, you can use *Tilekit* or another tiling package.

There are many ways of creating tessellations (see Chapter 6). This task focuses on the use of a computer. As with FCT 1, write-ups should describe the process students go through to produce the tessellations and, if *Logo* is used, include the appropriate code. There is an opportunity for students to demonstrate their grasp of concepts concerning angles round a point, interior and exterior angles of polygons, and perhaps also the ability to look at all possibilities within given constraints.

> 3) The matrix
>
> $\begin{pmatrix} 2 & 0 \\ 0 & 2 \end{pmatrix}$
>
> produces an enlargement with scale factor 2, and the matrix
>
> $\begin{pmatrix} 1 & 2 \\ 0 & 1 \end{pmatrix}$
>
> produces a shear with the *x*-axis as the invariant line.
>
> Use a transformations program on a computer to investigate the transformations produced by different matrices.
>
> You might want to start by restricting yourself to matrices of a particular type. For example, you could look at matrices where all four numbers are either 1 or 0. Or where all four numbers are either 1, −1 or 0.

This task is hard work unless a computer program such as *Geomat* is used. *Geomat* is better than *Moves* for this task because it allows the user to specify a matrix and then indicates the transformation the matrix produces.

Students need to be strongly encouraged to start with matrices of a particular type, such as those consisting of 0s and 1s as suggested in the task. The alternative, typing in four numbers more or less at random, is unlikely to give students a feel for what is going on. There are many different things that students can find out: some of these are hinted at in questions 16 and 17 of Section B.

Some students might want to look at the matrices of combined transformations (and combine this task with the task suggested at the end of Section B). Such students might then look at some of the properties of

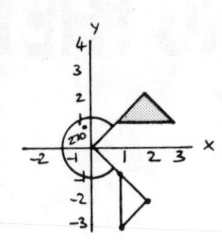

TELLING A COMPUTER WHAT TO DRAW

Matrix $\begin{pmatrix} 0 & 1 \\ -1 & 0 \end{pmatrix}$ Old position $\begin{pmatrix} 1 & 3 & 2 \\ 1 & 1 & 2 \end{pmatrix}$ New position $\begin{pmatrix} 1 & 1 & 2 \\ -1 & -3 & -2 \end{pmatrix}$ Y
-X

This is also rotation. Again the centre of rotation is 0,0. The angle is 270°

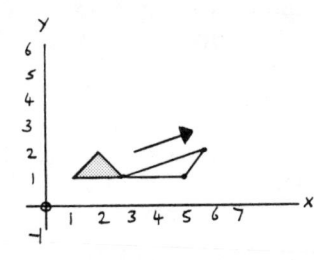

Matrix $\begin{pmatrix} 1 & 2 \\ 0 & 1 \end{pmatrix}$ Old position $\begin{pmatrix} 1 & 3 & 2 \\ 1 & 1 & 2 \end{pmatrix}$ New position $\begin{pmatrix} 3 & 5 & 6 \\ 1 & 1 & 2 \end{pmatrix}$ X+2Y
Y

This is shear with Y=0, and the shear factor of 2.

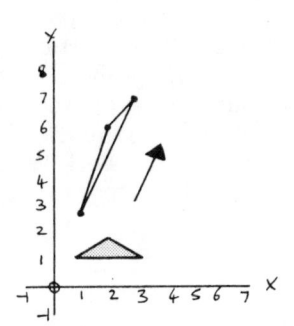

Matrix $\begin{pmatrix} 1 & 0 \\ 2 & 1 \end{pmatrix}$ Old position $\begin{pmatrix} 1 & 3 & 2 \\ 1 & 1 & 2 \end{pmatrix}$ New position $\begin{pmatrix} 1 & 3 & 2 \\ 3 & 7 & 6 \end{pmatrix}$ X
2X+Y

This is also shear, with x=0 and the shear factor 2

Transformation	Matrix (K is any number)	Old Position	New position
Enlargement Centre 0,0 Scale k	$\begin{pmatrix} K & 0 \\ 0 & K \end{pmatrix}$	$\begin{pmatrix} x \\ y \end{pmatrix}$	$\begin{pmatrix} Kx \\ Ky \end{pmatrix}$
Stretch x=0 Factor k	$\begin{pmatrix} K & 0 \\ 0 & 1 \end{pmatrix}$	$\begin{pmatrix} x \\ y \end{pmatrix}$	$\begin{pmatrix} Kx \\ y \end{pmatrix}$
Stretch Y=0 Factor K	$\begin{pmatrix} 1 & 0 \\ 0 & K \end{pmatrix}$	$\begin{pmatrix} x \\ y \end{pmatrix}$	$\begin{pmatrix} x \\ Ky \end{pmatrix}$
Reflection Y=0	$\begin{pmatrix} 1 & 0 \\ 0 & -1 \end{pmatrix}$	$\begin{pmatrix} x \\ y \end{pmatrix}$	$\begin{pmatrix} x \\ -y \end{pmatrix}$
Reflection X=0	$\begin{pmatrix} -1 & 0 \\ 0 & 1 \end{pmatrix}$	$\begin{pmatrix} x \\ y \end{pmatrix}$	$\begin{pmatrix} -x \\ y \end{pmatrix}$
Reflection x=y	$\begin{pmatrix} 0 & 1 \\ 1 & 0 \end{pmatrix}$	$\begin{pmatrix} x \\ y \end{pmatrix}$	$\begin{pmatrix} y \\ x \end{pmatrix}$
Reflection x=-y	$\begin{pmatrix} 0 & -1 \\ -1 & 0 \end{pmatrix}$	$\begin{pmatrix} x \\ y \end{pmatrix}$	$\begin{pmatrix} -y \\ -x \end{pmatrix}$
Rotation Centre 0,0 Angle 90°	$\begin{pmatrix} 0 & -1 \\ 1 & 0 \end{pmatrix}$	$\begin{pmatrix} x \\ y \end{pmatrix}$	$\begin{pmatrix} -y \\ x \end{pmatrix}$
Rotation Centre 0,0 Angle 180°	$\begin{pmatrix} -1 & 0 \\ 0 & -1 \end{pmatrix}$	$\begin{pmatrix} x \\ y \end{pmatrix}$	$\begin{pmatrix} -x \\ -y \end{pmatrix}$
Rotation Centre 0,0 Angle 270°	$\begin{pmatrix} 0 & 1 \\ -1 & 0 \end{pmatrix}$	$\begin{pmatrix} x \\ y \end{pmatrix}$	$\begin{pmatrix} y \\ -x \end{pmatrix}$
Shear Y=0 Factor K	$\begin{pmatrix} 1 & K \\ 0 & 1 \end{pmatrix}$	$\begin{pmatrix} x \\ y \end{pmatrix}$	$\begin{pmatrix} x+Ky \\ y \end{pmatrix}$
Shear X=0 Factor K	$\begin{pmatrix} 1 & 0 \\ K & 1 \end{pmatrix}$	$\begin{pmatrix} x \\ y \end{pmatrix}$	$\begin{pmatrix} x \\ Kx+y \end{pmatrix}$

TASK MATHS

Guide to Chapter 25: **GETTING THE MOST OUT OF LIFE**

Outline

The task for this chapter is maximising.
In the introductory activity students are asked to make a container with the biggest possible volume using only a sheet of A4 paper and adhesive tape.

Section A begins with problems about fencing off greatest possible areas. These are followed by a number of geometrical problems about maximising, some of which need Pythagoras' theorem, trigonometry (including the $\frac{1}{2}ab\sin C$ formula) and the volumes of solid shapes.

Section B is about maximising answers to problems involving the use of numbers. There are some straightforward questions about making biggest or smallest numbers according to certain rules. Later questions involve the use of trial and improvement, properties of multiplication, finding maximum and minimum values of functions from their graphs, and using the technique of completing the square.

There are five Further Coursework Tasks. They are all about maximising and most of them build on ideas first introduced in either Section A or Section B.

Strategies

The introductory activity is best done practically, because shapes which are not neat and tidy produce the biggest capacities. Class or group discussion is helpful with some questions in Section A, particularly question 12 (using geostrips) and question 13 (using circles of paper). Questions 1 to 4 of Section B provide a good focus for a class discussion. A coursework task could be based on questions 5 to 9. The rest of the questions in Section B are more challenging and some are very difficult unless a graph-drawing facility on a computer or graphical calculator, or a spreadsheet, is used. It is a good idea to use a class discussion to pull together the ideas students have worked on in Section B.

Equipment and Resources

For introduction to the task:
sheets of A4 paper
adhesive tape and/or stapler
measuring jug
peas, beans, rice or water (to measure volume)

For Sections A:
geostrips

For Sections A and B and FCTs 1 and 5:
graphical calculator or graph-drawing program on a computer
Spread or a spreadsheet

For FCT 2:
Spread or a spreadsheet

For FCT 3:
tennis balls

For FCT 4:
cardboard circles

I will now try another series, this time using...

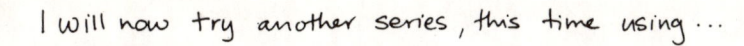

$\begin{pmatrix} 1 & x \\ 0 & 1 \end{pmatrix}$ $\begin{pmatrix} 1 & 0 \\ 0 & 1 \end{pmatrix}$ ▷ it stays the same

$\begin{pmatrix} 1 & 1 \\ 0 & 1 \end{pmatrix}$ ▷▷

$\begin{pmatrix} 1 & 2 \\ 0 & 1 \end{pmatrix}$ ▷ ◁

$\begin{pmatrix} 1 & 3 \\ 0 & 1 \end{pmatrix}$ ▷ ◁

Heres the table for the last series.

X	A	B	C	D
0	0	0	0	0
1	1	2	3	2
2	2	4	6	4
3	3	6	9	6
4	4	8	12	8
5	5	10	15	10

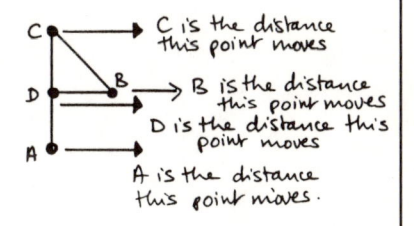

C is the distance this point moves
B is the distance this point moves
D is the distance this point moves
A is the distance this point moves.

After comparing this series with other commands, I have found out that this is a shear transformation, and x is the shear factor and the invariant line is $y=0$

The following extract illustrates the difficulties students face when describing the transformations that relate to given matrices, even when apparently simple matrices are chosen.

Here are some more which are not so easy to explain.

$\begin{pmatrix} -1 & 1 \\ 1 & -1 \end{pmatrix}$

I would think this is some form of stretch

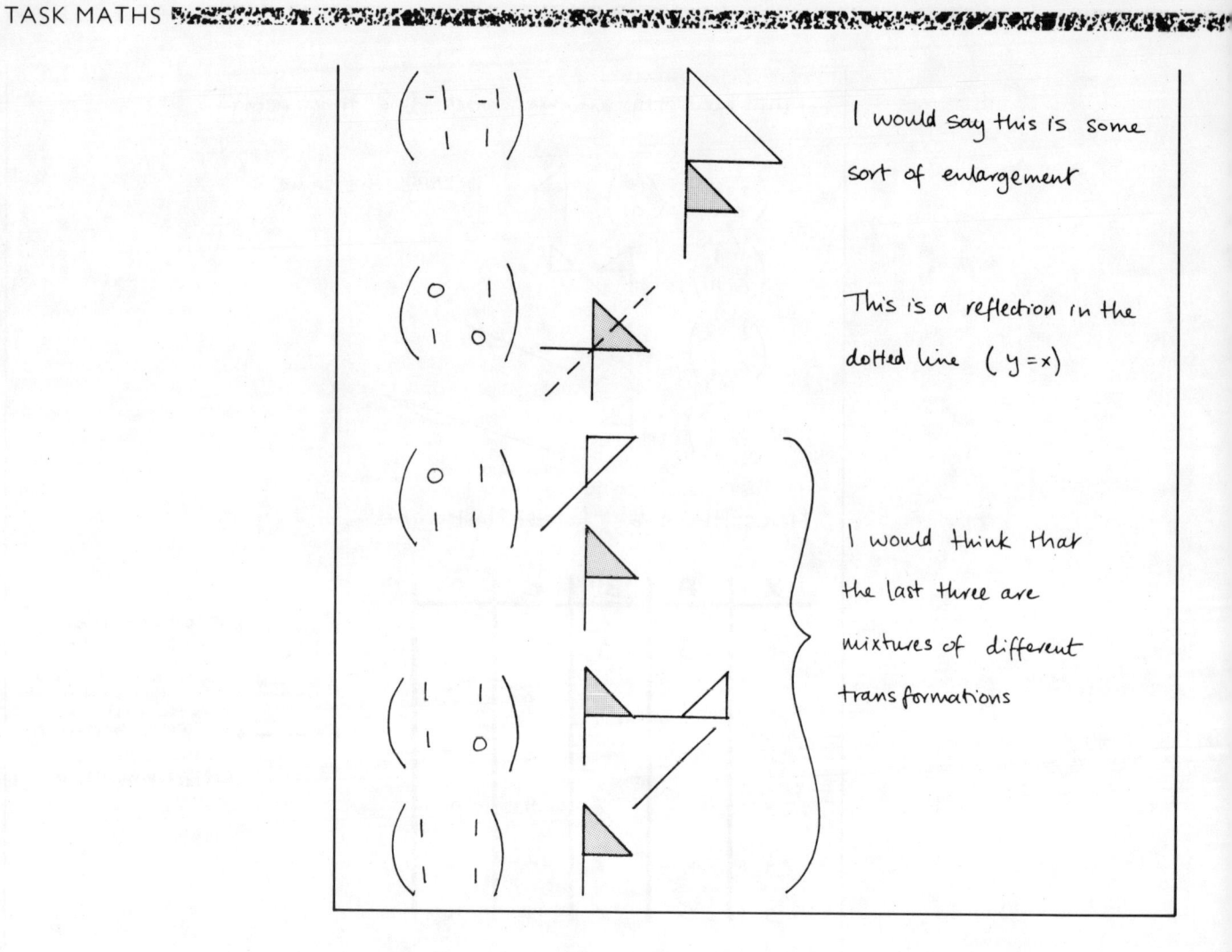

TASK MATHS

$\begin{pmatrix} -1 & -1 \\ 1 & 1 \end{pmatrix}$ — I would say this is some sort of enlargement

$\begin{pmatrix} 0 & 1 \\ 1 & 0 \end{pmatrix}$ — This is a reflection in the dotted line ($y = x$)

$\begin{pmatrix} 0 & 1 \\ 1 & 1 \end{pmatrix}$

$\begin{pmatrix} 1 & 1 \\ 1 & 0 \end{pmatrix}$ — I would think that the last three are mixtures of different transformations

$\begin{pmatrix} 1 & 1 \\ 1 & 1 \end{pmatrix}$

In this final extract the student has made commendable use of Section B to help her choose a set of matrices which are likely to lead her to a successful classification of the transformations. She first uses particular examples, noting their effect on a triangle. She then generalises her results, summarising them in a table.

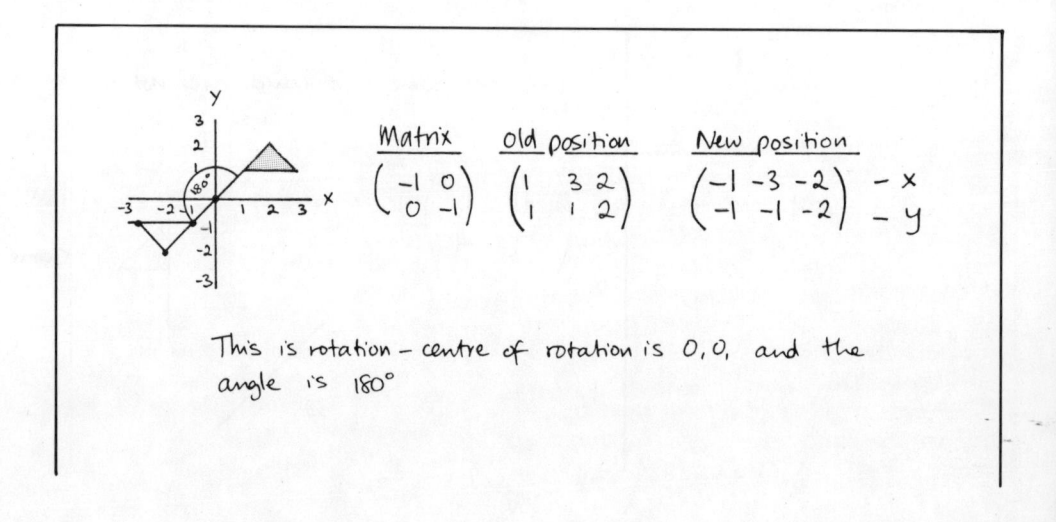

Matrix	Old position	New position
$\begin{pmatrix} -1 & 0 \\ 0 & -1 \end{pmatrix}$	$\begin{pmatrix} 1 & 3 & 2 \\ 1 & 1 & 2 \end{pmatrix}$	$\begin{pmatrix} -1 & -3 & -2 \\ -1 & -1 & -2 \end{pmatrix}$ — x — y

This is rotation — centre of rotation is 0,0, and the angle is 180°

GETTING THE MOST OUT OF LIFE

When there are four pieces of equal area there are four (essentially different) arrangements.

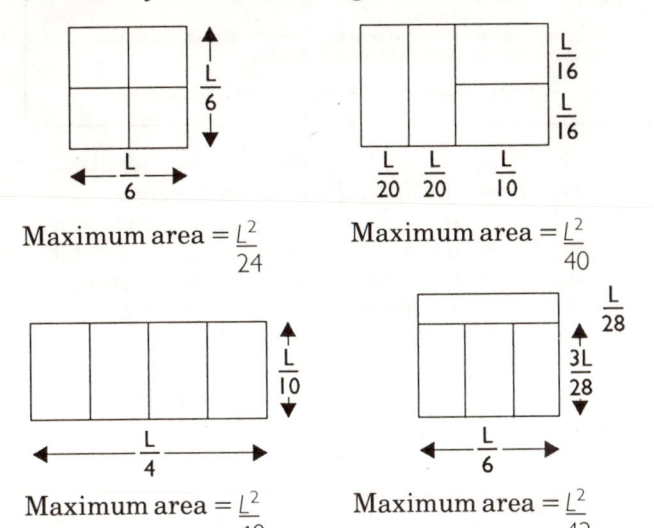

Maximum area = $\frac{L^2}{24}$

Maximum area = $\frac{L^2}{40}$

Maximum area = $\frac{L^2}{40}$

Maximum area = $\frac{L^2}{42}$

When there are five pieces there are seven different arrangements.

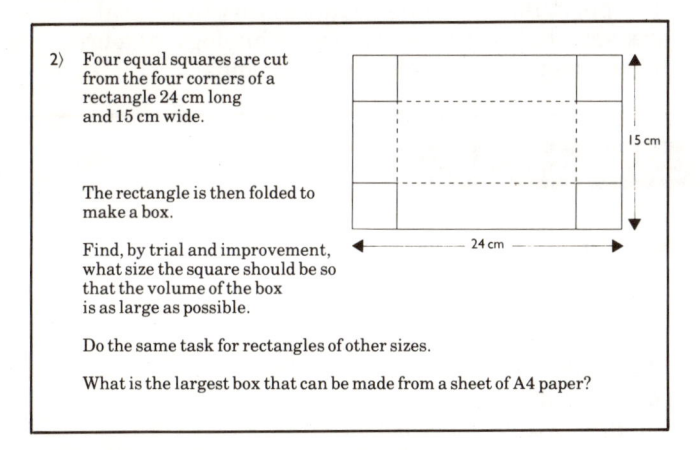

> 2) Four equal squares are cut from the four corners of a rectangle 24 cm long and 15 cm wide.
>
> The rectangle is then folded to make a box.
>
> Find, by trial and improvement, what size the square should be so that the volume of the box is as large as possible.
>
> Do the same task for rectangles of other sizes.
>
> What is the largest box that can be made from a sheet of A4 paper?

Many students find it helpful at first to actually cut the pieces out and make the box. This helps them to visualise what is happening. Once they have done this a couple of times they can manage without.

Spread or a spreadsheet can be used for this task. Alternatively, students could plot the graph of, for example,

$$y = x(24 - 2x)(15 - 2x)$$

and find out where the maximum is.

Some students will need reminding that the answer is not necessarily a whole number.

For a rectangle measuring 24 cm by 15 cm, removing squares of side 3 cm produces the maximum volume of 486 cm³. For a sheet of A4 paper (29.73 cm by 21.02 cm theoretically) squares of side 4.05 cm should be removed (4 cm is a reasonable approximation).

The maximum volume for a rectangle with dimensions m and n is achieved by removing squares of side

$$\frac{(m+n) - \sqrt{m^2 - mn + n^2}}{6}$$

Obviously students will not come up with this general result, which requires the use of calculus to derive. It is given here to make it easier for you to check students' results.

If students look at squares instead of rectangles it is much easier to spot the result that the maximum volume is obtained by removing four squares with side $\frac{1}{6}$ of the side of starting square.

The rectangle case does **not** produce a tidy result. What it does offer students is the opportunity to sort out how they are going to work, use trial and improvement and to consolidate work on volume and algebra.

> 3) Design a container which will hold 4 tennis balls. Make the surface area of the container as small as possible.
>
> Try the same task for different numbers of tennis balls.

This needs to be tackled practically, at least initially. Measuring just one tennis ball is not enough. Putting four in a row might need more room than four times the diameter of one ball. Obvious shapes to use for the box are cylinder and cuboids, but prisms with triangular or hexagonal sections could be used. Students could also consider a tetrahedral box.

Some students might want to concentrate on working largely experimentally and making one container well from card. Others will prefer to do a variety of mock-ups and then concentrate on calculating the results rather than on making the containers. (Some students are capable of working theoretically with little experimentation. Others *can* work theoretically after they have created some mock-ups which help them to visualise what is required.)

As well as looking at surface area of containers students can also consider the percentage of space 'wasted'. This provides an opportunity for students to demonstrate their skills with harder mensuration.

Students' write-ups can include sketches of nets, might include actual models, and can obviously show any calculations of surface areas and volumes.

A tennis ball has a diameter of somewhat less than 7 cm. Allowing 7 cm probably means that the balls will fit into the container designed.

On this assumption the surface area of a suitable cylinder ($r = 3.5$ cm, $h = 28$ cm) is about 690 cm². The volume of one tennis ball is about 180 cm³. About 33% of space is 'wasted' because the volume of the cylinder is about 1080 cm³.

The surface area of a square-based box (14 cm by 14 cm by 7 cm) is about 784 cm². About 48% of space is 'wasted'.

The surface area of a tetrahedron (edge length 24.1 cm) is 1009 cm². About 57% of space is 'wasted'.

TASK MATHS

4) Figure 4 shows 7 circles fitted into a rectangle. Each circle has a radius of 3 cm and the circles do not overlap.

Figure 4

What is the *smallest* possible area for a rectangle into which you can fit 2 circles? 3 circles? 4 circles? ...

We regard this task as a **harder** coursework task, because working experimentally does not seem to produce accurate enough results. Consequently, students need skills with trigonometry to calculate results. Students need to realise that two arrangements need to be considered: where the centres form a square grid, and where they form an isometric grid. This links with question 8 in Review Exercise A14, Sines and cosines, in Book 4.

The task only becomes really challenging if a large number of circles are considered. One way of refocusing this task is to look at the smallest number of circles (or rows) needed before a triangular grid is more efficient than a square grid.

5) Question 14 of Section A was about a channel made by bending a strip of metal 12 inches wide.

Investigate different ways of bending the metal to make a channel. Compare the cross-sections of several channels.

Try to make the cross-section of the channel as large as possible.

This task provides a good opportunity for students to use spreadsheets (or *Spread*) or alternatively a graphical calculator or graph-drawing program on a computer. Students can obtain a graph to get a rough idea of what is happening and then 'home in' using trial and improvement (or else zoom in on the graph).

Students can invent their own constraints (two bends, three bends, four bends, keep it symmetrical, make one angle twice another, etc.). The piece of work included in the next section shows the way one student developed his work on the task.

A semicircular cross-section is maximal (about 22.9 square inches for a strip 12 inches wide). But do **not** nudge students towards this result initially, or perhaps at all. It is far more profitable for students to devise their own sub-tasks and these should give them the opportunity to demonstrate ability in several areas, including the use of new technology, algebra, trigonometry and trigonometric graphs.

ASSESSING STUDENTS' COURSEWORK TASKS

Further Coursework Task 2

There are many different ways of tackling this problem, depending on the mathematical skills and knowledge of the student.

In the following extract the student is finding the maximum volume you can get for a 20 cm by 15 cm rectangle. She starts with squares with integer sides, and then homes in on a more accurate answer. She has done all her calculations using a four-function calculator. This means that progress was relatively slow, and it was difficult to generate enough data to make any generalisations.

The next size of paper I'm going to try is 20 cm × 15 cm

Square cut out	Length	Width	Height	Volume
1	18	13	1	234
2	16	11	2	352
3	14	9	3	378
4	12	7	4	336
5	10	5	5	250

GETTING THE MOST OUT OF LIFE

Relevant Review Exercises

C27	Fractions and decimals	page 93
C32	Algebraic manipulation	page 112
C38	Polynomial equations	page 128
C39	Rearranging formulae	page 132
C40	Nets and polyhedra	page 137
C41	Pythagoras' theorem and trigonometry in three dimensions	page 141
D43	Graphs of functions	page 249
D50	Trigonometry and triangles	page 272
D52	Algebraic fractions and dimensional analysis	page 277

National Curriculum Statements

Introduction to the task
2/4e1; 2/7c1

Section A
2/4a8; 2/4d2; 2/5c1; 2/6b; 2/7b1; 2/8c; 3/7a2; 3/8a2; 4/5d1; 4/6b2; 4/6b3; 4/7c; 4/7d; 4/8b; 4/9a4

Section B
2/4a1; 2/4a2; 2/4a8; 2/4d2; 2/7a; 2/7b2; 3/7a2; 3/7b4; 3/8c1; 3/10b; 3/10d2; 4/7c; 4/8b

Questions in Sections

Accessible to all students (no bars)	Somewhat harder (one bar)	More difficult (two bars)
Section A, 1–6	Section A, 7–9	Section A, 10–14
Section B, 1–7	Section B, 9	Section B, 10–15

Further Coursework Tasks

neutral: 1, 2, 3
easier:
more difficult: 4, 5

INTRODUCTION TO THE TASK: HINTS

Students can work individually or in small groups, and enjoy competing to see who can get the biggest volume. Chick peas or black-eye beans are accurate enough and less messy than rice or peas. If there are sinks nearby it might be easier to use water to test the result. The paper holds out long enough.

Folding an A4 sheet in half and joining it together with adhesive tape or staples to make a 'chip bag' produces a container with a capacity of approximately 1 litre. 'Cones' are tricky because the tops tend not to join up neatly and you get different results depending on whether you use water or a dry material. (For a 'cone' a capacity of about 700 cm^3 can be obtained using water and about 1000 cm^3 using beans). Some students will be able to follow up the practical approach with calculations of the capacities of cuboids, cylinders, cones and other shapes that can be made. Hence the task is suitable for students working at all levels.

The activity could conclude with a class discussion. What are the 'rules' for measuring capacity? Is biggest capacity an important criterion? Are other things, such as the convenience of the shape, more important?

SECTION A: ANSWERS

1 (a) Possible rectangles are $9 \times 1, 8 \times 2, 7 \times 3, 6 \times 4, 5 \times 5$ (b) 25 cm^2
2 (a) Possible rectangles are $36 \times 1, 18 \times 2, 12 \times 3, 9 \times 4, 6 \times 6$ (b) 24 cm
3 100 m^2
4 (b) 384 m^2 (three lengths of 16 and four of 12)
   (c) No difference
5 (a) (ii) 288 m^2 (four lengths of 12 and six of 8)
   (b) (ii) 288 m^2 (three lengths of 16, two of 18 and one of 12)
6 (a) 1 (b) 3 (c) 5 (d) 5 (e) 6
7 (a) $\frac{2}{3}$ (b) $\frac{1}{2}$ (c) $\frac{2}{5}$ (d) $\frac{9}{40}$

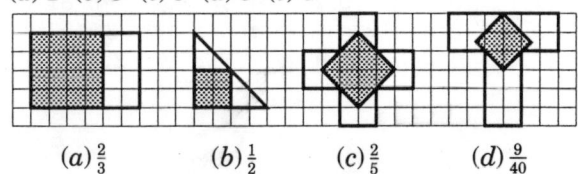

141

TASK MATHS

8 (a) Diagonal of square is $\sqrt{32}$ (approximately 5.6) (b) (i) 6 cm (diameter) (ii) $\sqrt{52}$ cm or 7.2 cm (diagonal) (iii) 5 cm (hypotenuse) (iv) 10 cm (longest diagonal) (v) 8 cos 30° or 6.9 cm (longer diagonal) (vi) 6 cm (both diagonals are 6)

9 (a) (i) $\frac{108}{x^2}$ (ii) $x^2 + \frac{432}{x}$ (b) 6 (c) 144 cm² (12 × 12)

10 (a) (i) $\frac{170}{\pi r^2}$ (ii) $2\pi r^2 + \frac{340}{r}$ (b) 3 (c) 226 cm²

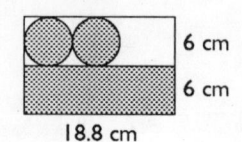

11 (b) (i) Square with side 7.1 cm (ii) 64%

12 (a) 15.6 cm² (b) (i) 31.2 cm² (ii) 36 cm² (iii) 36 cm² (c) (i) 24 cm² (rectangle) (ii) 24 cm² (two angles are right-angles)

13 (a) (i) $\sqrt{25-r^2}$ (ii) $\frac{1}{3}\pi r^2\sqrt{25-r^2}$ (b) 50.4 cm³, when $r = 4.08$ cm

14 (a) (i) 16 sinA(1 + cosA) (ii) 60° (b) (i) 9 sinA(2 + cosA) (ii) 68.5° (c) (a) is better (20.8 compared to 19.8)

SECTION B: ANSWERS

1 (a) 9931 (b) 1399 (c) 1, 2, 7
2 (a) 1024 (b) 9801
3 (a) 24.12 (b) 18.9 (c) 121.04 (d) 62.96
4 (a) 111 111 111 (b) 6210 (c) 18 (d) Impossible
5 (a) 16 (b) 56.25 (c) $\left(\frac{N}{2}\right)^2$
6 (a) 125 (b) 296.3 (c) $\left(\frac{N}{3}\right)^3$
7 (a) 3164.06 (b) $\left(\frac{N}{4}\right)^4$
8 $\left(\frac{N}{p}\right)^p$
9 (a) 81 (3 × 3 × 3 × 3) (b) 6.25 (2.5 × 2.5) (c) 172.1 (2.8⁵)
10 (b) $x = 0.5$ is a line of symmetry (c) −0.25
11 (b) Half-turn symmetry about (1,0) (c) 0.38 (when $x = 0.42$) (d) No, because the symmetry does not help to locate the maximum
12 (b) $x = 1.5$ is a line of symmetry (c) −1.0 (when $x = 0.38$) (d) 0.6 (when $x = 1.5$) (e) Symmetry helps with (d) But not (c)
13 (a) (i) 3 (ii) 16 (iii) −5 (iv) 3.75 (v) 5
14 (a) $\frac{\sqrt{100+x^2}}{2v} + \frac{\sqrt{100+(10-x)^2}}{v}$ (b) 7 (c) sin$i = 0.573$, sin$r = 0.287$
15 (a) (i) 2, 3, 5 (ii) 4, 9, 25 (iii) 6, 8, 10 (iv) 16, 81, 625 (b) (i) 2, 3, 5 (ii) $2^2, 3^2, 5^2$ (iii) $2 \times 3, 2^3, 2 \times 5$ (iv) $2^4, 3^4, 5^4$ (c) (i) 997 (ii) 961 (iii) 998 (iv) 625

FURTHER COURSEWORK TASKS

1) Questions 4 and 5 of Section A were about enclosing equal rectangular areas with a fixed length of fencing.

2 equal areas

3 equal areas   3 equal areas

Explore the situations described in these questions more fully.

If the rectangular area is to be divided into *four* pieces of equal area, several different arrangements are possible. Here are two of them.

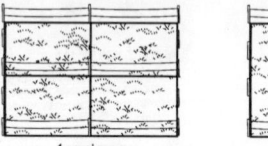

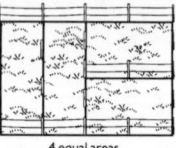

4 equal areas   4 equal areas

Explore the possibilities for each arrangement. What is the maximum total area which can be enclosed for a fixed length of fencing?

What if a different arrangement of four pieces is used? What if there are five pieces? Six pieces? ...

Most students will want to specify a specific length of fencing, so that they can use trial and improvement to find the *maximum* areas. 96 metres, which is suggested in questions 4 and 5 in Section A, is a good length to choose. *Spread* or a spreadsheet could be used for this task. It is not a trivial task to find *any* arrangement to give 4 or 5 pieces of equal area, let alone the maximum.

In the answers that follow it is assumed that the length of fencing is L.

The (total) maximum area when there are two pieces of equal area is $\frac{L^2}{24}$.

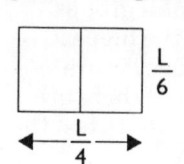

[rectangle with width $\frac{L}{4}$ and height $\frac{L}{6}$]

When there are three pieces of equal area there are two arrangements.

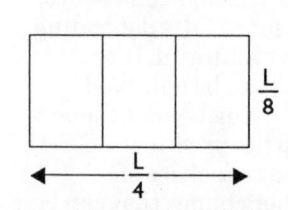

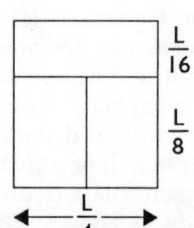

[rectangle with width $\frac{L}{4}$ and height $\frac{L}{8}$]

[rectangle with width $\frac{L}{4}$, heights $\frac{L}{16}$ and $\frac{L}{8}$]

Maximum area = $\frac{L^2}{32}$ Maximum area = $\frac{L^2}{32}$

half a square cut out

Square cut out	Length	Width	Height	Volume
2.4	15.2	10.2	2.4	372.096
2.5	15	10	2.5	375
2.6	14.8	9.8	2.6	377.104
2.7	14.6	9.6	2.7	378.432
2.8	14.4	9.4	2.8	379.008
2.9	14.2	9.2	2.9	378.856

The highest volume for paper sized 18cm x 15cm is 379 when 2.8 squares are cut out

She then attempts to find a way of working out the maximum volume for a rectangle with dimensions A and B. It is not correct and her use of algebra is clumsy. However, she has attempted to use algebraic symbolism in order to generalise her results. But she cannot achieve more than 5c because there is no justification.

From my table of results I have noticed that if you take away the length from the width of the rectangle, you are left with the width of the box with the largest volume.

e.g. A   B
     24cm x 15 cm paper

The largest volume is 486 cm³
          (= 18 x ⑨ x 3)
                L   W   h
24 - 15 = ⑨

Formula

$A - B = w$
$(B - w) \div 2 = h$
$A - (h \times 2) = L$
    h = size of square to cut out
$L \times w \times h$ = volume

145

TASK MATHS

Further Coursework Task 3

Like FCT 2, this task can also be tackled in many different ways depending on the knowledge and skills of the student. The following is the complete account by a student of how he made a mock-up paper container, using a practical approach. He can interpret information in a variety of forms (Ma1/5b).

In my maths group I chose to design a tennis ball container which can hold 4 tennis balls and make the surface area as small as possible.

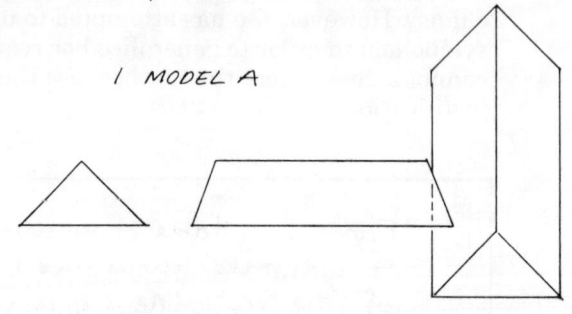

1 MODEL A

This my first idea. It was based on a equilateral triangle which mathematically is called a triangular prism. I rejected this one because there was too much space being wasted. Then I thought of a new shape which is like the model B

2 MODEL B

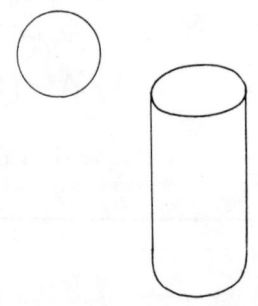

I chose this one because there was less wasted spaces. It might be harder but I liked the challenge. It is a cylinder shape.

First I chose a piece of paper and wrapped it around the tennis ball and enough space for the tennis ball to roll out freely.
After adjusting it I measured it. Its dimensions were 23cm. by 29.7cm. and I sellotaped it together.

> *Secondly* I placed this tube on paper and drew round the bottom in order to get the end shape right and cut it out and put it in place.
>
> *Thirdly* I just measured this by going straight across and got 7cm
>
> To get the area I times $3.5 \times 3.5 \times \pi$ which gave me an answer of 38.49 square cm.
>
> So for the 2 ends I needed a piece of paper which was 77cm².
>
> Which means the cylinder area was 683.1cm². I got this by multiplying 23×29.7
>
> ```
>   683.10  cylinder
>    38.49  top
> +  38.49  bottom
>   ------
>   760.08  total
> ```
>
> When I rounded it, it comes to 760cm²
> If you went into a shop you would have to have some wasted.
>
> [Diagram: rectangle 23cm × 29.7cm containing two circles of diameter 7, with wasted strip]
>
> total = $30 \times 29.7 = 891 cm^2$

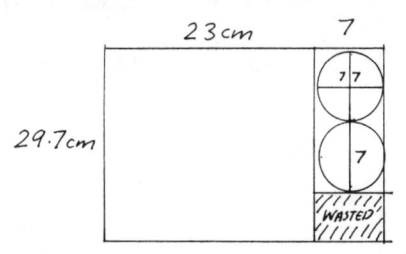

In the following extract the student is considering a container in the shape of an equilateral trianglular prism. He obtains the linear dimensions experimentally, and then uses his mathematical skill to work out the volume and surface area of his container. Earlier in his account he calculated the volume of four tennis balls, and he uses this fact again here to work out the volume of his container which is wasted. This prism was the third shape he considered. Earlier he looked at a square-based prism and a cylinder. He concludes that the cylinder is the most efficient container to make. He can give a logical account of his work with reasons for choices made (Ma1/8a).

TASK MATHS

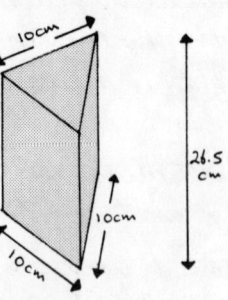

The length will be the same again 26.5cm. The width will be 10cm because I tried it with 6.5, the normal size, and the side of the container bulged out, and 10 it didn't.

I will do the volume first this time.

Volume of container = Area of end × length
Area of end ① = Pythagoras Theorem.

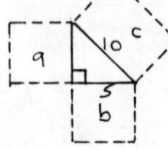

$a^2 + b^2 = c^2$
$c = 10 \quad \frac{1}{2}b = 5$
$100 - 25 = 75$
$\sqrt{75} = 8.66$

(A bit muddled? I don't blame you. To understand this bit you have to have done some work on it!)

I know why you half b now because to find the area of a triangle you ½ b×h. I also know why you take 25 from 100 because I'm not trying to look for (c) but (a). So the process is reversed...

$c^2 - \frac{1}{2}b^2 = a^2$ Sorry! The triangle is already halfed.
It should be $c^2 - b^2 = a^2$

Now that I have worked that out for I can carry on finding the area of the triangle in the normal way.

Area of triangle = ½ b × h
= ½ 10 × 8.66
= 43.3 cm²

Volume of the container = Area of lid × length
= 43.3 × 26.5
= 1147 cm³

From the shape of the container you don't think that much space is wasted but wait...

Wasted Volume = Volume of container − Volume of 4 tennis balls
= 571 cm³

% wasted = Volume of wasted ÷ volume of container × 100
= 571 ÷ 1147 × 100
= 50%

Shocked! Over half of the triangle container, the volume is not used.

Nearly forgot about the surface area:-
S.A = 3 × 10 × 26.5   (3 because of 3 sides)
= 795 cm²

Plus 2 lids = 795 + 43.3 + 43.3
= 882 cm²

Again the surface area is small compared to the volume of the container. Looking back at the answers the circle container was the best one to use because less surface area is used and the wasted volume is less.

GETTING THE MOST OUT OF LIFE

Further Coursework Task 5

The following piece of work is reproduced in full to show what can be achieved. This student uses his graphical calculator. He employs symbolisation to good effect. He could have made more effective use of his graphical calculator to obtain more accurate answers at each stage, but his attention was focused on finding the maximum cross-sectional area for an arbitrary number of bends. He devises the interesting method of increasing the number of bends and thus comes to realise that the semicircle is the shape which maximises the cross-section. He can solve problems and justify solutions involving a number of features (Ma1/9a and Ma1/9b). There is also some evidence for Ma1/10a.

WATER CHANNELS

A channel for water is to be made from a strip of metal 12 units wide.

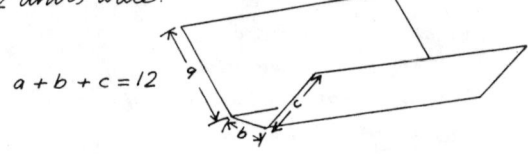

$a + b + c = 12$

The strip can be bent into any shape to produce as big an area as possible for the cross section of the channel.

I used a graphical calculator to work out the maximum area of the channel with the strip bent in different ways.

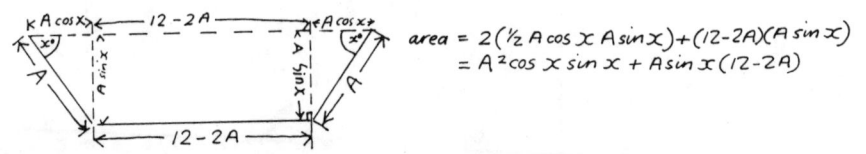

$$\text{area} = 2(\tfrac{1}{2} A \cos X \cdot A \sin X) + (12 - 2A)(A \sin X)$$
$$= A^2 \cos X \sin X + A \sin X (12 - 2A)$$

Using the graph function on the calculator, and substituting a value for A it is possible to draw a graph showing what values for A give what areas for the cross section.

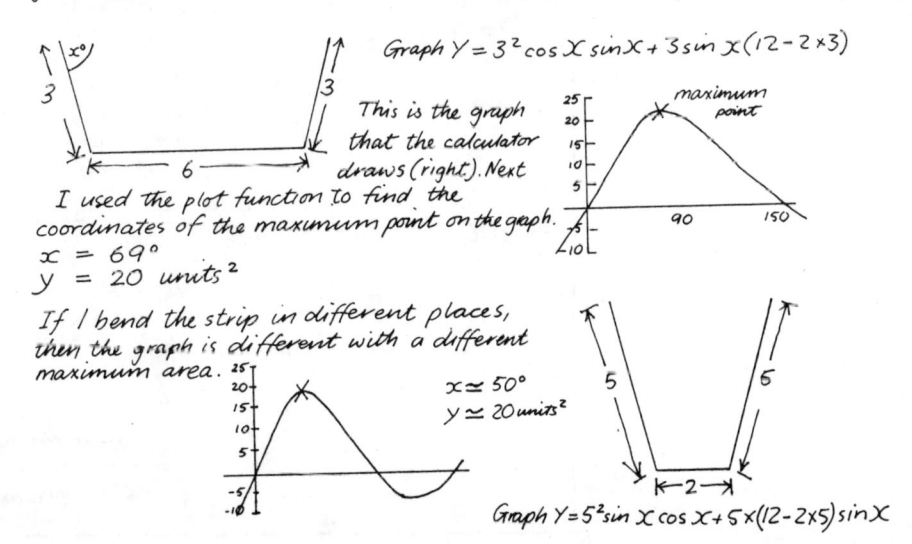

Graph $Y = 3^2 \cos X \sin X + 3 \sin X (12 - 2 \times 3)$

This is the graph that the calculator draws (right). Next I used the plot function to find the coordinates of the maximum point on the graph.
$x = 69°$
$y = 20$ units^2

If I bend the strip in different places, then the graph is different with a different maximum area.

$x \approx 50°$
$y \approx 20$ units^2

Graph $Y = 5^2 \sin X \cos X + 5 \times (12 - 2 \times 5) \sin X$

As the maximum areas of these two arrangements are about the same, I thought it reasonable to assume that the largest possible maximum area with the strip bent in two places, was to be found by taking the value for A between the two values I had already tried, ie. 4.

Graph $Y = 4^2 \sin X \cos X + 4(12 - 2 \times 4) \sin X$

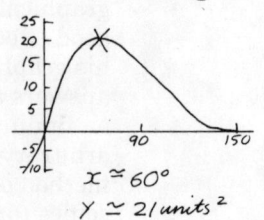

$x \simeq 60°$
$y \simeq 21 \text{ units}^2$

So the highest area of the cross section is about twenty-one. when the strip is bent in two places. Next I decided to see what it is with the strip bent only once in the middle.

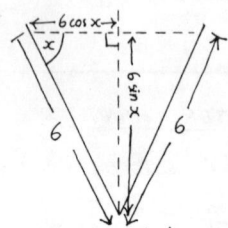

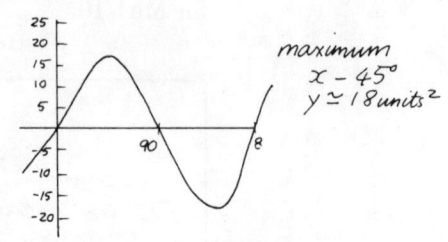

Graph $Y = 36 \sin x \cos x$

maximum
$x \simeq 45°$
$y \simeq 18 \text{ units}^2$

As this is smaller than the previous maximum, I decided that the biggest cross section will be found by having more bends in the strip.

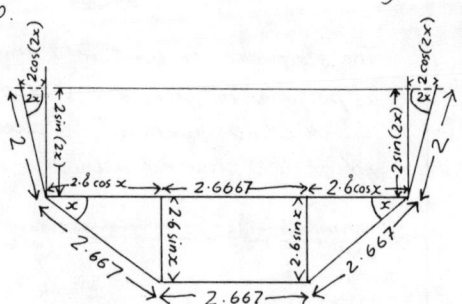

Graph $Y = 2\cos(2x) 2\sin(2x) + 2.\dot{6}\cos X \, 2.\dot{6}\sin X + 2.\dot{6} \times 2.\dot{6} \sin X +$
$\quad 2\sin(2x)(2 \times 2.\dot{6}\cos X + 2.667)$
$= 4\cos(2x)\sin(2x) + 7.\dot{1}\cos X \sin X + 7.\dot{1}\sin X + 2\sin(2x)$
$\quad (5.\dot{3}\cos X + 2.\dot{6})$

Hardly surprisingly, this complicated shape gives a complicated graph, so I won't draw it. I did plot the maximum point:

$x \simeq 45°$
$y \simeq 22 \text{ units}^2$

This shows that the more bends in the strip there are, the bigger the area is. Presumably then, the biggest area is that of a strip with ∞ bends ie. a semicircle

To work this out I had to first work out the radius
$2\pi r = 2 \times 12$
$\pi r = 12$
$r = {}^{12}/\pi$

then use this to work out the area
area $= \frac{1}{2}\pi r^2$
$= \frac{1}{2}\pi ({}^{12}/\pi)^2$
$= 22.918$
$\simeq 23$

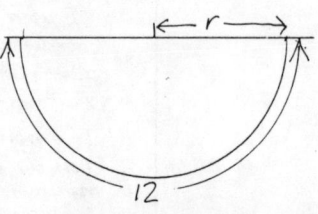

To conclude then, the semicircle gives the highest area for the cross-section, as it has the most bends, and they are all evenly spaced.

ANSWERS TO REVIEW EXERCISES D

EXERCISE 42 EVERYDAY GRAPHS

Relevant chapters

17 Managing the future
20 Repeating patterns
21 How do you decide?

National Curriculum statements

2/5d1; 2/7c3; 3/4c; 3/7b3; 3/8c2; 3/9c; 5/4b4; 5/5c2

Levels of difficulty of questions

Accessible to all students (no bars)	Somewhat harder (one bar)	More difficult (two bars)
1–12	13–18	19

Answers

1 (a) Vertical axis does not start at zero; line too thick (b) Between 260 and 275
2 (a) (i) Between 37% and 39% (ii) 1978 to 1980 (iii) 1974 (b) (i) 400 000 (ii) $\frac{2}{15}$
3 (a) 30 mpg (b) 8 gallons (c) 53 mph
4 (a) 12 m (b) (i) 75 m (ii) 55 m (c) 32 m
5 (a) 10 m/s (b) 20 s
6 (a) 50 mph for 1 hour, half an hour stop, 40 mph for 1 hour
7 (a) 6.3 km (b) 3.6 miles (c) About 41.9 km
8 (a) 490, 980, 1470 (c) (i) About 1715 francs (ii) About £82
9 (a) About 115 g (b) About 9 ounces
10 (d) (i) £39.50 (ii) 600 units (iii) £6
11 (a) 82 cm (b) 21 months (c) 176 cm
13 (a) About 3 m² (b) About £3 (£2.82 buys 3 m) (c) 500 l (d) Graph (iii)
14 (c) (i) About 54 mpg (ii) About 42 mpg
15 (b) (i) About 15 m (ii) About 6 s (d) (ii) About 8 s (iii) About 10 m/s
16 (b) About 8.8 m (c) About 3.45 am (d) 2
17 (b) (i) 40 °C (ii) 85 to 90 mins (difficult to be accurate) (d) About 1 °C per minute (e) About 25 °C
18

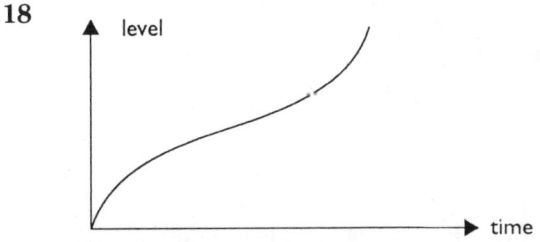

19 About 3.8 m

EXERCISE 43 GRAPHS OF FUNCTIONS

Relevant chapters

16 Every picture tells a story
20 Repeating patterns
25 Getting the most out of life

National Curriculum statements

2/8b1; 3/5c; 3/6c; 3/7b3; 3/8a5; 3/9b1; 4/9c1; 4/9c2; 4/9c3

Levels of difficulty of questions

Accessible to all students (no bars)	Somewhat harder (one bar)	More difficult (two bars)
	1–8	9–16

Answers

1 (a) $y = 4x+5, y = 2x+5$ (b) $y = 2x+2, y = 2x+5$
2 (a) $16-2x$ (c) 32, 31.5 (d) 32 chickens, 4 m by 8 m
3 (a) 5, −1, 1, 11 (c) 0.8 and −3.8
4 (a) £200 (b) £29 000
5 (b) $y = 2x^2$ (d) (iii) (1.5, 4.5) and (−1, 2) (e) (i) 4 (ii) −4
6 (b) 1008, 1056, 1000, 864, 672, 448, 216 (d) (i) 1056 (ii) 4
7 (d) 4.3 cm
8 (a) 8 m (b) 6 m/s (c) $d = 6t+8$
9 (a) $2l + 2w = 1$ (b) $w = \frac{1}{2}(1-2l)$ (c) $A = \frac{1}{2}l(1-2l)$ (e) $\frac{1}{4}$ (f) $\frac{1}{16}$
10 (b) 4 and −1 (d) Draw $y = 6-x$; 2.85 and 3.85
11 (a) (i) $y = 1, -7, 1$ (iii) Line of symmetry is $x = 3.5$; minimum value is −8 (b) (ii) 1.5 and 5.1
12 (a) 0.5, 2, 4.5, 11, 12, 7, 3, 0 (c) (i) About 2 m/s² (ii) About 2 m/s² (iii) About 30 m
13 (a) 5 0, 4.0, −1.5, −4.0, −5.0, −1.5, 1.5, 4.0, 5.0 (d) 5 cm (e) 0.5 s
14 $p = 3, q = 2$
15 (c) $(\sin x)^2 + (\cos x)^2 = 1$ (d) $\frac{40}{41}$
16 (a) 16 hours, 8 hours (b) Only 24 hours in a day

EXERCISE 44 BEARINGS AND LOCI

Relevant chapters

20 Repeating patterns
22 Knowing where you are

151

TASK MATHS

National Curriculum statements

2/5b3; 4/4b; 4/5a; 4/6c; 4/7b; 4/7d; 4/10a1

Levels of difficulty of questions

Accessible to all students (no bars)	Somewhat harder (one bar)	More difficult (two bars)
1–4	5–13	14–16

Answers

1. (a) (i) S (ii) School (iii) NE (b) (i) F4 (ii) Roundabout
2. $x = 90°, y = 170°$ and $z = 100°$
3. 98 km
4. (a) (i) 150 km (ii) 175 km (b) (i) About 059° (ii) About 317° (c) B
5. (a) 50 m^2 (b) 50%
6. (b) 10.1 cm
8. (a) 90° (b) Stays equal to 90°
9. (c) About 19.7 m (d) £9.60
10. (c) 43 m (d) 23 m
11. (d) (ii) 44 or 45 km
12. (a) 189 m^2 (b) 9500 g (c) £13.80 (d) 11.2 m
13. The locus is a quarter-circle with radius 3 m
14. (b) 1 (c) 4, but you can nearly do it with 3
15. (b) 120°, 462 m, 231 m (c) Angle APC is never more than 60°
16. (iv) (a) AB and the perpendicular bisector of AB (b) Midpoint of AB; 108°. Rectangle (v) (a) $8 - x$ (c) 4; 5 and 3

EXERCISE 45 STATISTICS 2

Relevant chapters

17 Managing the future
21 How do you decide?
23 What do you believe?

National Curriculum statements

5/4b3; 5/4c; 5/5c1; 5/5c3; 5/7a2; 5/7a3; 5/8b2

Levels of difficulty of questions

Accessible to all students (no bars)	Somewhat harder (one bar)	More difficult (two bars)
1–6	7–11	12–15

Answers

1. 8.5 hours
2. (a) Netball 12, Soccer 10, Hockey 14
3. (a) (i) 162° (ii) Other angles are 18°, 144° and 36° (b) $\frac{9}{20}$
5. (a) (i) $\frac{1}{6}$ (ii) £10 (b) 72°
6. (a) 21 (b) 2 (d) 30 (e) 37 (f) 28
7. (a) (i) 15 mins (ii) 12 (b) 7 (c) Frequencies are 4, 7, 11, 3
8. (a) 10 (b) 9 (c) 8
9. (a) (i) G (ii) 20.4 m^3 (b) (i) C (ii) 30.5 m^3 (c) (i) 3.0 m (ii) 4.1 m (iii) 2.0 m (d) (i) C (ii) 27%
10. (a) Angles are 90°, 72°, 144°, 54° (b) £81
11. (a) 24% (b) 53 cm
12. (a) (i) 10 (ii) 175 km^2 (iii) 28%
13. (a) $1.6 \leq w < 1.8$ (b) $1.2 \leq w < 1.4$ (c) 1.44 kg
14. (a) Type A: 37.5, 39.5, 33, 6.5; Type B: 25, 39.5, 15, 24.5 (c) B
15. (b) Maths 39 years, P.E. 36 years, difference 3 years (c) Maths 47.5 − 34.5 = 13 years; P.E. 43 − 29 = 14 years (e) About 15 300

EXERCISE 46 PROPERTIES OF CIRCLES

Relevant chapters

16 Every picture tells a story
20 Repeating patterns
22 Knowing where you are

National Curriculum statements

4/7c; 4/8a; 4/9a4; 4/10a1

Levels of difficulty of questions

Accessible to all students (no bars)	Somewhat harder (one bar)	More difficult (two bars)
	1–3	4–10

Answers

1. (b) (i) 70° (ii) 20° (iii) 70°
2. (a) (i) 13.1 cm (ii) 69.1° (b) 3.44 cm
3. (b) 36°
4. (a) 90° (b) (i) 50° (ii) 25° (iii) 25°
5. (a) 30° (b) 15°
6. (a) 52° (b) 12 000 km
7. (a) (i) 135° (ii) 270° (c) 11 cm
8. (a) (i) 40° (ii) 20° (b) (i) 17 cm (ii) 47 cm (c) 800 cm^2 (d) 4500 cm^2
9. (a) (i) $90 - x$ (ii) $2x$ (iii) x (b) 40°
10. (a) (i) 54° (ii) 54° (b) ACB = CAB = 54° (c) APB = RAB = 54°, B is common (d) CBA and ATB, CRB and PRA

REVIEW EXERCISES D

EXERCISE 47 ENLARGEMENT AND SIMILARITY

Relevant chapters

16 Every picture tells a story
23 What do you believe?
24 Telling the computer what to draw

National Curriculum statements

4/6b1; 4/7e; 4/8a; 4/9a3

Levels of difficulty of questions

Accessible to all students (no bars)	Somewhat harder (one bar)	More difficult (two bars)
1–5	6–10	11–16

Answers

1 (a) 1.5 (b) 9 cm
2 (a) 12 inches by 16 inches (b) 36
3 12 m
4 (a) 12 (b) 4 cm, 6 cm, 8 cm (c) 24 cm^3
5 (a) 80 cm (b) 45°
6 (d) 54, 1.5 (e) 36
7 (c) 2.5
8 (c) 2, −2
9 (b) E.g. 10% extra is only 92.4 g; or increases 12% (c) Increase height by 10% to 1.1 cm; increase radius by $\sqrt{10}$% to 5.2 cm; students could also use a combination of these.
10 (a) 90° (b) (i) 4 cm (ii) 6 cm
11 2025 g
12 48 kg
13 1:4000
14 1 : 2.5 × 10^9
15 (a) $\frac{1}{35}$ (b) 175 (c) 6.8 (d) 823 200
16 (a) (i) 268 cm^3 (ii) 0.065 cm^3 (iii) 4096 (b) 3.3 cm
   (c) (i) 0.5 cm (ii) 3.1 cm^2 (iii) 0.79 cm
   (iv) Remaining table entries are 0.5 cm, 0.79 cm^2, 6.3 cm^2, 3.14 cm^2, 0.065 cm^3, 0.52 cm^3, 0.52 cm^3

EXERCISE 48 INEQUALITIES AND LINEAR PROGRAMMING

Relevant chapters

23 What do you believe?

National Curriculum statements

3/8b1; 3/8b2; 5/10b

Levels of difficulty of questions

Accessible to all students (no bars)	Somewhat harder (one bar)	More difficult (two bars)
	1–4	5–14

Answers

1 (a) −3, −2, −1, 0, 1 (b) 0, 1
2 (a) 1, 2, 3
3 (a) 36 (b) −30 (c) −5
4 (b) −2 < x < 3
5 $x > \frac{1}{3}$
6 (a) A 2,2; B 3,2; C 3,4 (b) x = 5, y = 5; x = 6, y = 2
7 $x \geq 0, 5x+8y \leq 40, y \geq 2x$
9 (1,7), (2,4), (2,5), 2,6), (3,3), (3,4), (3,5), (4,2), (4,3), (4,3), (5,2), (5,3), (6,2), (7,1)
10 (b) −2.5
11 (b) $x \geq 1, y \geq 1, 3x+4y \leq 24$ (d) e.g. 5 wine, 2 spirit; 3 wine, 3 spirit
12 (c) 5x+3y = 33 (e) $y \leq 3x−3, x+2y \geq 8, 5x+3y \leq 33$ (f) 5 at (2,3)
13 (a) x = 187.5, y = 125 (b) $x \leq 250, y \leq 250, 60x+30y \geq 15000$ (c) $y \geq \frac{2}{3}x$ (e) 314 (188 double-decker, 126 single)

EXERCISE 49 TRANSFORMATIONS AND MATRICES

Relevant chapters

24 Telling the computer what to draw

National Curriculum statements

4/4a2; 4/5c2; 4/6b1; 4/7e; 4/8d; 4/10a3; 4/10a4

Levels of difficulty of questions

Accessible to all students (no bars)	Somewhat harder (one bar)	More difficult (two bars)
1–3	4–10	11–18

Answers

2 (b) Half-turn rotation about 0 (d) Reflection in horizontal line through 0
3 (a) (2,2), (1,6), (−2,1) (b) (−3,5) (c) (3, 5), (−1, 4)
4 (b) Rotation
5 (e) Reflection in y-axis
6 (b) Translation (−6,0) (c) Enlargement, scale factor 2, centre origin (f) Quarter turn anticlockwise about (3,3)
7 (c) Reflection in y = x

TASK MATHS

8 (d) (6,2)
9 (a) (0,1) (b) 90° anticlockwise
10 (b) $-\frac{2}{3}$ (d) (5,5), (1,−1) (e) Reflection in AB
11 (a) Translation (−1,2) (b) 90° rotation clockwise about 0 (c) Reflection in $y = x$ (d) Enlargement, centre 0, scale factor $\frac{2}{3}$
12 (d) (−4,0) (e) (0,1) (f) −90° rotation about (0,5); 180° rotation about (0,4)
13 (c) (i) −1 (ii) 180°
14 (a) (i) (0,0) (ii) (1,4)
15 (a) (−4,0), (0,−4) (b) Enlargement, centre origin, scale factor −4 (c) $\begin{pmatrix} 0 & 1 \\ -1 & 0 \end{pmatrix}$
16 (b) (i) (−1,−1), (−2,−1), (−2,−2), (−1,−2)
   (iii) Enlargement, centre origin, scale factor −1; or half-turn about the origin (c) (i) (1,−1), (2,−1), (2,−2), (1,−2) (ii) $\begin{pmatrix} 1 & 0 \\ 0 & -1 \end{pmatrix}$ (d) Reflection in y-axis $\begin{pmatrix} -1 & 0 \\ 0 & 1 \end{pmatrix}$
17 (a) $\begin{pmatrix} 2 & 0 \\ 0 & 2 \end{pmatrix}$ (b) $\begin{pmatrix} 0 & 1 \\ -1 & 0 \end{pmatrix}$ (c) $\begin{pmatrix} 0 & 2 \\ -2 & 0 \end{pmatrix}$
18 (a) Reflection in the line $y = x$. (b) (i) (−1,1), (−1,3), (−2,3), (−2,1) (c) (i) (−2,2) (ii) (−3,3), (−3,5), (−4,5), (−4,3)

EXERCISE 50 TRIGONOMETRY AND TRIANGLES

Relevant chapters

20 Repeating patterns
24 Telling the computer what to draw
25 Getting the most out of life

National Curriculum statements

4/7c; 4/8b; 4/10a2

Levels of difficulty of questions

Accessible to all students (no bars)	Somewhat harder (one bar)	More difficult (two bars)
	1–4	5–12

Answers

1 (a) 31°, 77°
2 7.6 m
3 36 km/hr
4 (a) (i) 550 m E, 430 m S (ii) 1050 m E, 430 m S (b) (i) 1140 m (ii) 292°
5 (a) (i) $\frac{4}{3}$ (ii) $\frac{16}{9}$ (b) $\frac{\sqrt{3}}{36}$ or 0.048 (c) $\frac{13\sqrt{3}}{324}$ or 0.069
6 75.5°, 75.5°, 29.0°
7 (a) 57 (b) 39 cm

8 (a) 21 cm (b) 580 cm
9 (a) (i) 110° (ii) 115 km (iii) 019° (b) 2260 km²
10 (a) 100 sin x (b) 90° (c) 30°
11 (a) 120 m (b) 30 m (c) 52°
12 (a) 6.4 cm, 7.2 cm, 7.8 cm (b) 70° (c) 22 cm² (d) 20 cm³ (e) 2.7 cm

EXERCISE 51 COORDINATES AND VECTORS

Relevant chapters

24 Telling the computer what to draw

National Curriculum statements

4/4a2; 4/5c2; 4/7a; 4/8d; 4/9b

Levels of difficulty of questions

Accessible to all students (no bars)	Somewhat harder (one bar)	More difficult (two bars)
	1–6	7–14

Answers

2 (a) (i) (6,6) (ii) (−2,0) (b) Parallel and 3 times length
3 (a) (2,−1) (b) (2,3) (c) (6,3)
4 (a) (i) (−3,−5) (ii) (−5,3) (iii) (−3,5) (iv) (5,3) (b) No
6 (a) (2,1,2), (2,3,2), (−4,3,2), (−4,1,−2), (2,1,−2), (−4,3,−2) (b) (−1,2,0) (c) 48
7 (a) (4.5,6,−18 (b) 19.5 m (c) 23° (d) (0,4,0)
8 (a) 3 (b) (0,1,−8), (0,7,−8), (6,7,−8), (6,1,−8), (6,7,−2), (6,1,−2), (0,1,−2), (0,7,−2) (c) 3 sides of cube could be (2,2,1), (−1,2,−1), (−2,1,2). Eight different opposite vertices can be obtained by adding or subtracting these three vectors to (3,4,−5).
9 (a) 63° (b) 50 (c) (50,100) (d) (2,−1) (e) (100,75)
10 (a) 8 (b) 79° (c) (−1,−5) (d) 18 m
11 (a) $q - p$ (b) (i) $\frac{p}{2}$ (ii) $\frac{(q-p)}{2}$ (c) MN parallel to BC, MN = $\frac{BC}{2}$
12 (a) $p + q, \frac{p}{3} + \frac{q}{3}, \frac{p}{3} - \frac{2q}{3}, \frac{p}{3}, \frac{p}{3} - \frac{2q}{3}$ (b) DL parallel to MB, DL = MB
13 (a) (i) $x + y$ (ii) $2x + 2y$ (iii) $2x + y$ (iv) $x + 2y$ (b) (i) $\frac{3x}{2} + 2y$ (ii) $\frac{3x}{4} + y$ (c) FNM is a straight line, N is midpoint of FM
14 (a) $\frac{a}{2} + c, \frac{c}{2} - a$ (b) $\frac{2}{5}, \frac{4}{5}$ (c) $\frac{1}{5}$

REVIEW EXERCISES D

EXERCISE 52 ALGEBRAIC FRACTIONS AND DIMENSIONAL ANALYSIS

Relevant chapters

16 Every picture tells a story
18 Equable shapes
25 Getting the most out of life

National Curriculum statements

3/8a1; 3/10b; 4/8c

Levels of difficulty of questions

Accessible to all students (no bars)	Somewhat harder (one bar)	More difficult (two bars)
		1–12

Answers

1 (a) 77 (b) 170
2 2 or −1
3 2
4 (a) $(4x+1)(x+4)$ (b) −4 or −0.25
5 (a) 4.2 m/s (b) $2x$ m/s
6 6.5
7 (a) (i) $2(x-4)$ (ii) $(x-4)(x+1)$ (b) −2.16 (c) (4,0), (−1,0), (0,−4)
8 (b) 16 or 1.5
9 (a) (i) $\frac{1}{4}$ (ii) $\frac{1}{2}$ (b) $\sqrt{\frac{2}{3}}$
10 $\frac{2h}{5}$
11 (a) $\frac{\pi r^2 h}{r^2} = \pi h$
   (b) Only one length (c) Height of square-based prism
12 (a) $\frac{4}{3}x^2z + 8x^3$ (b) $24x^2 + 4x\sqrt{2x^2 + z^2}$
   (c) $4\sqrt{2x^2 + z^2} + 24x$

RUNNING THE COMPUTER PROGRAMS

A disc of 5 programs can be obtained for use with *Task Maths* at Key Stage 4 (Books 4 and 5). The disc can be purchased in one of three versions:

- a disc for the BBC B or BBC Master
- a disc for the RM Nimbus
- a disc for the Archimedes

It is suggested that you make a back-up copy of the disc.

To start the BBC disc, put it in drive 0. Then hold down the **SHIFT** key with one finger and tap the **BREAK** key with another.

Before using the Nimbus disc you need to boot the system in the usual way, using your own system disc. Then place the disc in drive A and type RUN, and then press the **RETURN** (or **ENTER**) key.

To start the Archimedes disc, put it in drive 0. Then hold down the **SHIFT** key with one finger and tap the **BREAK** key with another. If this does not work, hold down the **CTRL** key with one finger and tap the **BREAK** key with another. (If this does not work, the Archimedes you are using has been set to start in a non-standard way. Seek advice about resetting the Archimedes.)

None of the programs on the *Task Maths* disc use files. This means that it should be possible to use them on a network if this is desired.

When you start the disc as described above you will see a Menu on the screen, listing the five programs on the disc. These are

A *Recurring decimals*
B *Circle patterns*
C *Spread*
D *Tilekit*
E *Estimating time*

To obtain one of the programs press the corresponding letter.

The rest of this section provides detailed notes about the use of each of the five programs. These notes include a sample use of the program, which are written for use at the keyboard to help you try the program out.

1 Recurring decimals

This is a straightforward program, used to find the exact decimal representation of any fraction. The title page explains how to use it.

Here is a sample use of *'Recurring decimals'*. What you type is in boxes. You press **RETURN** (or **ENTER**) at the end of each line entered.

TOP? $\boxed{3}$
BOTTOM? $\boxed{4}$
0.75

TOP? $\boxed{10}$
BOTTOM? $\boxed{4}$
2.5

TOP? $\boxed{1}$
BOTTOM? $\boxed{7}$
0.<142857>

TOP? $\boxed{2}$
BOTTOM? $\boxed{7}$
0.<285714>

TOP? $\boxed{1}$
BOTTOM? $\boxed{13}$
0.<076923>

TOP? $\boxed{7}$
BOTTOM? $\boxed{900}$
0.00<7>

TOP? 1
BOTTOM? $\boxed{7*7}$
0.<020408163265306122448979591836734693877551>

TOP? $\boxed{3}$
BOTTOM? $\boxed{16*16-1}$
0.0<1176470588235924>

As you can see from the sample use given above, expressions can be entered for **TOP** and **BOTTOM** as well as numbers.

To finish the program, press the **ESCAPE** (**ESC**) key. This will return you to the menu.

2 Circle patterns

This program allows you to create on the computer's screen patterns formed by joining points on the circumference of a circle. Such patterns can be created more quickly with a computer than with pencil and paper.

Here is a sample use of *'Circle patterns'*. What you type is in boxes. You press **RETURN** at the end of each line entered.

: $\boxed{\text{NUMBER}}$

Number of points? $\boxed{12}$

: $\boxed{\text{RULE}}$

Rule: N → $\boxed{\text{N+3}}$

: $\boxed{\text{GO}}$

The computer draws the pattern.

: $\boxed{\text{RULE}}$

Rule: N → $\boxed{\text{N+4}}$

: $\boxed{\text{FRESH}}$

The computer clears the screen.

: GO

Rule: N → N+6

: GO

The computer adds to the pattern on the screen.

: NUMBER

Number of points? 9

: RULE

Rule: N → N+4

: FRESH

The computer clears the screen.

: GO

The computer draws the pattern.

: RULE

Rule: N → N+3

: FRESH

The computer clears the screen.

: GO

The computer draws the pattern.

: FRESH

The computer clears the screen.

: CHAIN

Start of Chain? 2

: GO

The computer draws the pattern.

: CHAIN

Start of Chain? 1

: GO

The computer adds to the pattern.

: NOT CHAIN

: NUMBER

Number of points? 30

: RULE

Rule: N → 2N+15

: FRESH

The computer clears the screen.

: GO

The computer draws the pattern.

: RULE

Rule: N → N*N*N

: FRESH

The computer clears the screen.

: GO

The computer draws the pattern.

: PRINT

The computer prints the pattern, provided that an Epson-compatible printer is attached. This command is not available on the Nimbus version.

The key words illustrated by the sample use above are **NUMBER**, **RULE**, **GO**, **FRESH**, **CHAIN**, **NOT CHAIN**, and **PRINT**. Each of them (except **GO**) can be abbreviated to the first three letters.

Thus you can type **NUM** instead of **NUMBER**.

To interrupt the drawing of a pattern on the screen before it is complete, press the **ESCAPE (ESC)** key.

To finish the program, type **END** and press the **RETURN** key. This will return you to the menu.

3 Spread

This program allows you to create a table of numbers on the screen. The numbers in the table can be entered individually, or in a block, or using a formula.

Here is a sample use of '*Spread*'. What you type is in boxes.

First, press S, as instructed on the screen, to start the program.

>> E

>> Enter

Please type number: 6<RETURN>

The computer enters the number 6 into the table at the position shown by the red cursor.

Now use the arrow keys to move the red cursor to a different position.

>> E

>> Enter

Please type number: −17.5<RETURN>

The computer enters the number −17.5 into the table at the position shown by the cursor.

Now use the arrow keys to move the cursor back onto column A.

>> B

>> Enter a block of values

First number: 1<RETURN>

Step: 2<RETURN>

The computer enters the numbers 1, 3, 5, 7 and 9 into column A.

Now use the arrow keys to move the cursor onto column B.

>> B

>> Enter a block of values

First number: 4<RETURN>

TASK MATHS

Step: $\boxed{0\text{<RETURN>}}$

The computer enters the numbers 4 into all rows of column B.

>> $\boxed{C}$

>> Columns

Now many columns? $\boxed{4\text{<RETURN>}}$

The computer displays four columns labelled A, B, C and D.

>> $\boxed{N}$

>> Name

Give the column a new name: $\boxed{L\text{<RETURN>}}$

The computer renames column A as column L.
  Now use the arrow keys to move cursor onto column C.

>> $\boxed{N}$

>> Name

Give the column a new name: $\boxed{AREA\text{<RETURN>}}$

The computer renames column C as column AREA.
Now use the arrow keys to move the cursor onto column D.

>> $\boxed{N}$

>> Name

Give the column a new name: $\boxed{PERIM\text{<RETURN>}}$

The computer renames column D as column PERIM.
  Now move the cursor onto column AREA.

>> $\boxed{F}$

>> Formula

FORMULA AREA= $\boxed{L*B\text{<RETURN>}}$

The computer uses the formula to change the entries in column AREA.
  Now move the cursor onto column PERIM.

>> $\boxed{F}$

>> Formula

FORMULA PERIM= $\boxed{2*(L+B)\text{<RETURN>}}$

The computer uses the formula to change the entries in column PERIM.
  Now use the arrow keys to move the cursor onto column B.

>> $\boxed{B}$

>> Enter a block of values

First number: $\boxed{8\text{<RETURN>}}$

Step: $\boxed{-1\text{<RETURN>}}$

The computer enters the numbers 8, 7, 6, 5 and 4 into column B.

>> $\boxed{U}$

The computer updates the entries in columns AREA and PERIM, using the formulae for these columns.

>> $\boxed{R}$

>> Rows

How many rows? $\boxed{10\text{<RETURN>}}$

The computer displays ten rows.

>> $\boxed{S}$

>> Save

Name of file: $\boxed{RECT\text{<RETURN>}}$

The computer saves the table onto the disc, using the name RECT.
  The table can subsequently be retrieved from the disc as follows:

>> $\boxed{L}$

>> Load

Name of file: $\boxed{RECT\text{<RETURN>}}$

If you press $\boxed{O}$ the computer displays a list of options. Most of these have been illustrated in the sample use given above. You can experiment with the others for yourself.
  You finish the program as follows:

>> $\boxed{Q}$

>> Quit

Are you sure (Y/N)? $\boxed{Y}$

This returns you to the menu.

4 Tilekit

This program allows you to create tessellations on the computer's screen. Tessellations can often be created more quickly with a computer than with pencil and paper.
  Here is a sample use of '*Tilekit*'. You type only the first letter of each word. The **RETURN** key is never used with '*Tilekit*'.

Next: $\boxed{B}$ig $\boxed{H}$exagon
Next: $\boxed{B}$ig $\boxed{H}$exagon
Next: $\boxed{B}$ig $\boxed{H}$exagon
Next: $\boxed{M}$ove $\boxed{R}$ound
Next: $\boxed{B}$ig $\boxed{H}$exagon
Next: $\boxed{M}$ove $\boxed{R}$ound
Next: $\boxed{B}$ig $\boxed{H}$exagon
Next: $\boxed{M}$ove $\boxed{R}$ound
Next: $\boxed{B}$ig $\boxed{H}$exagon
Next: $\boxed{M}$ove $\boxed{R}$ound
Next: $\boxed{B}$ig $\boxed{H}$exagon
Next: $\boxed{M}$ove $\boxed{R}$ound
Next: $\boxed{M}$ove $\boxed{R}$ound
Next: $\boxed{B}$ig $\boxed{H}$exagon
Next: $\boxed{N}$ew picture

RUNNING THE COMPUTER PROGRAMS

Next: [B]ig [O]ctagon
Next: [B]ig [O]ctagon
Next: [B]ig [S]quare
Next: [M]ove [R]ound
Next: [B]ig [O]ctagon
Next: [C]reate program
Are you sure (Y/N)? [Y]
Next: [L]oop [8]
Next: [B]ig [O]ctagon
Next: [E]nd loop
Next: [E]nd program
(press spacebar)
Next: [G]o
Next: [C]reate program
Are you sure (Y/N)? [Y]
Next: [L]oop [6]
Next: [S]mall [S]quare
Next: [M]ove [R]ound
Next: [S]mall [T]riangle
Next: [E]nd loop
Next: [E]nd program
(press spacebar)
Next: [G]o
Next: [M]ove [R]ound
Next: [G]o
Next: [M]ove [R]ound
Next: [G]o

These are the shapes that can be drawn using '*Tilekit*'.

[B]ig [S]quare	[B]ig [T]riangle	[B]ig [P]entagon
[B]ig [H]exagon	[B]ig [O]ctagon	[B]ig [D]odecagon
[S]mall [S]quare	[S]mall [T]riangle	[S]mall [P]entagon
[S]mall [H]exagon	[S]mall [O]ctagon	[S]mall [D]odecagon

[R]hombus [1]   [R]hombus [2]
[O]blong [1]   [O]blong [2]
[P]arallelogram [1] [P]arallelogram [2]

Other commands not used in the sample use are:

[M]ove [F]orward   [M]ove [B]ack   [M]ove [H]idden
[M]ove [D]rawn   [T]urn [R]ound   [T]urn [S]lightly
[W]ipe off

To interrupt the drawing of a pattern on the screen before it is complete, press the **SPACEBAR**.

When [&] is typed the computer prints the current pattern on the screen, provided that an Epson-compatible printer is attached.

You finish the program as follows:

[F]inish

Are you sure (Y/N)? [Y]

This returns you to the menu.

5 Estimating Time

This is a straightforward program, which allows users to test how good they are at estimating time. Its use is self-explanatory. A rectangle is displayed on the screen for varying lengths of time and the user is asked to estimate the length of time on each occasion. After ten tries a table of estimates and actual times is displayed, which the user can then copy off the screen.

To finish the program, press the **ESCAPE (ESC)** key. This will return you to the menu.

TASK MATHS SOFTWARE FOR KEY STAGE 4

A software disk is available that contains five programs for use with Task Maths 4 and Task Maths 5. The programs are as follows:

CIRCLE PATTERNS

This program draws the patterns obtained by numbering equally-spaced dots around the circumference of a circle, and then joining them according to an algebraic rule. A printer dump is provided for the BBC and Archimedes versions.

SPREAD

This program allows the user to set up a table of numbers on the computer's screen. It has some of the characteristics of a spreadsheet, and some other characteristics of its own (including being easier to learn!). It can be used in connection with many of the problems for which a spreadsheet could be used. A more recent version of '*Spread*' which allows the user to print the tables is included on the Key Stage 3 disk.

TILEKIT

This program allows the user to create patterns composed of polygons, including tessellations, on the screen. It has a rudimentary programming capability. A printer dump is provided for all the versions.

RECURRING DECIMALS

This program displays the decimal representation of a fraction. The user types in the top and the bottom of the fraction and its exact (terminating or recurring) decimal equivalent is displayed.

ESTIMATING TIME

This program tests the user's ability to estimate short intervals of time (between 0 and 7 seconds). A rectangle is displayed on the screen and then cleared; the user estimates the length of time during which the rectangle was displayed and types this in. After ten trials a summary of actual and estimated times is displayed.

The software is available on disk in three formats; for the BBC B or Master; for the RM Nimbus; and for the Archimedes.

Task Maths software for Key Stage 4 is published by and available from: AVP, School Hill Centre, Chepstow, Gwent NP6 5PH, United Kingdom (telephone: 0291 625439).

Task Maths software for Key Stage 3 is available from Derek Ball, 8 Barrow Crescent, Gaddesby, Leicester LE7 4WA.